RESCUING MARY

Delta Force Heroes, Book 9

SUSAN STOKER

PROLOGUE

25 Years Ago, Age 5

"You listen to me, Mary, and listen good. Men are dogs. Good-for-nothing, low-down, rotten liars. All they want is to get in your pants. No matter what they say, they're incapable of love. You hear me?"

Mary didn't know why a boy would want to wear a girl's pants, but she knew better than to disagree with Mama so she said obediently, "Yes, Mama."

"And if they say they want to help you, what do you do?"

"Don't believe them."

"Right. Why?"

"Because they always have an ulteer motive." Mary had no idea what that meant. She'd asked once and Mama had started yelling at her and telling her not to question her ator-ity. Whatever *that* meant. So now she knew to simply answer the questions as she'd been taught.

"Right. They *always* have an ulterior motive. They never

do nothing for free. Remember that. And when they say they love you, what do you do?"

"Nod and agree. Take what they're willin' to give until they leave."

"Exactly. If you gotta open your legs to get what you want in this life, you do it. Money, drugs, a place to live...it don't matter what it is...but *never* get attached. Hear me?"

Mary nodded immediately. She was confused once more, but kept her mouth shut. She didn't know why opening her legs would make a boy give her money, but she knew better than to ask.

Her mom sat back on the couch and gulped down the clear liquid in the glass she'd been holding.

Mary bit her little lip and studied her mama. She was wearing the same clothes she'd had on the day before, and the day before that. She kinda smelled and didn't seem to notice that she hadn't eaten in a day and a half...or that she hadn't fed her little girl in the same amount of time. She'd been drinking the clear, nasty-smelling stuff for two days. And Mary hadn't seen Uncle Brad in two days either.

Mary wasn't an idiot. She knew Uncle Brad wasn't really her uncle, but since Mama asked her to call him that, she did. Brad was actually one of the nicer men who had stayed with them. He didn't hit, and sometimes he even smiled at her. Alan had hit Mama and made her cry. Harry had sat on the couch and drank the clear liquid all the time. And... Mary couldn't remember the name of the man before Harry, but he'd had a huge belly and burped and farted all the time. It was gross.

"Mama's tired now," her mama said. "Go to your room and play, okay?"

Mary nodded. She was tired of being in her room and she was hungry, but she agreed anyway. Mama was being kinda nice at the moment and she didn't want to do anything that would make that change.

Maybe Mama would remember to cook dinner tonight. Last night, she drank the clear liquid until she fell asleep on the couch, and Mary was afraid to go into the kitchen to try to find something to eat.

21 Years Ago, Age 9

"Get out!"

"Fuck you!"

"You already did. Now get out!"

"You weren't even that good. Newsflash, bitch, men don't like it when you scrape their cocks with your teeth!"

Mary heard her mama arguing with Uncle Ron and immediately slid off her thin mattress onto the floor and got under her bed. She put her hands over her ears, but could still hear them yelling at each other.

"You're nothing but white trash!" Uncle Ron yelled, then Mary heard glass breaking.

"That's better than being a stingy asshole!" Mama yelled back.

"Stingy? I've done nothing but give you money since I moved in," Uncle Ron replied. "I bought you booze. I bought groceries every week so you could fucking eat. You haven't even once said thank you. Not *once*. I even paid attention to your brat, which is more than *you* ever do."

"I knew you had your eye on her! Shame on you, lusting after a nine-year-old. You think she can suck your dick better than me?"

"Jesus H. Christ! I don't have an eye on your daughter. Are you sick or somethin'?"

"Don't bullshit me," Mama told him. "I knew from the second I introduced you that you wanted her."

"I feel sorry for you. No—I feel sorry for your poor daughter. It has to suck having you for a mom."

"Fuck you! I'm the best thing that ever happened to her."

"What a joke," Uncle Ron said, then laughed.

"I'm not a joke!" Mama screeched. "*You* are. All men are! You were all too happy to move in here because you knew you'd get your cock wet whenever you wanted. But the second I ask you for help, the strings come out. I'll buy you booze if you suck my dick, baby. I'll buy you food if you let me fuck you up the ass. You're all the same! You don't give a shit about me, selfish bastard!"

"Maybe if you opened your goddamned eyes, you'd see what's right in front of your face. You're gonna ruin that sweet little kid. Mark my words. She's gonna turn out just like you."

"Of course she is. I'm her mama!"

"I'm outta here," Uncle Ron said. "I'm sure you'll find another sucker to take my place within the week. Don't forget to feed your kid. She can't live on alcohol and drugs like you can."

"Good riddance!" Mama screamed.

Mary heard a door slam and she held her breath. The words weren't anything she hadn't heard before when Mama had fights with the uncles, but she was kinda surprised that Uncle Ron had brought *her* into the argument. Most of the men didn't care about her, and Mary had learned to stay quiet and out of the way.

She waited for her mama to come in and give her the

speech she now had memorized. She'd been giving her the same tired speech for as long as she could remember.

"Mary?" her mama called. "Get out here!"

Sighing, Mary rolled out from under the bed and headed for the door. She knew if she didn't, Mama would just come looking for her and drag her out.

"Men suck! Got that?" Mama asked when Mary was standing in front of her in the small living area of their trailer.

"Yes, Mama."

"All they want is to get you in bed. They'll take, take, take, and take, and won't give a flying fuck what *you* want."

"Yes, Mama."

"If a boy tells you he loves you, what does he really mean?" she demanded.

"That he wants to sleep with you." Mary was old enough now to know that when a boy slept with a girl, they weren't actually sleeping. They were having sex. She knew all about *that* too. Mama had described what that was in detail two years ago. It sounded gross to her, but Mama seemed to like it enough.

"And once he sleeps with you?" her mama demanded.

"He'll leave."

"Exactly. Now go away. My head hurts."

Without another word, Mary headed back to her room. Ignoring her growling tummy, she grabbed her thin comforter, the one Uncle Thomas got for her, and her pillow, and crawled back under her bed. Under there, she could pretend that she was someone different. That she lived in a big house, had a mama and poppy who loved her and said nice things to her. That they sat down at a big table heaping with food every night. She also pretended that she didn't have a different uncle living with them every month.

Sometime in the last four years, Mary had realized that her mama wasn't normal. Other kids had parents who would cook for them, wash their clothes, and wouldn't sit around the house all day drinking vodka.

The big thing she never understood was, if her mama didn't like men, why did she keep inviting them to move into the trailer with them?

15 Years Ago, Age 15

Mary shut the door as quietly as possible as she entered the trailer. Turning, she went to go to her room, but stopped dead in her tracks.

Mama was standing there. Her eyes were bloodshot and she swayed on her feet.

She was drunk. Again.

Not that it was any big surprise, but Mary had hoped she'd be passed out by the time she got home.

"You sleep with him?" Mama asked belligerently.

"No."

"Could'a fooled me. You look like a slut. Got a pile of makeup on your face. Your dress is short. What, he told you he loves you and you gave it up, right? After everything I've taught you."

"No, Mama. We went to the dance, hung out with friends, and he brought me straight home."

Mary took a step back as her mama came toward her.

Her arm flew up and she slapped Mary right across the face.

Mary brought a hand to her cheek and stared at her mama in shock.

"Don't lie to me! You're sleepin' around, I know it. Men suck. Why won't you get that through your stupid brain? You can't believe 'em when they tell you they care about you. You can't believe 'em when they say they want to help. They *don't*. All they want is to stick their dick inside you and get off."

"Brian's not like that," Mary said softly. "He likes me. He's nice."

"The hell he is," Mama sneered. "They're *all* like that. Mark my words. In the end, he'll hurt you, and I'll not give you an ounce of sympathy. I've warned you time and time again that you can't trust men. That they'll screw you over every single time. If you want to fuck him, fine, but don't pretend that you'll get anything out of it other than some mediocre sex. He'll leave you. They always do. Now, get out of my face."

Mary hurried around her mama to her room. She'd had a good time at the school dance and her mom had ruined it.

Brian was a junior, and two years older than her, but he'd done nothing more than kiss her. He'd said he liked her and enjoying spending time with her. He made Mary laugh and, more than that, she felt safe around him. She didn't need to worry about other boys trying to cop a feel or bullying her. Brian hadn't groped her when he'd kissed her and hadn't pressured for more. Her mom was wrong about him. She knew it.

14 Years Ago, Age 16

"I'm sorry, Mary, but it's over," Brian said in a cold tone she'd never heard him use with her before.

They were standing in the middle of the hallway at school. Mary had met him in their usual spot before lunch. She'd gone up on her tiptoes to kiss him hello, but he'd stepped away and said the last thing she'd expected to hear.

Especially since the night before, she'd given him her virginity.

She'd told Mama they were going to the basketball game and instead he'd rented a room at the rundown motel across town. He'd apologized and said he wanted their first time to be more romantic, but he didn't want anyone to recognize them and get her in trouble.

The actual act of having sex hurt, but Mary had pretended to enjoy what they'd done. Brian had seemed distracted, but Mary hadn't thought anything about it. He'd held her close afterward and eventually they'd left to go back to the high school. He'd said that he wanted to make sure people saw them at the game together so she wouldn't get in trouble.

Mary had loved that he was looking out for her. That he'd wanted to make sure her reputation didn't suffer. That was why his words now didn't make any sense.

Her brows came down in confusion. "What?"

"Me and you. It's not working out."

"But...you told me last month you loved me," she said.

He scoffed. "I thought I did, but I was wrong."

"I don't understand," Mary said, wanting to beg for him to take it back, but she had more dignity than that.

"We're too different," Brian said. "You're poor and live in that shithole trailer. My parents would never approve of us being together."

"But you told me that they liked me. That they were happy you were with me."

"I lied. There's no way they would *ever* approve of you. You're too white trash for me. They didn't care that I sowed my oats with you, but that's all this was."

8

Mary felt her heart break in half. He couldn't be saying what she thought he was. He'd been so *nice* to her. So tender and caring. He'd stuck up for her when other boys at school made fun of her.

She'd thought he loved her. That they were going to get married after she graduated.

"You're too young for me anyway," Brian continued callously. "When I go off to college, you'll still be here. You can't afford tuition, and you'll still be living in your shithole trailer with your whore of a mother. You guys are the laughingstock of town. No one is gonna marry the town hooker's daughter. Did you think I'd wait for you, that we'd get married?"

"You said you loved me," Mary repeated, too hurt to even address the whore comment.

"I only said that because you wouldn't give it up."

"Give it up," Mary echoed, staring at Brian.

Brian leaned in and tapped her on the nose before straightening. "Yeah. It took longer than I thought. The guys all thought for sure you'd be an easy lay because of who your mom is, so who would've thought your legs were all but chained closed? But I gotta say, once I got them pried open, you were one hot lay."

Understanding finally dawned, and Mary clenched her teeth before saying, "You said you loved me so I'd *sleep* with you?"

"Yeah, Einstein. There's no way I was gonna stick with you much longer anyway. The game had gotten old and there's a new batch of freshman cheerleaders I wanna take for a ride before I graduate."

"Fuck you," Mary said in a low, controlled voice.

All her mama's warnings echoed in her head. Her entire life, she'd thought her mama was a drunk, bitter old woman.

But she'd learned a harsh lesson—Mama was right. Men sucked. All of them. The boy she thought loved her, and who she'd wanted to marry and have babies with, had used her.

Thank God, she'd made him use a condom, even when he'd complained that it dulled his pleasure.

"No thanks," Brian said flippantly. "I've had my fill. You were a fun diversion, but way too much work. I gotta go. Andi is waiting for me in the lunchroom. I have it on good authority that she wants me, and who am I to deny a bitch my cock?"

And with that parting shot, he spun on his heels and walked away. Leaving Mary standing in the middle of the hallway.

Mary stared after him, her heart slowly hardening.

Despite everything her mom had told her. Despite seeing man after man parade in and out of their trailer, she'd still believed in fairy tales. She'd lain under her bed many nights, dreaming of her own Prince Charming. Dreaming of a man telling her and showing her without words how much he loved and cared about her.

But at that moment, watching Brian walk away the day after he took her virginity, after admitting he did it just to see if he could, Mary felt her heart shrivel up. She'd never believe tender words of love again.

Mama was right. She'd never trust another man as long as she lived. Never.

8 Years Ago, Age 22

"Men suck."

Mary turned to look at the woman who'd spoken.

She'd recently moved to Dallas after getting her college degree and was sick of sitting in her apartment by herself. She'd found the small hole-in-the wall bar and decided to go out for a drink or two. It didn't matter that she didn't have anyone to go with.

She'd been sitting there for about twenty minutes before the other woman plopped herself down on the barstool next to hers. She'd ordered a Midori martini before sighing and giving her commentary on men.

Mary grinned. Now here was someone after her own heart. "Agreed."

"I swear to God, I don't know why I keep trying."

"Because they make you feel good in bed?" Mary offered.

The other woman laughed. "Yeah, there is that." She turned to Mary and held out her hand. "I'm Rayne. Rayne Jackson."

Mary shook her hand and said, "Mary Weston."

"I think I like you, Mary Weston," Rayne said.

"Likewise."

They grinned at each other, and Mary held up her bottle of beer in a toast. "Here's to men sucking."

"I'll drink to that," Rayne said, and clinked her glass with Mary's bottle.

4 Years Ago, Age 26

Mary closed her eyes as another bout of nausea overtook her. She felt Rayne's hand on her back as she leaned over the toilet and dry heaved.

"Easy, Mare," Rayne said as she tried to soothe her. "When you're ready, let me know and I'll help you back to bed."

It took ten more minutes before Mary felt like the nausea had passed. Rayne helped her limp back to her bed and she fell onto it with a sigh. "I hate this," Mary said.

"I know," Rayne agreed.

"Not the cancer," Mary argued. "That asshole said he'd be here tonight."

"Men suck," Rayne murmured.

"I know. I can't believe I fell for his bullshit. Why didn't you kick me in the ass, Raynie?"

"Because I really thought he was going to be the one," Rayne answered, wiping Mary's brow with a damp cloth.

"My mama told me a long time ago that if a man says he loves you, he's full of shit. That I should never get attached and only use them for a good time."

"That's not true," Rayne protested. "I mean, yes, some men suck, but there's got to be some good ones out there."

"I don't think so. I mean, who tells a woman dying of cancer that he'll be there every step of the way and after the first sign she's struggling, he bails?"

"Reggie Milsap," was Rayne's dry response.

Mary chuckled, even though that made her head hurt even more. "Yeah. Him."

"Remember that promise we made to each other a few years ago?" Rayne asked.

"Which one?"

"That we'd wait to walk down the aisle until we both had men who had proven they were reliable, loved us for real, and we could do it together?"

"Yeah."

"I meant that," Rayne said, her eyes piercing in their intensity.

"I know."

"I'm not letting you use cancer as an excuse to get out of it either."

Mary chuckled again, but protested. "It's really kind of silly, Rayne. I mean, I don't think I'm ever going to get married. I can't trust anyone enough to go that far. And I would never want to hold *you* up from marrying someone you loved."

"Yeah, okay, I wouldn't want to hold you up either, but don't give up on finding someone. Men suck, but I'm holding out hope for a hero."

Mary rolled her eyes. "You and that song."

Rayne grinned. "How's this...if one of us finds someone that we really, really like, and there are no prospects for the other on the horizon, we'll go ahead and get married. But if the other is dating or something, then we'll wait."

"Deal," Mary said immediately. She knew there wasn't a chance in hell of her falling in love. It didn't exist. She'd been proven right time and time again. Reggie Milsap was simply the latest to dash her ridiculous hope that her mama was somehow wrong.

Mary knew Rayne would eventually find someone, she had no doubt. Rayne was a good person inside and out. She was adventurous, brave, funny...Mary could go on and on about her best friend. How could a man *not* fall in love with Rayne?

But her? Even if she lived through this bout with breast cancer, she knew deep in her bones no man would be able to get past the shields she'd put around her heart. She was too snarky and came across to others as a complete bitch. She couldn't help it. It was easier to keep people at arm's length than to risk them hurting her. Because they always hurt her. *Always*.

So she used sarcasm and snark as a shield. Mary knew the day she got married was the day she believed in fairy tales again. And it would be a cold day in hell before *that* happened.

CHAPTER ONE

"Mary! Kassie's having her baby! You need to get to the hospital, now!" The panic was easy to hear in Wendy's voice. Kassie was overdue by at least a week and was more than ready to have her baby.

Mary hadn't been sure anyone would even call to let her know when she went into labor, but Wendy and Casey hadn't taken sides in her current drama, and had kept her updated on Kassie's progress.

She'd done some shitty things in her life, but pushing her best friend away and getting married behind her back—*and* keeping it secret for months—was low, even for Mary.

"I'll be there as soon as I can. I'm not sure I can get off work early," Mary told Wendy. She knew frustration was leaking into her voice, but couldn't help it. She'd used up all of her sick and vacation time at the bank during her recent second bout of breast cancer, and she couldn't afford to take any more unpaid time off work. She couldn't be terminated because of the time she'd taken already, thanks to the Family and Medical Leave Act, but her boss wasn't exactly thrilled.

There was no way she'd approve of Mary leaving an hour early.

"Get here, girl!" Wendy practically yelled. "I think she's gonna have this kid sooner rather than later. You don't want to miss it!"

And Mary didn't. Even knowing most of the women in their circle were upset with her, she loved all of them.

Rayne had been her best friend for years. But through her, she'd gotten to know and love Emily, Harley, Kassie, Bryn, Casey, Sadie, and Wendy. She couldn't imagine not having them all in her life...so the last couple of months had been torture. Mary knew it was all her fault, for marrying Truck and not telling anyone, especially Rayne. But the last thing she'd wanted to do was admit to her friends that she was using the man for his insurance.

Okay, that was a lie. She never would've married anyone for money. No way in hell. The insurance was the reason she clung to, but the truth was that she cared about Truck a hell of a lot.

Shit, who was she kidding? She loved the man. She'd practically moved into his apartment. Now that the cancer was gone, she could've moved back home. She could've put space between them. She could've told him that she wanted a divorce, for God's sake.

But the truth of the matter was that Mary liked sleeping in Truck's arms. Liked waking up to his tousled hair and grumpy morning attitude. She liked coming home from work and having him there. She liked cooking for him, and letting him cook for her. She liked pretty much *everything* about him.

The bottom line was that Ford "Truck" Laughlin was a good man.

Way too good for the likes of her.

She was Ann Weston's daughter. The spawn of a town

whore. She was born white trash and she'd always *be* white trash. Too brash. Too snarky. Hanging out with Rayne and the other women made her feel less worthless, but when push came to shove, she was exactly like her mama. Using Truck for what he could give her.

But she couldn't quite make herself push him from her life. She couldn't imagine him *not* being there. And that scared the shit out of her.

If she felt this way about him now, when they were basically living as roommates and not lovers, not like a true man and wife would live, how would she feel if she let down all her barriers?

Mary didn't even want to get into the small fact that the thought of being intimate with Truck freaked her out. Not because of him; she could never be afraid of *him*. But because of what the cancer had taken from her. Namely, her boobs. It was silly. It wasn't like two mounds of flesh made a woman a woman, but the thought of baring herself to Truck now that she *wasn't* sick, letting him see exactly how disfigured she was, made her physically sick.

It wasn't as if Truck didn't know...he did. He was fully aware that she'd had a double mastectomy, knew what the radiation had done to her skin and nerves there. He'd see her when wearing clothes was too painful because of the radiation burns on her skin. But it was a whole different thing to willingly bare herself to him...or to anyone...now that she wasn't "sick" anymore.

"Mary?" Wendy asked.

Mary jerked back to the present. "I'll be there as soon as I can. If Kassie has her daughter before I get there, tell her congrats for me."

"I will. See you later!"

Mary hung up the phone and ignored the glare from her

boss. She wasn't allowed to make personal phone calls during work hours, but fuck that. Kassie was in the hospital having her baby. And it wasn't as if she'd been on the phone for hours.

Taking a deep breath, Mary gestured to the next customer in line.

An hour and a half later, Mary rushed into the hospital and ran up to the lady behind the reception area.

"I'm here for Kassie Caverly. She's having a baby. Might have already had it. Can you tell me what room she's in or where the waiting room is?"

The woman smiled, obviously having dealt with many panicked patrons over the years. "The waiting area for obstetrics is on the third floor. The elevator is behind you on the right."

"Thank you!" Mary told her and hurried toward the elevator doors. She pushed the button and turned to glance at someone she saw out of the corner of her eye—and froze.

It was Ghost. She hadn't been alone with him since it had come out that she'd married Truck.

She knew Ghost was pissed. Rayne had refused to marry him until she could walk down the aisle with Mary.

Ghost didn't take his eyes from her. He didn't look mad, not really, but his gaze on her was uncomfortable.

Because she felt uneasy, Mary did what she did best... brought out the snark. It was her defense mechanism, and how she'd been taught to deal with intense emotions. "Take a picture, it'll last longer," she told him, and inwardly winced at the childish taunt.

But her words didn't seem to faze the Delta Force soldier. He merely leaned against the wall and crossed his arms over his broad chest and continued to stare at her.

Mary fidgeted and prayed the elevator would hurry the

hell up. Of course, when it did arrive, she was going to have to get in the closed box with Ghost. That would be worse. She began to pray that someone else would arrive and get in the elevator with them. That way, he couldn't say anything that would slice her to ribbons.

Not that she would blame him. It was her fault Raynie wouldn't marry him. Well, that and the stupid pact they'd made while drunk one night. She'd tried to convince Rayne to marry Ghost, but she'd refused. Now it was a huge mess, and Mary was right in the middle of it.

The elevator dinged with its arrival and Mary bravely stepped in, Ghost right on her heels. The second the door shut, he spoke.

"How are you, Mary?"

"Fine."

"No residual effects from the cancer?"

Mary didn't understand why he was being so nice. She wished he would go ahead and lambast her and get it over with. "My fingers tingle, and some days I can't really feel them, but otherwise, I feel okay."

"Good."

She waited for the other shoe to fall. When he didn't say anything else, she took a deep breath and looked up at him. "Go on, say it already."

"Say what?" Ghost asked, looking completely unruffled.

"Yell at me. Tell me I'm a bitch. Tell me that you're pissed at me for hurting Raynie."

"Believe it or not, I understand why you married Truck and didn't tell anyone."

Mary gaped at the larger man. "You do?"

He nodded but didn't elaborate.

Hell, *Mary* hardly knew why she'd kept her marriage a secret. Well, part of it was that she simply hadn't wanted to disappoint Rayne by not having that double wedding she had her heart set on. Another part was because she was afraid. Rayne had put her entire life on hold the first time Mary had fought the cancer. Had spent every moment she could helping Mary get through it. The guilt Mary felt that her friend had done so much for her was almost overwhelming. She couldn't have put Rayne through that again.

But more than that, the last thing Mary had wanted was for Rayne to watch her die.

Mary had decided she wasn't going to go through the treatments again. And without the chemo, the cancer would eventually kill her. And she hadn't wanted her best friend to have to watch her fade away.

She'd kept the cancer from her best friend for Rayne's sake.

Mary had made peace with her life and was ready to die, but then Truck stepped in. Kept on her and wouldn't stop. He basically shamed her into fighting a second time. When he learned that she didn't have the money for the treatments, he offered to marry her so she could be on his Army insurance.

Mary wanted to decline, but in the end had taken him up on his offer. She wasn't an idiot, she'd known the man had feelings for her, but she'd pushed that to the back of her mind and put all her effort into the agony of going through the chemo and radiation treatments a second time...and keeping her best friend at arm's length so she didn't find out.

For Ghost to say he knew why she'd done what she had was laughable. He had no clue.

"You don't know me," Mary whispered. "You have no idea what my motives were."

Ghost took a step toward her then, and Mary retreated before she could stop herself. Once she realized what she'd done, she straightened and crossed her arms over her chest and glared up at Ghost.

"I know you love Rayne. I know you'd do anything in your power to look out for her. To protect her. You did it when I dicked her over, and you did it when you didn't tell her about your cancer returning. I don't know your history, I don't think even Rayne knows all of it, but what I *do* know is that you've probably been treated like shit. You love deeply, but have no idea how to express it. Your way of expressing that to your best friend was to push her out of your life when shit got tough, for her own protection. I understand that. I do. And to a small extent, I'm grateful, because Rayne would've done everything in her power to make sure you recovered. Would've put everything and everyone else to the side, including me.

"But you're also correct that I'm pissed. You denied Rayne the chance to be there for you. You essentially denied her love. I've already forgiven you, Mary. But you're going to have to work for Rayne's forgiveness. You hurt her. Bad. I've never seen her so devastated. She cried the entire night after she found out about you and Truck. About your cancer. Not because of a fucking wedding ceremony. But because you wouldn't let her be there for you. *That's* what she's upset about. Whoever taught you to be so selfish should be shot. Love freely given is the best kind of medicine out there."

Mary stared up at Ghost in dismay. His words slashing at her and hurting worse than the last bouts of radiation had, when her skin was already raw and burnt.

The elevator dinged and the doors opened on the third floor. Without waiting for a reply, Ghost strode out of the small box and headed down the hall.

Mary stepped out of the elevator in a daze. He was right, of course. Every single word out of his mouth was balls-on accurate. She *had* pushed Rayne away to protect her. And her mama had taught her to be selfish. But Mary hadn't thought she was being selfish when she'd kept her best friend in the dark about what was going on with her. Mary had thought she was doing the right thing. Seriously, who would want to watch their friend die?

But the more she thought about it, and because she knew Rayne, she knew without a doubt that Ghost was right. This wasn't about a wedding. She'd hurt her best friend, the woman who had always been there for her, who had never asked for anything in return, who had tattooed her own body in solidarity with Mary.

Mary wanted to fall down on the floor in a heap and bawl, but she couldn't. She had to be strong. She had to face Rayne and all the other women. Women who she knew without a doubt would've also stood by her side and helped her, if she'd only given them a chance.

She'd been alone for so long, and had let her mama's cynical ravings about men and people in general override her love for her best friend.

Mary heard voices raised in excitement down the hall, and she stilled. Everyone was happy and excited. Kassie had probably had her daughter by now. Mary walking in the room would make everyone uncomfortable and uneasy. She'd ruin the happy moment.

Mary needed to fix what she'd broken, but at the moment, she had no idea how. She wanted her best friend back. Wanted to babysit Annie and laugh at the little girl's hilarity. She wanted to hug Kassie and tell her how happy she was for her. Wanted them all to be able to sit together and drink wine and laugh and gossip.

She missed her friends. Tears sprang to her eyes as she realized that every single one of them would've done everything they could to keep her upbeat and positive. They wouldn't have felt sorry for her. They wouldn't have made her feel like a burden. She'd fucked up. Big time.

Feeling as if the weight of the world was on her shoulders, Mary turned and walked down the hall toward the stairwell. She needed to get out of there. Needed some fresh air. She would fix things, but not now. Not when everyone was celebrating the birth of Kassie and Hollywood's baby girl. She'd send a present to Kassie and her baby. The last thing she wanted to do was ruin everyone's happy mood.

Without looking back at the joyful group in the waiting room, Mary pushed open the door to the stairwell and disappeared.

Truck stood against the wall and grinned at his friends. Hollywood was passing out cigars as if he were a Mafia kingpin. He even had a bubblegum one for little Annie. Everyone was laughing and smiling and absolutely thrilled for Kassie and Hollywood. Even Karina, Kassie's sister, was there. She'd arrived with Jim and Donna, Kassie's parents.

Hollywood had come into the waiting room and told them all that Kassie was fine and that their little girl, Katherine Lauren, was perfectly healthy. That had set off another round of cheering and general happiness.

The only thing missing was Mary.

Truck had called the bank and found out she'd left fifteen minutes ago. She should've arrived by now. He knew Wendy had called and let her know Kassie was in the hospital and ready to give birth any minute.

He glanced at his watch and decided to wait another five minutes before heading out to look for her. Recalling how

Harley had disappeared after a car accident and had almost died before being found days after her wreck had made him paranoid.

"I rode up in the elevator with her," Ghost said softly from next to him.

Truck looked at his friend, not surprised Ghost knew why he was looking at his watch. "Was she...okay?"

Ghost nodded then pressed his lips together and sighed. "I upset her. I didn't mean to," he said quickly after seeing the pissed-off look on Truck's face. "She was defensive and obviously expecting me to lay into her. I told her that I forgave her, but I was probably too harsh in telling her how upset Rayne has been."

Truck sighed and ran a hand through his hair absently. He and Ghost had talked about the entire situation and they'd come to the conclusion that Mary had been protecting her friend, and that's why she didn't want Rayne to know about the wedding or the cancer.

"She was right behind me. But when I turned to let her enter the waiting room before me, I saw her heading for the stairwell."

"Thanks for letting me know," Truck told his friend. "I'm gonna head out. Will you tell Kassie congrats for me?"

"Of course. Are you okay, Truck?" Ghost asked.

Truck looked at one of his best friends, then turned to gaze at the others in the room. Rayne was standing next to Emily with her arm around her waist. Emily was within two months of having her own baby. Annie was running from one adult to the other, chomping on the bubble gum cigar she'd been given and smiling from ear to ear. Beatle and Casey were standing off to the side holding hands. Wendy was leaning back against Blade. Even Sadie and Chase were there. Chase had his arm around Sadie's waist in a comfortable embrace.

Truck wanted what his friends had. Wanted Mary to turn to him when she was feeling uncomfortable. Wanted her to hold his hand and look at him like his friends' women looked at *them*.

But it was about time to admit that maybe that would never happen.

He'd hoped that if he gave her enough time, Mary would come around. That she'd see how much he loved her, that he'd never let her down. But even after everything they'd been through, she still held him at arm's length. They slept next to each other every night, and they'd even shared a few kisses, but she still hadn't given him any indication that she wanted to move their relationship from the weird friend zone it was in to more.

Truck wanted more.

He deserved more.

He loved Mary. Knew he'd never find another woman who made his heart race every time he looked at her. She was prickly and had shields at least a mile high, and Truck had hopes he could scale those walls and they'd be inseparable as a result. But he was finally admitting to himself that maybe whatever had happened to make her so wary wasn't something he could overcome.

"I'm okay," Truck told Ghost.

It was obvious his friend didn't believe him, but to his credit, Ghost didn't say a word about it.

"Are we still headed out at the end of the week?" Truck asked.

Ghost frowned, but allowed the change in subject. "Yeah. Hollywood is staying here, but we're headed out with the other Delta team."

"Trigger and his crew, right?" Truck asked.

Ghost nodded.

"They're good people. Do we have any new intel on the area?"

"Not yet. Commander Robinson is working on it. You know how he is…he refuses to send us anywhere until he's got enough information to be sure of what we're heading into. Insurgents have been extremely active, and he's not happy about the situation as it is right now. The last thing he wants is an ambush."

Truck nodded. "Good." He slapped Ghost on the back. "I'll see you tomorrow at PT."

"Yup. Later."

"Later."

Truck made his way through the room and gave chin lifts to his friends and hugged the women. Annie ran over to him as he was leaving. He knelt down so he could be eye to eye with the almost eight-year-old.

"You leavin?" she asked.

"Yup."

"Where's Mary?"

"Something came up and she couldn't get here today." Truck hated lying, but he wasn't going to tell Annie what the issue was.

"I miss her. I haven't seen her in for-EV-er. Will you tell her I learned some new signs? Frankie taught them to me and I wanted to practice with her."

Truck blinked in surprise. He knew Annie had a little boyfriend who lived out in California, and that Frankie was deaf. They "spoke" to each other using a special program on their tablets. But he didn't know Mary had been practicing sign language with the little girl. "Of course I will. When did you last practice with her?"

"Last week," Annie said glibly. "She installed the same program me and Frankie have on her tablet and she calls me and I show her what Frankie taught me. We're learning together."

Truck was speechless. He hadn't known Mary was doing that.

Lately, it seemed as if everyone knew his wife better than he did.

"Mary told me that Frankie was lucky to have me for a girlfriend," Annie said proudly.

"She's right," Truck said.

"I was sad one day because a girl in my class was making fun of me for having a boyfriend who lives so far away. She told me to tell Carrie to stuff it. That having a boyfriend who lives in a different state is tough, but not impossible. And that if I really liked Frankie, I should do whatever it took to make him feel good. And he should do the same for me. I'm gonna marry Frankie, so I want to be sure to treat him really really good."

Truck was flabbergasted. Mary had told Annie to do what she could to make Frankie feel good. That was surprising. He knew Mary didn't exactly have a good track record when it came to men, and she'd said more than once that men generally had ulterior motives when it came to relationships. It was one of the reasons he'd been going so slow with Mary. He didn't want her to think he'd married her and put her on his insurance in exchange for sex.

"Well, she's right," Truck told Annie.

"I know," Annie said with a shrug. "I miss her. Tell her to call me so we can practice the new signs I learned."

"I will."

Annie leaned forward and kissed Truck on the cheek, right over his scar. Then spun and headed back into the room to find another adult to talk to.

Truck wiped the sticky bubblegum kiss from his face with

the back of his hand. He loved Annie as if she were his own. She'd never, not once, shied away from him because of the nasty scar on his face. The first time he met her, she'd put her hand on his cheek and asked if it had hurt.

Standing and walking out of the waiting room, Truck thought about Mary. He had no idea what to do. On the one hand, he loved having her in his space. Loved being able to talk to her every night, and he especially loved having her curl up against him as they slept.

But on the other hand, he needed more. He wanted to love Mary like she was meant to be loved. Wanted to make love with her, shower with her, laugh with her. He wanted to be her husband in more than just name only.

He'd thought after she got better that their relationship would morph into more. But it hadn't.

Pressing his lips together as he waited for the elevator, Truck knew he had to make a decision. Continue on like he had in the hopes Mary would eventually come to love him back, or let her go.

CHAPTER TWO

Two days later, Mary watched Rayne, Emily, and Casey come into the bank. She'd been trying to figure out how to approach Rayne, but she'd so far chickened out every time.

Not only that, but things with Truck had been weird. He'd been different since their friends had found out she and Truck were married, but lately he seemed distant. When he left for PT in the morning, he didn't wake her up to tell her he was going, and he didn't sit next to her on the couch at night either. In fact, he seemed to go out of his way to distance himself from her altogether.

Mary was worried that she'd lost not only her friends, but it looked like Truck had finally had enough of her bitchiness and wishy-washiness and was getting ready to dump her too.

It didn't help that he and the rest of the team were heading out of town this weekend for a mission. She hated when he left. Every single time, she worried that he'd never come back. That he'd be killed overseas. She knew he and the others were good at what they did, but something bad could always happen. Always.

Her life was out of control, and Mary wanted nothing

more than to throw herself in Truck's arms and beg him to love her forever, no matter what she did or said to fuck things up. She also wanted to prostrate herself in front of Rayne and beg *her* to forgive her.

Eyeing the women as they entered, Mary decided this was it. She needed to suck it up and ask Rayne if she'd come over so they could talk. It was time. Way past time. She'd never had a problem speaking her mind in the past; it was time she got back to *that* Mary.

She was on break and knew she had about fifteen minutes before her boss would give her the evil eye, indicating it was time for her to go back to work. The bank was busy as lunchtime was nearing. Taking a big breath, Mary walked up to Rayne and Emily. They were standing off to the side waiting for Casey to finish her transaction.

"Hi," Mary said uncertainly. She hated feeling this way.

"Hi," Rayne responded without the usual friendliness in her tone.

"Mary," Emily said, nodding at her.

"Do you have a second?" Mary asked Rayne.

Her best friend's gaze shot to Emily, then to Casey, who had walked up to them, before meeting Mary's. "Not really."

"Please," Mary whispered. "I have a lot of things I need to say, more than I can get through on my break, but I need to at least tell you how sorry I am."

Mary could tell Rayne was struggling with her emotions just as she was. She wanted to put her arms around Rayne and hug her, but knew she'd be rebuffed...rightly so.

Looking around, Rayne said, "Is there somewhere we can go so we aren't in the middle of the bank with everyone looking at us?"

Taking that as a good sign, Mary immediately nodded. "Yeah. The break room in the back. Typically it's off-limits to anyone but employees, but I've seen my boss bring some of her friends back there. I know she won't say anything."

"Fine. Come on, Em. Casey," Rayne said to the other women.

Mary nodded. She wasn't surprised Rayne wanted the others there for moral support. She would've too. Too bad it would make it feel like it was three against one, but Mary supposed she'd made her bed, now she had to lie in it.

She led the way to the back room. They passed two vaults —the money vault, and the one with all the safety-deposit boxes. The latter door was open. It stayed open during the day, except when a patron wanted to access their box. Then they were accompanied inside by an employee and the door was shut, giving the patron privacy. It had a thick rug on the floor and a table in the middle of the room. Mary hated that vault. With all the safety-deposit boxes lined up, and the subdued lighting inside, it always reminded her of a morgue, but on a smaller scale. The drawers were nowhere near big enough for a human, but she'd had a nightmare one night of opening one of the boxes and having a miniature body sit up.

Shuddering, Mary concentrated on the break room in front of her. The door was propped open and, once she was inside, she turned to face Rayne. "I'm sorry. I'm so fucking sorry for not telling you that I'd married Truck. It was a shitty thing to do."

"You think I'm mad about *that?*" Rayne asked incredulously. Her brows were drawn down and she was frowning.

"No," Mary said, looking at the floor. "I know why you're upset with me."

As if she hadn't spoken, Rayne continued, "I don't give a shit that you went behind my back and got married. Though I *am* pissed that you're leading Truck on. He's one of the nicest people I've ever met and deserves to be loved more than anyone. I know you care about him, but for some reason you're holding yourself back, and he doesn't deserve that. But, more than that, I'm pissed that the person I was closer to than anyone didn't tell me her cancer had returned."

Mary wasn't sure what to say. Her throat had closed up and she felt as if she was going to burst into tears any second. Having Rayne look at her as if she couldn't stand to be in the same room was the most painful thing she'd ever experienced.

Even more painful than when she'd been sixteen years old and learned her mama had been telling the truth about men all along. Even more painful than having Mama kick her out of the house the day she'd turned eighteen, even though she hadn't graduated from high school yet. Even more painful than the day she'd learned the cancer had returned.

"I don't understand why you pushed me away," Rayne continued. "Did I do something wrong? *Say* something? I know you've had problems trusting people, but I never in a million years would've thought that you didn't trust *me*."

"I trust you," Mary said after a beat.

"No. You don't. If you did, you would've told me the second you got that diagnosis. You would've let me come over and hold your hand while we dealt with it. You would've told me you couldn't afford the treatments and we could've done some fundraising to pay for it. Instead, you pushed me away and married Truck for his money. Were you ever going to tell me about *any* of it? Your marriage? The cancer? Or were you going to keep laughing it off when I told you I was waiting to marry Ghost until you sucked it up and admitted that you loved Truck as much as he loves you?"

Mary opened her mouth to respond, to deny Rayne's harsh words—but a weird noise from the lobby distracted her. The other women didn't even turn their heads, maybe because they weren't as familiar with the everyday sounds of the bank. Holding her hand up to the other women, she stuck her head out of the break room and looked over the heads of the tellers at the windows.

What she saw had Mary moving before she'd really even thought about it. She grabbed Rayne's hand and gestured for Emily and Casey to follow her. "Don't say a word!" she whispered urgently. "Follow me."

Without waiting for them to respond, she tugged Rayne out the door and headed for the safety-deposit vault. The safest place for them was there. Even though Mary hated the room, it was absolutely impenetrable.

Not only that, but if the two men with guns in the lobby decided they wanted more money than what was in the tellers' drawers, they'd ask to be let into the money vault, not the one with the safety-deposit boxes.

"Holy shit," Rayne exclaimed softly as Mary pulled her inside. "Is this really happening?"

Without answering, Mary gestured for Emily and Casey to hurry and the second they cleared the door, she shut it as quietly as she could, even though she didn't think the robbers could hear the door shutting over the sounds of the screams and crying now coming from the packed lobby.

Mary did what she'd been trained to do in a situation like this. She secured the door, trying not to shiver when it felt like the lid to a coffin shutting, and went straight to the phone on the wall. It was a separate line from the rest of the bank, for safety reasons. No one would see the red light on the desk phones indicating someone was using it. She dialed 9-1-1 and quickly explained the situation to the operator.

She didn't have a lot of details, but told the lady where she was, who she was with, approximately how many customers there were in the lobby as far as she knew, how many robbers she saw, and how many bank employees there were. The operator wanted her to stay on the line, but Mary hung up and immediately dialed another number.

Rayne, Emily, and Casey were murmuring behind her, but Mary ignored them for the time being. "Come on, come on," she chanted as the phone rang in her ear.

"Hello?"

The sound of Truck's voice immediately calmed her. "Truck, it's Mary. I need you."

"What's wrong?" His voice was hard, but composed. It kept her from losing her shit.

"I'm at the bank and there's a robbery in progress. Rayne, Emily, and Casey are with me, and I locked us in the safety-deposit vault. We can't hear what's going on out there, but the guys had guns."

"Are you all right?"

At his question, Mary's eyes filled with tears. How like Truck to worry about her first. "Yeah."

"And the others?"

Mary turned to look at her friends. They were huddled together and looked completely terrified. "They're good. We're all good," she told Truck, lying. She didn't think he needed to know they were on the verge of freaking out.

"Okay. I'm on the way. The guys are all here...and I'm gonna bring another Delta team with me. We've got this. Hear me?"

"Yeah. I called 9-1-1."

"Good. Mary...*we got this*," Truck said again, more urgently. "All you gotta do is stay safe. Can they get in?"

"Maybe. I've hit the panic button from inside the vault, which locks it down, but my boss has the override code. I'm hoping if they want money, they won't bother with this vault, they'll want the one with the money. My boss should steer them toward that one."

"Stay away from the door," Truck ordered. She could hear him moving in the background and hoped like hell he really was on his way right that second. "Can you barricade it in any way?"

"No. There's a table in here, but it's bolted to the floor, and it would be too heavy for us to move even if it wasn't."

"Fuck. Okay, that's okay. I bet those guys are already gone. They'll take what money they can and get the fuck out. We're comin' for you, Mare. You tell the others their men are comin' too. Okay?"

"Yeah."

"Don't do anything rash," Truck warned. "I love you."

Mary's stomach tightened at his words. He'd never come out and said it before. Oh, she knew he loved her, but she hadn't heard the words. Hearing them now was almost painful. "Be careful," she whispered, wanting to return his words, but not able to make herself say them.

"Always. You call me back if you need to."

"I will."

"You did good, Mare. I gotta go. Ten minutes and we'll be there."

"Okay."

"Bye."

Mary hung up the phone and took a deep breath and looked her friends in the eyes. "We need to get away from the door."

"They're coming, right?" Emily asked, her voice shaking.

Suddenly more than aware of how pregnant the woman was, and everything that could go wrong, Mary said, "Of course they are. They're also bringing that other Delta team they've been training with. Those asshole robbers won't know what hit them if they're stupid enough to still be here when the guys arrive. Come on, over here away from the door. Sit. You're not going to have that baby in here, are you? Because if you do, you're gonna have to name him Hank."

"Hank?" Emily asked as she waddled over to where Mary indicated, Rayne and Casey on either side of her.

"Yeah. You know, like bank, but with an H," Mary quipped.

Emily shook her head and rolled her eyes, but she was grinning while she did it. Rayne and Casey got Emily seated and looked up at her.

"Now what?" Casey asked.

Mary looked around the room and shook her head. "The table is bolted down, so we can't move it. There aren't any other chairs or anything else in here. All we can do is wait."

"Are those guys gonna want to come in here?" Emily asked.

Mary met her eyes. "As I told Truck, I don't think they will. I mean, the boxes are locked up tight and there are two keys needed for each one. The customer has one and the bank has the other. Yeah, there's probably hundreds of thousands of dollars' worth of jewels in here, but it would be tough to get at them easily. If I was a bank robber, I'd rather get into the money vault, where I could grab stacks of cash and go."

"You aren't just saying that to make us feel better, are you?" Rayne asked suspiciously.

Mary sighed and sat down about three feet away from the other women, making sure to put herself between them and the door. She met Rayne's eyes and said, "I'd say anything to make you feel safe, Rayne. I'd do anything in my power to protect you. When you were missing in Egypt, I almost lost my mind. So yeah, I'd totally fucking lie if it meant you were happy, safe, and secure. But I'm not lying to you right now."

The two women stared at each other without saying a word.

"You're talking about more than stashing us in here to get away from the robbers, aren't you?" Casey asked.

Not taking her eyes from Rayne's, Mary said simply, "Yes." This wasn't the time or the place that she'd planned on having a heart to heart with her best friend, but it was what it was.

"I never asked you to do that," Rayne whispered.

"I know. You're the best thing that ever happened to me," Mary told her. "My childhood was shit. I had so many 'uncles' coming in and out of our house, I stopped bothering to learn their names after a while. They, and my mama, taught me to never rely on anyone for anything because they'll always let you down. And it wasn't just that she told me that every fucking day...I saw it. Every one of those uncles promised my mama a better life. They promised they'd take care of her, and me. And every single one left. I can't really blame them because Mama was a bitch, but still.

"Teachers let me down by not noticing how hungry I was and how I hadn't showered in days. Social workers let me down too. They'd come around every now and then after one of the uncles reported Mama, but they were overworked and busy and didn't bother to really see me. Even the principal let me down after he found out Mama had kicked me out my senior year, by not giving a shit and threatening to have me expelled if I missed any more days of class. I told him it was because I was trying to find a place to live, but he didn't care.

"Then I met *you*, Raynie. I wasn't going to let you in, but you stormed the shields I had around my heart. I didn't know what love was until I met you." Mary knew she had tears in her eyes, but she didn't stop. "You got me. You didn't care that I used sarcasm to protect myself. You didn't care that I was snarky and a bitch. You loved me all the same. Then when I got cancer, you were there every step of the way. You came to my appointments with me. You were there when I was too sick to get out of bed. You forced me to eat, to stay positive, and to *live*. And the weirdest thing for me was that you didn't want anything in return."

"You tried to offer me money," Rayne remembered, her own face wet with tears. "As if I'd take your fucking money."

"I didn't know how to deal with that. No one in my life ever gave me anything without strings attached. Until you. You dropped your hours down at your job so you could be with me. You didn't date for months when I was sick. You went grocery shopping for both of us and you did all my laundry, cleaned my apartment, and practically moved in. It was overwhelming for me, but no matter how much I protested or how mean I was to you, you didn't leave."

"Nothing could've made me leave you when you were sick, Mare," Rayne said.

"I know. Then I got better, and you met Ghost. I was so happy for you, even though I was a dick to him after he got hurt. I couldn't stand to see you unhappy, Raynie. I didn't trust him, and I didn't want you to go through the pain that I'd been though. I hoped he was the man he seemed to be, but I also thought there was a chance he'd dump you once the honeymoon period was over."

"So why didn't you tell me the cancer was back? Did you not think I'd help you again?" Rayne asked.

"No. I *knew* you would. I couldn't go through it again," Mary said softly. "I couldn't do that to *you* again. It was hell on both of us, and it wasn't fair of me to put you through that twice. Not when you were living the dream. You had a man who doted on you and would give you the world if you asked."

"What wasn't fair was that you didn't even give me a choice," Rayne said with heat.

"You don't understand," Mary protested.

"So explain it to me," Rayne practically yelled. "I would've been there for you, Mare, just like I was the first time. I would've done *anything* for you, and you didn't give me that choice."

Mary clenched her hands into fists and squeezed her eyes closed as Rayne continued her harangue.

"You always go on and on about how people are selfish and users and only do things because they want something in return. But you *knew* I wasn't like that. I'd proven it already. So why, Mary? Why did you push me away? At least have the balls to tell me to my face. Open your eyes and face me!"

Mary's eyes popped open and she stared in Rayne's direction. She couldn't see her because of the tears obscuring her vision, could only see her blurry outline. All the pain she'd felt when she got the diagnosis that her cancer was back bubbled to the surface.

"I didn't want you to have to watch me die!" she yelled.

The words echoed in the room before she continued.

"The last thing I wanted to do was have my best friend, a woman I love more than anything in this world, have to see me waste away and know there was nothing she could do about it. I wanted your memories of me to be good ones." Mary closed her eyes once more and sniffed. "I didn't want you to have to experience that, Raynie. I couldn't take it. I *knew* you'd be there for me. You'd never let me push you away if you knew the cancer was back. You would've stayed by my side to the bitter end—and it would've killed me to see you so sad and upset."

There was silence in the vault after Mary's pronouncement. The soundproof room gave no hint as to what was happening out in the lobby. Mary had no idea if the robbers were still there, if there was a huge shoot out, or if the robbery was still in progress. All she could hear was her own heartbeat and her occasional sniffle. But she didn't dare open her eyes again.

She'd just laid herself bare to her best friend, and she was terrified Rayne would reject her for good. That this was the end of their friendship forever. She didn't know what she'd do without Rayne in her life. The last couple months had been hell. Absolute hell.

Mary jerked when she felt a hand on her arm and her eyes opened. She turned and saw Rayne crouched at her side.

"Thank you," Rayne said.

"What?"

"All this time, I thought I'd done something wrong. That you were mad at me for moving in with Ghost and loving him. I knew how you felt about men. But I had it all wrong. You were protecting me."

Mary nodded.

At that, Rayne shifted until she was sitting next to Mary and put her arms around her friend. Mary tucked her head into Rayne's shoulder and held on for dear life. The familiar smell of Rayne's favorite soap penetrated her senses and it felt like coming home.

"I'm sorry," Mary said into her shoulder. "I'm so sorry."

"It's okay," Rayne said. "I understand. I forgive you."

Mary pulled back. "Just like that?"

"Just like that. I love you, Mare. You're like the sister I never had. Chase is nice and all, but he's no sister."

Mary heard Emily and Casey chuckle, but she didn't take her eyes from Rayne as she continued.

"But don't do that shit again. If you get a fucking sniffle, I want to know about it. I love that you wanted to protect me, but don't do it again. Hear me?"

"Yeah, Raynie. I hear ya. *Please* marry Ghost. You guys are perfect for each other, and I know without a doubt that he'd never leave you. Ever."

"I know."

"So you'll get married?"

"Yes—on one condition."

Mary rolled her eyes and wiped her face. "What?"

"You and Truck renew your vows with us."

Mary froze, and the yearning that struck was almost painful. "I'm not sure—"

"That pact we made was bullshit. We both know it. I mean, there's no way I would've put off marrying Ghost if you didn't have a man in your life. But you do...Truck. I see the way you look at him when he isn't watching, and how he looks at you. I thought if I held off long enough, you'd see what was right in front of your face and we could have our double wedding ceremony."

"I'm sorry I didn't tell you about my marriage."

Rayne waved her hand in the air in dismissal. "I don't care about that. I'm glad you did it. It saved your life, so I can't be pissed about it. But...now that you *are* married, you can renew your vows with me and Ghost. You've got nothing to argue against. It'll be just like we planned all those years ago."

"Things between me and Truck aren't exactly husband and wifey."

"Husband and wifey?" Casey asked.

Mary nodded. "Yeah. I mean...we aren't..."

"Oh, shit, you haven't slept with him?" Rayne asked in shock.

"Well, we've slept, but that's it."

"Holy shit," Emily breathed. "I can't believe it. Truck

looks at you with such lust, we all thought for sure you were doing the nasty."

Mary winced. "Yeah, well, it wasn't as if we could get it on when I was sick. And now things are just...weird."

"Do you want him?" Rayne asked. Then added, "And don't lie."

Mary nodded.

"Do you love him?" she pressed.

"I don't know, Raynie. I don't know that I know what love is."

"Bullshit. You love *me*."

"That's different."

"It's not. Look. I get it. From the first time we met, we agreed that men suck. But even back then I knew that for you, it wasn't just something you were saying because you'd just had a breakup. You truly believed it. Your bitch of a mom planted that seed when you were nothing but a kid. But Truck is *not* those guys from your past. He's not one of your childhood *uncles*. I think he's more than proved he's with you because he loves you and not because he wants something from you."

"I know."

"Then what's holding you back?"

Mary bit her lip then looked at her best friend. "I'm scared to let him see me. You know...without..." She gestured to her chest. "But it's not just that. I mean, I know he has his own scars and if anyone would understand, it'd be him. The last time I told a guy that I loved him, he dumped me the next day. I'm scared to death that if I say it again, the same thing will happen."

"You're selling Truck short, and that's not fair to him," Rayne said with conviction. "I get it. It's scary to open yourself up, both physically and emotionally. But Truck is not that guy. If you told him you loved him, I have a feeling it would change both your lives. For the good. Give him a chance, Mare."

"I'll try."

"Ooh..." Emily moaned from nearby, and both Mary's and Rayne's heads turned to stare at the pregnant woman.

"What? What is it?" Rayne asked urgently.

"I'm not sure," Emily said, the concern easy to hear in her voice.

"Lie down," Casey ordered, already helping the other woman to the floor.

Rayne and Mary moved to her side. Mary grabbed one of her hands and Rayne grasped Emily's leg. "Deep breaths," Rayne ordered. "Try to relax."

"I think I'm okay," Emily said. "It was just a twinge. I've still got two months to go. I'm not in labor."

"Damn straight you're not," Mary said. "I am *not* delivering Annie's brother in the middle of a bank robbery in this cave of a room."

"You don't know it's a boy," Emily said.

"It is. Annie wants a brother, so it's a boy."

Emily rolled her eyes, but quickly looked up at Mary. "Thank you for not distancing yourself from Annie. She loves you so much, and she wouldn't have understood."

Mary nodded. "Annie is my soul sister. She's precious and can be snarky, just like me. Do you...will you forgive me?" Mary hadn't ever been so unsure in all her life. Usually she didn't give a damn what people thought about her, but this was too important to be flippant.

"Of course I do," Emily said immediately. "I was upset because Rayne was upset. But I never hated you."

"Thank you," Mary told her softly.

"And I'm too new to even know what all the hub-bub was about," Casey piped in. "So I forgive you too."

Rayne laughed. "Girl, you never even took sides. In fact, you constantly bugged me to talk to Mary and mend our rift."

"True," Casey said cheerfully. "And now you have. I can't wait to call Wendy, Kassie, and Harley, and tell them all is well."

Mary grimaced. "I need to talk to them too. To explain."

Rayne put her hand on Mary's arm. "I'll do it."

"Thanks. But that's not cool. Maybe we could both do it? Take them to lunch or something?"

"That sounds awesome. And we can call Bryn together too."

Mary shuddered. "That woman. I love her, but jeez, you know she'll analyze the situation to death and then get side-tracked and want to know all about my cancer, what it's like to have no boobs, and what the doctors said...in detail."

Everyone chuckled. They all knew Bryn, and knew she'd do exactly that. Her curiosity was voracious and typically their phone calls always went off on a weird tangent because of the way Bryn's mind worked. But she was refreshing and didn't have a mean bone in her body.

"How long has it been?" Emily asked, one of her hands resting on her rounded tummy protectively. "What do you think is going on?"

Mary looked at her watch. "About fifteen minutes. I'm gonna call Truck back." She stood and went over to the phone on the wall. She knew it was a risk. If he was in the middle of doing his Delta Force thing, he wouldn't be able to answer, and she could even take his attention away from what he was doing, but she needed to know what was happening on the other side of the wall.

Besides, she was worried about Emily. Even if the other

woman thought she was okay, she needed to see a doctor to make sure. Mary hadn't been kidding when she said that she didn't want to deliver a baby.

She dialed Truck's number and he answered on the second ring.

"Mary?"

"Yeah, what's happening?"

"Are you guys all right?"

"Yeah. We can't hear a thing though. And Emily's having some pain."

"Shit. The cops are clearing the scene now. We should be able to get to you guys in about five minutes. Will she be okay until then?"

"Yeah. I think so. She seems to be all right at the moment. She's lying down. Clearing the scene? So everyone is safe?"

Truck's voice lowered, his tone calming her again, just as it had earlier. "Yeah. We got here at the same time as the cops, and luckily we knew them. They let us take point. Trigger's team breached through the back door and we came in through the front. Those assholes didn't even resist, simply dropped their weapons when they saw they were surrounded."

"And all the customers?"

"They're fine. Shaken up, but no one was hurt. The assholes were trying to get your manager to open the money vault, like you said. She was in the process of opening the vault when we rushed in. No one was hurt."

"Thank God."

"Yeah. Okay, four minutes and we'll be there. I'll get the code from the manager. You guys just stay back from the door. We'll come to you. Tell Em to hang on, okay?"

"I will."

"Mare?"

"Yeah, Truck?"

"Are you all right? I mean, you and Rayne haven't exactly been getting along. Is everything okay?"

"Surprisingly, yeah."

She heard Truck breathe a sigh of relief. "Good. See you soon, baby."

"Bye."

The endearment was surprising, but welcome. Truck usually called her Mare when he was being loving, but lately she hadn't even heard that much. So hearing him call her baby made her heart swell.

She might've mended her relationship with her best friend, but she still had a ways to go with Truck.

She'd get there. She had to; the alternative was unthinkable.

She turned to the others. "Truck and the guys are on their way. They came in with that other Delta team and surrounded the robbers. They gave up without shooting anyone."

"Yay!" Casey exclaimed, and everyone laughed.

"Emily, I know you heard me tell him that you were having some pain, so prepare yourself for going to the hospital," Mary ordered.

"I wish you hadn't said anything," the other woman murmured. "I'm fine."

"As if," Mary said, rolling her eyes. "You're going to the hospital and that's that. Again, the last thing I want is poor Hank coming out in the bank."

Everyone burst out laughing at the intentional rhyme.

Mary hadn't felt as good as she did right this moment in months. She wasn't sick, she had her best friend back, and she had a new mission...tell Truck that she wanted to change the nature of their relationship.

Four and a half minutes later, all four women turned to look at the door as it slowly opened. Before Mary could blink, Truck was there. He pulled her up from the floor where she'd been sitting, holding Emily's hand, and had her in his embrace.

He buried his face in her hair and backed away from Fletch, Ghost, and Beatle as they reached for their own women.

Mary's feet weren't touching the floor, but the only thing she could concentrate on was Truck and the way he felt and smelled. His arms were like steel bands around her back. With a flash of insight, Mary realized that there was nowhere in the world she felt safer than right here in Truck's embrace. When he held her, she felt as if nothing and no one could hurt her. The epiphany was a bit late, considering how long she'd been living with him, but it was no less heartfelt.

He smelled amazing too. The body wash he used was nothing fancy, but it permeated every inch of his apartment, even his sheets. Mary frequently switched his pillow with hers right before he came to bed so she could have his scent in her nostrils as she fell asleep.

"Are you sure you're okay?" Truck murmured in her ear.

Mary nodded. "The second I realized something was going on, I got all of us in here and closed the door."

He eased her away from him and put her back on her feet. Mary felt a twinge of remorse at losing his arms around her, but he grabbed her hands and held on as they talked, making her feel a bit better. "How did you know to come in here?"

"Training," Mary said immediately. "We've had a few security experts come in and teach us the best things to do and what not to do in case of a robbery. Corporate had this vault outfitted with an external phone line. The expert said it was an almost perfect place to hole up since it has its own climate control, soundproofing, and phone line."

"Thank you," Ghost said from next to them, obviously overhearing her explanation. "I don't know what I'd do without Rayne." He looked down at her and squeezed her waist affectionately.

"And my thanks too," Beatle piped in from next to Casey. "You thought fast, and I'm grateful."

Embarrassed now, and not used to people praising her, especially not lately, Mary simply nodded.

"I told you, I'm fine," Emily complained from the floor behind them. Everyone turned in time to see Fletch pick her up as if she weighed as much as a child, rather than a seven-months-pregnant woman.

"And I heard you, but you're still going to the hospital," Fletch countered.

Emily rolled her eyes, but didn't complain further as her husband carted her out of the vault and into the bank on his way to an ambulance.

"You want to meet the other Delta team?" Truck asked Mary.

"Hell yeah!" she exclaimed. Mary was fascinated by the dynamics of the Special Forces teams. The men were the best of the best and they were extremely loyal. To each other and the Army. She'd never pass up the chance to meet more men like Truck.

They walked hand in hand through the lobby of the bank, which looked remarkably normal. There were only a few papers on the floor and a couple of handbags, but otherwise it could've been any other day. Mary didn't see any of her coworkers or her boss.

Seeing her confused look, Truck informed her, "Most of

the employees and some of the customers were taken to the hospital. They seem to be okay, but some had elevated blood pressure and the paramedics just wanted to be sure they didn't have anything else going on."

"And my boss?"

"She went too."

"Oh. Okay. I should stay and lock up then...I guess," Mary said.

Truck kissed the side of her head. "No, the manager called in someone from corporate. I think that's him over there." He motioned to a man in an expensive three-piece suit standing next to a group of police officers.

"Already? That was fast," Mary commented.

"I guess when your bank gets held up by armed thugs, damage control is implemented immediately," Truck said dryly.

Mary shrugged. "I guess."

"Come on, the others are over here."

Mary let Truck lead her through the parking lot toward a group of men standing on the outskirts. As she got closer, she snorted in disbelief.

"What?" Truck asked.

"Seriously?"

"What?" he repeated patiently.

"They're all hot. I mean, *really* hot. What is it with you Special Forces people? Are you *all* good-looking?"

Truck chuckled. "I don't know about that, but we're all in shape. We kinda have to be, considering what we do for a living."

"It's not just your muscles," Mary protested. "It's everything. You're all tall, handsome, and built. Shit, you could all be movie stars."

"Present company excluded," Truck said, gesturing toward his face.

Mary stopped abruptly and put her hands on her hips as she scolded him. "Don't. That scar on your face does nothing to take away from how hot you are, Ford Laughlin."

Instead of frowning at her, Truck smiled indulgently.

"And don't laugh at me!" Mary told him huffily.

"I can't help it. You're so fucking cute," Truck told her.

"Whatever. I am not."

"You're right. You're not. You're hot. Beautiful. Gorgeous. Not cute."

Now Mary knew she was blushing. "Hush. I thought you were going to introduce me."

"I was. Now I don't think I will. Not when you think they're all hot," Truck told her, turning to walk back the way they came.

Mary grabbed his arm and looked up at him, expecting to see him smiling at her.

But he wasn't smiling at all. He looked completely serious.

Mary spoke without thinking, wanting only to reassure him. "I don't have eyes for anyone but you, Truck. The first time I saw you, I knew you were trouble. That you could be the man to break me."

"I don't want to break you, Mare," Truck said quietly.

"I know." She reached up and put her hand on his scarred cheek. "I don't want anyone but you," she said softly, opening herself up, just a tiny bit, for the first time.

He understood exactly how much her words meant too, because his eyes got heavy and one hand came up to rest on her nape. "Yeah?"

Mary nodded. "I'm scared."

"Of me?"

"Yes." When he frowned, she quickly said, "But not how

you think. I haven't told anyone other than Rayne that I loved them since I was sixteen years old. And believe me when I say, *that* didn't go so well. It's hard for me...but I'm trying."

Truck closed his eyes and rested his forehead on hers. "Thank you, baby. You have no idea how much that means to me."

They stood like that for a moment longer, before Truck straightened and took her hand in his once more. "Come on. I'll introduce you and then take you home."

"Don't you have to get back to post and report in or something?"

"I do, but that can wait until I get you settled and make sure you're okay."

"I'm okay."

"Humor me, Mare. Let me take care of you. Hearing you say that you were in the bank when it was being held up by men with guns knocked me for a loop. I need to make sure you're home safe and sound before I get back to work."

What could she do other than nod?

With that, he started toward the group of men once more. They all turned to face them as they approached.

"Hey, guys. I'd like you to meet my wife, Mary."

She startled at that. It was the first time Truck had introduced her that way to anyone. They'd been keeping it a secret for so long, she hadn't thought about the fact that, now that everyone knew, they didn't have to keep their relationship on the down low any longer.

One by one, she shook the seven men's hands. They were all tall, as she'd observed, and good-looking. She could tell they were muscular even though they were wearing their long-sleeve BDUs.

Their nicknames were just as crazy as those in Truck's

group, but she didn't comment on it. Trigger, Lefty, Oz, Grover, Lucky, Brain, and Doc. They greeted her warmly, and Mary's head swam trying to keep them all straight.

"So you guys are headed off at the end of the week too, huh?" she said, trying to make conversation.

"Yup," Trigger said with a wink. "Truck and his team decided they needed us to show them how things are done."

Mary rolled her eyes. She knew he was teasing but couldn't resist messing with the other man. "Yeah, Truck mentioned that. Said they needed someone to flush out the bad guys. You know, like when hunting dogs run into the field and make the birds scatter so the hunters can shoot them?"

Lefty and Oz—at least she thought that was their names —threw their heads back and laughed, while the others simply smirked at her.

Feeling uncomfortable, like maybe she shouldn't have shown her snarky side immediately upon meeting the other men, Mary did her best to smile gamely back at them. Truck pulled her against him and kissed the side of her head once more.

"Here's some advice, Trigger. Don't go up against my wife in a game of wits. She'll win every fucking time."

"She thinks *we're* the dogs," Lefty said between chuckles. "But you're the ugliest dog out of all of us."

And just like that, Mary's humor vanished. She stepped out of Truck's light hold and marched up to the other man. She poked him in the chest, punctuating each word with a finger to his sternum. "That's not funny."

"Hey," Lefty said, taking a step away from the pissed-off woman and holding up his hands in capitulation. "I didn't mean nothin'."

"Then why'd you say it? Truck has a scar. Big fucking deal. It's not okay to make fun of him for it. If Brain over there lost his leg, would you start calling him Crip instead? No. You'd respect him and everything he went through. Don't make fun of the way Truck looks. It doesn't make you cool. It makes you an asshole."

Everyone was silent for a second, before Mary heard chuckles erupt all around her, which pissed her off even more. She spun, ready to tell off the others, but Truck was there. He wrapped his arms around her and pulled her against his chest. He hugged her close and lowered his head so he was speaking right into her ear. "Easy, Mare. He didn't mean anything by it, and I didn't take offense."

"Well, you should," Mary protested, squirming in his arms. "It's not cool. You got injured serving your country and they should respect you for it, not make fun of you."

"We *do* respect him," Trigger interjected. "But more than that, we respect *you* for coming to his defense."

Mary blinked and stopped struggling to get away from Truck. She stared at Trigger then met the eyes of the other men. They were all looking at her with expressions that ranged from humor to admiration.

Suddenly she blushed. Shit, she'd done it again, spoken without thinking. It would be a miracle if the men didn't think she was a raging bitch.

She forced a smile on her face and grabbed hold of Truck's forearm, digging her nails in to try to ground herself. "All right then. Now that *that's* settled. Thank you for coming over and helping out today."

Everyone nodded at her and mumbled various renditions of "of course" and "wouldn't have it any other way."

Truck kissed the top of her head and stepped to her side as a paramedic sauntered up to them. She was tall and slender with long brown hair, which was currently up in a ponytail on the back of her head.

Mary smiled, thinking she was coming to make sure she was okay—but instead the woman went up to Truck and smiled flirtatiously.

"My name is Ruth, and I wanted to make sure you were okay. Reports said that there were shots fired. Were you hit?"

Mary blinked at the woman. Shots fired? She hadn't heard anything, but then again, she'd been inside the vault. The paramedic didn't look at any of the other men standing around, and she certainly didn't look at Mary. She only had eyes for Truck.

"I'm fine," Truck told Mary, seeing her concern. "A piece of the door we busted down broke off as we were breaching the building."

"Are you sure?" Ruth asked, ignoring the fact Truck wasn't talking to her. "You have some dried blood on your head." And with that observation, Ruth reached up and touched his temple with her fingertips.

Truck reacted instantly. He jerked away and glared at her with a look so intense, *Mary* would've stepped backward if she didn't know Truck as well as she did. He looked like he was about two seconds away from hauling off and slugging the pretty paramedic.

Deciding she needed to do damage control, pronto, Mary stepped into Truck's side and put an arm around his waist and looked at Ruth. "He's okay. I'll be sure to check him over when we get home."

For once, the words didn't come out snarky. It was obvious the other woman was attracted to Truck, but for some reason, Mary wasn't intimidated by her. She felt kinda sorry for her. Truck was hot, and she couldn't blame the other woman for flirting with him. But Truck was *hers*. He'd made that more than clear time after time.

"He should be checked out by a professional," Ruth

pushed. She fluttered her eyes up at Truck. "It won't take long at all. We can just go over to the ambulance and I'll take care of you."

Mary felt Truck tense under her, and before she could run interference again, he spoke.

"Are you insane?"

Ruth blinked. "What?"

"Are. You. Insane? I'm standing here with my woman, who was inside the bank when those assholes decided to start waving guns around, and you come up to me, bold as you please, and *hit* on me?"

"Truck, it's okay," Mary soothed.

"It's *not* okay," he countered. "We're obviously together. You're in my *arms*, and she has the nerve to come on to me?"

"She didn't mean anything by it. I mean, you're so handsome, I don't blame her for trying."

Truck kept his eyes on Mary's, dismissing the paramedic as if she wasn't standing there. "Mare, I'm with you. I'm *always* gonna be with you. It's not cool for anyone to try to pick me up, *especially* not in front of you."

Mary turned into Truck and looked up at him, petting his chest with her hands soothingly. "Okay, Truck."

"I just thought—" Ruth began, but Truck cut her off.

"That's the problem. You clearly *didn't* think. You're not hard on the eyes, but it's damn presumptuous of you to think any man you want will choose you over the woman he's already with. Let me make it clear. I don't want you. I want Mary. I'm *with* Mary, and I'll always *be* with Mary."

"Uh...okay...sorry...my mistake." Ruth looked behind her desperately. "I gotta go. Be sure to see your personal physician if you get headaches or feel dizzy or anything." And with that, she turned on her heel and headed for one of the ambulances.

"Fuck," Truck said, closing his eyes, frustration easy to see on his face. "You were right here. I can't believe she did that. I mean, it's more than obvious I'm crazy about you. Stupid bitch."

Mary smiled up at Truck. She wasn't thrilled that the other woman had hit on him, but she'd be dead if she wasn't happy with the way he'd immediately rebuffed her. "Are you okay?" she asked softly, raising a hand and trying to wipe off the blood on the side of his head she hadn't really noticed before the paramedic had brought it to her attention.

Truck took her hand in his and brought it to his mouth. He kissed her palm and nodded. "I'm fine."

"He always did have a hard head," Trigger quipped.

"Damn straight," Truck retorted.

Mary nodded and turned to the other Delta Force team. "If it's okay with you guys, I think I'm gonna have Truck take me home now. It was nice meeting you. Take care of my husband this weekend, yeah?"

They were all smiling at her now, as if she were a comedian on a stage rather than someone who was trying to regain her dignity.

"Of course we will," Doc said. "It's what we do."

After a last round of "Nice to meet yous," Truck took Mary's hand and led her away.

"God, shoot me now," Mary muttered.

Truck wrapped an arm around her neck and pulled her into his side. She threw one of her arms around his waist to keep her balance and leaned against him. "You're amazing," Truck told her as they walked toward his car.

He opened the passenger door for her and got her settled then walked around the front to the other side. After he closed his door and started the engine, Truck turned to Mary.

"Wait until I tell the guys that you told Trigger to look after me like I was a wayward child."

"You'd better not," Mary warned, as threateningly as she could.

"Or what?"

"I don't know. But I'll think of something," she said, trying hard to think of a suitable threat, but coming up blank.

Truck reached out and snagged her behind the neck and brought her into his personal space. "I can't wait," Truck said against her lips, before pulling her the rest of the way into his arms and kissing her senseless.

When Mary was breathing hard and trying to remember they were in a public parking lot, Truck finally let her go. It made her feel better that he was breathing just as hard as she was.

"Thank you for coming for me," Mary said softly.

"I'll always come for you," Truck returned.

"I'm sorry I've been a pain in the ass," she continued. "I'm not sorry I married you, and I want to make this marriage work." The words were some of the hardest she'd ever said, but the way Truck's eyes lit up made them all worth it.

"You have no idea what that means to me," he told her before kissing her on the forehead then settling back into his seat. "Unfortunately, I have to get back to post. There's nothing I'd like more than to stay home with you, but I can't. We're in the middle of planning the op and we're running out of time before we have to leave."

"I understand."

"But hear this, Mary. When I get back, I'm going to do everything in my power to show you how much you mean to me. That includes in our bedroom. You okay with that?"

"Yeah, Truck. I'm definitely okay with that," Mary told

him, even if she wasn't one hundred percent okay with him seeing her naked yet.

They drove home in a comfortable silence, fingers intertwined. Mary was scared out of her mind that she'd somehow screw things up, but for the first time in her life, she felt as if she was making the right decision.

Truck loved her. That somehow made things easier. He'd be more forgiving if she made some mistakes in their relationship. Hell, he'd already been more forgiving than he should've been. She knew that.

Truck knew about her double mastectomy. He knew she was standoffish with most people. Knew she used snark as a shield. She had no idea how he'd fallen in love with her in the first place, but was extremely thankful he had. He'd done all the hard work in their relationship and had made all the first moves.

Mary knew if he didn't already love her, and she had to put her best foot forward in order to try to woo him, she'd fail miserably. She'd never chased after a man in her life, and would have no idea where to start with Truck if she had to do it all over again. She'd lucked out when it came to Truck. Big time.

Laying her head against the back of the seat, Mary turned to watch Truck drive, and simply enjoyed being next to him. Feeling safe and protected. She didn't know what she'd do without him.

CHAPTER THREE

The day after the men left for parts unknown for an undisclosed period of time, Emily invited everyone over to her new house. She and Fletch had moved after construction was completed on their old place. Too much had happened there for either of them to be comfortable staying.

They'd purchased a ranch-style house. Fletch refused to live in anything above one story after hearing about how Annie and Sadie had to climb out his daughter's second-floor window after the house had been hit with a rocket-propelled grenade. It was surrounded by ten acres of land, which Fletch had outfitted with enough cameras and spy equipment to keep the President of the United States safe, if he felt the urge to visit.

It was large, almost five thousand square feet. It had five bedrooms and a gourmet kitchen. The backyard was big, and Fletch had plans to put in a swimming pool at some point. Emily said it felt too big when she'd first moved in, but now she loved the extra space and couldn't wait to fill it up with more kids.

Mary was sitting with her legs crossed on the floor with

Annie on her lap. Rayne was on the couch with Wendy and Sadie. Emily was in one of the extremely comfortable armchairs, and Harley and Casey were squished together in a huge beanbag in the corner. Everyone but Emily and Annie had a glass of wine, and they were all feeling mellow and relaxed.

"How's Kassie and little Kate?" Casey asked no one in particular.

"I talked to her this morning," Harley said. "They're both doing great. They got home yesterday, and Kassie and Hollywood are adjusting to life with a baby."

"That's cool that Hollywood didn't have to go on the mission," Emily said a little wistfully.

"The guys are fine," Sadie said gently. "You know there's nothing that will keep Fletch from getting home to you and your little one." She gestured at Emily's belly with her head.

"I know. It's just...I miss him when he's gone."

Everyone nodded in agreement. They all knew exactly how Emily felt.

Mary hugged Annie tighter in her arms. It was almost weird to be with the group during a time like this. She'd been invited in the past when the men went on missions, but because of her health, and the fact she'd been concealing her sickness from them, she'd always declined when the girl-friends and wives got together for a pity party. It was the one and only time they'd do it when the men headed off to their jobs. Afterward, they'd put on their brave faces and get on with life without their men by their sides.

Now that Mary was better and the secret of her marriage to Truck was out, Rayne told her that if she didn't join them, she'd come over and physically drag her to the gathering. It wasn't much of a hardship to agree. Mary liked these women. A lot. She'd missed them terribly when they'd found out about her and Truck, and had stopped talking to her for a while.

Taking another sip of her wine, Mary propped her chin on Annie's head and listened to the chit-chat going on around her.

During a lull in the conversation, Annie dropped a bombshell on them all.

"What happens if Daddy doesn't come home?"

Emily turned to look at her daughter with big eyes. "What?"

"What happens if the bad guys kill him? Will we have to move back into an apartment? Will we be able to afford food? Will I have to sell my Army man?"

"Come here, baby," Emily said, holding out her hand.

Mary helped Annie stand and tried to blame the tears in her eyes on the alcohol.

Annie padded over to her mom and climbed into the armchair with her. It was a tight fit since Emily's belly took up so much room, but they managed. Annie placed her head on her mom's shoulder and one of her hands on her belly. Her thumb brushed idly back and forth over where her new sibling rested.

"Your daddy is way smarter than the bad guys," she told her daughter. "Not only that, he's got all the others there to help keep him safe."

"Sometimes bad things happen to good people," Annie said sadly. "Amber's daddy was killed when he was in Afney-Stan and she has to move."

Amber was a girl in Annie's class at school. Mary wanted to smile at the mispronunciation of Afghanistan, but there was absolutely nothing amusing about the conversation. Not in the least.

Emily raised tortured eyes to the others. It was more than

obvious she was at a loss for words and had no idea how to console her daughter without making promises she couldn't possibly keep.

"Remember when Harley was missing, and we all made sure Coach was eating?" Rayne asked Annie.

The little girl nodded.

"And when Kassie and her sister disappeared, and your daddy and the others did whatever they could to find her?"

Annie nodded again.

"And when Casey was in trouble? What happened then?"

"I went to the safe room and daddy and Bug Man raced to save her."

"Right," Rayne agreed. "And when Chase was hurt when the bad guy came and blew up your old house?"

Mary winced. She wasn't sure Rayne should remind Annie of that day, but the little girl didn't get upset.

"Me and Mommy made a ton of food and brought it to his place so Sadie didn't have to cook."

"And when the bad guys took you and your mommy from your car and put you in that metal box? You remember that *all* of the guys came and got you out, right? They worked together, making sure everyone was safe, and everyone went home safe and sound."

Annie nodded again, a little more vigorously.

"No matter what, you and your mommy aren't alone anymore," Rayne said, shifting so she was sitting at the edge of the couch. "Your daddy and Ghost, and Coach, Beatle, Truck, and Blade and everyone else, are going to do everything in their power to come home to us. But if something happens and they can't, you better believe Truck and Chase and Hollywood will still be here for you. You and your mom will never be hungry. You'll never be lonely. And you'll always have us as friends. Understand?"

Annie nodded, but looked up at her mom. "I miss Daddy."

"Oh, baby. So do I."

"But he's protecting the world from the bad guys."

"He is," Emily agreed.

"It's important."

"Yup."

"Do you think..." Her voice trailed off.

"What, Annie?"

"Do you think he'll be back before my brother is borned?"

"I think he'll do everything in his power to make sure that happens," Emily reassured her daughter. "But, Annie, you don't know this is a brother," she said gently. "It might be a sister."

"It's not," Annie said stubbornly. "It's a boy."

Emily sighed and looked up at the ceiling in exasperation. Mary knew she'd had the same conversation with Annie more than once in the past. Annie was set on having a baby brother, and nothing anyone said could change her mind.

Mary thought they were crazy for keeping the gender of the baby a secret until he or she was born, but they'd decided as a family to wait, and Emily was determined to do just that.

"I heard your dad changed out the motor in your tank to a more powerful one. Want to show me?" Sadie asked Annie, changing the subject.

And as if she hadn't just asked about her father dying and never coming home again, Annie nodded and quickly climbed out of the armchair. She ran over to Sadie and grabbed her hand, pulling her up from the couch. "Yeah! Come on!"

"Thanks," Emily mouthed as the other woman was towed past her.

Sadie blew her a kiss and then they were gone, leaving the

women alone to talk about subjects little Annie shouldn't necessarily be privy to.

"How do you feel?" Casey asked Emily. "What did the doctor say after that thing at the bank?"

"I'm good," Emily said. "He explained that the pain was probably stress related. He told me to go home and put my feet up and relax."

Everyone chuckled. "As if," Rayne said.

"Right?" Emily agreed. But her smile quickly died. "Anyone know where they went?"

Everyone knew who and what she was talking about.

"You know we don't," Harley said softly. "The guys are really careful about not giving us information that would make us freak out if we saw anything on the news."

"I know. I just...it feels different this time for some reason." Emily rested her hand on her belly.

Mary didn't know how it had felt for the others in the past because she'd always dealt with Truck leaving on her own. But she had to agree with Emily. It *did* feel different this time. More ominous for some reason.

She shook her head. She was being silly. This was what their men did. They went out, kicked ass, then came back and were their usual protective alpha selves. This time would be no different.

Standing, she said, "Who needs another round?"

Everyone's hands went into the air.

Mary went to grab two bottles of wine and she topped off everyone's glasses.

When everyone's glass was full once more, she raised hers in an impromptu toast. "To our Deltas. May they kick some terrorist ass and get home sooner rather than later."

"In one piece," Harley added.

"Healthy and whole," Rayne piped up.

"Amen to that," Wendy agreed.

Everyone took a sip of their wine and fell silent, thinking about the men they loved more than life itself.

Finally, Casey cleared her throat and said, "So...Beatle and I have been talking weddings."

Everyone screeched in delight, and Casey held up a hand to shut everyone up. "Okay, okay, pipe down." She chuckled and turned to Wendy. "I wanted to know if you and Blade might be interested in a double ceremony?"

The question came out tentatively, but Wendy didn't hesitate to reassure her. She bounced from the couch and leaped for her friend. Harley was laughing and trying to get out of the way, but because she was in the enormous beanbag with Casey, it was impossible. Wendy ended up in the beanbag with both Casey and Harley, and she hugged Casey hard.

"Yes, a thousand times yes. I'd love to!"

"Shouldn't you ask Blade first?" Casey asked dryly.

"Nope. He's been bugging me about getting married but I couldn't begin to think about planning. It stresses me out. This way *you* can plan the whole thing and I'll just show up and smile!"

The two women grinned at each other. "I'd be honored," Casey said. "And then we'll be sisters for real."

"Oh, shit," Wendy said with a sniff. "You're gonna make me cry, bitch."

Mary watched with a huge grin on her face. She knew she probably looked a little silly, but she didn't care.

Wendy turned to stare at Rayne. "What about you, Rayne? You want in on this?"

Rayne looked startled for a second. "On what?"

"Wanna get married with us?"

Mary's eyes widened in surprise, almost as big as Rayne's were.

"Seriously?"

"Yeah. If we're gonna party, might as well make it one big-ass celebration!" Casey said, beaming.

Rayne put her glass down on the little side table and said, "Okay. But..." Her voice trailed off.

"What?" Casey asked.

Rayne turned to Mary. "Mary has to get married with us too."

Mary stared at her best friend.

"You said that you'd renew your vows with Truck, and we'd have a double wedding ceremony. Are you opposed to a quadruple ceremony?"

Mary swallowed hard and looked from Rayne to Wendy to Casey, then to the others. Everyone was smiling encouragingly and nodding.

"You really want me with you after what I did?"

Rayne got up and went over to Mary. She sat on the floor and took her in her arms. "Hell yeah. We're best friends, Mare. You pissed me off, and I know I'll piss you off in the future too. It's what friends do. But I absolutely want you to stand up with me when I marry Ghost. You were there from the very beginning. Remember, I texted you all the details when I decided to have that one-night stand with him in London. Please say yes."

Mary turned to Wendy and Casey. "Are *you* guys sure? Blade and Beatle might not be thrilled at having to share your day."

"I probably shouldn't admit this," Harley interjected, "but Coach let it spill that the guys all decided they wanted to have a huge quadruple wedding the day that asshole shot up the Organizational Day on post."

"They did?" Rayne asked, surprised.

"Yup."

"Seriously?" Mary questioned.

"Yeah. Don't ask me how I know, because I might've used sexual torture to get it out of Coach."

The women all chuckled. "So? Mary, what do you think?"

Mary slowly nodded. "If Truck is game, so am I."

"Holy shit," Rayne said softly. "We're getting married together, Mare."

Mary knew things weren't quite that simple, but she nodded anyway. She probably wouldn't have agreed so easily if she hadn't had four glasses of wine, but she knew deep down there was nothing more that she wanted than to marry Truck for the right reasons. She might not be ready to admit to his face that she loved him, might not ever be ready, but she was more than ready to spend the rest of her life with him. She couldn't imagine *not* having him by her side.

Any thoughts she might have had of divorcing him had long since disappeared. If she was honest with herself, from the second he'd stood across from her at the courthouse and said "I do," she'd been lost. She'd felt like crap and knew she might not live to see the marriage become a real one, but even though she'd bitched and moaned, she'd been thrilled that Truck had insisted on marrying her.

"The second they get back, I'll let Beatle know what's going on," Casey said with glee. "He's gonna be ecstatic. He's been bugging me for weeks to set a date."

"I think Blade's been talking to Beatle, because he's been a pain in the butt about setting a date too," Wendy agreed.

"Can I ask a favor?" Emily piped up.

"What?" everyone asked.

"Can we please wait until I have this baby? I don't want to be the only beached whale at this giant wedding ceremony."

"Of course!" Casey told her.

"We can't plan a quadruple wedding in two months anyway," Wendy added.

"Don't bet on it," Rayne said. "I think the second Ghost hears I'm finally going to marry him, he'll have everything planned and ready to go within twenty-four hours."

Everyone laughed. Mary agreed with Rayne, but she kept quiet. She wasn't sure what Truck was going to think about the entire situation, but she hoped he'd be happy. She wanted to start their married lives over. To get rid of the old excuses for marrying each other and do it because they both wanted to spend their lives together.

The rest of the evening went by quietly. Sadie and Annie came back in, more wine was consumed, Annie learned about the upcoming quadruple wedding ceremony, and that she was going to be a bridesmaid, and they all ate way too much sugar and junk food.

Late that night, Mary snuggled under the covers in one of Emily's guest rooms with Rayne on the twin bed across from her.

"Are you really okay with this?" Rayne asked quietly.

"Surprisingly, yeah," Mary said.

"I'd understand if you weren't."

Mary turned on her side and faced her best friend. "I'm more worried about what Truck will think. He hasn't exactly been happy lately."

"Really?"

"Really. After the thing at the bank, I thought things were fine between us, but they're not."

"He loves you, Mare."

"I know. But I'm afraid he's getting tired of waiting for me to reciprocate. What if he comes back and decides he's done?"

"He won't," Rayne said, her voice full of conviction.

"I don't think I'd survive if he left me," Mary whispered.

Rayne propped herself up on an elbow. "I thought you guys talked. I saw you two at the bank. It didn't look like he had any plans to leave."

"We did. But...he doesn't hold me at night anymore." Mary was embarrassed to admit it. But this was Rayne. Her best friend in the world. If she couldn't talk to *her* about what was going on with Truck, who could she talk to?

"What do you mean?"

Mary sighed. "He's seen my naked chest. When I was sick, he'd pull me into his arms and hold me all night. Even when I felt like shit and told him to go away, he wouldn't. When the radiation hurt so bad I couldn't even stand having a tank top or sheet touching me, he'd wrap his arm around my belly, sleeping with his feet sticking off the end of the bed, just so he could be next to me. He never seemed to care that my chest was as flat as a kid's. He always kissed me in the morning, on the forehead, and he'd constantly touch me. My arm. My hand. The small of my back. It used to drive me crazy...but now it's like I have the plague. He's right next to me, but he might as well be miles away."

"Have you asked him about it?"

"No. How do I ask for something I always pretended I hated? I miss him, Raynie. I mean, of course I miss him now that he's on this mission, but I missed him before that, and he was right next to me. I know he was happy I wasn't hurt at the bank, but then I think he started having second thoughts when I didn't immediately open up to him afterward. I'm afraid he's trying to figure out how to tell me he's setting me free. That he's going to give up on me."

Rayne sat up and threw the covers back. She padded across the small space between the beds and pushed Mary over. Without a word, she climbed under the covers and hugged Mary close. They lay like that, their arms around each other in the small twin-size bed, and Mary did her best to keep the tears from falling from her eyes.

After several minutes, Rayne said softly, "That man loves you, Mary. I'm one hundred percent sure of that. You have to open yourself up to him. Talk to him. Tell him everything you haven't told *me* about your childhood, no matter how hard it is. Tell him what a bitch your mom was. Tell him about the uncles."

"Then what?"

"Seduce him."

Mary choked, and it took a couple of moments to compose herself. "Seriously? That's your advice?"

"It worked for me and Ghost."

"That's different."

"Not really."

"I don't exactly have the equipment to seduce him anymore, Rayne," Mary said dryly, more than aware of her completely flat chest.

"He doesn't give a shit that you don't have boobs," Rayne retorted.

"I do."

"What does your surgeon say about reconstruction?"

Mary realized that because of the rift between her and Rayne, they hadn't talked about this. "It's possible. But it'll take about a year and a half for the entire process. They have to do liposuction and insert fat cells from my thighs and belly into my chest to stretch the skin first. That'll take several sessions and months. Then he'll put in expanders, and I have to go in every week to have them filled. I'll do that until I either get to the size I want, or the skin starts to deteriorate and the doctor says we need to stop. After several months, the expanders will have created a pocket the implants will fit into, and I can have *that* surgery."

"And?"

Rayne knew her too well. "I hate the way I look right now. I can't even look in the mirror. I can't imagine exposing myself to Truck. I mean, he's seen me, but I felt so awful at the time, I didn't really care. I told you that first time I couldn't stand to have anything against my skin when the radiation burns were so bad, but this is different. And the thought of getting fake boobs makes me feel like such a hypocrite. You know me. You know how I always made fun of women with implants."

"This is different."

Mary closed her eyes. "It's karma, Rayne."

"What do you mean?"

"My mama had her breasts done so she could get men. We didn't have enough money to eat, but somehow she conned one of her boyfriends to pay for the surgery. She always said that men would do anything for a pair of good tits. Guess she wasn't wrong. When I was old enough to understand, I told her she was pathetic. That only whores got breast implants. She smacked me and told me that I was a stupid bitch, and that if I didn't understand by then that men only care about tits and pussy, I would never make it in the world."

"She was wrong," Rayne said immediately, pulling back and putting her hands on Mary's face. "Mare, your mom was *wrong*."

Mary couldn't hold back the tears anymore. "I'm damned if I do and damned if I don't, Raynie. I want Truck to love me, but I know boobs are important to men. I don't want to look like a ten-year-old kid when I'm naked, but at the same time, if I get implants, I feel as if that'll make me no better than my mama."

"Your mother was a bitch. I'm sorry, but she was also a whore. She used men, plain and simple. The men she dated *were* only with her because of what she looked like and probably because she was good at sucking cock. But Truck isn't like that. I think he's proved over and over again that he's with you because of *you*. But you know what? Forget about him for a second. This has *nothing* to do with him or any other guy."

"How can you say that?" Mary asked.

Rayne dropped her hands and pulled Mary's head against her chest. "This is about you, Mary. How *you* feel. It doesn't matter what I think. It doesn't matter what Truck thinks. It doesn't even matter what your doctor thinks. All that matters is what *you* think. If having the reconstruction will make you feel more comfortable or prettier, then you should do it. If you want to stay exactly how you are right now because of women's lib or whatever, then do that. You can wear boob inserts in your bra, or don't, and screw everyone who might look at you weirdly. The Mary I know wouldn't give a shit what anyone else thinks about her. If you want to go and get tattoos over every inch of your chest and walk around bare-ass naked, then you should do it. If you want to get Dolly-Parton-size implants, then do *that*. Fuck what everyone else thinks."

Mary smiled. "So if I asked what *you* think I should do, you'd refuse to answer me, right?"

"Right," Rayne said immediately. "I'll love you no matter what size gazingas you have, Mary. Flat as a board or huge as watermelons, it'll make no difference to me. And it'll make no difference at all to the people who know and love you, including Truck. The only people who will judge you are those who don't know you...and fuck them anyway. Their opinion doesn't matter."

"Are you quoting me, bitch?" Mary asked, her words muffled because she was lying on Rayne's chest.

"Abso-fucking-lutely. You told me that same thing when I was worried about people finding out about me and Ghost's one-night stand."

"You know I love you, right?" Mary asked after several minutes had gone by.

"Yup. I wouldn't be lying in this small-ass bed if I didn't love you right back," Rayne retorted.

"You'll stay?" Mary asked.

"Of course."

"I'll be okay in the morning." Mary felt the need to explain. "It's just that I've missed Truck so much and—"

"You don't have to explain," Rayne said, and tightened her hold on her friend.

"When Truck gets back, I'll tell him again that I want a real relationship," Mary decided. "Hopefully this time I can use the right words so he'll truly believe me. I'm not sure how sex will go, but I'm willing to try."

"That's the Mary that I know and love. It's good to have you back," Rayne told her.

"I'm really trying to curb my bitchiness," Mary said. "It's not easy, but if I've learned anything over the last year or so it's that life is short. And I want to try to stop being so angry and snarky all the time."

"Just don't lose the Mary we all know and love," Rayne said. "I mean, I think there are times when you could use a little more tact, but we still love you exactly how you are. It's nice to have someone who isn't afraid to say what we're all thinking."

"Deal," Mary said with a smile. "Do we have any idea when the guys will get back this time?" Mary asked.

Rayne shook her head. "Unfortunately, no."

"I get why everything is so secret, but it still sucks," Mary grumbled.

"Welcome to life as the wife of a Delta Force soldier," Rayne said dryly.

Long after Rayne fell asleep, Mary remained awake. She was more than happy to have her best friend back, but despite the way Truck had acted toward her after the robbery, he'd still maintained a distance between them at home. It was confusing and frustrating and made her unsure about where she and Truck stood. She was happy for Rayne's advice about the reconstructive surgery, even if she didn't know what her decision about that was going to be yet. But she couldn't help thinking the worst when it came to Truck.

She'd been awful to him. Horrible. If a man had done to her what she'd done to Truck, she'd never forgive him. But by some miracle, Truck hadn't given up on her...yet. He loved her. He'd said it even that week, but Mary knew that loving someone didn't mean things would automatically turn out well in the end.

Sighing, she resolved to apologize to Truck and show him that he hadn't made a mistake in marrying her. To let him know that she could be more than the snarky bitch people thought she was.

CHAPTER FOUR

Truck raised the binoculars and peered through them at the clearing below. He knew his team was nearby, as was the other Delta Force group. They'd spread out and surrounded the area. Along with the commander's meticulous research, they'd been doing reconnaissance for a few days now, and they knew the routines of the men holding the seventy-plus girls hostage as well as they were going to know them.

They'd been sent to this hotter-than-hell country in Africa because a French diplomat's daughter had been kidnapped, along with seventy or so other girls. Rebels had stormed the international school in the middle of the afternoon, threatening to kill everyone if anyone interfered. The diplomat just happened to be visiting the school that day, of all days. And he'd brought along his ten-year-old daughter with him on this trip to show her how people around the world lived.

The rebels had taken the French girl right along with the others. Many of the students were from the nearby villages, but there were also around ten girls who belonged to the international aid workers helping out in the area. The students had been held hostage for over a month by the time the Deltas had been called in.

The rebels had been demanding the government release several hostages in exchange for the girls' safe return, but so far, negotiations had failed to bring an end to the standoff. The French Special Forces were currently on the other side of the country, checking out another tip, but it had turned out the Deltas were on the right track after all.

Truck glared at a rebel through the lenses. He'd just smacked a girl—around twelve, if Truck had to guess—and was laughing at her tears. They'd seen some awful things over the last few days and everyone was eager to make a move. Truck thought about Annie being in this situation and it made his blood boil. No one had seen the little French girl, but there was no doubt she was there.

There were about forty or so rebels guarding the camp. At any one time, there were ten watching over the tents with the girls. There were three tents holding the hostages—and the guards took turns dragging the girls out one by one and taking them into a smaller tent nearby.

All the Deltas knew what was going on, but they couldn't make a move to stop the abuse until they were sure they could take out the rebels without any retaliation against the hostages.

Truck couldn't wait to kill the men. He wasn't usually bloodthirsty, but he couldn't help it in this situation. Anyone who hurt little girls deserved to die a slow and painful death. He'd always hated violence against women and children, but after getting to know Annie, and getting to know his best friends' women, *and* after having met and married the love of his life, he abhorred it even more.

If anyone dared to look at Mary the wrong way, he wouldn't hesitate to put them in their place. Mary could take care of herself, but she shouldn't *have* to. It wasn't cool that men thought it was okay to smack a woman's ass because of what she might be wearing. It wasn't okay for them to make suggestive remarks or to tell her that she'd look better on her knees in front of him.

Truck hadn't always been an angel. Before his friends started meeting their women, they'd gone to strip clubs, picked up women in bars. He'd wrapped his arm around a woman's waist without asking if it was okay first. He'd palmed asses, stolen kisses, and pulled women onto his lap, even when he knew they'd feel his hard-on under them. But now that Mary was in his life, as well as all the others, he'd never disrespect a woman like that again.

Watching the rebels hurt the children they were holding hostage was unbearable. He wanted to move immediately and stop it. If they could prevent even one girl from horrible memories she'd have for the rest of her life, it'd be worth it. But he had to wait. They had to make sure they had their plan down pat. If they didn't, those kids he wanted to save could end up dead.

Along with his hatred for the rebels, his frustration over his relationship with Mary wasn't helping his emotions. While he was thrilled as could be for Hollywood and Kassie and their newborn daughter, he couldn't help but be jealous of his friend as well.

He wanted that. Wanted to be able to hold Mary's hand in public and not worry if she was comfortable with that or not. Wanted to have a family with her. Because of her cancer, he had no idea if she'd be able to have kids naturally, but that didn't matter. They could adopt. Or if she didn't want kids, they could go to the shelter and find some cats and dogs that needed homes. It didn't matter what kind of family they had, as long as they had one.

He'd thought that, after the robbery, Mary would loosen up toward him, but things remained awkward between them. He could tell she was still holding back—and he wanted more from her. Wanted her to stop fighting what she felt for him.

"You all right?" Beatle asked after he'd crawled up next to him.

"Yeah."

"You don't look all right."

"I'm. Fine," Truck bit out between clenched teeth.

"How're things with Mary?"

Truck let out a breath of frustration and turned to Beatle. "You think now is the time to discuss this? We're about ten minutes from storming the castle, so to speak."

Beatle shrugged. "We know what the plan is. We're just waiting until it's time to kill all those motherfuckers. I want to know how my friend is doing. Things looked good between you and Mary at the bank."

Truck knew Beatle was fishing, but he needed someone to talk to, so he didn't put him off like he might've at any other time. "I thought so too. But something's off. I don't know what."

"You or her?"

And that was the question. Mary had definitely softened toward him, but he wasn't sure if it was enough. "Me."

"You regret marrying her?"

"No." The answer came immediately. Truck didn't regret what he'd done. Mary was still alive because she'd gotten the treatment she'd needed.

"Then what?" Beatle asked.

"I don't want a pity wife. I want a real one. I want what *you* have, Beatle. A woman who looks at me as if I'm her everything. A woman who's happy to see me when I come home at the end of the day. Maybe has dinner waiting and who doesn't mind when I don't want to talk after a tough mission. I want someone who isn't afraid to touch me, and to be touched in return."

"So you want the Disney version of a relationship," Beatle drawled.

"I guess," Truck mumbled.

"You might as well divorce Mary the second you get back then," Beatle said. "Because there is no such thing as a Disney relationship."

Truck looked at his friend in surprise. "Don't tell me that Casey doesn't love you more than anything."

"Oh, she does. But there are plenty of times when she's not happy to see me at the end of the day. She's tired and cranky from teaching and driving all the way back home from Baylor. I'd move in a heartbeat, so she could be closer to work, but you know as well as I do that I can't. I have to be near the post in case we get called up for a last-second mission. And there are plenty of nights when I go to bed, ready to love my woman, and find her dead to the world or she tells me she's just not in the mood. Relationships are messy, Truck. You might see me and Casey holding hands and smiling at each other in public, but you don't see the times we fight or when she refuses to get anywhere near me. When I'm so tired from work all I want to do is sit and watch football on television, and she tries to talk to me and I snap at her to leave me alone."

Truck stared at Beatle with wide eyes. "You two having trouble?" he asked.

Beatle blew out a silent breath of frustration. "No. You're missing the point."

"Then make it clearer, asshole," Truck huffed.

"Being with someone you love means you deal with the shit as well as the roses."

"I think I've dealt with more than my fair share of Mary's shit," Truck told his friend.

"Yeah, Mary having cancer sucks, but just because she's better doesn't mean that everything is going to come up roses from here on out. How does she feel about her diagnosis? Is she scared it's going to come back? Does she have other side effects from the disease or drugs that are making her irritable? She had a mastectomy, right? How does that make you feel? How does *she* feel about it? Does she have to wear different clothes now?"

Truck was silent for a beat, then admitted, "I don't know. We don't exactly talk about that stuff."

"Communication is key," Beatle said. "I screwed up when Casey first moved in. I didn't ask her how she was feeling about a lot of stuff. Her new job, leaving Florida, if she had any residual fears from her LSD trip...I just assumed she'd talk to me about that stuff if it was bothering her. Turns out, she thought I wasn't asking because I didn't care."

"I care," Truck said immediately. "I want to know everything about Mary. About her childhood—which I know was shitty—about her job, about how she's feeling. I love her."

Beatle leaned in closer and hissed, "Then *talk* to her, man. If she won't touch you, you reach out to her. Tell her how much you love the feel of her hand in yours. Tell her when you're feeling vulnerable about your scar. Remind her that you chose to be with *her* over every other woman."

Truck thought about Beatle's words for a long moment and realized he was right. He'd been afraid to talk to Mary, *really* talk to her, because he didn't want to hear her say that she wanted a divorce. That since she was better, she didn't need to be married to him anymore. But maybe she was waiting for *him* to make the first move. That made more sense. As much as she was brash and bold, she wasn't all that confident when it came to relationships. He knew it was because of how she was brought up, but he hadn't ever come out and asked her point-blank about it.

She needed reassuring as much as he did. And the second he got back to Texas, he was going to be a different kind of man for her. He wouldn't force her to talk to him, but he was going to make sure she knew how much he loved her, and that he was there to talk whenever she needed it. He'd open up to her about his own life, his own feelings. Not about her —although he was going to make sure a day never went by without him telling her how important she was to him—but how he felt about work, his family, their friends...everything.

"Thanks," Truck said softly.

"You're welcome," Beatle responded, then picked up his binoculars and gazed down on the rebel camp.

"Moving in sixty seconds," Ghost's voice said through their earbuds.

"You ready to kick some ass?" Beatle asked as he grinned over at Truck.

"More than," Truck responded. "Those fuckers are as good as dead."

"Damn straight," Beatle said.

The two men shifted and got into position. Their job was to attack from the back side of the chow tent. Twenty or so of the rebels were inside eating lunch. If they could take them out, it would cut the number of rebels in half, making the rest less likely to turn on the girls and more likely to flee for their lives.

Beatle and Truck heard Ghost counting down from ten in their ears, and at the word *Go*, all hell broke loose.

Time had no meaning in the middle of battle. If asked, Truck would be hard pressed to say if minutes went by or seconds. He focused entirely on the task at hand and everything else faded into the background. He focused on covering his teammates and getting the job done. Truck didn't know how many rebels he'd taken out once the shooting started, but ultimately, it didn't matter. He lost track of Beatle in the chaos of battle, but knew the man was to his right somewhere. The air was full of smoke and the smell of gunpowder, and he could hear yelling outside the tent, but he didn't take his concentration from the men hiding behind overturned tables. Every time a head popped up from behind a table to try to shoot at them, Truck fired.

He heard a yell from his left and turned to aim in that direction, then hesitated for a split second—because he wasn't expecting to see what he did.

One of the rebels hadn't just popped up from behind a table to shoot at him. No. He'd leaped over it and was running toward him as fast as he could.

Truck squeezed the trigger of his weapon, taking the man down, but not before he'd gotten way too close for comfort.

The man went down on his knees and swayed. His hate-filled eyes met Truck's for a split second—and then he grinned. An evil, nasty grin that made the hair on the back of Truck's neck stand up. He raised his weapon to fire again... and noticed too late what the man held in his hands.

Grenades. Two of them. And the pins were nowhere to be seen.

Truck had enough time to yell "Gre—" but before he could finish the warning, the chow tent exploded in a shower of body parts, wooden table pieces, and metal.

"Sitrep! Sitrep!" Ghost yelled, his voice echoing through the earbuds of the other Delta Force men.

Trigger and his team had secured the girls and gathered them all together in the largest of the three tents they'd been held in. Three had been killed in the raid, but Lefty, Doc, and Brain had taken out the men guarding them before they'd been able to shoot any more. Brain was put in charge of speaking to the girls, as he was the only one who *could* communicate with them. He was a language savant and spoke more than thirty different languages, hence his nickname.

Doc was tending to the injured girls, and seemed to be doing his best to keep his temper under control. The girls were beyond freaked out. They were emotionally scarred, and it was more than obvious which ones had been abused, as they cringed away from the Deltas anytime they got close. The little French girl was found hiding amongst them as well. They weren't yet sure if she'd been assaulted. During the short time the teams had been watching the rebel camp, the captors hadn't seemed to differentiate between the local girls and the international ones.

Oz and Grover were standing guard outside the tent holding the former hostages, and Lucky and Lefty were doing their best to get the trucks started so they could get the hell out of there.

Coach and Blade had disappeared into the surrounding trees, chasing after the rebels who had decided to cut and run rather than stay and fight.

"Dammit, Beatle. Truck. Sitrep!" Ghost barked harshly, even knowing they probably wouldn't answer. He looked over at Fletch, who was staring at the smoldering tent that used to be standing thirty feet away, but was now nothing more than a smoking mess.

"Coach and Blade, get your asses back here. Pronto," Ghost ordered as he and Fletch made their way cautiously toward where the tent had been standing.

"You need us?" Trigger asked.

"Hold," Ghost said, his eyes scanning for his teammates. He'd heard the gunfire coming from inside the tent, but he'd been busy taking out his own share of the rebels. Beatle and Truck knew what they were doing, and he hadn't been concerned. In all their surveillance, they hadn't seen any weapons other than the rifles the rebels were constantly holding. No RPGs, no explosives. The rebels were prepared, but they weren't exactly a well-oiled Army machine. Their clothes were worn and torn and the highlight of most of their days seemed to be chow time.

Ghost gestured to Fletch to go to the right and he went to the left, his eyes constantly checking for any kind of movement. He came upon a few rebels who were still alive and dispatched them without mercy. He'd seen for himself the terror in the little girls' faces. He had no sympathy for the men who'd kidnapped and abused them. None.

At one corner of the smoldering rubble, he saw a leg wearing a pair of black pants.

Kneeling, Ghost frantically tore boards and debris away from the man. He sighed in relief when he saw a pair of familiar eyes blinking up at him.

"Beatle? You okay, man?"

Beatle nodded and slowly sat up, with Ghost's help. He shook his head sluggishly and said, "Holy shit."

"Where's Truck?" Ghost asked, more relieved than he could say that Beatle seemed to be all right. There was a trickle of blood coming from the side of his head, but otherwise all his limbs seemed to be good, and he was quickly becoming more and more aware of his surroundings.

"He was over there the last time I saw him," Beatle said, pointing to where they could see Fletch cautiously combing through the debris. "We were picking them off one by one when a rebel ran right toward him. Truck shot him and the guy went down to his knees. Truck yelled something, then kaboom."

Ghost hauled Beatle up and kept one hand on his teammate's elbow and the other on the trigger of his weapon. The last thing they needed was one of the rebels to pop up and shoot them. They made their way toward Fletch, their eyes constantly on the lookout for either bad guys or Truck.

By the time they made it to Fletch, Beatle was walking almost normally. He'd regained his balance and was kicking at wood planks that used to be tables as he went.

"Where exactly did you last see Truck?" Ghost asked, well aware that time was running out. They'd made enough noise for any rebel in a ten-mile radius to hear them, and they wanted to get the hell out of dodge before reinforcements showed up.

"There," Beatle said, gesturing to a point about ten feet away from them. Without a word, the three men fanned out and began lifting every piece of wood they came in contact with.

"Oh, shit. Found him!" Fletch said urgently. "Help me!"

Ghost tasted bile in the back of his throat at the tone of Fletch's voice, but didn't hesitate to close in on him. With Beatle's help, they threw off a large wooden tabletop, two arms, a leg, and someone's intestines before completely uncovering Truck.

He was lying on his back, his arms outstretched, his weapon nowhere to be seen. He looked like he was sleeping, but all three Deltas knew that wasn't the case.

Ghost leaned down and put his fingers on Truck's carotid artery and held his breath.

He immediately breathed out a sigh of relief at feeling the strong pulse. "He's alive," Ghost told the others.

"Injuries?" Fletch asked.

"Not sure," Ghost said. He looked up and saw a metal box lying nearby. At one time it probably held ammunition, but it was empty now. It did have a huge dent in the side...about the size of a human head. "Help me turn him over so I can check his back. Careful, keep his spine straight."

With Fletch and Beatle helping, Ghost did a quick battle-field survey of their friend. His spine seemed all right, no protrusions of his spinal cord, and Ghost didn't see any blood pooling under him either. Glancing down at his limbs, nothing looked obviously broken.

But with the way he'd been buried by debris, he probably had some fractures of some sort.

"Truck?" Ghost said loudly as he squeezed his friend's shoulder.

Truck moaned but didn't regain consciousness.

"Come on, buddy. You gotta wake up. You're huge, and it'll take too many of us to haul your carcass out of here."

No answer.

Beatle leaned down and lightly slapped Truck's face. "Stop fucking around, Truck. We've got seventy freaked-out girls here that we need to move. This is no time to sleep on the job."

Remarkably, Truck's eyes fluttered and he moaned again, even as he shook his head.

"Easy, man," Fletch soothed. "Open your eyes, buddy."

They all watched as Truck opened his eyes, then immediately closed them again. "Fuuuuuck," he swore. "Mother-fucker, my head hurts."

Ghost sighed in relief. If Truck was awake enough to bitch and moan, he was going to be just fine. "Yeah, well, that's because the tent you were standing in exploded."

"Awesome," Truck muttered. "Sitrep?"

"The girls are good. Rebels are either dead or have fled," Fletch said, filling him in.

Truck opened his eyes in a squint and looked up at his friend. "Girls?"

"Yeah, they're okay," Fletch repeated. "You look a bit banged up, but your spine is good. No broken legs or arms, although you'll have to tell us if anything is fractured or not."

They watched as Truck moved each of his legs, then his arms. He tried to sit up, and moaned in pain and collapsed backward. "Extremities are good, but feels like I have at least a couple of broken ribs. Fractured at the very least."

"Anything else hurt? You think you have internal injuries?" Ghost asked.

Truck pressed his large hands on his abdomen. After a moment, he said, "I don't think so. Although my head is pounding. It hurts. Bad. Can hardly keep my eyes open, the light hurts so much."

"Concussion," Beatle said. "You dizzy or nauseous?"

"Both," Truck told them.

"Can you walk?" Ghost asked.

Truck took a deep breath and nodded. "If that's the only way to get out of this shithole and back to civilization, then yeah, I can walk."

"Fuck yeah, you can," Fletch said softly. "Come on, we'll help you stand."

The three of them helped Truck stand and held on when he wobbled in their grip. It took a minute or so before they felt he was steady enough to stand on his own.

Just as they let go of him, Truck turned his head and puked.

He wiped his mouth and swore. "Fuck, I hate throwing up."

"Come on, let's get the hell out of here," Fletch said.

Ghost took the lead, with Truck following and Beatle and Fletch at the rear. Truck was in no shape to defend himself against any rebel who might still be lingering. They walked toward the trucks and, as they got near, Coach and Blade materialized out of the surrounding trees.

"We heard," Blade said, gesturing to his earbud. The group had an open mike, and they'd obviously been listening to the situation with Beatle and Truck. "Good to see you have a hard head," Blade joked.

"That's what she said," Truck replied.

Everyone chuckled, and they continued toward the vehicles with the girls and Trigger's Delta Force team.

Lefty stepped out from between two trucks as the group approached—and everyone watched in disbelief as Truck moved faster than they would've thought possible for a man with his injuries.

He grabbed the pistol out of the holster at Ghost's waist and had it pointed at Lefty before he could say a word.

"Don't move, asshole," Truck ground out.

"What the fuck?" Lefty said, but obediently raised his hands in surrender.

Within seconds, Trigger, Oz, Grover, and Lucky appeared, and quickly had their weapons drawn, which made Coach, Beatle, and Blade pull *their* pistols.

"Everyone calm the fuck down," Ghost ordered, holding his hands up and stepping in front of Lefty, facing Truck. "Put down the gun, Truck."

"Who the fuck are they?" Truck asked, not lowering the gun.

"What do you mean, who are they?" Ghost asked.

"I mean, who the fuck are they? When we came in here, it was just the six of us. Speaking of which, where's Hollywood? Do you assholes have him?"

Ghost stared at Truck in dismay. "Truck...Hollywood's not here. He stayed back stateside this time."

"No, he didn't. We were talking right before we called in for air support to kill these motherfucking terrorists."

Ghost swallowed hard. Fuck. Fuck, fuck, *fuck*. "What were you talking about?" he asked.

"About tonight. About how we're finally gonna get some R&R, pick up some chicks, and get some pussy."

"Oh, shit," Fletch said, and Ghost saw him lower his weapon.

"Truck, put down the weapon," Ghost demanded again and took a step toward his friend. "I'm ordering you to stand down."

Truck's eyes met Ghost's and the confusion was easy to see. And the pain. "Did they get Hollywood? What aren't you telling me?"

Just then, one of the girls in the truck sobbed loud enough to be heard from where the standoff was happening. Truck turned toward the sound, his brows furrowed in confusion.

Ghost didn't hesitate. He leaped toward his friend and slammed his hand down on Truck's forearm, making him grunt in pain and, more importantly, drop the pistol he'd been holding. Ghost swept his leg out, taking Truck's feet out from under him.

The large man fell to the dirt like a rock and grunted in pain once again when he landed. Ghost immediately went to his head and cradled it, while Beatle, Coach, and Trigger leapt on top of him to keep him down.

"Watch his ribs!" Ghost yelled. They needed to subdue and control their friend, but not hurt him more than he already was.

But Truck wasn't moving. He stared up at Ghost in confusion. "What's going on?"

"You were hurt, buddy. You hit your head."

"Yeah, it hurts," Truck agreed.

"Where are we?"

"What?"

"Where are we, Truck?"

"Iraq."

"Fuck," Ghost heard someone swear from above them, but he didn't take his gaze from his friend's. "How old are you?"

"Why?"

"Humor me."

"Thirty-five."

Ghost closed his eyes for a second in despair, then opened them again.

Truck was thirty-eight. Three years ago they *had* been in Iraq. They'd been on a mission that had complications, just like this one, and they'd had to call in the Air Force to drop some bombs to give them cover and to help dispatch the terrorists who'd surrounded them.

"Does the name Rayne mean anything to you?"

Truck's brows furrowed again. "Like the water from the sky? Just that we've been in this damn country so long, I think I've forgotten what it looks like."

"What about Emily? Kassie? Annie?"

"Are those the chicks you've lined up for when we get to Kuwait for our R&R?" Truck asked.

"No. Think, Truck. What about Mary?"

"I don't *know* anyone named Mary. What's going on?"

Instead of answering, Ghost patted Truck's chest. "These are our friends," he told him, gesturing to Lefty and the others. "They were helping us. Don't shoot them, okay?"

"Where's Hollywood?"

"He's fine. I swear. He's traveling ahead of us, making sure the coast is clear."

Truck seemed to ponder that information for a moment before nodding.

"You ready to get out of here?" Ghost asked.

Truck nodded again. "Think I can get a painkiller? My head really hurts. It's hard for me to even see straight."

"Of course." Then for the second time, Truck was helped to his feet by his teammates. But this time they all exchanged worried glances. They helped Truck to a beat-up truck nearby, one without any kids in it, and got him situated in the back seat.

Ghost watched in silence then turned when he felt a hand on his arm.

"Amnesia?" Trigger asked softly.

"Looks that way. He must've hit his head on a metal box we found behind him." Ghost shook his head. "Rattled his brain. Fuck. This is bad."

"I'm sure it's temporary. Once his brain has had a chance to heal, he'll remember," Trigger offered tentatively.

"I hope so," Ghost said. "I sure as fuck hope so."

CHAPTER FIVE

Mary was sitting on the couch watching the first season of *Stranger Things* on Netflix. She couldn't wait for Truck to get home to watch it with her. Of course, she wasn't going to wait for him to get home to watch it herself. She'd be more than happy to see it again and catch all the things she was sure she was missing this time around.

She was still binging on it when there was a knock on the door.

Surprised, Mary paused the show and headed for the door. Truck's apartment felt more like home than her own did at this point. Of course, without Truck there, it simply felt empty...much like her own apartment.

Looking through the peephole, she saw Hollywood standing there.

Internally freaking out, Mary quickly unlocked the door and took the chain off. She whipped the door open and before Hollywood could say anything, she blurted, "Is Kassie okay? Kate?"

Hollywood nodded and said, "Yes. They're both fine."

"Thank God," Mary said, resting a hand on her chest in

relief. Opening the door wider, she gestured for him to enter. "Come on in."

"Thanks."

Mary followed Hollywood inside and locked the door behind them as Truck had taught her. She never used to worry about locking up when she was home, but since living with Truck, and watching him constantly worry about her safety, it had become a habit.

Hollywood stopped just inside the living room and turned to her. "I have some bad news."

Mary's legs nearly collapsed under her. Her eyes got wide and she heard a ringing in her ears. "Truck?" she asked.

Hollywood nodded.

The room spun and Mary wavered on her feet.

Not Truck. No. Not when she was finally ready to open up to him and tell him that she cared about him and wanted to be his wife for real.

Seeing her sway, Hollywood swore under his breath and put a hand on her elbow, and led her to the couch. As soon as she was sitting, he pulled the coffee table closer and sat on it. He reached forward and took her cold hands in his large warm ones and squeezed. "I didn't mean to scare you. Truck is alive. He's okay."

When Mary didn't respond, but simply stared at him with wide eyes, he said, "Did you hear me, Mary? Truck is okay. He was injured, but he's alive."

Mary's breath left her in a rush. She'd been so scared that Truck had been killed she hadn't been able to think about anything else. At Hollywood's words, she relaxed a fraction. "Where is he? Can we go and see him?"

The man in front of her shook his head. "It's not that simple."

Mary's brows furrowed. "What do you mean? He's at a

hospital, right? Is he in Germany? I know that's where a lot of soldiers go when they're injured overseas."

"Yeah, he's in Germany at the moment."

Mary tried to stand. "Then let's go. I'll pack a bag real quick."

Hollywood's fingers squeezed hers once more, preventing her from standing. "You can't go and see him, Mary. I'm sorry."

"Why not? I'm his wife. The Army can't keep me from him!" She knew she sounded hysterical, but she was feeling extremely shaky and off-kilter. The possibility of Truck or one of the other guys being hurt or killed was always there when they went on a mission, but experiencing it firsthand was a hundred times more horrible than she'd ever thought. "Was he hurt worse than what you're saying? Is he dying? Dammit, Hollywood, tell me!"

"He has amnesia," Hollywood said sadly without beating around the bush. "He doesn't remember who you are...much less that he's married."

Mary stared at the handsome soldier in shock. "Amnesia?"

"Yeah. He hit his head really hard on the mission and it rattled his brain something awful."

Tears formed in Mary's eyes, but she blinked them away. "What *does* he remember?"

"Basically, he's lost the last three years of his life. He knows me and the guys. Knows he's in the Army. He knows everything up until one of our missions in Iraq about three years ago. When he woke up, he thought that's where he was."

"But he's okay otherwise?"

"Yeah, Mare. A doctor in Germany has checked him out and said other than the concussion, a few cracked ribs,—and the amnesia, of course—he's fine."

"Maybe seeing me will jog his memory," she said somewhat lamely.

The compassion in Hollywood's eyes nearly did her in.

"I talked to Ghost today, he and the others are staying with Truck in Germany until he's released...and he said that Truck got extremely agitated when Fletch told him he was married. He refused to believe him, thought the guys were playing a joke. The doctor's recommending, for now, to bring him home but to limit his interactions with others for a while. They want to see if coming back to his apartment will trigger his memories naturally. It can be extremely jarring for someone in his situation to be confronted with people who know him, but who he doesn't remember."

"But he *will* remember, won't he?" Mary whispered.

Hollywood's lips pressed together before he said, "They just don't know, Mary. Sometimes patients like him get their memories back all at once. Other times they remember bits and pieces, but not everything. And there are also cases when the person never remembers what they lost. They just forge a new life from the time the injury happened."

Mary ripped her hands out of Hollywood's grip to cover her mouth in horror. "He might not *ever* remember me? Everything we've been through?"

"I'm sorry...but it's possible that he'll never remember."

"Oh, God."

Mary felt Hollywood's hand on her shoulder, but she couldn't process what was happening. She'd assumed Truck would get home, she'd tell him that she wanted to make their marriage work, and they'd live happily ever after. But if he didn't know her, didn't know anything about her fight with cancer, their marriage, or that he'd sworn to love her forever... how in the hell would they live happily ever after?

She had no idea what she'd done to make him love her in the first place. No clue how to get him to do it a second time.

"I've lost him," Mary said in a barely there whisper. "The only reason I caught his eye was because of Rayne. If he doesn't know any of us, how can I make him love me again?"

Hollywood moved to the couch next to her and took Mary into his arms. For the first time since she'd heard the second diagnosis of cancer, Mary felt completely discouraged.

"He loved you from the first moment he saw you," Hollywood told her. "And I have every confidence that he'll get through this. He'll remember."

"You don't know that," Mary said.

"I do. Truck is stubborn, but so are you. And the rest of the team."

"But if you aren't supposed to expose him to people who might agitate him, how are you going to get him to remember?"

"I don't know. We're as shocked by this as you are, Mary. But I swear to you, we're gonna figure this out."

Something else Hollywood said finally settled in her brain. "If he's supposed to come back here to his apartment, I'm going to have to move out, aren't I?"

Hollywood sighed. "I'm sorry, but...yeah. Just for the short term. We're hoping when he gets back here, his subconscious will kick in and he'll remember all the time he spent with you here, and the rest of his memory will return."

Mary looked around and winced. Over the last few months, she'd slowly moved most of her things here. There were pictures of her and Rayne on the walls. Her favorite books on the shelves. Her sheets were on their bed. Her hair stuff was in the shower. Even her favorite foods were in the cupboards. Thinking about removing every single thing from Truck's apartment was extremely painful. Removing her very presence felt like a permanent step. An extremely agonizing one.

Hollywood went on, unaware of the blow he'd inadvertently dealt her. "The girls are going to come over to help later today. We don't know when Truck and the others will return but we thought it'd be better to be prepared. Emily said you could stay at her place if you wanted."

Mary shook her head, feeling numb. "No, I still have my apartment."

She didn't tell Hollywood that she'd planned to call her landlord and officially end her lease after she talked to Truck when he got home. It was silly to keep it when she was living with Truck full-time.

No need to do that now.

Hollywood's phone vibrated in his pocket and Mary pulled back, giving him room to pull it out. He read the text and winced. "I have to go, Mare. That's Kassie. She's freaking out because she thinks Kate is making weird noises."

Mary nodded. "Go. It's fine."

"I don't want to leave you. Come with me."

She immediately shook her head. Mary didn't want to be around anyone. Especially not Kassie, who was blissfully happy with her new daughter. She loved the woman, but she couldn't deal with that right now. Not when her own world was crumbling around her. "I'll be fine."

"Mary," Hollywood chastised.

Mary didn't like the note of pity she heard in his tone and straightened her spine, pulling the old Mary up from somewhere deep inside. "I'm fine. Seriously. Go. You have more things to worry about than me. You did your duty and told me what you had to. I'm sorry you got the short end of the stick on that, Hollywood. Sucks that you were here and not in Germany with the guys. I'll just pack up my shit and get out of here. We both knew this was too good to last anyway. Truck deserves better than me."

She was unprepared for the way Hollywood gripped her shoulders and turned her to face him. Or for the look of frustration on his face. "*Don't*. Don't pull out the bitch with me. Truck loves you, and I understand that I just laid some heavy shit on you and you're trying to adjust, but I swear to God, me and the others are going to do everything possible to help him regain his memories. We need your help. Don't give up on him so easily. You know if the tables were turned, he wouldn't give up on *you*."

"He only married me so I could use his insurance," Mary protested weakly, knowing, even as she said it, that she didn't really believe it. "It's better that he doesn't remember that."

"Bullshit. I know this is your defense mechanism talking, but you don't have to do that with me. I know you."

Mary stood, dislodging Hollywood's hands. She moved away from him until the small kitchen table was between them. "Believe me, he doesn't need to remember all the nights he knelt behind me as I puked into the toilet. Or my hair falling out. Did you know when you go through chemo you can lose *all* your hair? Not just the stuff on your head. I didn't care so much about the arm hair or my pubes, but losing my eyebrows and nose hairs sucked. You have no idea how much those little suckers do until you don't have them. I sneezed all the time because of the shit that got into my nose and I sniffed so much I know people probably wondered if I was doing drugs. I won't even get into how many nose bleeds I had as a result."

Hollywood looked shocked, but Mary kept going. "I've been nothing but trouble for Truck. I'm not exactly the right kind of woman to be an Army spouse. I'll eventually say the wrong thing to the wrong person and it'll hurt his career. This is his chance to start over. Find a nice shy woman who'll treat him gently and won't be a pain in his ass. If he does eventually remember, he'll probably be relieved to have gotten out of his marriage so easily."

Hollywood shook his head in disappointment. "We hoped you'd feel differently."

Mary was having a hard time feeling *anything* other than crushing despair. She was barely aware of his words. She just wanted him to *go*. In reply, she merely shrugged.

"I'm still going to call the others. They'll be here in a few hours to help you pack and to help get you settled back into your apartment. I know you're just trying to push me away, and I'm not going to let that happen. Put the bitch aside and fight for your man, Mary. He needs you." And with that, Hollywood walked toward the front door. He unlocked it and turned to her before leaving. "Lock this behind me," he ordered gently, then left.

The click of the door shutting was all it took to break Mary's composure. She crumpled to the floor where she stood, although no tears fell from her eyes. She deserved Hollywood's frustration. He had every right to be disappointed, but he'd actually gone pretty easy on her. As he'd pointed out, she'd unleashed the bitch, but it was to protect herself. She couldn't deal with his pity.

She wanted Truck. Wanted him to put his arms around her and tell her that everything would be fine. But she wasn't going to get that. Maybe not ever again.

She had no idea how she'd ever get Truck to love her a second time. She wasn't like other women. She didn't dress up, had never "simpered" in her life, and she certainly wasn't a damsel in distress anymore.

Curling up into a ball, Mary racked her brain for ways she

could get through to Truck. How she could make him remember her.

How long she lay there, she had no clue, but when there was a tentative knock on the door, she couldn't muster up the energy to get up and answer it.

"Mary?" she heard Rayne call out.

She didn't bother to answer.

"Mary?" her best friend said again, this time closer. She'd opened the unlocked door and entered the apartment. When she saw Mary on the floor of the dining room, she rushed over.

"Oh my God, Mary, are you okay?"

Mary looked up at her best friend and the tears she hadn't been able to shed finally formed. "What am I going to do?" And with that, Mary burst into tears. Cried like she hadn't cried since she was five years old and one of the nicer uncles had left.

Four hours later, Mary sat on her couch in her own apartment on the other side of town. Rayne had called the others and within thirty minutes, Harley, Casey, Sadie, and Wendy had arrived at Truck's apartment to help her.

Emily stayed home because she wasn't feeling that great and Annie was in school, but the other five women had systematically gone through Truck's apartment and packed all of Mary's belongings, and even changed the sheets on the bed and put the dirty towels and linens in the washer.

Mary was thankful, because she didn't think she would've been able to do it. Wouldn't have been able to find and pack every single thing that she'd brought over in the last few months. Definitely not as quickly as her friends had.

But a small part of her was resentful. *They* didn't have to move out of their houses. *They* didn't have to pretend not to know their men. *They* didn't have their hearts ripped out of their chests. Their men would come home and their lives would resume as normal.

She'd tried to be nice, though. The last thing she wanted was to alienate the best friends she'd ever had, but she was at the end of her rope and wanted to be alone. To wallow in her misery.

When Mary had walked through Truck's apartment one last time before she left, she'd broken down again. It was as if she'd never existed there. Hadn't spent the best and worst times of her life in that apartment. She felt just as devastated as she had when she was sixteen and Brian admitted he'd only said he loved her to get between her legs.

"I'm staying," Rayne declared after the others had left.

Mary shook her head. "No, I'm okay."

"You're *not* okay," Rayne countered. "And I don't care what you say, I'm not leaving."

Mary ground her teeth in frustration. She wanted to be alone. She had to go to work the next day and needed time to push everything that had happened to the back of her mind. But she knew Rayne wasn't going to let her do that. No matter how mean she was to the other woman or what she said.

Instead of lashing out and being a bitch—she really *was* trying to change—Mary sighed and put her head back on the couch. She closed her eyes and after a long moment, said quietly, "Thank you."

Rayne picked up her friend's hand and threaded their fingers. "You're welcome. I know you don't want to talk about it, but too bad. We need a plan."

Mary shook her head but didn't open her eyes. "There's

nothing we can do. The doctor said that Truck needs time and it wouldn't be good to try to force his memories to come back."

"I understand that. But that doesn't mean we can't *subtly* try to get his memories to come back."

Mary's eyes popped open and she looked over at her best friend. "What do you mean?"

"I mean, we activate *Operation Make Truck Remember His Life*."

"I won't do anything that'll hurt him," Mary said firmly.

"Me either. I know we can't just go up to him and introduce you as his wife and tell him he loves you. We need to be sneakier about it."

Despite her depression, Mary was interested. "I'm listening."

"I talked to Ghost this morning about the situation, and he told me the doctor said it was okay to bring Truck to some of his old hangouts. The places he and the guys go to all the time. Restaurants, the gym and beach where they do PT in the mornings, bars, things like that. So when they do, we'll just happen to be there. We won't necessarily even talk to him, but maybe if he sees you enough, something will click and he'll remember."

"And if he doesn't?"

"Then you're no worse off than you are right now. Look, I can't imagine what you're going through, and what I'm about to say in no way negates your feelings, but I've lost him too, Mare. We all have. We can't have any get-togethers with the guys because he doesn't know they're married, and no one is going to leave him out of things. Truck can't get to know baby Kate. He can't be there when Emily has her baby. And poor Annie, she won't understand why she hasn't seen Truck around. We *all* want him to regain his memory because of what he means to us."

Mary nodded. She got it. She did. Truck was well loved in their circle. But she had more to lose. The others could eventually become his friends even if he never remembered them. They could have him back. But if he didn't remember her, and what they went through together, she knew she didn't have a shot in hell of making him love her again. Of being his wife for real.

"I know, Raynie."

"So you're in? *Operation Make Truck Remember* is a go?"

Mary nodded. "Yeah, I'm in. I'd give up everything to have him back."

"You'll get him if I have anything to say about it." Rayne held out her pinky. "Pinky swear."

Mary rolled her eyes at her best friend, but linked her pinky to hers anyway.

"Love you, Mare."

"Love you back, Raynie."

"We're gonna get through this and have our quadruple wedding."

"I'm less concerned about the wedding at this point. I just hope to get Truck to not hate me on sight."

"He won't."

Mary wished she could be as confident as her best friend.

CHAPTER SIX

Truck used his keys to open his apartment door and stepped inside, Ghost right on his heels. The last week had been a whirlwind of flights, doctors, blood draws, and psychologist sessions. All he'd wanted to do was get home to his own bed and sleep for a week.

His head still throbbed, but not as badly as before.

The doctor had informed him that he was missing some time, but Truck wasn't too worried. If he'd lost his entire memory, that would've been bad. But losing a few years wasn't that big of a deal.

It was a bit odd to find out he was actually three years older than he'd thought, but having Ghost, Fletch, and the others there with him was a comfort. He remembered everything about them. How Ghost had a thing for brunettes, Fletch was a neat freak, Coach could complete logic puzzles faster than anyone else on the team; how Hollywood could collect at least ten phone numbers from women every time they went out, that Beatle hated bugs, and how Blade got his nickname.

It was also a bit strange to learn in the hospital in

Germany that the team hadn't been about to go on R&R and pick up chicks after completing their mission, but instead they'd been in Africa on a completely different mission, three years in the future. But he'd dealt with it then, and he could deal with it now.

Scratching the scar on his face absently, Truck looked around his apartment. Things weren't quite where he remembered them being, but he supposed that would happen since a few years had passed.

When he'd first been told he had amnesia and was missing three years of his life, he'd laughed and accused the guys of playing a prank on him. But when not one of the men had cracked a smile, he'd realized they were serious. The doctors and the poking and prodding of his head were more proof.

The most frustrating part was that Truck knew his friends were keeping things from him. Beatle and Blade seemed to be even closer than he remembered them being, and they were constantly whispering to each other far enough away that he couldn't hear them. Ghost was on the phone all the time, and he'd yet to get a good explanation as to why Hollywood hadn't been on the mission with them.

Truck had liked the other Delta team. Trigger and his men were competent and had taken over getting the girls reunited with their families and, where necessary, out of the country when he'd been flown to Germany to be admitted to the Army hospital.

Ghost had told him the other team were also stationed at Fort Hood, and that they'd see them when they got back. It had been a long week, and Truck was more than happy to be out of the hospital and home.

"Welcome home, man," Ghost said.

When Truck turned to him, his friend was looking around the space as if he'd never seen it before.

"You've been here," Truck said. "Why are you examining it as if there might be tangos hidden behind my furniture?" Truck asked.

Ghost laughed nervously and brushed off the question. "I made arrangements for your cabinets to be filled, as well as your fridge. You should be good to go for a while."

Truck nodded. "Thanks. Any chance the commander will ignore the doctor's orders for me to take a month off from the team?"

Ghost shook his head. "No way in hell. You need to rest, Truck. Your brain took quite a beating. You might feel as if you're good as new, but you can't push it. Take the time off and be happy for it. It's been a long time since you've had a vacation."

Truck sighed. "Me being sidelined means no missions for the team, right?"

Ghost nodded. "Yeah, but that's okay, we're happy to stay home for a bit."

"Why?"

Ghost's eyes dropped from his and roamed the room.

Truck seethed inside. Even more sure his friend was hiding something from him, he wasn't surprised when he changed the subject.

"I'll come over tomorrow and we can watch a movie or something."

Deciding now wasn't the time or the place to get into it, as his head was really starting to throb, Truck asked, "Anything good come out in the last three years that I need to see?"

Ghost looked at him in surprise, then smiled. "Oh, man, it's kinda cool that you'll get to see movies for the first time again. *Deadpool*, a few new *Star Wars* movies, *American Sniper*, *Hidden Figures, Logan, Sully*...and of course, *The Lego Movie*."

"Are you shitting me?" Truck asked.

"Yup," Ghost said with a grin. "Only about the fucking *Lego Movie*. The rest are all kick-ass. I'll see you tomorrow, Truck. Get some sleep. Call me if you need anything or if your head starts to hurt more than it is right now."

"How do you know my head hurts?" Truck asked.

"Because we're best friends. And because you're squinting and tilting your head to the right."

"Fuck. Okay, yeah, it hurts. I'm gonna take a pill or two and crash. Thanks for everything. I owe ya."

"You owe me nothing," Ghost returned. "You hear me? I'd crawl through hell for you, *have* crawled through hell, just as you've done for me."

That was true. Truck was thankful once more that he hadn't lost his memories of his teammates. He held out his hand and Ghost took it in a tight grip. When Ghost went to let go after shaking it, Truck held on.

"I know you're keeping shit from me, and I hate it. I get why you're doing it. The doctor told me that suddenly finding out huge pieces of my life that I've lost could be detrimental —but I need you to promise me that if there's something I really need to know, you'll tell me. Or if I do or say something that is out of line based on something that's happened in the last three years, you'll let me know."

Ghost sighed. "You're missing a lot, Truck."

"You think I don't know that?" Truck asked. He dropped his friend's hand and sighed in frustration. "One part of me wants you to just tell me all of it so I can start to deal. But the other part of me knows that I'm not ready yet. I just...I don't like this feeling inside that something's wrong. That I'm missing out on something big."

Ghost put his hand on his friend's shoulder. "You're gonna

remember," he vowed. "Just the fact that you feel something missing is huge."

"I guess."

"It is. I heard what the doctor said. That your brain is swollen and when it heals, you'll either remember or you won't, but fuck that. You're gonna remember, Truck. That doctor doesn't know you. Doesn't know what we've been through. You're a fucking Delta, we aren't like most men. We're smarter, quicker, stronger, and tougher. But you don't have to remember *tonight*. Get some sleep. It's been a long fucking week. I'll come by tomorrow with some of the guys and we'll hang out."

"I'd like to see Hollywood," Truck said.

Ghost pressed his lips together. "I'll see if he can get away."

Truck wanted to ask what Hollywood needed to get away from, but he didn't. He knew whatever his friend was doing, it had to be important for him not to have been on the mission in Africa. Though, Hollywood was the only one he hadn't seen or talked to since waking up after hitting his head, and he was still half afraid his friends were lying when they'd said he was alive and well.

"Sounds like a plan. See you tomorrow."

Ghost nodded and left. Truck locked the apartment door behind him and sighed in relief. He was finally alone for the first time in a long-ass week. He'd always loved being by himself. At least, he had three years ago. But, looking around, Truck had a niggling feeling in the back of his head. Something was there...but the second he tried to concentrate, a stabbing flash of pain shot through his skull.

Not bothering to check out what Ghost had gotten for him to eat, Truck went straight to his bedroom, swallowed two pain pills, then flopped down on his mattress. The sheets smelled freshly washed and he reveled in the fact they were clean. He was happy that he'd been smart enough to do laundry before he'd gone on the mission.

Truck pulled a pillow closer to him and turned over onto his side, trying to alleviate the pain in his skull. He inhaled deeply, doing his best to relax—and froze.

The pillowcase smelled like laundry soap...but there was something more there too. He couldn't place it though.

Sitting up and ripping the pillowcase off, Truck brought the pillow to his face. He had no idea why, but the scent made him sad and aroused at the same time.

Had he brought a woman home right before the mission and had sex with her here, and now her scent lingered on his pillow? It made no sense. But the more he tried to remember why the smell triggered such a feeling of coming home, the more his head hurt.

Succumbing to the pain, Truck lay back once more, this time clutching the pillow to his chest. He buried his nose in the material and eventually fell asleep with the comforting scent surrounding him.

CHAPTER SEVEN

"I don't know about this, Rayne," Mary told her best friend as they sat down in the corner booth in Truck's favorite steakhouse. It wasn't a chain restaurant, rather a locally owned business that Rayne had told her Ghost and Hollywood were taking Truck to for lunch.

"You said you were down with *Operation Make Truck Remember*," Rayne informed her.

"I am. But...what if he sees me and falls to the ground with blood leaking out his ears or something?" Mary asked semi-hysterically.

"That's not how amnesia works," Rayne told her.

Mary knew that, but she was so nervous about seeing Truck for the first time. It had been two days since he'd returned home, and other than the updates she'd gotten from Rayne and the other women, she had no idea how he was doing.

All of the other women were doing everything they could to pass on information about Truck. The notifications on Mary's phone were out of control. She'd gotten more texts in the last two days than she'd ever gotten in her life. The women all grilled their men when they came home, then reported back to Mary every single thing that Truck had said or done.

She knew all about how he'd loved the movie *Deadpool*, apparently especially the sex scenes. He'd gone to the gym to work out with the guys, and was irritated because the doctor had said he needed to take it easy and Fletch kept telling him to chill out. Casey had told her that Beatle had told *her* that Truck's head was still bothering him, alternating between stabbing pains and a ringing sensation.

Mary both loved and hated the updates, wanting to see for herself that he was all right, but they were killing her. She was scared to death of what might happen when Truck saw her, but her desire to see him in the flesh overrode her fears.

"Breathe, Mare," Rayne said softly when they'd gotten settled in the booth.

"What if seeing me hurts him?" Mary asked.

"Then we'll call the doctor and deal with it."

That wasn't the kind of hurt that Mary meant, but she didn't contradict Rayne.

Her best friend reached across the table and grabbed Mary's hand. "It's gonna suck if he doesn't recognize you," Rayne warned.

"I know."

"No, seriously. I know you. You're gonna pretend that it doesn't matter. That it's not a big deal. But it is. I saw him yesterday in the grocery store, and he looked right through me. The man carried me, bleeding and scared out of my mind, out of that building in Egypt, and I didn't see one spark of recognition when he walked past me. It sucked for *me*, and that's why I know this is going to be doubly painful for you."

"Jeez, why don't you get some lemon juice and rub it in my open wounds?" Mary quipped.

Rayne squeezed her hand tighter. "All I'm saying is that it's okay to break down. I'm not going to judge you. This is a no-judging zone." Rayne whirled her free hand in a small circle, indicating the booth they were sitting in.

Mary gritted her teeth. "I know. You think it already doesn't hurt, Raynie? Sleeping by myself in my bed that seems way too empty? Waking up and turning over, expecting to see him there next to me? Not one second goes by that I don't regret the way I've treated him, that I didn't get the chance to say thank you or try to tell him that I care."

"You mean you're sleeping?" Rayne retorted.

Mary shook her head at her best friend in exasperation. Rayne knew her too well. Either that or the dark circles under her eyes told their own story. She *wasn't* sleeping. Not very much. She'd been having the worst dreams. Some involved Truck lying on the ground and bleeding out, others starred her mama saying over and over that men were no good and that love didn't exist. Still others were nothing but weird noises and spooky shapes that had her sitting up in a panic, thinking someone had broken into her apartment.

But she didn't tell Rayne any of that. She simply nodded her head and tried to look sincere when she said, "Of course I am."

"You're such a bad liar," Rayne told her.

"So what's the plan?" Mary asked, trying to head off another lecture.

"You walk by their table a couple times."

"That's it?"

"Well, yeah," Rayne said. "I mean, it's not like you can drop yourself in his lap and announce that you're his wife and you want him to take you home to bed."

"Tempting," Mary quipped under her breath.

Rayne smiled. "I heard that."

"I know. Should I stop and talk to them? Maybe I can pretend to know Ghost or something and talk to *him*."

"Hmmm, not a bad idea, but I'm thinking this first time you just walk by. Let's ease into this. See what his reaction is."

Mary knew that was probably best, but it was going to be so hard to not do something stupid—like get down on her knees and beg him to remember her.

Rayne flagged down their waitress and ordered them both iced teas and they got a plate of cheese fries to munch on.

Mary knew the fries were more for Rayne's sake than hers. She couldn't eat a thing, and she had a feeling Rayne knew it, but she appreciated her friend trying to make things seem as normal as possible.

Ten minutes later, the door to the restaurant opened and Ghost, Hollywood, and Truck walked in.

Mary sucked in a breath. Truck stood head and shoulders above his friends. His mouth was pulled down in its usual scowl because of the scar on his face. He was wearing a black T-shirt and his biceps strained against the material. Mary immediately noticed the way his brow was furrowed, as if he fought against a headache.

"Oh, shit," Mary whispered. "I can't do this." Seeing him in person, standing tall and looking exactly like he had when she'd last seen him, was painful. He was just as handsome in her eyes, looked exactly like the Truck who'd promised that they were going to move their relationship to the next level.

His eyes took in the restaurant, and Mary held her breath as his gaze met hers for a split second before moving on.

Without thought, one of her hands came up to press on her chest over her heart. The blankness in his gaze was a blow. Rayne had warned her it would be, but nothing could've prepared Mary for the lack of recognition she saw in his eyes.

The entire time she'd known him, Truck had looked at

her with intense emotion, even the very first time she'd met him. Caring, worry, amusement, love, tenderness...the list went on and on. But him dismissing her as if he had no idea who she was almost broke her. Of course, he *had* no idea who she was. It wasn't as if he was purposely hurting her.

At that moment, Mary knew she had two choices. The first option was to set Truck free. If she let him go, it would destroy her. She would probably turn back into the cynical woman she'd been before he'd decided she was worth the effort.

Or she could fight for what she wanted.

It was an easy decision.

She wanted Truck.

She might not ever be able to verbally say the words, but she could show him every day how much he meant to her and how much she loved him. She could be there for him. She could support him. She could be a woman he would be proud to have at his side. She'd show him every night how much she loved him with her body. He'd understand. Of course he would, he was Truck.

She wouldn't give up on him. He hadn't given up on *her* when the odds were way more stacked against her with something far more serious than memory loss. Truck wasn't dead. By some miracle, *she* wasn't either. She was going to fight for him. She might not succeed, he might not want anything to do with her, but she'd be as pathetic as the damsels in distress she loved to make fun of in movies if she didn't at least *try*.

Mary followed the trio with her eyes as they were seated. She couldn't tear her gaze from Truck, even though she knew if he caught her, he'd think she was a creeper.

"Are you okay?" Rayne asked from across the booth.

Reluctantly, Mary looked over at her best friend. "Yes."

Rayne blinked and then narrowed her eyes. "You are, aren't you?"

"Yeah. That sucked, there's no doubt. But you know what?"

"What?"

"I almost died. Twice. I had my body filled with so many poisons and crap, I would've glowed if someone held a black light up to my body. I dry heaved so much it felt as if I'd done a thousand sit-ups in a row. I puked all over myself, the floor, Truck, and my bed. I went five days without eating anything and only drinking enough to survive. But I beat that fucking cancer. Twice. Amnesia? *Pbfft*." Mary made a scoffing noise then continued. "Amnesia's got nothing on me. It's like someone pulling out a cute little derringer when I've got a Desert Eagle."

"I don't know what that means," Rayne said with a confused look on her face.

"It means, amnesia is *not* going to beat me. No fucking way. I'm gonna fight it as hard as I fought my cancer...well, okay, there was a point when I didn't really fight it all that hard, but Truck did for me. So I'm going to return the favor."

"Um...that's all well and good, and I'm thrilled you're not curled up in a ball on the other side of this booth, but I don't know how you can fight this. It's not as if you can inject him with drugs and fix it."

"No, you're right, I can't. But I can fight for what I want. And I want Truck."

Rayne didn't react for a second, then a huge grin broke out on her face, and she squealed and leaped out of her seat and plunked herself down next to Mary and hugged her as tight as she could. "God, I'm so glad to hear that."

Mary hugged Rayne back and chuckled.

"I was so afraid you'd give up. That you'd decide you couldn't handle this. That you'd think love wasn't worth it."

"I handled cancer. I can handle this. I'm not saying it'll be easy. It won't. And, Rayne, I know I'm going to need your help. But Truck didn't fight to keep me alive, only to have me turn my back on him now."

"Damn straight."

"Damn straight," Mary agreed.

The waitress chose that moment to return and put the plate of cheesy goodness down on the table. Rayne moved back to the other side of the booth and the two women proceeded to plot their plan of attack.

It wasn't lost on Truck that Ghost kept looking over at the booth in the bar area where two women were sitting. He'd noticed them the second he'd walked in, but had done his best to look disinterested. He wasn't here to pick up women; he was here to talk with his friends and to hopefully remember something from the last three years.

One thing Truck *hadn't* forgotten was the way women sometimes looked at him. They either immediately wanted to jump his bones because he was a bad boy, or they acted as if he were a serial killer who was going to pull a knife out from behind his back and start slashing at everyone around him. His height, and the scar on his face, had turned more women off than he could even count. And the college-aged girl who'd led them to their table was no exception. She'd taken one look at his face and had immediately turned her eyes away and spoken to Hollywood instead.

But the woman sitting in the bar with short brown hair with the pink streak in it hadn't looked away from him when he'd caught her eye. In fact, she'd stared at him with such intensity, he almost walked toward her to find out what was wrong.

When Ghost looked over at the other table for the fifth time, Truck asked, "You know them?"

It took his friend a while to answer, but Truck was glad he didn't try to lie to him. "Yeah."

"Hmmm." Truck wasn't sure what to say. He wanted to ask *how* Ghost knew them, but he had a feeling the other man wouldn't tell him. It wasn't hard to tell that his friends were watching what they said around him very carefully. They were treating him as if he were a ticking time bomb and if they said the wrong thing, his head would literally explode. It was beginning to irritate the fuck out of him.

Deciding to let it go for now—his head still hurt and he had an appointment to see the doctor on post before he could go home—Truck looked down at the menu. It was different than he remembered, but that wasn't too surprising since he remembered a menu that was three years old.

He settled on a ten-ounce steak with a loaded baked potato and a salad. The waitress did her best to not make eye contact while he was ordering, concentrating on the notepad in front of her instead. Of course, she didn't have any problem flirting with Hollywood as he ordered. Truck mentally rolled his eyes. *That* was familiar.

Their salads arrived after a while and the three men were talking about the PT session they'd had that morning. Ghost had just asked about his afternoon doctor's appointment when his friend said "shit" under his breath.

Looking up, Truck saw the woman who had caught his eye earlier walking toward them. Her eyes were glued to his—and Truck stilled.

She had the most expressive brown eyes he'd ever seen.

He held his breath as she neared, forgetting all about Hollywood and Ghost sitting with him.

She wasn't looking away. Wasn't pretending she didn't see the gnarly scar on his face. When she got close, her lips curled up in a slight smile.

Truck could feel his hands begin to sweat—what the hell? — but he couldn't tear his gaze from hers.

When she got close, she said, "Hi," in a low voice. Truck thought for sure she was going to stop and talk to them, but she continued walking, obviously headed for the hallway, which had a large "restrooms" sign above it.

Truck watched her ass as she headed away from the table. She was fairly tall...probably around five eight or nine, exactly the height he liked best in a woman, and slender. Almost too slender for his taste. She didn't have much in the way of tits, but her hips were nicely rounded. Her hair was short, but the pink streak gave it character. It told him a lot about her. That she wasn't afraid to go out on a limb. That she wasn't so into societal norms. That she was a bit of a risk taker. He liked all of that.

But it was the fact that she wasn't afraid to meet his eyes and truly *look* at him that really made him interested. Oh, he'd seen her eyes flick to his scar, but then she looked right back into his eyes. And that was truly unique. Most women either retreated, mentally or physically, or tried to check out his package. As if they thought they might be able to put up with his ugly mug if he had a big cock.

He did, but that was beside the point.

"What time is your appointment?" Ghost asked. "I can come with you if you want."

Truck didn't take his eyes off the woman until she'd disappeared into the restroom. Then, instead of answering, for some reason he turned his head and looked back at the table in the bar area where the woman had been sitting. He caught her friend looking in their direction, but she quickly ducked her chin and picked up a French fry from the almost empty plate in front of her. She was trying to look nonchalant, but he saw a blush work its way up her cheeks at being caught staring.

Truck wasn't an idiot. He knew he fascinated women. Once upon a time, he'd been easy on the eyes. He'd had no problem picking up women when he went out. Sure, he attracted the freaks who wanted to get it on either because he was damaged or out of pity, but at least he'd been able to get off.

But he hadn't seen pity in the woman who'd just passed their table. He wasn't sure what he saw in her eyes, but it wasn't pity or a sick kind of curiosity.

The throbbing in his head intensified as he thought about the woman.

"Truck?" Ghost questioned.

"Two-thirty," Truck told his friend, answering his earlier question. "And I don't need you to go with me and hold my hand."

Ghost chuckled. "I wasn't going to offer," he said, pretending to be offended.

Truck kept up a witty back and forth with his friends, all the while attuned to the back hallway. He was curious as to whether the woman would walk by their table again or if she'd go the more obvious route to her table via the back of the restaurant.

Within minutes, she reappeared—and walked straight toward him again.

Truck couldn't stop the small smile. He knew it was lopsided, but he didn't care. Having this unique-looking woman check him out felt good. Really good.

This time when she passed the table, he nodded at her. She didn't speak again, but gave him another small smile in return. Truck wanted to turn and watch her ass as she passed, but he refrained.

"She was checkin' you out," Hollywood observed.

"Yup," Truck replied.

Hollywood opened his mouth to say something else, but the waitress appeared with their steaks. They smelled as good as Truck remembered, and he was glad the quality of the food hadn't diminished in the last three years.

When she was done setting their lunches down on the table, Truck snuck a glance over to the bar. He was surprised to find the women's booth vacant. All that remained was an empty plate, two glasses, and what was obviously the signed bill on the table.

Feeling disappointed, Truck turned his attention back to his food and his friends. It wasn't as if he could have strolled over to the woman and given her his phone number, not when he was missing such a big chunk of his life. It felt wrong, somehow, to even be interested in anyone. He had no idea why that was, but knew if he tried to explain himself to Ghost and Hollywood, they'd change the subject.

They'd taken the doctor's orders to heart, to not rush his memory. To let him recall things on his own. Which was super frustrating because so far, he hadn't recalled shit. He didn't remember anything about the other Delta team or the mission in Africa. The last thing he still remembered with any clarity was being in Iraq...which was apparently years ago.

It was maddening—especially when he caught his friends communicating silently, as Hollywood and Ghost were right now.

Deciding to not call them on it—maybe if he pretended he didn't know they were keeping shit from him, they'd relax a bit and actually talk to him—Truck took another bite of steak and pretended to be interested in what his friends were saying.

"So?" Rayne asked when they were outside.

Mary shrugged, still reeling from her small encounter with Truck. She'd been sure he would ignore her presence as she walked by the table. But instead of ignoring her, he stared, his brown eyes piercing in their intensity. For a second, she thought he was going to stand up and take her in his arms and tell her how much he'd missed her.

She'd squeaked out a small "hi" when she passed him, and he didn't move. Didn't come after her. Didn't declare that seeing her had cured him. But Mary felt his eyes on her ass as she walked away and entered the restroom.

It had taken a couple minutes to regain her equilibrium, and she'd frantically texted Rayne, asking if she should walk past his table again, or if she should go the other way. Rayne had encouraged her to walk by Truck again, so she had. And the second time he'd nodded at her.

It was depressing and exciting at the same time.

She had never, not since she was fourteen years old, made the first move in a relationship. Not once. She'd always let the guys come to her. But...it felt good. Empowering.

"Mary!" Rayne demanded. "What happened? I couldn't really see much."

"Nothing to get excited about. I said hi when I went by the first time, and he nodded at me when I went back by."

"That's good," Rayne declared.

"Is it?"

"Oh, yeah. They went out to eat last night, just to get him

out of his apartment and to make sure he was okay. When the waitress hit on him, Ghost said he didn't even look twice at her."

"What?" Rayne hadn't told her that. Neither had any of the other women. "When were you going to tell me?"

"Oh...uh...soon. But I wanted you to get the first contact out of the way before I said anything," Rayne said quickly.

The thought of anyone hitting on Truck made her want to pull their hair out by the roots, but what really was scary was wondering about Truck's reaction. She remembered how he'd acted when the paramedic at the bank had hit on him. He'd been offended that anyone would dare make a move when he was with her.

But now that he didn't *know* he was with her, Mary wondered if it was only a matter of time before he sought attention from the opposite sex. After all, she knew how long it had been since he'd *had* sex. At least a year. She wasn't sure what his bedroom activities were before that, but she had a feeling he'd been celibate since he'd met her.

"When are they going out again?" Mary asked Rayne as they walked to their cars.

"Um...I'm not sure."

"Don't lie to me, Rayne. Seriously, you suck at it, and I can tell every time. Tell me."

Rayne sighed and said, "This weekend. Ghost said Truck wanted to go to that sleazy bar near the post they used to go to all the time. Of course, he doesn't know they stopped going there when everyone got girlfriends. He still thinks that's their usual hangout spot."

"I'm going," Mary declared.

"I'm not sure that's the best idea," Rayne said. "I mean, I know we're working on *Operation Make Truck Remember* and all, but I know you."

"What's that mean?" Mary asked with her hands on her hips.

"It means that if someone hits on Truck, you're going to lose your shit. I know it's been a while, but I also know that you'll have no problem getting into a brawl, and that's the last thing you need, both health wise and because it'll draw unwanted and unflattering attention to yourself. Do you want Truck to see you rolling around on the nasty floor of that bar? No, you don't." Rayne was talking faster and faster, as if by continually talking, she could keep Mary from disagreeing. "And you just made the first contact today, and it went well. Let Casey and Wendy go. They'll chat up the guys and see if they can jog Truck's memory."

Mary knew Rayne was trying to do what she thought was the best thing for her—but she was wrong. "He looked interested in me," Mary told her.

"Truck?"

"Yeah. We made eye contact, and I could tell that he was curious about me. There wasn't any recognition, not really, but I think if I saw him again, I might be able to *keep* him interested."

"It's not a good idea to start dating him, having sex, if he doesn't remember you. What would happen if he *did* suddenly remember? It could be a disaster. He might think you were deceiving him...which you would be," Rayne argued.

"Maybe. It's a chance I'm willing to take. If our roles were reversed, and I lost my memory, I'd rather Truck seduced me and I woke up in *his* bed than in some stranger's. Can you imagine how awful that would be? To regain your memory and realize you'd slept with someone other than your wife? He'd be devastated. I know him. Besides, there's no way I'm gonna let any bar-hopper bitch get with *my* man," Mary finished heatedly.

When Rayne didn't answer, but instead smiled a weird smile at her, Mary asked belligerently, "What?"

"It's just that the shoe is on the other foot."

"Whatever."

"No, seriously. For years, Truck has pursued you. He's gone out of his way to do everything he can think of to make you his. And now, here you are, doing the same thing in reverse. Calling him your man. Claiming him. It's kinda funny."

"This isn't funny."

"Yeah, Mare, it is. And forgive me for being a bitch, but it serves you right."

Mary knew she should be pissed at her friend for being so blunt, but she couldn't be. Her lips twitched, then curved upward in a grin. Then she was laughing. Rayne joined in and the two of them laughed until they were crying.

"Shit. Anyone who says karma doesn't exist is so fucking wrong," Mary said when she'd controlled herself.

"Right? Seriously, it so does. But you got this, Mary. I'll help any way I can."

"You'll go to the bar with me this weekend?"

Rayne sighed in mock exasperation. "You know I will. I'll see if Harley or any of the others want to come too. We'll make it a girls' night out."

"Thank you," Mary said with heartfelt gratitude. She had no idea what she'd do without Rayne. She'd missed her so much over the last couple months. She'd been an idiot to push her out of her life when she'd needed her the most.

"I'm headed out on an overnight on Sunday though," Rayne warned her. "It's a flight to New York City. So you'll have to continue *Operation Make Truck Remember* without me."

"I'll text you updates."

"You better."

The two women hugged and Mary waved as she got in her car and started the engine. She had to get back to work as her lunch hour was over. Her boss had been a little more lenient after the robbery, but Mary could tell her gratefulness no one had gotten hurt was waning, and her bitchy attitude would return sooner rather than later.

The news had reported that the two men who'd held up the bank were members of a local gang and the robbery was some sort of initiation or something. They were in jail...but since then, there had been two different instances of customers coming in wanting to rent safety-deposit boxes that hadn't sat well with Mary. They'd both worn nice slacks, long-sleeve shirts, and ties, but Mary had seen tattoos on the sides of their necks that made her nervous.

She was profiling, and she knew it, but she couldn't shake the weird feeling about the men. She'd mentioned it to her manager, but the woman had told her she was being paranoid.

There was nothing Mary could do about it. If someone wanted to rent a safety-deposit box, and was able to pay for it, it didn't matter if they were the President of the United States or a felon. There was no discrimination at the bank.

Thinking about work made Mary think about Truck again. And thinking about Truck made her more determined than ever to make him want her. Even if he only wanted to sleep with her, that was better than nothing, and it would keep any other woman from warming his bed. And if Truck, God forbid, never regained his memory, she'd do whatever she could to start their life over. Even if she had to propose to *him* this time.

CHAPTER EIGHT

Truck was looking forward to the night. He enjoyed hanging out with his friends at the bar near post. It wasn't the most trendy place, pretty much a hole in the wall, but he and the others hung out there all the time, and he'd even picked up a girl or two. Of course, Hollywood usually got first choice of the women since he looked like a fucking movie star, but inevitably there'd be someone who was willing to go home with him, despite his scars.

Hollywood and Fletch weren't there tonight though. It seemed they weren't partiers anymore. Truck could understand Fletch not wanting to come, but Hollywood bailing surprised him. He'd made up some excuse that sounded totally made up, but Truck didn't want to think about what the real reason was behind his friend bailing. He was sure it had to do with whatever everyone was keeping from him, but for once, he didn't want to worry about it. Ghost was there, as were Beatle, Blade, and Coach.

Truck didn't want to worry about the doctor telling him there was a chance he'd never regain the three years he'd lost.

Or about how his head was still throbbing...had never *stopped* throbbing since he'd woken up in Africa in the middle of the op. All he wanted to do was hang with his friends, flirt with some women, and try to feel normal once again.

He was going stir crazy sitting in his apartment. There were times he'd look around and feel as if something was missing...but as soon as he'd have the feeling, it would disappear. Every now and then, he'd also swear he could smell some sort of flowery scent, but when he inhaled deeply, it was gone.

Truck wanted to be back at work, but he still had a few weeks to go before the doctor allowed him to return on a part-time basis. He'd also been warned about drinking alcohol, but he needed a beer. Just one. He hated how off-kilter he felt.

Truck had been playing darts with the others for about half an hour when he felt a hand on his back.

Resisting the urge to turn and take out the person with his leg, Truck turned to see who was dumb enough to touch him while he was holding, and about to throw, a lethal dart.

A woman was standing there, one he didn't recognize. Not that *that* meant much, since he didn't recognize a lot of people these days. She had long brown hair and had curves in all the right places. She had a nice rack and was pretty. She was wearing a blouse that was a bit too low cut for an innocent night out. The look in her eyes as she ran them up and down his body made it clear what she wanted from him.

In the past, Truck wouldn't have hesitated to throw his arm around her shoulders and pull her in close. Hell, if a woman hit on him, Truck was all about seeing if they had enough chemistry to take her home, but tonight felt different.

He was different.

Truck had no idea why, but the thought of taking a woman home, *this* woman home, didn't sit right with him.

"Hey," the woman drawled as she flirtatiously ran a finger up his biceps.

"Hey," Truck returned, and his eyes skipped to Ghost. The other man was doing his best to ignore Truck and the woman at his side. He'd get no help there.

"My name's Ruth," the woman said.

"Truck," he said in return.

"Truck," she purred. "I like it. Maybe later you can rev my engine."

Truck wanted to roll his eyes, but he refrained. Barely.

"Can I buy you a drink?" Ruth asked. "You seem to be the only one not drinking over here." She giggled. A high-pitch sound that grated on Truck's nerves.

"No thanks," he told her, not wanting to get into why he wasn't drinking. He'd finished the one and only beer he was going to have. It tasted awesome, but like the doctor had warned, it also made his head throb more.

"Come on," she cajoled, then leaned into him, pushing her tits together so her cleavage was prominently on display. "Have a drink with me."

"I'm in the middle of a game," he told the woman, who was now officially annoying him.

"Okay, babe. If it's all right with you, I'll just sit over here and watch." Her eyes went back down his body and rested on his crotch for a beat too long. She licked her lips then looked back up at him.

Truck mentally sighed. She was way too obvious. She wanted to see his cock. Wanted to know if it was as big as he was. He'd encountered women like her all too often. They didn't care about him, per se, they just wanted to sleep with the giant and get their freak on. One such woman had even told him it was a good thing he had a big dick since his face was so fucked up.

He turned to Beatle and quipped, "I see *this* hasn't changed in the last three years."

Beatle almost spit out the beer he'd just taken a sip of, but managed to swallow it so he didn't spew all over the bar table they were standing near.

The other men chuckled, but didn't help him get rid of the annoying woman. Knowing he couldn't be rude—it just wasn't his style—he merely nodded at the woman, and then sighed in frustration when she beamed up at him and shimmied onto one of the barstools nearby. She leaned over until her elbow was resting on her knee, which made her tits just about fall out of the shirt she was wearing.

Truck turned his back on her and rolled his eyes at Blade. The other man smirked at him, then said, "Still your turn, Truck."

"Right," he said, then tried to turn his concentration back to the game. Darts wasn't exactly a challenge for the Deltas, all of them got bullseyes with almost every throw, but it passed the time. And it got Truck out of his apartment... which had been his goal. For the first time that week, he felt almost normal.

Going out had been a great idea. Spending time with his buddies in their usual hangout felt like putting on an old familiar coat. He liked it. Except for the bar bitch waiting nearby. He could practically feel her stripping him with her eyes. If she thought he would be taking her home later, she'd be extremely disappointed.

She could go home with one of the others. Maybe Coach would like her. He liked chicks with dark hair.

"That fucking bitch," Mary said between clenched teeth.

Rayne, Casey, Wendy, Harley, and Mary were sitting on the other side of the bar. They'd gotten there before the men and, so far, had kept their presence low key.

But Mary knew that was about to end.

"Easy, Mary," Rayne soothed. "Remember, we talked about this. You don't want Truck's first—well, second impression to be of you rolling around on the floor fighting."

"She touched him," Mary bit out. "She knows he's taken, and she fucking touched him. And her boobs are about to fall out of her bra. It's disgusting."

"He doesn't look all that interested," Casey observed. "I mean, she's practically throwing herself at him, and he hasn't looked at her again."

"He made it more than clear he was with *me* at the bank that day," Mary went on. One of her hands was clenched into a tight fist on her lap and the other clutched her bottle of beer.

"She either has balls of steel to come on to him after the smackdown you told us Truck gave her," Wendy said, "or she somehow heard about his amnesia and is trying to take advantage."

"How would she have heard about it? It's not like it was in the papers or anything," Mary said. "But whichever's the case, it makes her a *bigger* bitch than I already thought she was if she's trying to get with my man. I was nice last time. Wasn't I nice at the bank, Rayne?" Mary asked.

"You were," her friend immediately agreed. "I was kinda surprised when you told me what happened, actually. But then again, you said that Truck told her in no uncertain terms he was with you and that was that."

Mary inwardly seethed. She took a sip of her beer and tried to calm herself. It was bad enough the paramedic had dared to hit on Truck when they were at the bank and she was supposed to be working, but to go up to him bold as brass tonight, and hit on him a *second* time, was low. Really low.

"So, what's the plan tonight?" Harley asked. "*Is* there a plan?"

The four women all looked at Mary. "The plan is for me to introduce myself to Truck and flirt with him."

Casey's eyes got big. "Are you gonna sleep with him?"

Mary almost choked on her beer. After swallowing, she said, "No. Jeez. I'm just gonna flirt with him and see if I can catch his interest. I hadn't really thought about anything else yet. God."

"She hasn't slept with him yet," Rayne informed the others.

Mary whipped her head around and stared at her best friend incredulously. "Rayne!"

"What?" she asked not so innocently.

"I really don't want to talk about that right now."

"Look, if you can't talk to your friends, who *can* you talk to?"

Mary scrubbed a hand over her face and stared down at the scarred table. "It's embarrassing."

Rayne covered her hand with her own and said, "No, it's not."

"We're married. It's not normal," Mary insisted.

"You were sick," Harley said. "When were you supposed to have sex? Between bouts of barfing? How about when your chest was so burnt from the radiation your skin was peeling off? Then?"

Mary stared at her in shock. She loved Harley, but the

woman wasn't usually so forward. She was more apt to keep her nose buried in her computer screen writing code for the video games she loved so much. How did she even know that much about breast cancer treatments, anyway?

"Rayne talked to us," Wendy explained. "She wanted us to understand why you did what you did. It's not a big deal."

It wasn't a big deal? It was a *huge* fucking deal! She was going to tell everyone eventually, but she wanted it to be on her terms and when she was ready. Mary turned accusing eyes to Rayne. The other woman held up her hands in capitulation, but she was grinning and didn't seem the least bit repentant for sharing such intimate things with the others.

"It's not a big deal that you guys haven't slept together yet," Rayne said. "Besides, we all know you're not a one-night stand kind of woman."

"I used to be," Mary mumbled.

"Yeah, before you met Truck," Rayne reiterated. "But all that aside, I think your plan is good. I argued with Ghost tonight about Truck. I told him that he was babying him too much. I asked how he'd feel if it was *him* who'd lost his memory, and his friends didn't tell him about me."

"And how did he take that?" Harley asked.

Rayne wrinkled her nose. "He wasn't thrilled. But seriously. Those guys are taking this too far. I mean, yeah, they shouldn't give him too much information at one time, but admitting that they have girlfriends, or are married, isn't going to kill Truck. Ghost didn't agree."

Mary slumped in her seat. "So if the guys don't want me around him, this'll never work."

"What the hell?" Rayne said harshly.

Everyone's eyes went to her.

"Mary, you can't seriously be giving up. What happened to the take-no-prisoners best friend I used to know? The one who told me to go for it when I texted you about Ghost when I was in London? The woman who wasn't afraid to stand up for what she wanted and to hell with the consequences? I know I was the one who tried to talk you out of coming tonight, but I can admit I was wrong about that. I have a feeling the more Truck sees you, the more curious he'll be. All that notwithstanding, I hate to be the one to tell you this, but you've gotten soft. And it isn't pretty. I want my bitch friend back."

"First of all, I didn't say I was giving up," Mary huffed. "I was *inferring* that trying to get to know Truck in public places like this bar, with all the guys watching us, isn't going to work. But secondly..." Mary glared at Rayne. "You want the bitch?"

"Yes!" Rayne snapped. "At least *that* Mary wasn't afraid to go toe-to-toe with Ghost when he was being an ass. She had no problem standing up to Truck and the others when they were being idiots. Well, they're being idiots again, and you're sitting here all frowny-faced and sad. I don't necessarily like it when you make a scene, but now, in this case, I'm not sure it wouldn't be warranted."

Mary wanted to protest. Wanted to tell Rayne that she was scared no matter what she did, Truck wouldn't take a second look at her. That he'd pick Ruth the paramedic over her. But something deep inside stirred at her best friend's words. She'd had a hell of a year, but the cancer was behind her now. Hadn't she decided earlier in the week that she was going to fight for Truck? So why was she sitting here moping? Why *wasn't* she standing up to Ghost and the others? *She* was the one married to Truck. Not them.

"You're right."

"Damn straight, I'm right," Rayne fired back.

Mary's lips twitched and she turned to look in Truck's direction—just in time to see Ruth plastered to his side as she stood on her tiptoes to whisper something in his ear before she stepped back, patted his chest, then sauntered off toward the restroom.

"Oh, fuck no," Mary growled.

"Oh, shit," Harley said. "You've awakened the beast, Rayne."

Mary downed the rest of her beer then stood and headed for the restroom. She didn't wait for any of the girls to go with her or to stop her. This shit had to end. Once she took care of the skank trying to steal her man, she'd make sure Ghost and the others knew what she thought of them keeping so many damn secrets from their teammate.

Mary waited outside the bathroom for Ruth to reappear. She was not going to get into this inside the nasty restroom. She'd been in there earlier, and never wanted to have to go in again.

Within minutes, Ruth opened the door and, upon seeing Mary waiting for her with her arms crossed over her chest and a scowl on her face, stopped in her tracks.

"That's right, bitch," Mary said. "It's me."

But Ruth recovered and flipped her hair behind her shoulder and sneered at her. "What do *you* want?"

"I want you to stay away from my husband," Mary fired back.

"Doesn't look like he feels the same."

Mary stepped into Ruth's personal space and said in a low, hard tone, "I think he made himself more than clear the other day where things stood with you. *Nowhere*. He's mine, and if you insist on embarrassing yourself, you'll regret it."

"I know all about his amnesia." Ruth smirked. "One of my coworkers is married to someone on post, who heard about it from one of the nurses at Darnall Army Medical Center. Truck doesn't even *remember* you. If you were so tight, don't you think he'd instinctively know and push me away? But he's not—so you obviously aren't as close as you thought you were. I'm taking my shot."

"Look, Ruth, I know you think you're smart and all, but you don't know shit. Truck has *amnesia*. He doesn't have Spidey senses or anything. That's not how the brain works. But make no mistake. He's mine. He's always *been* mine. And he might not remember me, but that doesn't change the fact that we're still married. I'll protect him from anything—or anyone—who tries to hurt him."

"He didn't seem upset to have me by his side earlier," Ruth said with a smug smile. "Besides, you can still have him. I just want him for a night or two. I've never been with someone as big as him...if you get my gist."

Mary saw red. She was done trying to be nice. Rayne wanted the bitch back? Fine.

"Truck is *not* a piece of meat to pass around. And if you were paying attention, you'd have noticed how he leaned away when you pressed your tits against him. His lip curled when you couldn't take your eyes off his dick. You aren't fooling him. Truck isn't stupid. He knows that you don't give one little shit about him as a person. All you care about is how big his dick is. If you really want to get fucked, you can go to any sex shop and *buy* a big dick."

Mary took a breath and continued, "I'm here to tell you that Truck is the most amazing person I've ever met. He'd give the shirt off his back to anyone who needed it. He's also the kind of man who would be polite to a pushy bitch who's horning in on his bro time and isn't getting the obvious hints he doesn't want her. So, because you're clueless, and a chick, and my friend Rayne is always telling me that there's some unspoken girl code that says women need to look out for each other, I'll let you know straight up—*Truck doesn't want you.* He would rather play darts with his friends then go home to an empty bed and jack off than be anywhere *near* you. Was that clear enough?"

"You're a bitch," Ruth hissed.

"Thank you," Mary responded. "But that doesn't change the fact that Truck doesn't want you. He'll *never* want you, no matter how much you throw yourself at him. Go home while you still have some dignity left."

Instead of answering, Ruth pressed her lips together and took a step toward Mary. She swung her arm back to slug her.

Mary grinned in anticipation and shifted her weight, readying herself for a fight. It had been a long time since she'd gotten to take a bitch down a peg or two.

But before Ruth could follow through with her swing, her wrist was grabbed and her arm twisted behind her back.

Her boobs almost popped out of the shirt she was wearing with the movement, but somehow she stayed decent as Blade spun her around and pressed her face to the wall of the hallway.

Mary turned—and saw that Beatle, Coach, Ghost, and Truck were all standing at the end of the narrow hallway, staring at them.

She swallowed hard. Shit. There were times she didn't mind letting others see how much of a bitch she could be, but now really wasn't one of them.

"How much did you all hear?" Mary whispered to Blade as he easily held the struggling Ruth against the wall.

"Truck isn't a piece of meat," Blade told her with a smirk on his face.

Mary relaxed a little bit. So they hadn't heard the part when they'd talked about his amnesia or when she'd called him her husband.

Lifting her chin, refusing to be ashamed of what they'd

heard, especially since every word was the truth, she turned toward the others as confidently as if she had smackdowns in the hallways of bars every night of the week. She walked right up to Truck and held out her hand.

"Hi. I'm Mary."

Truck didn't hesitate. He grinned down at her and took her hand in his own. Instead of shaking it though, he brought it up to his mouth and kissed the back. "I'm Truck. But you obviously know that."

"I do. Wanna buy me a drink?"

His grin got bigger, and he didn't let go of her hand.

"I'm not sure—" Ghost began.

But Mary didn't let him finish. She turned and glared at him. "You're my friend, Ghost—but butt out."

"Mary, you can't just—" he tried again.

"Seriously," Mary interrupted. "I got this. You're just going to have to trust me. I'm not going to do *anything* to hurt Truck. Hear me? I may not have made the greatest decisions in the past, but I have nothing but his best interest at heart."

"Leave them alone," Coach told Ghost. "After the way she just stuck up for him, I'd say he owes her at least one drink."

Ghost frowned and ran a hand through his hair, but finally nodded. "Okay, but we're gonna be watching."

Mary rolled her eyes. "Thanks, Dad. I'm sure Truck appreciates you guys protecting him from big bad me."

Truck chuckled—and the sound went straight between her legs. It seemed like forever since she'd heard it, and when he shifted their hands until their fingers were intertwined and their palms were smushed together, she couldn't think about anything but how good he felt.

"Come on, Mary," Truck said. "We'll let my dads play more darts while you and I get acquainted...or re-acquainted, as the case obviously is."

Mary nodded, then turned to glare at Ruth, who now looked appropriately cowed. A little too late, but whatever. "Don't come at me again, Ruth. Ever. I'm a lot tougher than I look. And I won't hesitate to defend myself." And with that, Mary turned back to Truck and said, "I'm parched."

Without another word, Truck led them out of the small hallway where they'd been attracting quite a bit of interest to a spot at the far end of the bar. Mary caught Rayne's thumbs-up and the smiles of the other women at their table, and she relaxed. Ghost might not think she was doing the right thing, but her friends did. And that felt good.

How could something that felt so right be wrong? She wasn't going to blab that they were married, and she would definitely tread carefully, but Truck was tougher than his friends thought.

Truck waited until the spunky woman was settled on the barstool before scooting the one next to her a little closer and sitting. The bartender immediately came over and Mary ordered a beer. She then ordered a water for him, in a martini glass, with extra olives.

Surprised, Truck merely stared at her.

She shrugged at seeing his confused look. "You always said that when in a bar and not drinking, it was better to make it look like you were, simply to get people to leave you alone and not get on your case about it. This is what you usually order."

Truck nodded. Yeah, he did say that. Of course, he didn't remember telling the spitfire sitting next to him, but there was the whole missing-the-last-three-years-of-his-life thing.

Instead of getting mired in self-pity, he was curious. Curious as to how well he knew Mary.

He was attracted to her, but it was more than her looks. He'd seen her head into the hallway and immediately recognized her as the woman from the steak place earlier that week. When he'd heard raised voices, he'd gotten concerned, and he and the others had made their way to check on her. If someone had been assaulting her, they'd have regretted it.

But instead of Mary being assaulted, *she* was verbally haranguing the skank who'd been hitting on him—and her words were a surprise. Not only because she was so staunchly defending him, which felt good, but because it was more than obvious she knew him. Very well.

Standing there listening to Mary give Ruth a verbal beat down, and not give one fuck that she was being a bitch as she did it, stirred something deep inside Truck. He'd spent much of his childhood letting people get away with rude remarks about his size. Even after he'd grown into his body and had been able to defend himself, he typically kept silent. After he'd been injured, the rude comments started up again, although this time mostly behind his back rather than to his face.

Even when his parents had been incredibly harsh to him when they'd come to visit him in the hospital, he'd bitten back the bitter words that were on the tip of his tongue.

It was just who he was. He'd never be the kind of man who would stand up for himself, for the simple reason that he knew he'd never change another person's mind. But listening to this woman—Mary—say exactly what was on *her* mind was amazing.

Truck realized at that moment what had been lacking in most of his relationships in the past. The women weren't strong enough to stand up to him. Or his friends. Or anyone, really. He intimidated most people. But apparently not Miss Mary. He felt excited that he'd known her before. He had an in to get to know her all over again.

"Thank you," he told her. "You obviously know me pretty well."

"I do."

Truck grinned at her.

"Why are you smiling?" she asked.

"Because I'm fucking thrilled someone is being honest with me."

"They mean well," Mary told him.

"I know. But it's still annoying. I'm not an idiot. I might not remember the last three years, but I'm assuming I didn't live in a bubble. It's extremely weird to have people smile at you and not know if they're just being polite, or if you're supposed to know them. I went to the grocery store the other day and the check-out lady smiled at me, and then engaged me in a ten-minute conversation. I still have no idea if she was just super friendly or if I know her from before."

"That sucks," Mary said.

"Yup. So thank you."

"You're welcome. But you should know, I'm not exactly going to tell you your entire three-year history tonight. We'll work into it."

"Good. That means you'll have to see me again. And again. Don't want to overload my poor brain and have it explode."

Mary laughed. "Smooth, Trucker. Smooth."

"Trucker?"

She blushed, and Truck thought it was the cutest fucking thing he'd ever seen. He had a feeling she didn't blush much.

"Yeah, uh...it's what I call you when you exasperate me.

Or when I'm upset with you. Or when I just want to rile you up."

It was Truck's turn to laugh. "I take it you call me Trucker a lot then, huh?"

She shrugged. "Often enough."

"I think I like it."

Mary rolled her eyes. "Figures that you don't *remember* the nickname, but the first time you hear it, you act just like you have every other time I've tried to annoy you by using it."

"What's your last name?" Truck asked, suddenly wanting to know everything about the fascinating woman in front of him.

For some reason, she looked away from him, then answered, "Weston."

"Mary Weston. I like it," he told her.

"Thanks."

"Tell me more," he demanded.

"Like what?"

"I don't know...everything. You probably know all there is to know about me, and I don't know anything about you."

"I don't know all that much about you," Mary mumbled and picked at the label on her beer bottle.

Without thought, Truck reached out and lifted her chin so she had to look at him. The second his finger touched her skin, he felt a jolt of...something. Her skin was soft, and he wanted to palm her cheek in his large hand but he refrained. Barely. "Why?"

She shrugged. "Our relationship has been...complicated."

"Were we dating?"

"Sort of."

Truck didn't like the ambiguous answer, but forged onward. This was more information than he'd gotten from his friends in the last week, and he didn't want to make her clam up. He was desperate to hear more about his missing three years. "So...complicated?"

She gave him a half grin. "Yeah. Very."

"Okay, so we get to know each other now. We can start new. A blank slate, so to speak."

"Really?"

"Really."

"Why?"

She was a prickly thing. Truck liked it. "Because. I want to get to know you...again. You said things were complicated, so let's make them uncomplicated."

"I'm not going to sleep with you," Mary said a little defensively.

Again, her honesty was refreshing. "Good, because I don't want a one-night stand," he shot back. "Look. I get that this is weird for you. But it's even stranger for me. I have no idea what 'complicated' means. Were we in an open relationship where we could both sleep with others? Do we like ménages? Maybe we're married and you've got our twelve kids stashed away somewhere. I just don't know."

He noticed the way Mary paled, but continued, "But I *do* know that I'm drawn to you. I don't need protecting, never have, but hearing you stand up for me back there," he motioned to the restroom hallway with his head, "both aroused and fascinated me. It also made me yearn to get to know you. You're literally the first person who's admitted we had some kind of relationship before I lost my memory. I'm flying blind here, and you're going to have to tell me if 'complicated' can be overcome, or if starting over with me from scratch is too much for you."

"It's not too much for me," Mary said immediately.

Truck breathed out a sigh of relief. "So, we'll start fresh. I'll be as open as I can with you, more open than I obviously was before, and I can get to know you all over again as well. I'm not promising anything other than friendship for now. I'm attracted to you, Mary, I won't lie about that, but until I either remember or someone tells me everything about my life that I'm missing from the last three years, I can't commit to anything serious or long term."

"I can live with that," Mary said. "But you should know...I like you too. We may have been complicated, but that doesn't mean that I didn't care a great deal for you. I wasn't always the best at showing you, for lots of reasons, but I'm going to try harder this time. I can't exactly turn off my feelings because you don't remember."

They stared at each other for a long moment. Truck was more impressed with her now than he was before. It couldn't have been easy for her to admit that.

"I can live with that," he echoed.

Just then, someone jostled Mary from behind, making her knock over the bottle of beer she'd been drinking. Luckily, it tipped away from her and spilled over the back side of the bar instead of all over her.

Truck looked around and realized that the bar had gotten a lot more crowded since they'd sat down. He saw Ghost and the others, no longer playing darts but sitting at a table in the corner with four women, including the one who had been at the restaurant with Mary.

He should've guessed. None of the guys had been the least bit interested in checking out the women at the bar like they used to. Some Special Forces soldier *he* was. He should've known they had girlfriends.

Suddenly feeling sick that his friends hadn't told him they'd found women, Truck wanted to get away from their prying eyes. Wanted nothing more than peace and quiet.

He turned back to Mary. "Want to get out of here?"

"Yes," she said immediately, not taking her eyes from his.

Standing, Truck put his hand on her elbow to help her off the stool. "Do you need to tell your friends where you're going?"

She shook her head. "No. It's none of their business."

Truck's lips twitched. "I think Ghost and the others would disagree."

Mary stepped close and tilted her head back so she could look up at him. It made Truck feel ten feet tall, and that was saying something, considering he was already so much taller than she was. She was jostled again, and Truck put his arm around her back to steady her.

"Ghost is like a brother to me. The others too. They should know that I'd never do anything to hurt you, and that you'd never hurt me. But at the moment, I don't give a shit what they think. Your head is bothering you, it's loud in here, and you and I need to start getting to know each other."

"My place or yours?" Truck asked. He knew it sounded presumptuous, but he'd already told her that he wasn't going to sleep with her. Besides, she was right, his head *was* pounding, and he wanted to get to know her without watchful eyes on them.

"Mine," she said immediately.

"Did you drive?"

Mary shook her head. "No. I came with Rayne."

"Do you trust me enough to come with me?"

Then she blew his mind. She put her hands on his chest and stood on her tiptoes. Truck instinctively leaned down and she put her lips over the scar near his mouth. She kissed him gently and said softly, "More than I trust myself." Then she took a step back, smiled at him, took his hand in hers, and started for the door.

Truck looked over at the table where his friends were

sitting—and almost laughed out loud at the eight pairs of shocked eyes watching him and Mary walk toward the door. He gave Ghost a chin lift and then turned his attention back to the woman walking in front of him. He was sure he'd get the third degree later, but for now, he was going to enjoy being in Mary's presence.

CHAPTER NINE

"It's nothing fancy," Mary said as they entered her apartment. And it wasn't. She hadn't bothered to empty the boxes the guys had helped her pack at Truck's place. Her heart wasn't in it, and she knew that every time she saw something that had been displayed at Truck's, it would hurt. So she'd left everything in the boxes.

"Are you moving?" Truck asked.

Mary wrinkled her nose. "No."

To his credit, he didn't push, but merely shrugged and headed for her couch. It was the one thing that Mary had regretted leaving behind when she'd all but moved in with him. It was brown suede and the most comfortable thing she'd ever owned. It had cost a fortune, but was worth every penny. It had huge cushions, and even Truck's feet almost didn't touch the floor when he sat on it.

"Want something to drink?" she asked, standing next to the couch.

"No. Sit, Mary."

Loving the bossiness in his tone, and realizing for the first time how much she'd missed it, Mary kicked off her shoes and went over to the other side of the couch. She curled her jean-clad legs under her and leaned against the back cushions, facing Truck. He scooted over until he was within touching distance and sat sideways to face her.

"Does your head feel better?" Mary asked.

Truck nodded. "Now that we're out of the noise, yeah."

"Does it always hurt?"

"Unfortunately, yes."

"What did the doctor say about it? You did tell him, right?"

"Of course. He said it was normal. My brain was knocked around quite a bit when I fell and it's bruised and swollen. He says that's why I can't remember the last three years. He's hoping that when the swelling goes down and my brain heals completely, my memory will return."

"Is there anything you can take for it?" Mary asked. She didn't even want to talk about the possibility of Truck not remembering. She wasn't being selfish either...okay, a little. But she couldn't imagine losing that much of her life. Although, forgetting the hell she went through while she was fighting cancer might be a blessing, but then she'd also have forgotten Truck. And she'd take the awful memories of the cancer if it meant she could have memories of how amazing Truck had been.

At least it wasn't worse. She supposed Truck could've lost all his memory and not even remembered that he was a soldier, or that Ghost and the others were his friends. *That* would've been tragic, and would be a lot harder to come back from.

"I don't like painkillers," Truck said. "I'd rather deal with the slight headache than take something that makes me tired or crabby."

Mary smiled. She knew that. She'd also tried to put off

taking the painkillers and anti-nausea pills for as long as possible when she was sick because they made her feel as if she was out of it, and she didn't want to get addicted, but Truck wouldn't let her. They'd argued about it, with Mary declaring that if Truck could decide not to take drugs when he got hurt on a mission, she could make the same decision in regards to her cancer treatment. He'd agreed to her point— then pleaded with her to take them, since seeing her in so much pain hurt *him*. She'd relented.

"What?" Truck asked.

She should've known he'd figure out she was remembering something. "I've heard you say that before. Do you remember what happened when you got hurt?" she asked, wanting to change the subject.

"No. When I woke up, I thought we were in the Middle East."

"Must have been a surprise to find out you were in Africa, huh?" Mary knew that's where they'd been because Rayne had told her. She'd heard the basics from Ghost. She didn't know exactly where or why, but knowing Africa was where he'd been hurt was enough.

"Yeah. I pulled a gun on one of the other Deltas."

"One of your team?" Mary gasped.

"No. The other one that was with us."

"Seriously?" Mary asked. When Truck nodded, she said, "Holy shit."

Truck chuckled. "It was tense there for a minute or two. I pulled a gun. He didn't pull out his own weapon, but his teammates sure did. Then Coach, Beatle, and Blade reciprocated. Ghost stood between me and the other team, trying to calm me down. There we were, in the middle of an op, all ready to blow each other away."

Mary couldn't help but smile at the image he'd put in her mind.

"Of course, calmer heads prevailed, and here I am," Truck said wryly.

"I'm glad," Mary told him honestly.

Truck rested his head on his hand and stared at her.

"What?" she asked after a moment, uncomfortable.

"I'm trying to figure out how in the hell I could've forgotten you," Truck said.

That was probably the nicest thing anyone had said to her in a long time, and Mary tried to blow it off. "Probably because I'm a bitch and hold people at arm's length."

"Why?"

"Why?"

"Yeah. Why?"

This was it. The start of the new them. Mary knew she could either deflect his question, or she could take the opportunity to let him know why she was the way she was.

Taking a deep breath, she felt the shield she'd kept wrapped around her for so long crack the slightest bit. "I didn't have a good childhood." That was the understatement of the year, but he didn't say anything, just kept watching her with his intense brown eyes. His quiet contemplation, and the fact he didn't immediately start asking questions, gave her the courage to continue.

"My mama was a whore. And I don't mean that in the general name-calling sense. She was literally a whore. She didn't stand out on street corners or anything, but she went after men who she knew were vulnerable and had money. She'd seduce them, move them in so they could pay her bills, and she milked them for all they were worth. In return for them buying groceries, paying the phone and cable bill and electricity, she slept with them. One of my earliest memories is of Mama fighting with one of my 'uncles'—that's what she told me to call them—and when he got fed up and left, she lectured me for hours about how awful men were and how all they wanted was sex. She said that as long as I didn't expect them to love me, it was okay to spread my legs for them, especially if I got as much out of them as I could. I didn't know what that meant, I was only four or five, but eventually I understood, because the lecture remained the same for years."

"That's awful," Truck said in a tone that showed no pity, only compassion.

"Yeah. My entire childhood, she pounded into me that men were no good. That they were only useful for money and they only wanted sex. She told me over and over, and showed me by her actions, that they weren't capable of loving women. I didn't want to believe her. I mean, I knew she wasn't the nicest mama in the world, she sure didn't take care of *me*, I had to do that on my own. I thought she was full of shit."

Mary stopped talking. She hadn't ever told anyone this. Not even Rayne. Oh, her best friend knew her mama was a whore and that she wasn't very nice, but Mary had never gotten into the details. And now here she was, basically telling a stranger her life history. But somehow that made it easier. He didn't know anything about her. Had no preconceived ideas about her.

Truck reached out and put his hand on one of her knees. "Go on," he urged. "Get it all out."

"This is crazy," Mary murmured. "We should be talking about our favorite foods or some shit."

"We're past that," Truck said.

Mary rolled her eyes. "You didn't know I existed an hour ago."

"But I know you exist now," Truck countered. "And I can't

explain it, but I think a part of me remembers you. It's not a memory, per se, but a feeling. Now, what happened?"

Mary sighed. She wanted to believe him, but she knew how stubborn he was. Truck used to hate not knowing what she was thinking, which happened all the time because Mary was just as stubborn as he was. She didn't like to talk about her feelings or about the shit that she'd been through.

Closing her eyes, Mary decided to just get it done. "When I was fifteen, I met a boy. He was so nice to me. He stood up to bullies for me, and he made me feel so pretty and wanted. We dated for a while and one day, he told me he loved me. I was so happy. I told him I loved him back. I thought we'd get married and I'd live happily ever after. I slept with him. Gave him my virginity." Mary ground her teeth together and tried to calm herself down to finish the story.

It was Truck's hard grip on her knee that did the trick. She opened her eyes and saw the hard, furious look on his face, and weirdly, it made her feel better that he was upset for her. She reached down and picked up his hand and held it in both of hers while she finished. "The next day, he broke up with me. Told me I'd held out longer than he'd thought I would, considering I was the town whore's daughter, and that he was moving on to the freshmen cheerleaders who would sleep with him without all the dramatics. That was the last time I ever told a guy that I loved him."

She bravely looked up and met Truck's gaze. It was as if he could read her mind. Knew what she was trying to say without saying it. "That guy didn't deserve your love," he said after a beat.

"Duh."

"I'm sorry you went through that, Mare. That sucks."

Mary beat the tears back at the endearment. Had something deep inside him *really* remembered her as he'd claimed?

She cleared her throat and said, "He was the first man to hurt me, but he wasn't the last. I tried to prove my mom wrong time after time, but eventually I realized she was right. All the men I dated were using me for one thing or another. Some wanted something tangible—a place to live, for example—but others just wanted sex or to try to make an ex jealous. I didn't want to admit that Mama was right, but I didn't really have a choice."

"If it makes you feel any better, my childhood wasn't exactly idyllic," Truck said. "Although at least my parents didn't flaunt their affairs in front of me."

Mary sat up straighter. Truck had never talked about his family. *Ever*. She'd even asked Rayne to ask Ghost about it, and she'd reported back that Ghost didn't know much about Truck's life before he'd joined the Army. He never talked about his parents. Even to the men who were like brothers to him.

Truck looked away from her uneasily. "Although you probably know that already."

"I don't," Mary said, holding his hand tighter when he tried to pull away from her. "You never talked about your family."

"Really?"

She nodded.

"Yeah, probably because I don't like to even think about my parents anymore."

"What'd they do?"

Truck sighed. "They kept me fed and clothed, but they were never very loving. I started growing in middle school. I grew so fast, they had to keep buying me new clothes so I didn't show up to school in high-water pants. I was super skinny, no matter how much I ate. I was a beanpole and the other kids definitely noticed.

"My dad wanted me to play basketball since I was so tall, but I was also uncoordinated back then. I didn't make the team, not that I was surprised. After that, it was as if my dad gave up on me. He wasn't interested in anything I did. If I couldn't succeed in sports, he couldn't be bothered to pay attention to me. Neither him nor my mom wanted to hear about the bullying I went through. I learned to take it. If I pretended the words didn't hurt, then they usually gave up taunting and teasing me."

"I don't understand why kids are so awful," Mary said quietly. "I really don't."

"It didn't help that my sister was super popular and beautiful."

Mary jerked back and stared at him in surprise. "You have a *sister?*"

Truck nodded. "I guess I never told you that either, huh?"

She shook her head. "No. I had no idea. How old is she? What's her name? Where is she now? I take it you aren't close?"

Truck pressed his lips together. "Mercedes. But she hates that name. She always went by Macie. And once upon a time, we were extremely close. She's almost five years younger than me. She was going into ninth grade when I graduated and left for boot camp. I haven't talked to her since the night before I left."

"Why? If you were so close, what happened?"

"I'm honestly not sure. We had a fight the night before I left for basic training. I didn't like the boy she was dating, and she thought I was being too overprotective. We yelled at each other, and then I left. But I wrote her. I figured she'd get over it. I guess she never did, because I never heard from her again."

Mary tightened her hand on his. "Truck...something had

to have happened. I mean, you were both so young. She never wrote you back?"

He shook his head. "No." His voice lowered. "It hurt. It had been us against the world—and our parents—for so long, and it felt as if she'd abandoned me when I left. Even when I got this," he fingered the scar on his cheek, "I never heard anything from her. I wrote her for years. I think I was around thirty when I finally gave up. I had begged her to contact me, told her that whatever it was I'd done, I was sorry. Told her that I loved her and wanted her to be a part of my life. I thought about hiring a private detective to try to find her after I got hurt, after I realized just how awful my parents were, but after I thought about it for a while, it was more than obvious she didn't want to be found. Didn't want me in her life."

"Do you... Never mind."

"What?"

Mary paused, then asked the question that was on the tip of her tongue. "Is she still alive?"

"Yeah. My parents had no problem telling me what a perfect daughter she was every time they saw me. Granted, I haven't talked to them in a long time, but I'm guessing she's fine."

Mary's mind was racing. She couldn't believe Truck had a sister that no one knew about. "Maybe if your parents were so awful to *you*, they did something to prevent her from contacting you. Maybe they were mean to her too, or threatened her in some way. Did you ever think about that?"

Truck stared at her for what seemed like forever before he said, "No. And what kind of brother and man does that make me, that I was so locked in my hatred for them that I didn't even think about what they could be doing to Macie?"

"Don't," Mary warned, sorry she'd even brought it up.

"Whatever they did isn't on you. So...Macie was popular and you weren't?" she asked, wanting to change the subject slightly and get back to what they were talking about before his huge revelation...namely, his bullying. It was hard to believe a man like Truck was *ever* bullied.

Truck nodded and continued, "When I was in the tenth grade, I finally started filling out, but by then it was too late. I was the weird, tall, quiet kid. I was lonely a lot, as I didn't have any friends. I joined the local YMCA and started doing weights and running, just to keep my mind off how miserable I was. I joined the Army right out of high school, and my dad actually laughed at me when I told him what I'd done. He didn't think I'd be able to cut it."

"But you did," Mary said.

"Yup. Decided I was going to show him. I signed up for Delta Force and was thrilled when I was chosen. The training sucked, but every time I wanted to give up, I thought about those kids making fun of me and my dad telling me I would never amount to anything. I was going to go home and throw it in my dad's face that not only had I done it, I was a force to be reckoned with. I even thought about how proud Macie would be of me, and it kept me going. But then I got this." Truck gestured to his face once again.

"The Army contacted my family, and my parents came to see me in the hospital. It looked a lot worse back then, believe it or not, and my dad took one look at my ruined face and turned his back on me. They didn't know I was conscious...and he told my mom that at least they still had *one* good-looking kid. He couldn't stop talking about how hideous I looked, how no woman would have me now, even if I was some 'hotshot killer'."

"That asshole!" Mary exclaimed. "He should've gotten down on his knees and thanked God you were alive."

"Yeah, well, that was the last time I saw them. They were surprised when they found out I wasn't unconscious and told them to get the fuck out, and that I was done with them. For good."

"What did they say?"

"Nothing. They simply left."

"I can't believe that!" Mary said again, standing up and pacing in front of the couch. "I mean, you were hurt serving your country! How could they turn their backs on you?"

Truck grabbed her hand when she paced by and yanked her toward him. Mary shrieked, not expecting the move, and landed with an *umph* on his lap. He wrapped his arms around her and lay back, resting his head on the arm of the couch. He shifted her until she was lying with her back to the cushions and her front plastered against his side.

Mary froze. All she could think about was her boobs. Were they still where they were supposed to be inside her bra? What if they'd shifted? The last thing she wanted was for Truck to look down and see one of her inserts sticking up from her shirt, or a lump in the middle of her stomach.

But all thoughts of her chest flew out the window when Truck lifted his head and buried his nose in her hair.

"What...what are you doing?" she asked shakily.

"You smell so good," Truck told her.

"Um...you know this is weird since we just met," she said, trying to put some space between them. She didn't *want* the space, she'd missed him terribly, but she was trying to do the right thing.

"How long have you known me?" Truck asked, keeping his nose right where it was.

"Um...a couple of years."

"So this *isn't* weird," he concluded.

"Truck!" Mary protested.

"Mary!" he countered. "Relax. I need this right now. I hate thinking about my parents, about my childhood. And you smell so good. Comforting. Give me a second."

How could she keep resisting when he said things like that? She couldn't. Besides, she loved being here with him. They'd lain just like this many times in the past. He'd held her when she'd felt sick from the chemo. They'd watched television or simply slept.

Mary melted into him and shifted one leg up and over his. Her arm wrapped around his huge chest and she let her head relax until it rested on his massive shoulder.

"You know, that explains so much," she said after a minute or two.

"What explains what?"

"You never call people out when they're being rude. When they stare at your scar like it's the most fascinating thing ever. When people look down their noses at you. I've always wondered why."

"It's just not worth it. Besides, I have a feeling *you* probably stuck up for me more than once, didn't you?"

Mary stiffened. Did he remember?

"I don't remember you doing it, but after hearing you lay into Ruth tonight, I'm guessing you aren't so reticent when it comes to people staring."

She sighed. "Unfortunately, no."

"Why unfortunately?"

"Because it makes people think I'm a bitch. And then they look at you with pity because you're with me."

"I don't mind that you're a bitch. How about this, you keep calling people on their rudeness, and I'll make sure they know how happy I am to have you at my side."

"Shit," Mary said softly.

"What?" Truck asked.

"I'm not sure I can handle all this openness," she said honestly.

"I take it we weren't exactly chatty Kathys, huh?" Truck said with a chuckle.

"Uh, no."

"I like this new version of us."

"But you don't remember the *old* version of us," Mary said.

"True, but if we didn't talk like this, and if I didn't know about your bitch mama and you didn't know about my horrible parents and Macie, then what we had was probably based on the wrong things."

Boy, did he have *that* right.

Before she could agree, he inhaled deeply again. "You smell so...familiar. It's like I'm having déjà vu."

"Do you think that could be good?" Mary couldn't help but ask.

"I have no idea. But at the moment, I don't care."

They stayed like that on the couch for another couple of hours. Mary told him a few details about her friends, without mentioning names or many specifics...except about Rayne. They also talked about their likes and dislikes. They discussed the movie *Deadpool* and had a spirited argument about whether or not it could be classified as a romance. When they finally seemed to run out of things to talk about, Mary asked, "How's your head feel?"

"Good," Truck slurred.

"Really?"

"Yeah. I should go."

"Don't," Mary said swiftly. "Stay."

"I told you, young lady, that I wasn't going to have sex with you," Truck teased.

Mary giggled, then said softly, "I haven't felt this good in months."

"You really want me to stay?" Truck asked.

"Yeah."

"Then I will. You want to get up and go to bed?"

Mary shook her head. "I'm comfortable here."

His arms tightened around her for a moment before relaxing again. "Me too."

"Truck?"

"Yeah, Mary?"

"We haven't had sex together."

He lifted his head at that. "Why not?"

"It's a long story," Mary prevaricated.

"But we've slept together." It wasn't a question.

"Yeah."

"I thought so. This feels familiar to me. You in my arms. Snoring."

"I don't snore," Mary protested, smacking his chest.

Truck's hand came up and flattened her palm against his chest, his thumb brushing back and forth over it, as if to calm her.

"I'm glad," Truck told her.

"Glad we haven't had sex?" Mary asked in disbelief.

"Yeah. Because I think I would've hated knowing I'd been inside you and not remembering it. It makes me feel as if we're more on the same level since we haven't seen each other naked yet."

"I didn't say that," Mary muttered.

His brow arched. "You've seen me naked?"

She shook her head. "No. Dammit. But you've seen me."

"Fuck. I *hate* that I don't remember."

"I'm not much to look at."

This time when his head came up, his eyes were sparkling with anger. "Don't say that."

"It's true."

"Look at me, Mare. Out of the two of us, I'm the one who isn't much to look at."

Mary scooted her hand out from under his and palmed his cheek. "You're perfect."

"As are you."

"But you don't know—"

"Shhhhh," Truck soothed, cutting her off. "No one is getting naked right this second, so just relax."

Mary put her head back on his shoulder but kept her hand on his cheek. He was so warm and alive under her. She knew that if he'd hit his head any harder, he might not be here at all.

"There you go," Truck murmured. "Relax, Mare. This is the first time I get to sleep with you...and actually remember it. Let me enjoy it."

"Brute," Mary complained without heat.

She felt him chuckle, his chest rumbling under her, but she was too relaxed and happy to argue with him anymore. "I'm glad you're here," she told him.

"Thank you for defending me against that scary woman," Truck returned. "I don't know why she couldn't figure out that I wasn't interested."

"Because you're a catch," Mary told him. "Of course she wanted you."

"But I'm with *you*," Truck complained.

Mary felt warm inside at his words. He hadn't known he was with her when the other woman had come on to him, but something wouldn't let him be attracted to her regardless. It felt good. Like hope. Hope that they might work out after all.

"Yes, you are," Mary agreed.

"I'm glad you're here too," Truck told her. "Now, go to sleep."

"Yes, sir," Mary said cheekily.

"That's more like it," he said with satisfaction.

"Don't get used to it, Trucker. I'm not usually so compliant."

In response, he hugged her and ducked his head so his nose was in her hair once more. Mary had no idea why he liked smelling her shampoo so much, but she wasn't going to complain.

CHAPTER TEN

Truck woke up like he always did, all at once and completely awake. He had no idea where he was, but he knew he was comfortable and something smelled delicious.

Without opening his eyes, he inhaled deeply—and just like that, an image flashed through his head.

He was sitting behind a naked woman in a bathtub. He was wearing a pair of sweatpants and holding a washcloth, running it over her arms. The woman was sniffing quietly, and he knew she was crying, but trying to hide it from him.

Truck felt helpless. When he'd heard her crying, he'd entered the bathroom without a second thought and had only taken the time to whip off his shirt before joining her. The scent of the shampoo he poured into his hand wafted up to his nose as he gently massaged her head. There were only short little strands of hair poking up through her bald scalp, but she didn't react as he worked the shampoo over her carefully.

"I've got you," he said soothingly. "You're okay."

But it was obvious she wasn't okay, and Truck had never felt so helpless in his life.

"Good morning," a voice said, and Truck would've jumped ten feet in the air if he wasn't as well trained as he was.

As soon as the woman's voice sounded in his ear, the vision disappeared. Truck wasn't sure if he'd been dreaming or remembering. He didn't know any bald women, or at least hadn't met any since he'd been back home. The images didn't make sense.

He looked down at the woman in his arms. Mary. The night before came back to him, and he smiled. "Morning, Mary."

She beamed. "You remember me."

Truck chuckled. "I should hope so, considering you lured me into your home and kept me prisoner by pinning me to this couch all night."

She giggled, as he'd intended. "Are you hungry?" she asked. "I can make us something."

"I need to go," Truck told her regretfully. He didn't like the look of sadness that appeared in her eyes at his statement.

"Oh, okay. Sure." She tried to sit up, but Truck tightened his arm around her waist to keep her where she was.

"I know it's Sunday, but I arranged to meet the guys for PT this morning. I think you know as well as I do that if I don't show, they'll freak. They've been a bit...protective of me. But just because I'm leaving, doesn't mean that I want to go."

The hollow look in her eyes cleared and she nodded. "You're right. I'm just being selfish. I'll see you later, I'm sure. I know my friends will be wanting to talk to me too."

"Don't let them talk you into staying away from me," Truck warned. "Because it won't work. I know where you live and...um...where do you work?"

Mary laughed. "At Central Bank, downtown."

"Right. I know where you live and work. There's nowhere you can hide from me."

"I don't want to," she admitted somewhat shyly.

"Right. So let's go and deal with our friends then we can figure out when we're going to see each other again."

"Sounds like a plan."

Truck helped Mary stand up...and couldn't take his eyes from her ass when she was finally upright.

"Are you looking at my ass?" she questioned, putting her hands on her hips.

"Yup," Truck admitted unapologetically.

"Whatever," Mary said, rolling her eyes. "The bathroom is down the hall to the right," she informed him.

Still grinning, Truck leaned down, kissed her on the forehead, then headed down the hall.

When he came out a few minutes later, Mary was waiting for him.

"What are their names?" Truck asked.

"Who?"

"The guys' women."

"Oh...um...I'm not sure—"

"Mary, after last night, it's more than obvious to me that the women you were with are all connected to my teammates. My head isn't going to explode if you tell me."

"How does it feel this morning?" Mary asked.

"It's throbbing. Now tell me."

"Stubborn," Mary grumbled under her breath. "Fine. Rayne, Harley, Casey, and Wendy."

"Who's with who?"

Mary looked at him for a beat, then said, "I guess their names didn't jog your memory, huh?"

"Mare, if *yours* didn't, and you said we were together—even if the togetherness was complicated—there's no way the names of women who belong to my friends would make me suddenly remember the last three years."

"Whatever," she huffed. Then added, "And they don't 'belong' to your friends."

Truck grinned. "You know what I mean."

"Whatever. I hate when guys say that."

"I apologize. Now, who's with who?"

"Why do I have the feeling that you're just apologizing to appease me and the second my back is turned, you'll be telling people I *belong* to you?"

"Because you're smart? Now stop stalling."

Huffing out a cute breath, Mary rolled her eyes then told him what he wanted to know. "Rayne's with Ghost. Harley's with Coach. Casey and Beatle are together, and Blade is Wendy's boyfriend."

"And Hollywood? I know Fletch is married...even if it's hard to believe." Truck pushed.

Mary held up her hands. "No, they'll kill me if I tell."

Needing to know now, Truck backed Mary up against a wall and clasped her wrists in one of his hands above her head. He tilted her chin with his free hand and pressed his body against hers. "I'm not going to freak out, no matter what you tell me. I just need to know. It's driving me crazy. Hollywood's not acting like normal. Is something wrong? Is he okay? What aren't you telling me?"

"Easy, Truck," Mary soothed, not trying to get out of his hold. "They're fine. Hollywood hasn't been around much because his wife just gave birth."

"Holy shit!" Truck said, dropping his hands and staggering back. "Hollywood's married? And he just had a *kid*?"

"Yeah. A girl. She's adorable. Kate. His wife's name is Kassie."

"Wow. Seriously? Hollywood *married*. That's crazy. I never thought he'd settle down."

"Fletch's wife is pregnant too," Mary said gently. "She's due in about a month and a half and is having a difficult end of her pregnancy. Her name is Emily."

"Damn," Truck said, trying to absorb what Mary was telling him. "I didn't know she was pregnant."

"And they have another daughter. She's eight. She's Emily's, but Fletch adopted her. Annie is amazing. She's refreshing and cute and exasperating all at the same time."

"Annie," Truck mused.

"Do you remember her?"

Truck shook his head. "No. But I feel kinda the same weird feeling inside when I hear that name as I do when you're in my arms."

Mary blinked up at him but didn't comment.

"And now it makes sense why Ghost asked me over in Africa if I knew anyone by the name of Rayne, and then spit the other names at me. Thanks for telling me," Truck told her.

Mary flung herself at him, and Truck caught her by reflex. "You're gonna remember, Truck. I know it." She looked up at him. "I just hope you don't regret anything when you do."

"None of that," Truck scolded. "I told you I wasn't going to have sex with you yet, so there's nothing to regret." He didn't like the look of unease on Mary's face and wanted to tease it out of her.

Luckily, she smiled up at him, and he relaxed.

"That's right, Trucker. I'm not that kind of girl."

"I know it. And with that, I really do need to go. I'm already late and I can feel my phone vibrating like crazy in my pocket. The guys have probably already called the cops and reported me missing."

Mary smiled. "Okay. I'll text you some more details about the women, okay?"

"I'd like that."

"It won't be everything, but just a few important things about them. Maybe you can get all the details from the guys. They won't be happy I told you anything."

"Tough shit. *I'm* happy you told me. And that's all that matters."

Mary grinned. "All right then. I'll see you later."

Truck stepped back. "Yes, you will."

"Have fun storming the castle," Mary quipped as she waved at him.

"*The Princess Bride*," Truck said. "Love that movie."

"I know you do."

"Bye, Mary." Truck reluctantly turned and headed for her front door before he decided he never wanted to leave. There was something about the woman that made him feel protective and proud at the same time.

"How's Emily doing?" Truck asked Fletch later that morning when they were running along a dirt path in the middle of Fort Hood.

His friend whipped his head around to stare at him and nearly face-planted in the dirt when he tripped over his feet.

"Goddammit," Ghost swore from nearby. "She wasn't supposed to tell you that shit!"

"Why not?" Truck asked. "Because I'm weak? Fuck that.

As my best friends, you guys should've told me that you didn't want to go to that bar to pick up chicks. You should've told me that you've all got women of your own. I thought we never kept secrets from each other. What happened to that, huh?" Truck stopped running and his friends all followed suit. "Is that how we operate now? Because that's not what we did three years ago. We told each other every-fucking-thing." He was breathing hard, and not because of exertion.

"Wow, this is kinda eerie," Beatle remarked dryly.

"Shut up, Beatle," Fletch admonished then faced Truck. "Of course it's not. But this isn't exactly a normal situation. We didn't want to make you have a setback. And I'm not sure it was that smart of Mary to blab."

"Don't," Truck warned, glaring at Fletch. "Do *not* badmouth Mary. She's the only person who's been honest with me since I got back here."

"Honest, huh? Did she tell you that you were——"

Fletch's mouth was covered by Ghost's hand before he could finish his sentence.

"More secrets?" Truck asked, frustrated with his friends. He had no idea what Fletch had been about to say, but he had a feeling it was big. Huge.

"We were only doing what the doctor told us to," Ghost said. "He warned us that if we all told you at once that we're married or have girlfriends, it could be harmful."

"So what, you were never going to tell me? You were going to continue to go out to bars with me and pretend to go home with chicks?" Truck asked.

"Of course not," Blade mumbled.

"My memory might not ever come back. So were you going to *pretend* you'd just met Wendy somewhere and started dating her? Maybe you'd have a second marriage ceremony, Hollywood, just to keep up the pretense?"

No one said a word, although their eyes said plenty.

Truck knew he was being harsh and tried to rein in his emotions. "You've hurt my feelings," Truck admitted in a gentler voice. "Hollywood, I hear congratulations are in order. I bet your baby girl is fucking beautiful. I'd like to meet her, if you think I can do that and not have my head explode." He turned to Fletch. "And I was serious when I asked how Emily was doing. Mary told me she's having a hard pregnancy."

"She's okay," Fletch said softly. "She's had some pain recently and we're worried that the baby might come too early, so she's basically on complete bed rest."

"That sucks," Truck told his friend. Then he turned to the others. "I'd like to meet Casey. I find it hilarious that you hate bugs as much as you do and ended up with an entomologist. I also want to meet Wendy and Harley."

Beatle, Blade, and Coach all nodded. "We'd like that too," Coach said for them all.

Then Truck turned to Ghost. "And I understand you had a one-night stand with Rayne, and then we ran into her in the middle of an op?"

"Mary sure was chatty," Ghost grumbled, but relented and nodded. "Yeah. Rayne's amazing."

"That explains the new tattoo," Truck said, glancing at Ghost's leg.

Ghost nodded again.

Truck took a deep breath. "I get that this is awkward, and that you don't want to do anything that will hurt me. But, guys, I'm either going to regain my memory or I'm not. The last thing I want is for you to live your lives disingenuously. You're the best friends I've ever had, and I want to get to know your women for the second time. I want to hang out with all of you. I realize it'll be awkward at first, but don't block me from your lives."

They all nodded. "We won't," Hollywood said. "Kassie's been bugging me. Wants to see you."

"Emily too," Fletch added. "Although you'll have to come to our place, since she's not allowed out of bed at the moment."

"You buy that big house you had your eye on?" Truck asked.

Fletch winced. "Yeah. That's how I actually met my Em," he said. "But we've since moved."

Truck raised an eyebrow.

"Long story, man. *Really* long story."

Truck nodded and turned to the others. "I want to know how you all met your women. Mary told me some, but I need all the details. I still can't believe you fuckers are all pussy whipped."

"Like *you* should talk," Coach groused, and Ghost smacked him on the back of the head.

Truck's eyes narrowed. "Mary told me that we were together, but that it was complicated."

"She's right," Ghost said. "Look, we'll stop hiding our women from you, but you and Mary have to work out your relationship on your own."

"So we *are* in a relationship?" Truck asked, wanting clarification.

"Yes," Ghost told him.

And with that, Truck punched him in the jaw so quickly, he didn't have a chance to defend himself.

Ghost landed on the ground with a grunt but was back on his feet immediately. "What the fuck?" he asked, holding his jaw.

"You knew I was in a relationship, and you let me go to that bar and let that woman hit on me," he growled. "That's not cool. Not cool at all. No wonder Mary was so upset."

"You didn't want anything to do with that other woman," Ghost retorted, defending himself. "We weren't going to let you go home with her, or anyone else."

Beatle nodded. "We may not have told you about your relationship with Mary, but we aren't assholes."

"Are you attracted to Mary?" Beatle asked.

"Yes." Truck didn't have to think about his answer. It was immediate and earnest.

"Right...so you took one look at her and you were interested. That's pretty amazing, considering you have no recollection of her."

"What's your point?" Truck asked.

"That's exactly the way it happened the *other* first time you met her."

Truck's brows went up. "Yeah?"

"Yeah. And that's all I'm going to say about it," Beatle said. "But I thought you should know. It might make you feel less weird about knowing you already had a relationship with her, so you can get to know her now without worrying about what happened in the past."

Truck had to admit he *did* feel better about his instant attraction to Mary, knowing it had happened the same way when he'd first met her. Almost as if he and Mary were meant to be. "Anything else you guys want to tell me?" Truck asked.

"Did Mary tell you about Fish?" Blade asked.

"Who?"

"Guess that answers that. He's an unofficial member of our team. Long story short is that he's living out in Idaho with his wife, Bryn. She's incredibly smart and socially awkward. We all love her. Whatever you do, do *not* get in a discussion with her about your amnesia. She'll talk your ear off and you won't have the heart to stop her."

Everyone chuckled, and Truck felt himself smiling.

Looking at each of his friends, he said, "I'm happy for all of you. We've seen our share of military relationships crash and burn and it's awesome to see you all so happy."

Ghost clapped Truck on the back and said, "Thanks. Now, can I ask you something?"

"Of course."

"How do you *really* feel about Mary?"

Truck frowned. "Why?"

"Don't get defensive," Ghost said. "I'm just asking."

"I like her. She's refreshing. She's not intimidated by me, and I like how she has no problem standing up to you assholes."

Ghost grinned. "You've certainly got her pegged after such a short time."

Truck shrugged. "She's funny, interesting, and I can tell she's a fighter."

"Interesting. Why?" Fletch asked.

"Because she doesn't back down from anyone or anything. We also talked a lot last night. She had a shit childhood, and it's only made her stronger."

"Yeah?" Hollywood asked.

"You don't know?" Truck asked in surprise.

"She's not very open," Hollywood said. "Kassie doesn't know a lot about her. Only pretty recent stuff."

"Agreed," Ghost said. "Rayne is her best friend, and even she doesn't know a lot of details. She knows that her mom wasn't the greatest and that she's been on her own since she was eighteen."

"That's the understatement of the year," Truck agreed. "We have that in common."

"Come on, you guys, let's continue on while we talk," Beatle urged.

The six men continued their run and Truck said, "Mary

mentioned that I hadn't told her about my parents. That got me wondering if I've told *you* guys in the last three years, because I know I never said anything before that."

"No. All we know is that they aren't in your life," Coach said. "I mean, we know they came to see you after you got hurt, but you made it clear when they left that talking about them was a no-go. We didn't push."

"Right. So you should know, I haven't been purposely keeping them a secret from you. It's just that I never think about them anymore, since they're not part of my life."

He took a glance at the others and saw they were paying attention even as they were running. So he continued, "I also have a sister."

Ghost tripped over his feet and almost fell flat on his face. The others stared at Truck with their mouths open.

He held up a hand to forestall their questions. "I know, I know. Mary's reaction was much the same as yours. Mercedes —Macie—is almost five years younger than me and I haven't seen her since I left for boot camp. We used to be close, but for some reason, she never tried to contact me after I joined the Army. And yes, I wrote her, but she never wrote back."

"And you never went home?" Coach asked.

"No." Then he proceeded to explain about growing up as the skinny, picked-on kid and how his parents didn't seem to care. He told them about their visit when he was in the hospital after he'd been disfigured, and what they'd said. It wasn't easy, but it felt good to open up to his friends.

He'd gotten a second chance at life. He was more than aware that he could've died instead of just losing three years. He wanted these men to understand he valued their friendship, and he couldn't think of a better way to let them know than truly opening himself up to them.

By the time they got back to the parking lot, Truck's head

felt as if there were little sledgehammers inside it, but he still felt lighter somehow.

"If you ever want help in finding Macie, if nothing else but to clear the air, you know we're more than willing to do what we can," Ghost told him. "I'm sure the commander would have no problem using his connections to help find her as well."

Truck didn't immediately reject the offer. Ever since his talk with Mary, he'd been seriously thinking about calling their friend, Tex. The man could find anyone, no matter how deeply they'd hidden themselves. But maybe he'd start with the commander first. It was a good idea. "I'll think about it."

Ghost nodded then held out his hand to Truck and they shook. "Rayne was right," Ghost said.

"How so?"

"We've been babying you too much. I'm sorry we kept shit from you. I'm still worried about your health, but we'll try to chill, right guys?"

Everyone agreed.

"Want to come over and meet Kassie and my Kate?" Hollywood asked.

"Fuck yeah," Truck told his friend.

"Great. I'll make that happen."

"Uh...you should know that there's a group wedding in the works," Beatle informed Truck. "My fiancée, Casey, is his sister." He pointed to Blade.

"Holy shit," Truck said, his eyes wide. "That's awesome!"

Blade beamed. "I think so."

"Congrats, Beatle," Truck said, slapping the other man on the shoulder.

"Thanks. The double ceremony was the girls' idea," Beatle told him.

"When?" Truck asked.

"We're not sure. They want to wait until Emily has her baby," Blade said.

"Cool. I'll have time to get to know them again," Truck said.

"Yup."

"So that makes us the only un-engaged ones left, huh?" Truck asked Ghost.

"I guess so," was Ghost's response. Truck heard a note of something in his tone, but couldn't place it.

"We gotta get going," Coach said, interrupting the moment. "The commander wants to talk to us about something this morning."

"Should I be there?" Truck asked.

Coach shook his head. "No need. I asked the same thing, and he said it was about the Africa mission, and since you don't remember it, you're excused."

Truck wanted to insist that he be there too, that maybe if he listened to what happened it might jog his memory, but his head was killing him and he needed to lie down for a while. So he let it go. "Okay. I'll talk to you guys later then?"

"Definitely. Truck?" Fletch asked tentatively.

"Yeah?"

"Do you think I might... Shit."

"What, Fletch?"

"Did Mary tell you about Annie?"

"Yeah. Your daughter."

"Right. Well...she misses you and has been begging to see you. Do you think we might come over for a while later this afternoon? I'll keep the visit short so you aren't overwhelmed."

"Does she know about me?" Truck asked. "The last thing I want to do is hurt the kid by not recognizing her."

"She knows," Fletch told him.

Truck wasn't entirely comfortable with it, but he couldn't refuse his friend. "Sure."

The look of relief on Fletch's face was telling. The man loved his daughter, that much was obvious. Truck hoped the girl wasn't annoying. He wasn't so sure about kids, they tended to freak over his scar, or ask irritating questions. But since Fletch said Annie had been begging to see him, he figured she'd probably be okay with the way he looked.

"I need to get to the meeting with the commander. I'll see you later," Fletch said as he hurried to his car.

The others all said their goodbyes as well and before he knew it, Truck was headed back to his apartment. What he really wanted to do was see Mary, but he knew he needed to give her some space.

The morning had been good. He'd cleared the air with his teammates and hopefully made his point about them not keeping shit from him anymore, no matter what the doctor said they should do. But he hadn't remembered anything new, and that frustrated him.

He hoped as time went by he'd slowly start to remember things here and there, but that hadn't happened yet. The doctor had told him to be patient, that a week wasn't enough time for his memory to return, but he'd been hopeful the doctor was wrong. Unfortunately, he wasn't. The last three years were just as blank as they'd been when he'd woken up after hitting his head.

The names of his teammates' women didn't jog his memory. They meant nothing to him. Just names of random people. He hated that, as they obviously meant a great deal to his friends. He felt as if he was missing out, and that sucked.

Truck brooded all the way back to his apartment and instead of feeling better when he got inside, seeing his apartment made his head hurt more. He looked around, trying to figure out what was missing. Something was, he was sure of it, but as hard as he tried, he couldn't remember.

"Fuck," he swore.

Because his head hurt so badly, he decided he was going to take one of the powerful painkillers the doctor had prescribed. He hadn't taken many of them because, as he'd told Mary, he really didn't like taking the hard drugs, but he was almost desperate to escape the pain and nothingness that was in his head at the moment.

Looking at his watch, he saw it was almost eight in the morning. Fletch said he'd be over in the afternoon, so he had plenty of time to take a nap before Fletch arrived with his daughter.

Truck knew taking the pill would knock him out completely. He'd be dead to the world for at least five hours. Good.

Suspecting he was slipping into a depression, Truck swallowed the pill dry. The faster he got some sleep and escaped the constant throbbing of his head, the better.

"Easy, squirt."

Truck frowned at the voice in his head.

Then he felt something touch his face. The scarred side.

Jerking his head back, he then felt a weight settle on his belly. His eyes popped open—and he stared up into a pair of blue eyes.

A little girl was straddling his stomach. Her dirty-blonde hair was loose around her shoulders and long enough to brush his chest as she leaned over him. She had on a scruffy pair of jeans and a T-shirt with a silhouette of a military tank on it. One of her small hands was on his face, over his scar, and she looked completely serious as she gazed down at him.

"Hi, Truck. I'm Annie."

"Hi," Truck croaked out, feeling emotional for no reason he could think of.

"Sorry, man," Fletch said from above him. "I knocked but you didn't answer. I used my key—one you gave me, by the way—to come in. I wanted to make sure you were all right."

"It's okay," Truck said, still looking up at Annie.

"Do you 'member me?" Annie asked.

Pressing his lips together, he felt awful that he had to tell this little angel no. "I'm sorry...but no."

"I'm Annie Elizabeth Grant Fletcher. I'm eight. I have a boyfriend named Frankie. He's deaf and lives in California. I talk to him with my hands over the Internet. He's teaching me how. Daddy Fletch gave me some Army men the first time I met him. I don't like wearing dresses, I prefer pants. Mommy and me moved in with Daddy Fletch when she got sick, and then the bad guys stolded us, but you and Daddy came and got us. 'Member now?"

God, this girl was precious. How could he have ever assumed she'd be annoying? Truck felt guilty even though he hadn't met Annie yet when he'd thought that.

The hand on his cheek didn't waver. She kept eye contact with him the entire time she was talking. She had what Truck would have to say was an "old soul." The weird feeling of déjà vu came back with a vengeance. He knew this little girl, but he didn't. It was a frustrating and weird feeling.

"Sorry, Annie. I don't. But you know what?"

"What?"

"Just because I don't remember you, doesn't mean that I don't like you."

"Of course you like me," Annie said with conviction. "I'm likable. Everyone says so."

Truck heard Fletch chuckling. He looked up at his friend and saw him standing next to the couch. He looked both relieved and worried at the same time.

"How about you let Truck sit up, squirt."

Instead of climbing off him, Annie lowered herself onto Truck's chest. She lay her head on his shoulder and kept her hand on his cheek. "I'm sorry you were hurt, Truck."

"Me too."

"Are you scared?"

Truck swallowed and put his hand on her back, holding her to him as he sat up. Annie clung to him like an octopus, not moving even an inch away.

"I'll get us all something to drink," Fletch said, giving him some privacy with his daughter, now that he knew she was in good hands.

"A little," Truck told the girl honestly.

She nodded against him. "I think it'd be scary not to 'member things. But we'll take care of you."

"Thanks."

"Mommy told me that being scared means you're about to do something brave."

Truck closed his eyes and tried to control his emotions. "She did, huh?"

"Yeah. And when the bad guys had us, I was really scared, but I was brave too. You were there, and you made sure we were safe."

"Good."

"Truck?"

"Yeah?"

"Are you gonna make Mary smile again?"

"Annie!" Fletch scolded from behind the couch. "We talked about this."

Annie picked her head up from Truck's shoulder and glared at her dad. "I wasn't going to tell. I just miss Mary too! She hasn't been over in forever. I want to see her and practice my sign language with her in person. It's not the same over the Internet. And she was sad the last time we FaceTimed."

Truck's mind was spinning. The dull throb was back, but not as bad as it had been this morning. Holding Annie felt good. Right. Even listening to her talk was soothing. It wasn't that he remembered the little spitfire, but it was as if his *body* remembered her. There was something about her little hand on his cheek that made him melt inside and felt very familiar.

"Annie Elizabeth," Fletch warned.

The little girl's eyes dropped. "Sorry, Daddy," she said contritely.

Truck wanted to laugh. She had Fletch wrapped around her little finger, and she knew it.

"Damn, Fletch, I never thought I'd see the day," Truck said.

"That's five bucks!" Annie yelled, and held out her hand expectantly.

"Huh?"

"Five bucks. You said a bad word. Now that I have my tank, it goes toward my college fund. Daddy says that when he's having an adult conversation with his friends that it doesn't count, because sometimes the bad words just come out, but when someone's talking to *me*, like this, then it totally counts. So...you owe me five dollars!"

Truck chuckled. "How much do you have so far?" he asked the little girl.

"Almost four thousand dollars," she told him proudly.

Truck choked. "Seriously?"

Annie nodded. "Daddy's friends say a lot of bad words," she said nonchalantly, then wiggled her fingers impatiently.

Truck leaned over, pulled his wallet out of his pocket, took out a five-dollar bill, and put it in Annie's hand. She beamed at him and climbed off his lap. She ran over to Fletch and waved the money in front of him. "Look, Daddy!"

"I see, squirt."

Annie smiled happily and went back over to where Truck was sitting on the couch. "Does your head hurt?" she asked.

Truck immediately envisioned Mary asking him the same question. He should be sick of people asking him that by now, but for some reason, he didn't mind if Annie or Mary asked. "A little."

"Oh. Then you should rest some more. Mommy says when something hurts that there's nothing like a good nap to fix it."

"Your mom sounds smart."

"She is. Her belly hurts all the time so she sleeps a lot right now. But that's just my brother being impatient to come out and meet me."

"Your brother, huh?" He looked up at Fletch. "You didn't tell me you were having a son."

"That's because we don't know the gender of the baby. Annie just *hopes* it's a boy. She wants a brother she can play with."

"It *is* a boy," Annie insisted. "I know it."

"Just because you want something, doesn't make it true," Truck said gently. He had no idea where the words were coming from, but he had a vague recollection that he'd had this exact thought in the past. About what, he had no idea, and that frustrated him. "I might really, really want to remember you and my other friends, but just because I want to, doesn't make it happen."

Annie pouted. "But...girls are stupid! And mean. I want a baby brother I can show my Army man to and play in the dirt with. I want to teach him how to do the obstacle course at Daddy's work."

"You can teach a baby sister to do those things," Fletch told her. "And who's being mean to you, squirt?"

Annie's lips pressed together before she mumbled, "No one."

Fletch sighed.

"You know what drives bullies crazy?" Truck asked Annie.

"No, what?"

"When you ignore them. When they can't get a reaction out of you."

"How do you know?" she asked.

"Because people were mean to me when I was in school."

"They were?" Annie's eyes got huge in her face. "But you're so big you could squash them like a bug. I'm littler than *everyone*."

"I wasn't always this size," Truck said. "I was always tall, but I was skinny. So skinny people would call me bean pole."

"Really?"

"Really. I learned to ignore the people who said that about me. Besides, if they were mean, I didn't want to be their friend anyway."

"Even if they were popular and everyone liked them?" Annie asked in a quiet voice.

"Even then. Do what you like to do, Annie. And to hell with what they think. Having one real friend is so much better than having ten fake friends."

"I like Amy. She's in my class and she's nice."

"Then be Amy's friend, and don't worry about everyone else. Besides, if kids don't like you, they're missing out. I've only known you for a little while and I think you're amazing."

She giggled. "You've known me for longer than that, Truck."

"Nope." He tapped his temple.

"Oh, yeah! I forgot."

Truck smiled at her. "That's the nicest thing anyone's said to me in a long time."

"Thanks, Truck," Annie said, and gave him a hug. "Oh, but one more thing."

"What's that?"

"You owe me another five dollars. You said h-e-double hockey sticks."

Truck mock scowled at her. "Guess *your* memory is really good, huh?"

"Yup," she said happily.

Truck hadn't yet put his wallet back in his pocket, so he pulled out another five and handed it to Annie.

"Come on, squirt, we've bilked Truck out of enough money for one day, I think."

"Bilked?"

"Conned, swindled, bamboozled."

"Bamboozled! I like that word," Annie screeched, then proceeded to repeat it over and over as she headed for the door to Truck's apartment with his five-dollar bills in her hand.

Truck stood and followed Fletch and his little girl to the door.

"Can I start the car?" Annie asked, looking up at her dad with big pleading eyes.

"Sure," Fletch said and pulled a key fob from his pocket.

Annie grinned and turned to Truck. "I love pushing the magic button!" And with that, she was out the door and running for the parking lot.

Truck watched as she went straight to a Highlander that

was a couple years old and climbed inside. They heard it start up and saw Annie wave at them from inside the car.

"She's amazing," Truck told his friend.

"Thanks. I can't take too much credit for that. That was all Em."

"She's also a handful," Truck observed.

"Now *that* I'll take some credit for," Fletch said with a laugh.

"She being bullied?" Truck asked.

"I guess so. She hasn't said anything at home, but then again, we've been pretty worried about Emily. Annie's a naturally happy kid and doesn't complain much about anything."

"Keep your eye on her," Truck said. "It might not be a big deal now, but it can be hell on a teenager with raging hormones."

"Sorry you had to go through that," Fletch told his friend.

Truck shrugged. "Long time ago."

"Still."

Truck nodded.

"You okay?" Fletch asked.

Truck turned to him and raised an eyebrow in question.

"She said a lot in there. Did it bring anything back?"

"No. But..." He paused, not sure how to explain the weird feelings of déjà vu.

"What?"

"I feel as if the memories are there. It's like when you can't think of a word, but you know you know it. It's on the tip of your tongue but you can't spit it out."

"Is that different from how you felt last week?" Fletch asked.

"Yeah. At first it happened only occasionally. But lately it gets triggered by smells, by seeing random things, like when I went to that meeting last week on post and sat inside the meeting room, or when your daughter laid her hand on my cheek."

Fletch nodded. "That's good."

"I hope so."

A horn sounded from the parking lot and both men turned to look at the Highlander. Annie was smiling and waving at them again.

"Guess that's my cue to get my ass in gear."

"Five bucks," Truck quipped.

"It only counts if *she* hears it." Fletch grinned, then clapped his hand on Truck's shoulder. "Thanks for being so great with her."

"Wasn't a hardship," Truck said dryly.

"Thanks anyway. You made her day. Week. Month. See ya later."

And with that, Fletch headed for his car and his little girl.

For a second, Truck was jealous of his friend. They'd all been single for so long, it hadn't occurred to Truck that everyone might have found women to make their lives complete.

He felt left out. As if he'd been left behind. Which was stupid, but he couldn't help the thought. And that led him to thinking about Mary and the nature of their relationship. He couldn't deny he had feelings for her. But defining them was harder. A part of him felt as if he loved her. Which was crazy, since he didn't really even know her any longer.

But another part of him was wary. As if his brain was cautioning him to go slow with her, to hold back for some reason. He had a feeling Mary could really hurt him. He never let women get too close because he'd been let down by them time after time. It was frustrating not knowing exactly what his relationship with Mary had been like.

But watching Fletch with Annie, and knowing he was

going home to his pregnant wife, made Truck want that too. He wanted to come home to Mary. Wanted her to smile when he came through the door and welcome him with open arms.

Hearing his stomach growl, Truck smiled ruefully. Wanting things wasn't going to magically make them happen. He'd been given a fresh start with Mary, and he was going to take it. Pretend as if whatever had happened between them in the past was just that...in the past.

He might never remember where they'd been, but he looked forward to seeing where they'd end up in the future.

Smiling, Truck shut his apartment door and wandered into the kitchen to make a late lunch/early dinner. He had time to get to know Mary before he had to go back to work, and that's just what he was going to do. He'd spend the next couple of weeks going on dates with her. Talking. Getting to know her.

He'd either regain his memory or not. Either way, he wanted to have Mary at his side, as his girlfriend, when he went back to work.

CHAPTER ELEVEN

Mary stood in the doorway of the safety-deposit vault and warily watched the young man inspect it. She'd had her suspicions a couple weeks ago that something was going on at the bank, but now she was sure of it.

This was the tenth young man who'd come in asking about renting one of the boxes in the last two and a half weeks. They had all dressed in suits and ties, but they couldn't cover up all of their tattoos. They were on their necks and the backs of their hands. Some even had a few on their faces.

She hadn't seen the two men who had tried to hold up the bank a month or so ago. Last she knew, they were still in jail, pending a trial, but if she had to guess, she'd say that these men were in the same gang. She'd once again brought it up to her boss, Jennifer, who'd said that she didn't think it was anything to worry about, but she'd look into it.

Mary didn't believe her, but what could she do?

This young man was a bit more obvious in asking question about the security of the vault and the boxes than the others had been. He also wanted to know who else had a key to the boxes and what would happen if he ever lost his key. She explained there were two keys needed to open each box. The bank had one and the owner of the box had the other. They had to be inserted at the same time and left in the box as it was removed. There were procedures in place if someone lost their key, but it took a couple days to make a new one.

It was impossible to open more than three boxes at once, because that was how many master keys the bank had on hand, but she didn't tell the customer that though.

"What happens if there's a fire?" the man asked. "Would my stuff be protected?"

"If you're asking if the boxes are fireproof, they are," Mary said as calmly as she could.

"Hmmm," the man said. "And if me and my buddy wanted to get to our stuff at the same time, could we do that?"

"No. Only one patron is allowed in the vault at a time."

"That's stupid."

Mary shrugged. "It's company policy."

"What if—"

"Mary!" Rebecca, one of the other tellers, yelled as she came down the hallway toward the vault.

She turned and saw the other woman was holding her cell phone. "Your phone's been ringing off the hook. Jennifer is pissed, but I saw it was your friend, Rayne. I thought it might be important and— Oh...sorry, I didn't realize you were still giving the tour."

"We're just about done here, I think."

"I can finish for you, if you want," Rebecca said tentatively. Mary knew the other woman was just as uneasy about all the young men coming in and inquiring about the safety-deposit boxes, so she shook her head. "Not necessary." She turned back to the man. "Mr. Smith," she mentally rolled her eyes at the obviously fake name he'd given them, "you've got the application. You can drop it off anytime between nine and four-thirty, Monday through Friday."

"Right. Thanks," the man said, then walked out of the vault. He brushed against Mary as he passed. "Sorry," he said belatedly—and with a suggestive smile on his face.

Mary bit the inside of her cheek to keep herself from saying something she might regret. She walked Mr. Smith out to the lobby, and she and Rebecca watched as he sauntered out into the afternoon heat.

"Something is definitely up," Rebecca said.

"Oh, yeah," Mary agreed.

"Did you hear the latest rumor about the bank?" Rebecca asked.

"No, now what?"

"Corporate wants to get rid of the tellers and put automatic machines in the lobby. They think it will deter robberies like the one last month."

"Shit. So we'll all lose our jobs?"

Rebecca shrugged. "I don't know. I guess most of us would. They need to keep some of us to run the drive-through and to take care of things the machines don't do... like people ordering foreign money and things like that. But they want to automate as much as possible, like deposits, withdrawals, and balance inquiries."

"Damn," Mary said, then shrugged. "Guess it's time to see what else we can find, huh?"

"But this is all I've ever done," Rebecca said. "I mean, it's not exactly my dream job, but after eight years, and a degree in general studies, I'm not sure what else I can get."

Mary shared her fellow teller's concerns, but tried to stay positive. "We're organized and trustworthy. We'll find something."

Just then, the cell phone in her hand rang again, and Mary

saw it was Rayne calling once more. "I'll just be a second," she told Rebecca.

The other woman nodded and headed for her position behind the counter.

"Hello?" Mary answered.

"Em's at the hospital," Rayne said, not bothering with a greeting. "She started bleeding this morning and Fletch called nine-one-one."

"Oh no! Is she okay?" Mary asked.

"We don't know yet."

"Are you at the hospital?"

"Yeah. Can you get here?"

"I still have three hours left on my shift."

"Tell your boss it's an emergency."

"I don't think she's gonna care," Mary said almost hysterically. "Where's Annie?"

"She's here, and she's freaking out."

The thought of Em being in the hospital with complications was heartbreaking, but knowing Annie was stressed was beyond anything Mary could handle. "I'll be there in thirty minutes or less," Mary told Rayne.

"What about your boss?" Rayne asked.

"As you said, this is an emergency. I'll think of something."

"Don't do anything drastic," Rayne ordered.

"Who, me?" Mary quipped.

"Yes. I know you."

"Whatever. Are the guys there?"

"Beatle is. The others were in a meeting and couldn't get out of it. They'll be here as soon as they can."

"And Truck?"

"I haven't called him yet."

"I'll call him," Mary told Rayne. She and Truck had been spending a lot of time together in the last two and a half weeks. They were officially dating, and it felt good and weird at the same time. She'd never dated Truck. They'd gone from picking on each other in the way two kids in elementary school would, to him forcing her to move in when he found out how sick she was, to them getting married.

But over the last couple weeks, they'd gone out to eat, watched movies at each other's apartments, taken walks, and had even gone on a weekend trip to Enchanted Rock in nearby Fredericksburg. It was fascinating getting to know Truck without her sickness being a factor. She already knew he was funny, protective, and bossy, but she'd also found out other little things about him. Like the armadillo was his favorite animal of all time, and that he was ticklish, and she'd heard countless stories about his sister, Macie, and how close they were growing up.

Mary had fallen even harder for the man, if that was possible.

They'd made out a couple of times, but she'd stopped things before they went too far, scared he'd feel her fake boobs and ask questions. Mary knew she needed to talk to him before someone else blabbed about her cancer, but she hadn't been able to find a good time to do so.

Besides, she was enjoying being "Mary" and not "Mary who has cancer" for once.

"Cool. The girls will also get here as soon as they can, other than Kassie, who isn't comfortable bringing Kate to the hospital with all the germs yet," Rayne told her. "I'll see you soon."

"Bye," Mary said and clicked off the phone. She thought fast. What could she do to get Jennifer to let her leave work early? She didn't have a lot of sick time saved up after coming back to work, but she had to have at least three hours she could use.

Sighing, she decided to just suck it up and talk to Jennifer. It wasn't as if she loved this job anyway. If she got fired for having an emergency and needing to leave, so be it.

Taking a deep breath, Mary went to Jennifer's office and knocked.

Her boss looked up and impatiently asked, "Yes?"

Mary quickly outlined what was happening and waited to see what her boss's decision would be.

"You've already missed a lot of work, Mary."

"I know, but I wouldn't ask if this wasn't really important."

"Between this and harassing our customers, you're pushing your luck," Jennifer said.

Mary swallowed the harsh retort on the tip of her tongue. She wasn't harassing customers. She'd brought her safety concerns to her boss—like she was supposed to do. Biting the inside of her cheek, she kept silent.

Finally, Jennifer sighed. "Fine. But no more. I mean it."

Mary nodded quickly, extremely relieved. "Thank you," she said and turned to leave.

Jennifer stopped her. "Mary?"

Mary spun back around to face her boss. "Yeah?"

"I appreciate you asking, and not making up some lame excuse or resorting to theatrics to get your way."

Mary simply nodded and left, not telling the other woman how close she'd come to doing just that.

As she headed quickly for her car, Mary couldn't help but think about what her friend was going through. Driving like a bat out of hell toward the hospital, she called Truck.

"Hey, Mare," Truck said as he answered.

"Hi. Emily's at the hospital. She started bleeding this morning and Fletch called an ambulance."

"Shit. Where are you?"

192

"I'm on my way."

"Slow down."

Mary blinked in surprise. "How do you know I'm speeding?"

"Because I know you. Just take a deep breath and try to relax. You getting there three minutes faster isn't going to change anything. I'd rather you slowed down and got there safely."

Now Mary was blinking back the tears that had formed in her eyes. How like Truck to be more worried about her than Emily. Sure, Rayne and the others cared about her and wanted her to be careful, but Truck's caring was different. "Okay. Are you coming?"

"Of course I'm coming," Truck said, sounding exasperated now. "Why wouldn't I?"

"I just...all the women are going to be there. And Annie's already there. I know it's all still kinda weird for you, and I didn't want you to be uncomfortable being around everyone at the same time."

"Are you going to be there?"

"Uh...yeah. I already told you I was on my way."

"Then *I'm* going to be there," Truck said with conviction.

His words settled in her stomach and spread throughout her body with a warmth she'd never felt before.

She wanted to tell him that she loved him. That no one had cared about her as much as he did in her entire life, but she couldn't. She physically couldn't say the words. Saying them opened herself up to being hurt, and Mary wouldn't do that. Couldn't.

Clearing her throat to try to push away the urge to cry, Mary said, "I know you don't like hospitals. I'll be okay."

"I need to jump in the shower real quick," Truck said, ignoring her attempt at giving him an out. "I was working out when you called, but I'll be there in half an hour or so. If something happens, call me."

"I will," Mary said, happier than she could put into words that he was coming.

"Drive safe, baby. I'll see you soon."

"Okay."

"I've missed you."

Mary smiled. "It's only been like a day and a half since we've seen each other."

"A day and a half too long. Later."

"Bye, Truck."

Mary clicked off the Bluetooth on her steering wheel and shook her head. She missed Truck too. It was crazy. She was independent, had always lived by herself. But she'd gotten used to having him around before his accident. His presence in her life made her feel calmer, less defensive about the world in general. They used to sit together in the same room and not even talk, which was peaceful, and Mary would catch herself looking up every now and then, just to make sure he was still there.

He was comforting. Generous. Relaxing. But more than that, he made her feel safe. Growing up, she'd hadn't felt that way. She never knew if the uncles would try to get in her room and treat her like they did her mama. Once she was eighteen and kicked out of the house, she didn't feel safe because she didn't have a place to live. And even after finding space of her own, none of her apartments had ever felt completely safe. Maybe that was a result of her upbringing, maybe it was because she was a single woman. But she'd gotten used to the feeling.

Being with Truck made her feel as though she didn't need to look over her shoulder. She didn't need to get up and check to make sure the door was locked, because he'd already done it. She didn't need to worry about pulling the curtains, because Truck closed them as soon as it got dark outside. He slept on the side of the bed that was closest to the door, putting himself between her and anyone who might enter.

He had his faults. He was too bossy. Too used to getting his way. He hogged the remote and had a habit of blowing his nose in the shower, which was just disgusting. But those were all little things. Everything else he did more than made up for his quirks. Besides, Mary knew she had way more annoying habits than he did...and he put up with all of them.

Ten minutes later, Mary pulled into the hospital lot. She hurried toward the entrance and took a deep breath before entering. After all she'd been through, she really didn't like hospitals. They brought back so many bad memories, but she pushed through them, knowing Annie was inside and worried about her mom and her little sibling.

Without bothering to ask the receptionist where she should go, Mary headed for the elevator. She remembered where the obstetrics waiting room was from when she'd come here after Kassie had her baby, but this time she was alone in the elevator.

After arriving on the correct floor, Mary strode toward the waiting area. This time it wasn't filled with happy, laughing people. The second she entered, Annie popped out of the chair she'd been sitting in and ran over to her, throwing her arms around Mary's waist and burying her face in her belly.

Mary rocked back on a foot, but immediately clamped her arms around the little girl's shoulders. "Hey, Annie."

She mumbled something in her belly, but didn't raise her head.

Looking around, Mary saw Rayne, Beatle, Wendy, and Harley.

"You call Truck?" Beatle asked.

Mary nodded. "He was going to jump in the shower then come over. He said about thirty minutes about fifteen minutes ago."

Beatle nodded.

"Truck's comin'?" Annie asked.

Mary ran her hand over the little girl's mussed hair and nodded. "Yeah, he's on his way."

"Good."

Mary shuffled over to one of the chairs with Annie still holding on to her. She sat on a chair that didn't have any arms and lifted Annie so she was sitting sideways on her lap. It was a little awkward, as Annie wasn't exactly a tiny thing anymore. "Any word?" Mary asked Rayne as everyone sat back down.

She shook her head. "They took her back to do a C-section a bit ago. Fletch is in there with her."

Mary wanted to ask more. Wanted all the details. But wouldn't while Annie was there. The last thing she wanted was for the little girl to hear something scary about her mom.

As the minutes went by, the room filled up. Ghost and the other guys got there, obviously having finished with their meeting on post. Hollywood was there, even though Kassie was still at home. When Truck entered the room, he made a beeline for Mary and Annie.

Crouching down in front of them, he put one hand behind Annie's back and he palmed the side of Mary's neck with the other.

Mary felt surrounded by him. His fresh, clean scent wafted up to her nostrils and she inhaled deeply.

"How're my girls?" he asked softly.

He'd come straight to them. Hadn't said hello to his team-mates first. Hadn't stopped to greet anyone else. His gaze had swept the room looking for her and he had come straight over when he'd found her.

"Hangin' in there," Mary said in a shaky voice.

"Why's it takin' so long?" Annie asked, her lower lip trembling.

Truck stood then reached down and took Mary's hand in his. He helped her stand, and sat down on the seat where she'd been. Then he tugged Mary down onto his lap. She was still holding Annie, and she wobbled a bit trying to get situated. But she wasn't going to fall, no way. Not while Truck was near.

He held her steady and Mary leaned back against him, trusting him to keep both her and Annie safe. Annie curled into a little ball in Mary's lap.

"Having babies is a long process," Truck said softly. "And the doctors are taking the best care they can with your mom and your new baby sibling."

"Brother," Annie said defiantly. "Baby brother."

Truck chuckled and Mary felt it rumble through her.

"Sorry. Brother."

Annie fell silent, and Mary couldn't think of anything to say to Truck that wouldn't upset the girl. So the three of them sat curled up together in silence. Ten minutes later, Annie was snoring slightly in Mary's lap.

"Is she heavy? Do you need me to take her?" Truck asked quietly in her ear.

Mary shook her head. "She's okay."

"What's going on? Any new news?"

"No."

"This feels familiar, but not," Truck said out of the blue.

Mary lifted her head and stared at him. They were practically nose to nose now. "How so?" she asked.

"Being here in this room with all the guys...and even the women too. But it's different somehow."

"You were here when Kassie had her baby," Mary said softly, not sure she was doing the right thing, but forging ahead anyway. She'd been sharing little things like this with Truck over the last two weeks, and he hadn't seemed to be any worse for the wear as a result. "But everyone was laughing and happy that Kate was born healthy. Hollywood was passing out cigars, and even Annie was here."

"Hmmmm," Truck mused. "I'm not sure that's what seems familiar."

"Then what?"

"I think it's the smell of this place. It doesn't bring back good feelings. It's as if I've spent a lot of time here, and the second I walked into the hospital I felt a sense of dread."

Mary's stomach lurched. Could he be remembering the times he came with her to get chemo and radiation? She bit her lip.

"Mary?"

"Yeah?"

"What aren't you telling me?"

"Now isn't really the time or place."

"This isn't because of my amnesia, is it?" Truck asked with crazy insight.

Mary opened her mouth to answer, but was interrupted by a doctor appearing in the doorway. "Are you all here for Emily Fletcher?"

Choruses of "yes" responded and the doctor held up his hand. Mary wanted to wake Annie up, but didn't want her to hear bad news from a doctor...if it *was* bad news. She'd break it to the little girl later if she had to.

"Emily is fine."

"And her baby?" Rayne asked, wringing her hands.

"Also fine. He's a bit premature, so we're keeping him in the NICU for monitoring for now as a precaution. But he's big, which was part of the issue, so we think he'll be all right."

"I knew it was a boy," Mary said, smiling up at Truck.

As everyone began talking at once around them, Truck didn't take his eyes from Mary's. "A boy," he said softly.

Mary could only nod.

Then Truck leaned toward her slowly. Mary licked her lips in anticipation. When his lips touched hers, Mary melted.

She leaned toward him, trusting him to keep her safe on his lap, as she couldn't hold on because her hands were full with a sleeping Annie. She felt the arm around her back tighten as he tilted his head and deepened the kiss.

Right there in front of all their friends, Truck claimed her. That was the only way to explain it. He didn't seem to give one shit that everyone could see them. He devoured her mouth as if he'd never have it again, and Mary reciprocated. She'd always been a bit reserved with him, not wanting to lead him on, but right then, Mary didn't care. She loved Truck. Loved him as she'd never loved anyone before. As she'd never love anyone like this again. She wanted this man by her side for all time.

After a long moment, Truck pulled back abruptly. He was breathing heavily, and if Mary wasn't mistaken, she could feel his thick, hard cock under her ass. She licked her lips again and tasted Truck there. She felt her libido return with a vengeance. She wanted this man. Was desperate to feel him deep inside her.

"What's going on?" Annie asked, sitting up and rubbing her eyes.

Mary jerked in surprise. She hadn't even heard the noise around them, she'd been so focused on Truck.

He smiled at her obvious befuddlement and ran a hand over Annie's head. "Looks like you have a new baby brother."

"Really?" she asked, sitting straight up and almost clipping Mary's chin in the process.

"Really," Truck confirmed.

Annie leaped off Mary's lap, almost sending her tumbling to the floor. Only Truck's hand on her back kept Mary from falling.

"Yipee!" Annie yelled, jumping up and down. "Iknewit-IknewitIknewit!"

Mary smiled at the little girl's enthusiasm.

"When can I meet him? I want to show him my Army man. Oh no, I left him at home! Rayne, I need to go home and get my Army man so I can show him to my brother!"

"You'll have time to do that later," Rayne said, grinning from ear to ear.

"A brother," Annie said a little more sedately. "I'm so happy." Then she burst into tears.

Rayne gathered her up in her arms and beamed at Mary.

"I have no idea how I could've forgotten that beautiful little girl," Truck said into her ear. "But more importantly, I have no idea how I could've forgotten how it feels to have my mouth on yours. To feel you squirming in my lap like you were earlier."

Mary knew she was blushing, but she had to be honest with him. "It hasn't been like that between us before."

Truck didn't respond verbally, but instead raised one of his eyebrows in question.

"It's...complicated," Mary finished lamely.

Truck's hand ran up and down her arm in a gentle caress. "It doesn't feel complicated now."

Mary shook her head. "No, it doesn't."

She would've said more, but just then a voice rang out above the boisterous celebration in the room.

"Mary?"

Mary turned toward the voice—and froze. Literally every muscle in her body clenched.

"What's wrong?" Truck asked urgently, obviously having felt the tension in her limbs.

"Nothing, I'll be right back."

Mary awkwardly climbed off Truck's lap and made her way toward the nurse standing in the doorway to the waiting room. "Hey, Donna. How are you?"

"I'm good. The question is, how are *you?*"

"Fine." She gestured toward the room. "I'm here because my friend just had her baby. There were complications and she had a C-section, but the doctor just told us that she and her baby are fine."

"Awesome," Donna said. "You missed your appointment."

Mary grimaced. She knew she had. She was supposed to come back and talk to her doctor about the reconstruction surgery. She had to make a decision on what to do, but she'd skipped the appointment because of everything happening with Truck. If she was honest with herself, she'd been glad to have an excuse to ditch it. She had no idea what to do and didn't want to even think about it.

"What appointment?" a deep voice asked from behind her.

Mary pressed her lips together in annoyance and spun around to face Truck. "Nothing."

"Doesn't sound like nothing if you skipped an appointment with a doctor," he said, frowning.

"I'll call to reschedule," Mary told Donna, then turned her back on her and grabbed Truck by the arm and towed him away from the other woman. The last thing she wanted was

Donna blurting out what the appointment was for, or anything else about her cancer. She hadn't gotten up the courage to tell Truck about that yet, and she didn't want him learning about it now.

"Mary, talk to me," Truck said as he allowed her to move him away from the doorway and off to the side of the room.

"It's not important."

"Everything about you is important," Truck said in an intense voice, leaning closer to her.

Mary didn't know how to respond. She simply stared up at him.

"You're not going to tell me," he said in surprise after a moment.

Mary shook her head.

"Out of everyone, you've been the most honest with me from the start. You got on Ghost's back for keeping shit from me. You've told me bits and pieces here and there, giving me my life back, and now you're keeping something from me?"

"It has nothing to do with you," Mary told him, knowing the bitch was creeping back into her tone, but she couldn't help it. This was too soon. She was enjoying being normal with Truck. She didn't want that to end. Not yet.

Truck took a step back at her words. "Nothing to do with me? *Everything* that affects you has to do with me," he said, sincerity lacing his words.

"You've only known me a few weeks," Mary said lamely.

"Bullshit," Truck fired back. "We've known each other a hell of a lot longer than that. I might not remember details, but I know it here," he said, putting a hand over his heart. "Talk to me."

"Now's not the time," Mary told him.

"Then when is?"

"I don't know!" Mary yelled—then paled when the conversation in the room died down. She looked around and saw that everyone was looking at them. Great, just great.

Feeling trapped, Mary fell back to her old ways. She did what she always did when things got too intense. She retreated behind the shields she'd put up and spoke without thinking.

"I'd think you have enough to worry about with your *own* health issues," she said. "Your headaches aren't going away. In fact, they're getting worse. Have you talked to your doctor about that, huh? What about your commander? You can't go back to work if your head feels like it's gonna explode, can you?"

She could see Truck's jaw flexing as if he was grinding his teeth together. She flinched, realizing that she probably shouldn't have outed him like she had. No, she didn't want to talk about her missed appointment, but she also didn't want to throw him under the bus in the process.

"Your head's been hurting?" Beatle asked.

"Shit, Truck. That's not good," Ghost added.

"The last thing you want is to lose any more of your memory," Coach added.

Truck glared at Mary before turning to his friends and holding up his hands. "Easy, everyone. I'm fine. The doc said I'd continue to have some pain for a while. It's not as bad as Mary's makin' it out to be."

She felt worse and worse as Truck fielded questions about his health. The old her would've been glad she didn't have to talk about her appointment and happy the attention was deflected from her. But she'd promised herself she would try to curb her bitch tendencies. She hadn't meant to out Truck, but she had anyway. And now she felt like shit about it.

Rayne came over to her as Truck was reassuring his friends. "Did you do that on purpose?" she asked.

Mary didn't even try to pretend she didn't know what Rayne was talking about. "No." When Rayne looked skeptical, Mary went on. "I didn't. It just came out, I wasn't trying to get him in trouble with the guys."

"Why?"

"The nurse wanted to know why I hadn't rescheduled the appointment I'd skipped."

"And you haven't told Truck about the cancer yet," Rayne correctly deduced.

"Nope."

"Oh, Mare. You need to."

Mary sighed. "I will."

"When?"

"I don't know, okay? I want to enjoy being just *me*. Not the poor woman with no boobs who almost fucking died."

Instead of being put off by Mary's harsh words, Rayne glared at her. "Boo-fucking-hoo," she said.

"What?" Mary asked in shock.

"You heard me. We've already had this conversation, but it seems as if we need to have it again. I want to know where my kick-ass friend went. The girl who never let anything get her down. Who was like one of those fucking weird Weeble toys."

"Huh?" Mary couldn't get over the fact that the shoe was on the other foot, and Rayne was being a bitch to *her*.

"You know...Weebles wobble but they don't fall down. Mary, I've always admired you because when the shit hits the fan, you don't stand there and cry about it. You deal. But you are *not* dealing with this cancer situation at all."

Now Mary was getting mad. "You don't understand."

"Bullshit. I do."

"No, you don't. You haven't almost fucking died—twice. You haven't had your tits try to kill you so you had to chop them off. You've got a killer fucking body with beautiful curves that your man loves to put his hands all over. I'm still too skinny, I'm flat as a board. Excuse the fuck out of me for wanting Truck to keep looking at me the way he does now. Without *pity*."

"He's never *once* looked at you with pity," Rayne fired back. "If you'd open your eyes and see him, you'd know that. He loves *you*, Mary. Not your body, not your boobs."

Mary wanted to keep the bitch up, but couldn't. She wanted to believe Rayne, so fucking badly, but she was scared. Scared that the second she let down her guard, Truck would come to his senses. Or he'd remember everything. How awful she'd been to him when she was sick. How he'd seen her at her lowest. How he thought she'd married him only for his insurance when the fact of the matter was that she'd married him because she loved him.

She needed to apologize to Truck. To tell him she hadn't meant to blab about his continued headaches. "I need to talk to Truck," she told Rayne.

Rayne's voice gentled. "Tell him about the cancer," Rayne urged. "It's eating you alive, Mare."

"I'll think about it," Mary told her.

Rayne leaned forward and hugged her, hard. "You do that," she said. "Call me tonight, bitch. I'll give you the update on Emily and the baby."

Nodding, Mary knew she didn't deserve a best friend like Rayne. They might fight, but they always made up and never held grudges. She loved that about their friendship.

Mary took a deep breath and walked over to where Truck was standing talking to Ghost. "Truck?"

He turned to her, and she almost flinched at the frustrated look on his face. Ghost stepped away, giving them some privacy.

"I'm sorry," she said immediately. "It just popped out."

Truck ran a hand over his jaw and nodded.

Mary swallowed. In the past, Truck would've immediately told her it was okay and let her off the hook...thus making it easy to keep being a bitch, because she didn't suffer any consequences from it. But now that she had to own up to what she'd done, and he wasn't giving her an automatic out, it hit home just how much she'd taken advantage of his easy-going nature.

Feeling uncomfortable, and knowing she needed to retreat to lick her wounds, she bit her lip. "I need to get going," she said.

Truck simply stared down at her.

Shifting awkwardly, Mary knew she was doing what she always did—running—but couldn't help it. "I'll talk to you later."

When Truck didn't respond, just continued to look at her with that disappointed expression on his face, she couldn't take it anymore. "Tell Annie bye for me," she whispered, then turned and headed for the exit.

Truck watched in frustration as Mary left. She was keeping something from him. Something big. And he hated it. He believed her when she'd said she hadn't meant to tell the others about his headaches, and he'd already forgiven her for that. But he'd wanted her to explain why she'd felt the need to change the subject earlier.

He wanted to find the nurse Mary had been talking to and demand she tell him about the appointment Mary missed, but he knew she wouldn't talk to him. It was frustrating as hell.

"You're sure you're all right?" Ghost asked for the tenth time.

"I'm fine," Truck said...again. "Enough."

"It's been three weeks," Coach said. "The headaches should be receding."

"The doc also said there was a chance they wouldn't. That it would take longer for the bruises on my brain to heal," Truck told his friend.

"Are you remembering anything more?" Beatle asked.

"Maybe."

"Maybe?" Blade asked. "What kind of answer is that?"

"An honest one," Truck said with a chuckle. "I don't remember anything specific, it's more like feelings, as if I've been somewhere before or done something before."

"Like?" Ghost asked.

"Like earlier today when I entered this waiting room, it felt as if I'd done it before."

"You have," Coach confirmed. "When Kassie had her baby."

"Right. That's what Mary said," Truck agreed. "But it's more too. Scents are big for me. I can smell something and get an immediate sense of déjà vu. I might hear something and get the same feeling. It's...odd."

"It's good," Ghost said.

"Yeah, I think so too. Which is why I'm not too concerned about my headaches. They're really just a nuisance."

"So why did Mary make such a big deal out of them then?" Blade asked.

"Because she's worried about me," Truck said without hesitation. "I honestly don't think she meant to get me in trouble with you guys, but she missed an appointment of some kind and the nurse was asking her about it. When I asked what the appointment was for, she clammed up, which isn't like her. She usually has no problem answering my questions, especially when it's something she knows I've forgotten."

He waited for someone to tell him what he wanted to know—but suddenly everyone was extremely interested in their watch. Or the floor. Or the walls.

Damn it all to hell. He was done with this shit.

"I'm out of here," Truck told his friends.

"Truck, wait," Ghost implored.

"I'm sick to death of being kept in the dark about things from my own fucking life. I thought we'd gotten past that shit?"

"It's not our place to tell you," Coach said. "It's Mary's."

"It was *your* place to tell me about your women," Truck fired back. "But you didn't do that either. Mary did. Someone tell me. Right fucking now."

He gave his friend ten uncomfortable seconds, and when no one said anything, Truck shook his head and headed for the door.

He was pissed. Beyond pissed.

A woman was about to enter the room when he stormed out the door, and she squeaked in alarm when she saw him. But Truck didn't care. He usually did his best to not seem intimidating when he was out in public, but he was beyond caring about that at the moment.

He was sick of all the secrets.

Sick of not knowing what the hell was going on around him.

But more than that, he was worried.

About Mary.

He couldn't stop thinking about her on his way home.

He thought about her as he went up to his apartment.

He thought about her as he made something to eat for dinner.

He thought about her as he sat on his couch and watched the news.

He thought about her as he brushed his teeth.

And he definitely thought about her as he lay in his bed.

When he closed his eyes, Truck could swear that he felt Mary's body next to his. He actually reached for her, but when his hand encountered nothing but cool sheets, he knew he was hallucinating.

Or was he?

Could he be remembering?

Mary had stayed the night twice since they'd slept together on her couch, but both times they'd stayed out in his living room.

So why could he practically sense her here in his bedroom?

Opening his eyes and turning over, Truck flicked on the light next to his bed. His eyes slowly roamed the room, looking for something, *anything*, that would tell him he wasn't making things up that he just wanted to be true.

His eyes stopped on a section of wall next to the door leading out to the hall.

He stared at the white wall for several minutes, trying to bring something into focus that was just out of reach.

Sighing in frustration, Truck flopped back on the bed and stared at the ceiling.

Mary was his. He knew it down to the marrow of his bones, but he didn't know how to break through the barrier that was still between them. It was frustrating. He wanted to tell her that no matter what had happened with them in the past, it didn't matter now.

But he had a feeling it *did* matter. A lot.

Tomorrow, he'd start getting to the bottom of things. He was a Delta Force soldier, for God's sake. One who was currently on a forced break. It was time he tried to find out about his and Mary's past on his own.

Feeling better now that he had some sort of plan, Truck closed his eyes once more. His imagination kicked in, and his hand moved of its own volition. He brushed it against his dick and felt himself immediately harden.

"Fuck it," he whispered and pushed his boxers down, freeing his cock. Then, bringing the feeling of having Mary against his side to the forefront of his mind, Truck got himself off. After he'd gone to the bathroom and cleaned up and returned to his bed, he felt much more relaxed.

Mary was his.

Period.

And no one would keep him from her.

Not his friends, and certainly not Mary herself.

CHAPTER TWELVE

The next morning, after Truck had made a pot of coffee and a spinach and mushroom omelet, he heard a knock on his door. He was shocked to see Mary standing on the other side when he looked through the peephole.

He opened the door quickly and said, "Mary."

"Surprised to see me?" she asked a little hesitantly.

"Actually, yes," Truck told her. But he was just glad she was there. He'd had time to think about what had happened the day before, and he'd realized the more abrupt she was, the more emotional she was feeling. Whatever had happened right before she'd told the others about his continued headaches had obviously touched her deeply.

"Can I come in? We need to talk."

"Of course," Truck said, opening the door wider. He inhaled deeply as she walked past him and, once again, the feeling of familiarity swept through him.

Mary was lying in bed in front of him. Her head was resting on his arm, using it as a pillow. His chin was resting on top of her head and his free arm was curled around her waist. She was moaning softly, and Truck was murmuring quietly to her.

He felt helpless to help her. He couldn't take away the nausea. He couldn't magically fix her. All he could do was hold her and let her know that she wasn't alone. That he was right there with her. Loving her.

He moved his hand to run his fingers lightly up and down her arm. Neither spoke, but he was letting her know without words that he was there. That she could lean on him. That he'd take care of her.

"Truck?"

He blinked and the vision was gone. It had been so real, he knew it had to be a memory.

Keeping it to himself, Truck said, "Sorry. Did you say something?"

"Are you okay?" she asked.

"Yeah. Just haven't had enough coffee this morning."

She smiled at that. "You do love your coffee," she said under her breath. Then louder, "I have to get to work, but I didn't want to leave things between us the way they were, and I didn't want to text you or talk over the phone."

Truck was surprised. He didn't know why, but this didn't seem like the Mary he knew. She was more likely to hold a grudge forever, and he'd have to make the first move. "I always have time for you, Mary," he said gently.

She looked at the floor. "I'm sorry about yesterday. I know I said it before, but I need to say it again. I'm not only sorry for blabbing about your headaches, but I know it's not fair of me to tell you some things then clam up about others. I...I want to talk to you, but I'm scared."

Truck took a step toward her and put his hand on the side of her neck. "Do *not* be afraid of me," he ordered a bit gruffly, put off by the mere thought that she might be scared of him.

"I'm not scared of you, per se," she said immediately, without pulling away from him. "I know you won't hurt me...physically."

"You think I'd hurt you emotionally?" he asked.

Mary nodded. "Every man I've ever gotten close to has."

"I'm not them," Truck said, willing her to believe him.

"I know. Which is why I'm here," she admitted.

Not able to stop himself, Truck leaned down and kissed her on the forehead. It was a chaste kiss, but it felt more intimate than almost anything they'd done. It was a promise of sorts. "Whenever you need me, I'm there."

She gave him a shaky smile. "Okay. As I said, I have to get to work. We have a meeting this morning with our boss. I think she's going to announce layoffs, which sucks."

"Fuck. Are you going to lose your job?" Truck asked with concern.

Mary shrugged. "I don't know. Probably. But I think I'm okay with it if I do. I...missed a lot of work last year, and it just hasn't been the same since I've been back. I was surprised my boss let me leave early yesterday, but I think it's because she's just collecting reasons to can me. I think she's bitter that she couldn't fire me, and I've found that I just don't have the same kind of drive to work there as I used to. Not to mention the assholes we've had to deal with recently are making things really tense."

"What kind of assholes?" Truck asked, his hand tightening on her neck.

Mary shrugged. "That's just it, I'm not sure. I mean, I'm sure they're assholes, but they haven't really done anything to make my *boss* do anything about them."

"Mary. Spit it out," Truck said.

"Sorry. It's just that there have been lots of young men coming in and asking questions about renting safety-deposit boxes. Which, on the surface, is fine, but they're sketchy. They seem too young to really care about renting one— statistics show that most renters are older—and I just get a bad vibe from them. And I've told Jennifer, but she says that I'm just being paranoid."

"This doesn't sound like something to fuck around with. What if they're casing the place?" Truck asked. "They could be coming in to get information, to see the layout of the bank, to see how many employees are working, stuff like that. The last thing you need is someone holding up the place."

Mary's eyes fell from his, and he wondered what that was about, but she simply nodded and said, "I know. But for some reason, as I said, my boss doesn't seem to think it's an issue. Anyway, so all of that stuff combined makes me not so upset at the idea of being laid off."

"What would you do instead?"

"I'm not sure. But there are a ton of organizations around here that I could probably volunteer for until I figure it out."

Truck had a feeling she knew exactly what she wanted to do, but wasn't comfortable enough telling him yet. Again, he let it go. "You want to come back over after work?"

"Yeah, if that's okay."

"Of course. My home is your home," Truck said, and he got the impression that he'd said that to Mary before.

She smiled. "Okay. I'll text before I come over. Thanks, Truck. I'm sorry that I'm so bitchy sometimes. I...it's just how I am."

Truck leaned forward and put his forehead on hers. Their breath mingled together and he could feel the warmth of her body against his. Her fresh smell was sharper this close and he reveled in it. "I like how you are, Mary.

And your bitch doesn't bother me. I know what's under her."

"What?"

"My Mary," Truck said simply.

She swallowed hard and closed her eyes. They stood like that for a long moment before Truck reluctantly pulled back.

Mary looked up at him and nodded. "I'll see you later then."

"You will. And, Mary?"

"Yeah?" She paused with her hand on the doorknob.

"It's going to be okay. Whatever you need to tell me, I'll treat you with care."

She stared at him for a few seconds, then nodded. "I know. I'm just scared you're gonna be pissed enough to not want to do this anymore."

"Nothing will make me pissed enough to not want to do *this*," he gestured between them with a hand, "anymore."

"We'll see," Mary said.

"Yes, we will. Later. Drive safe."

"I will. Later, Truck."

Truck stared at the door after it closed behind her. Another image came to him then, of Mary sitting on the couch. She looked ashen—and was completely bald.

He leaned over her with a bowl of soup and said, "You have to eat, Mary."

"I'm not hungry."

"I don't care. You're going to eat this."

"I'm just going to throw it up later, Truck. Let it go."

"No. Eat."

She sighed and took the bowl from his hands. "Okay, but I'm going to say I told you so later when you're holding me up as I puke."

"Deal."

Truck leaned down and kissed her pale, bald head...

Then the vision blinked out and he was once again staring at the door of his apartment.

"Son of a bitch," he swore. His headache had returned with a vengeance, but he knew without a doubt that his memory was coming back. The blips and spurts were annoying and confusing, but with each and every one, he understood more and more what Mary meant when she'd said their relationship had been complicated.

He hoped like hell she was going to explain everything that evening. He was beginning to make his own deductions, based on the things he'd been remembering lately, but he hoped he was wrong.

His stomach clenched and he prayed as hard as he ever had before that whatever had been wrong with Mary was in the past. He couldn't have found her, again, only to lose her now.

Mary wasn't surprised when Jennifer announced the new direction the bank wanted to take with the machines as tellers instead of humans. She said that all but five of the tellers would be laid off in the next month or so. Everyone would receive two months' severance pay, and help would be available applying for unemployment benefits if anyone needed them.

She thanked Rebecca after the meeting for giving her a heads-up. Everyone's mood was subdued that day, but all

Mary could think about was Truck and what he was going to say when she talked to him later that night.

She wasn't ready to break the news that they were actually man and wife, but she was going to tell him about her cancer. One thing at a time. She was hoping that maybe learning about her cancer would somehow jog his memory enough that he'd remember their wedding ceremony all on his own, so she wouldn't have to tell him and try to explain why he'd asked and, more importantly, why she'd finally said yes.

She guiltily thought about their framed marriage certificate still buried deep in one of the boxes she'd brought back to her apartment. She'd thought more than once about digging it out and hanging it up, but she didn't want Truck to accidentally see it when he was over at her place.

But with every day that went by, it got harder and harder to keep things from Truck. She was pissed the day before, and deliberately dodged telling him about her appointment, but by the time she'd gotten home she'd felt so guilty, she'd already planned to head over to his place this morning to beg him to talk to her. Luckily, he hadn't made her beg.

But now she had to find the courage to spill the beans. She didn't want Truck to look at her with pity or treat her differently. It was hard to be the full-speed-ahead Mary all the time that people had come to expect. There were days where all she wanted to do was stay in bed and not see or talk to one single person.

Throughout the workday, her phone was constantly buzzing with incoming texts from all the girls. Rayne sent a selfie of her and Emily. Emily looked amazing after giving birth only the day before. But it was the picture of Annie holding her new brother that made tears well up in Mary's eyes.

The little girl looked positively ecstatic. It was adorable

and beautiful at the same time. The thought that she might've missed seeing this if Truck hadn't browbeat her into marrying him was painful. He'd done the right thing. As hard as going through the treatments again had been, seeing Annie and her baby brother made it worth it.

When Mary had asked Rayne what Emily and Fletch had named their son, she'd reported back that no one knew yet. The Fletchers were throwing a welcome-home party when Em and the baby were released from the hospital, which should be by that weekend, and they were going to reveal it then.

Mary had merely shook her head. Emily loved having people over, loved even more when *everyone* was there. Despite what had happened at her wedding, she loved a big, boisterous party.

By the time four-thirty came, Mary was done mentally. The day had sucked. Everyone was depressed, it had seemed like there were more customers than normal, and Mary had to give another tour of the safety-deposit vault to another shady potential customer.

She'd tried to talk to Jennifer once more, to explain that something was very wrong and she needed to get extra security in or something, but her boss once again blew her off. She tried to tell herself it was because Jennifer was knee-deep in the reorganization of the staff and trying to figure out when the new machines for the lobby were going to arrive, but something didn't sit right with Mary.

There was a feeling of wary anticipation in the air that Mary couldn't help but think was going to bite them all in the ass. Not one of the young men who'd toured the vault had come back to return the application and actually rent a box. Not a single one. Which gave more credence to the fact that they were up to no good. Why Jennifer was ignoring all the signs pointing to something big, Mary couldn't fathom.

When Mary left the bank at the end of the day, she was fried. Mentally done. The stress of knowing she was most likely going to be unemployed, worrying about if, or when, the gang members were going to make a move, and thinking about what she was going to tell Truck, not to mention skipping lunch, had all worked to make her want to go home and bury herself in her bed covers and not come out for a week.

But she'd told Truck she'd be over after work, and she wasn't one to go back on her word. Knowing she should probably wait until she was in a better frame of mind, Mary knocked on Truck's apartment door anyway.

It opened almost immediately and Truck smiled down at her with his lopsided grin. An urge to collapse against him and let him take care of her swept over Mary, but she resisted.

"Hi," he said. "How was your day?"

"Shitty," Mary said bluntly.

He looked surprised at her answer, but then his face gentled and he reached out and grabbed her hand. "I'm sorry, Mare. Come in. Let me get you something to drink. You hungry?"

Mary allowed him to pull her into his place and shut the door behind her. She didn't answer him as he walked toward his kitchen, her hand secure in his.

It felt good.

It reminded her of how he'd always taken care of her when she'd been sick.

And suddenly she was tired of it all.

She didn't like keeping secrets from Truck, but she really hated having to tell him about her cancer. She didn't like to talk about it, would prefer to pretend it never happened at all...and she resented that she was in this position in the first place.

Mary knew her feelings were irrational, but she couldn't help it. She'd gone to see a therapist at her doctor's urging when she'd been diagnosed a second time. He'd assigned her the task of writing down her feelings in a journal, then bringing it in so they could talk about what she'd written. Mary had gone back once then stopped altogether.

She didn't like sharing her feelings. She'd continued to write in the damn journal here and there, but ultimately it didn't make her feel any better. Mary had no idea where the stupid thing was now, probably at the bottom of one of the boxes the girls packed up when they'd moved her out of Truck's apartment, but she suddenly had the urge to write in it again. To pour out everything she was feeling right now.

"Mare?" Truck asked again. "Want me to fix us something for dinner?"

He'd let go of her hand and was standing in front of the refrigerator looking at her, waiting for her to answer.

"I had breast cancer," she blurted. "Twice. I had a double mastectomy. I know almost all of the nurses at the hospital because I was there so much. That's what that nurse was talking to me about yesterday. I missed my appointment with my doctor to talk about my breast reconstruction because I just can't deal with that yet."

She stared at Truck defiantly. That wasn't exactly how she'd planned to tell him, but the words simply spilled out of her. She couldn't deal with making small talk and pretending everything was all right. She just needed to tell him. And now she had. The ball was in his court.

Mary's words caused Truck's stomach to clench painfully. After his flashbacks, or memories, or whatever they were, he'd had a hunch that was her big secret, but hearing her confirm it so bluntly was jarring.

He slowly lowered his hand from the fridge and stepped toward her.

His heart broke when Mary moved away from him, rejecting the comfort he wanted—no, *needed* to give her.

"Do you want something to drink?" he asked.

"Did you hear me?" she asked, and Truck could see her hands shaking. "I had breast cancer. There's a chance it could come back a third time."

"What do the doctors say?"

She shrugged. "They don't know. They think they got it all this time, but no one knows. I'll have to take drugs for the next eight to ten years to manage it. They'll do tests every year to check to see if it's returned."

Truck struggled to find the right words that would comfort her. He loved her. The thought of her not being here, not standing in front of him right this second, was so abhorrent, he grimaced. "How are you feeling?" he asked inanely.

"Fine. Well, except for the numbness in my toes, which is fucking annoying. And before you ask, I prefer my hair short. I was bald for a while, but I'm not trying to grow my hair out longer than this. I like it short."

"I like it too. It's cute."

Mary rolled her eyes. "Just what I want. To be cute. Gag."

His lips twitched at that. He took another step toward her, and she either didn't notice or didn't feel the need to keep the distance between them. He liked that. "I take it I helped out when you were sick."

She nodded. "Yeah. You...you helped a lot."

"Good." Another vision of walking into his apartment after work and finding Mary sprawled on the living room floor flashed through his brain. She'd fallen and hadn't had the strength to get up. She'd tried to pretend as if she'd purposely decided to take a nap on the floor, but he'd seen right through her. "You're amazing," he said softly.

"No, I'm not."

"Yeah, Mare. You are. Cancer sucks. Fighting it *once* breaks people. But you not only beat it once, you beat it twice. That's amazing."

"I didn't want to do it the second time," she admitted. "Rayne was there for me the first time, but I decided I couldn't do it again. I was ready to give up."

"But you didn't."

She shook her head. "No. Because *you* wouldn't let me."

The words hung in the air for a moment...

"No! You're talking crazy!" Mary yelled.

"I'm not, and you know it. It's the only way," Truck returned as calmly as he could. He couldn't believe she was arguing about this. Not now. Not after everything that happened recently.

"No!"

"Yes!"

"No!"

Truck could've argued all night, but seeing the tears in Mary's eyes, coursing down her cheeks, was his undoing. "Say yes, Mare," he cajoled. "Please. For Rayne. For Annie. For me."

Mary stared at him for the longest time, and Truck forced himself to stand still, even though he wanted to haul her into his arms and hold her tight. She had to say yes. But he couldn't force this, no matter how badly he wanted to.

Finally...she nodded. Truck immediately went to her and gathered her into his arms and held her as she cried.

He blinked as he abruptly came back to himself and realized that Mary was staring at him nervously, obviously waiting for him to say something. He had no idea what they'd been arguing about in his flashback, but it didn't matter.

"Thank you for fighting," Truck told her. "Thank you for not giving up. I'm sure you wanted to, but thank you for letting me help you."

Mary looked at the floor then. They stood silent for a minute or so before Truck risked taking another step toward her. When she didn't retreat, he took another. Then another. When he was right in front of her, he reached out and gently pulled her into his arms and held her just as he had in his memory.

She immediately wrapped her arms around his waist and put her head on his chest. Truck sighed in relief and shut his eyes. The only time he felt completely at ease since he'd been hurt was when he had Mary in his arms. It didn't make sense; he only knew it was true.

"Tell me about the reconstruction," he urged, sensing it would be easier for her to talk about it if she wasn't looking at him.

"I have to decide if I want boobs," she said succinctly.

"What're the pros and cons?" Truck asked. "Talk it out with me."

"Pros, I won't look like an eight-year-old little girl," she said dryly. "I'll have perky tits that won't sag when I'm eighty. I could get a stripping job and cater to all the pervs out there who want to get it on with an elderly woman."

Truck chuckled. "Yeah, not going to happen, babe."

"Pros, I could wear V-neck shirts again. I'd have cleavage. I'd be able to wear normal bathing suits and not have to worry about making sure I put in my waterproof boobs. I wouldn't have to worry about leaning over and having my boob fall out of my bra. I'd feel...attractive again."

The last part was whispered, and Truck knew that was the most important thing she'd said. He tightened his grip on her. As much as he immediately wanted to tell her to do it, he wanted her to *feel* as beautiful as she already *was*. Wanted her to see herself as he did...absolutely stunning. But he worried about the risks as well. "And the cons?"

"It would take over a year for the entire process. They'd have to take fat cells from my thighs and stomach and inject them into my chest to try to stretch out the skin there, so they can even put in the implants. I'm paranoid that getting implants will somehow mask the cancer returning. And I've always hated women who have fake tits. It seems like something women do to try to attract men. And that's fucked up. They're just blobs of fat on our chest...it shouldn't matter."

He understood. And unfortunately, he had absolutely no advice for her. This wasn't something he could decide. The process didn't sound pleasant, that was for sure. He hated the thought of her going through more pain simply to conform to society, but if it made her feel better about herself as a woman, it could be worth it.

"So? What should I do?" she asked.

Truck had dreaded the question. "I can't make this decision for you, Mare."

She snorted against his chest and pulled away abruptly. "Yeah. Whatever."

He took hold of her upper arms and kept her from moving away from him. Her hands came up to push at him, but he held on. "I like you exactly how you are, Mary. I don't give one little shit if you have boobs or not."

Another memory flashed through his brain, of lying next to her in his bed, trying to find a place he could touch her that wouldn't hurt. Of Mary being bare from the waist up because she couldn't stand anything against her chest. It was red and her skin was peeling off from the radiation. He'd never seen anything so horrific in all his life, and he'd seen a lot in his time as a medic in the Army.

"Right," she drawled. "Men like boobs. They like to squeeze them, suck on them, and love to see them bouncing up and down. Cleavage is like crack to men, they can't look away."

"I like *you*," Truck said with a hint of impatience. "I like what's in here," he said, putting his hand on the side of her head. "And in here." He put his other hand over her heart, noticing for the first time that her breasts weren't natural. "The rest is just window dressing."

Mary knocked his hands off her body and stepped back. "I don't believe you. All men want a beautiful woman by their side."

"Look at me," Truck ordered.

"What?"

"Does my scar make you ashamed to be by *my* side? Does it make you less attracted to me?"

"It's not the same," Mary protested.

"It's exactly the same," Truck countered. "I can't tell you how many times women have refused to look me in the eyes because of it. Or how many women have gone straight for one of my friends, dismissing me because of this hideous scar. But the bottom line is, I don't give a shit. If they can't see past my scar, then I want nothing to do with them. Mary, when I lost my memory, you could've taken the opportunity to avoid me altogether. You could've pretended you didn't know me. But you didn't. When that chick at the bar made a play for me, you were right there, defending me and claiming me. Why?"

Mary looked away from him then. "Anyone would've done that."

"No, they wouldn't. They haven't. *You* did though. Why?"

She pressed her lips together, then said, "What do you want to hear, Trucker? That I can't live without you? That I owe you my life? What?"

"How about that you care?" Truck said softly. "Can you admit that you care about me? Even a little?"

Mary stared at him with big eyes. He could see the emotions churning there. But he knew she wasn't going to give him what he wanted. What he needed.

He pulled out his ace card.

"I love you, Mary Weston. Even not knowing our history, I love you."

Tears welled in her eyes, but she stayed stubbornly silent.

"The last few weeks have been great. I've loved getting to know you...again. Everything is new for me, and it's been exciting to learn your likes and dislikes and your quirks. I love your hair. I love the way you smell. I love your snarkiness and the way you'd do anything for your friends. I love how you look at little Annie, and I love how you think of everyone but yourself first. You stand up for the little guy, the oppressed. I see you, Mary. I see how you might tell off a man who didn't bother holding open the door for someone after he went through it, but then turn around and be polite and respectful to a single mother who looks like she's at the end of her rope. I love the way you snuggle up to me when we're watching television, and I love how you argue with me about every fucking thing. It's you, Mary. Not what you look like. Not how big your tits are. *You*."

She stared at him for a beat, then said, "I need to go."

"Dammit, Mary! Don't."

"It's been a hell of a day and I should go. I need to call Emily and see how she's doing. And Annie too. They're having a party this weekend, if the baby is home by then, and I need to see what she needs me to do."

This seemed familiar too. Mary backing off when things got intense between them. Truck didn't like it, but he knew he wasn't going to get anywhere now. Not when the iron shields she held around her were up.

He stood back and gestured to the door. "Running isn't going to make me love you less, Mare," he told her. "Running isn't going to make your decisions any easier, either."

"Thanks, Einstein," she mumbled, then headed for the door.

She didn't say goodbye, and neither did he. She just opened the door, walked through, and softly closed it behind her.

The second he heard it click, Truck let out an exasperated yell and turned and kicked the couch as hard as he could.

Mary heard Truck's yell of frustration before she'd taken three steps away from his door, but she didn't slow down. Didn't go back, even though everything in her was screaming to do just that.

She could barely see where she was going because of the tears in her eyes. She wanted to tell him that she cared. That he'd literally saved her life. That she couldn't imagine her life without him in it. That his apartment felt more like a home

227

even without her things in it than her own did. That she was proud and happy to be his wife...but she couldn't.

There was something seriously wrong with her. Every time she opened her mouth to tell him, she froze up. Maybe it was the years of conditioning by her mama when she was little. Maybe it was because the one and only time she'd told someone she loved them, that love was thrown back in her face. She didn't know.

But she knew she'd just walked out on her one shot at being loved. *Truly* loved. And she had no doubt Truck loved her. He'd proven it again and again with his words and actions. She knew he wouldn't give a shit that she didn't have boobs. Knew that he'd stand by her no matter what her decision was about the reconstruction.

The tears fell from her eyes in a steady stream. Her phone rang with Rayne's special ring tone, but she ignored it. She couldn't talk to her best friend right now. Rayne would tell her she was being an idiot. That she should go back and talk to Truck. But she couldn't. She wanted to be alone. Needed to be alone.

She needed to get *used* to being alone, because after walking out on Truck, there was no way he'd want to be with her. She was a pain in the ass and she'd just rejected him.

It was better he didn't know they were married.

CHAPTER THIRTEEN

Truck stood in the middle of his destroyed bedroom with his hands on his head, panting. He'd gone a little crazy after Mary left, kicking things, turning over furniture, breaking shit. When he'd run out of things to take his frustration out on in his living room, he'd moved to his bedroom.

He was frustrated that he didn't remember all the details about Mary being sick. Frustrated that he couldn't take away her pain. Frustrated that he couldn't shield her from having to make tough decisions like whether or not to have her breasts reconstructed. But above everything else, he was frustrated that his memory wasn't coming back as quickly as he wanted.

Taking out those frustrations on his belongings felt good. Turning his dresser over. Picking up his mattress and flipping it up against the wall. The lamp next to the bed had broken, but Truck didn't give a shit. There were clothes all over the floor and the one picture he had on his wall now had a fist-sized hole in the glass covering it.

Truck was irritated with his doctor and his teammates. He wanted things to be the way they had been...even if he couldn't remember them. They might not have been perfect, but they had to be better than this.

How could he be with a woman if she wouldn't even tell him how she felt?

The bottom line was that he wasn't sure he could be. He needed the words as much as she did.

But the shit thing was, he *knew* Mary cared about him. She wouldn't have defended him so staunchly at the bar if she didn't. She wouldn't have spent the last few weeks letting him get to know her if she didn't. She wouldn't have told him about her cancer if she didn't.

Cancer.

She'd had fucking *cancer*. And he'd forgotten about it. How in the hell could he have forgotten that? The woman he loved more than life itself had suffered for months, and he'd fucking forgotten it. And if the few memories that had flitted through his brain were to be believed, it had been one hell of a fight. And he'd been there every step of the way. He had no doubt about that.

The truth hit him like a sledgehammer—and Truck backed up until he hit the wall and slid down it. He sat on the floor and stared blankly at his bed. The box spring was still in place, but the mattress was pushed up against the far wall.

Mary loved him.

She might not be able to say the words, but she did. He knew that as well as he knew his own name was Ford Laughlin.

He was an ass for even thinking he couldn't have a relationship with her if she didn't come right out and tell him her feelings.

She'd told him with her actions over and over that she cared. More than simply cared. Even in the last month, he'd seen it. The way her eyes lit up when she saw him. The way she sparkled when they argued. The way she called him Trucker and smiled when she did. The way she sat next to him and played with a thread on his pants. The way she looked right at his scar yet didn't seem to see it.

Truck closed his eyes and sighed. He'd fucked up tonight. He should've waited to tell her he loved her. He'd pushed her too hard. Had pushed for something she might not ever be able to give him. The question was...could he deal with that?

He opened his eyes and nodded. Yeah, he could deal with never hearing the words as long as he had her in his life.

Truck went to stand up, to start cleaning the mess he'd made of his apartment and his life, when something caught his eye. It was a notebook. A plain black and white notebook on the floor by the bed. It must have been dislodged when he'd had his temper tantrum and flipped his mattress.

Truck didn't think it was his. He could be wrong, though. Lord knew there were a lot of things he didn't remember about his own life. He walked over and picked up the notebook. For some reason he had the weird feeling he was standing in front of a locked door. On his side, it was dark and rainy. But on the other side, he just knew it was sunny and beautiful.

And the notebook he held in his hands was the key to getting to that other side. Of stepping out of the darkness and into the light.

Slowly, as if a snake would come out of the pages and bite him, Truck opened the cover.

He stared at the writing and instinctively knew it was Mary's. He couldn't remember seeing anything she'd written before, but there was no one else he could've let have free rein in his home other than her. No one else who would've had the opportunity to put a notebook under his mattress for safekeeping.

He read the words on the first page.

Mary's journal

If your name isn't Mary Weston and you're reading this—stop it. Seriously. I'll find you, gut you, and make you wish you could turn back the clock and make a better decision. I'm only writing this shit down because my doctor told me it would make me feel better. I'm not sure about that, I mean, I have breast cancer for fuck's sake. How is writing my feelings down going to make me feel better? It's certainly not going to magically cure me. Whatever. Here goes nothing...

The words made Truck smile. They were quintessential Mary. Taking the journal with him, Truck left his bedroom and went back into the living room. Taking a seat on the couch—which was thankfully still in one piece, albeit shoved halfway across the room from where it had been before his temper tantrum —Truck didn't even hesitate to turn the page and start reading.

It might be wrong, but he was desperate to understand the woman he loved. Wanted to know everything about her. To figure out the missing pieces of his memory. This might be his one and only shot to get answers. He wasn't going to pass it up, even if he was trespassing on her private thoughts.

Mary hadn't dated any of the entries. She'd just started writing, as if she couldn't get the words on the page fast enough.

The cancer is back. The motherfucking cancer is back. I can't do this again. I can't put Rayne through this again. This must be payback for me being a bitch my entire life. Having a whore of a mama wasn't enough punishment. Being screwed over by men time and time again wasn't enough either. Whatever I did in a past life, I'm sorry. Do you hear me, I'M SORRY! Fuck. Damn it all to hell.

Her pain was easy to feel. They were only words on a page, but Truck could physically feel her terror. She was scared to death and that gutted him. Truck had an inkling of what she felt. Not that he'd ever been told he had a deadly disease, but when the doctor in Germany had informed him that he had amnesia, and that he might never remember the last three years of his life, he'd had many of the same thoughts Mary did when she'd heard her diagnosis. It wasn't fair. Why him?

The next entry was just as emotional as the last.

I've decided. I'm not going through chemo and radiation again. I can't. It almost killed me last time. I'd rather die on my own terms than go through that again. I'm also not going to tell Raynie. She'll put her entire life on hold for me again. She'll browbeat me until I agree to treatment. But I'm tired. So fucking tired. She doesn't understand. I might have considered treatment if I knew my insurance would cover it, but after spending so much money on the treatment before, I'm pretty sure it won't all be covered this time. They said something about a payment cap, which is bullshit. I might make pretty good money, but it's not enough to pay for all the treatments without insurance help. Hell, one damn anti-nausea pill costs $300. It's ridiculous. So I'm just going to go about my life and when it's my time, it's my time. I won't put Rayne through the pain of watching me die. I'd never do that to her. It'd scar her for life. When I get too sick, I'll quit my job and head to the beach somewhere. Some hotel maid will come in one day and find my body. And that's okay. Better her than my best friend.

Truck felt sick. The thought of Mary going off to some damn hotel to die made him want to puke. He was not surprised in the least that Mary had wanted to spare Rayne. He knew how close the two women were. But he also had a feeling if Rayne had known what Mary was thinking, she would've pitched a royal fit. He quickly kept reading.

This sucks. I was supposed to be babysitting Annie tonight and I got so sick I couldn't. Everyone was down in Austin at an Army Ball, and I had to call Truck and tell him I needed help. I hate asking for help. I hate that I'm sick. I fucking hate cancer!

Truck came, of course he did. He's freaking perfect in every way, but I'd never admit that to him. Of course, instead of bundling up Annie, taking me home, then bringing Annie back to her house and staying with her, he made me stay at her house with him. And of course I ended up puking all over the bathroom floor because I didn't make it to the toilet in time. And it figures I was too weak to get up so I got it all over my clothes.

I hate my life.

I try to be so fucking brave and tough, but it's hard. So hard.

And it's even harder when the most perfect man I've ever known comes into the bathroom and sees me lying in my own puke and has to not only help clean me up, but has to clean up the bathroom too.

I wouldn't wish cancer on my greatest enemy. Not even Mama.

"Holy shit," Truck said. He didn't remember the Army Ball or the incident Mary described, but just reading about it made him tear up. She had to have felt so helpless. It was obvious to him, just by reading her words, that he'd loved her then. If she asked for his help, of course he would've given it to her. He'd give her anything.

It was also obvious that her asking for help was big. *Huge.* Mary didn't ask for much, even now that she wasn't sick. He hated thinking about her being so weak she couldn't make it to the bathroom. The only reason she'd asked for help in the first place was because she was watching Annie. If the little girl hadn't been a factor, she probably would've lain on the floor of her own bathroom until she somehow magically found the strength to get up. God, he hated that.

Did I say Truck was perfect? I lied. He's insane. Crazy. Has a screw loose. After the incident at Emily's house, when I puked in the bathroom, Truck came over to my place and told me he had a question for me.

The daft man asked me to marry him!

All I could do was stare at him in disbelief. I'm dying. Why the hell would he want to marry me? But...the more I thought about it... the more I wanted to say yes. The man drives me crazy, but I think I love him. Heh, I know, I know, I said I'd never love another man for the rest of my life, but this is TRUCK. He doesn't get pissed when I'm snarky, in fact he seems to find it amusing (which is annoying). He doesn't let me push him away (again, annoying), and he tells me how pretty I am all the time (which I know is a lie, because hello...chemo hair!!).

But you know what? The second I opened my mouth to tell him yes, that I would marry him and spend the rest of my (limited) days with him, loving him, he had to go and open his mouth again.

I'd stupidly spilled the beans while I was sick at Emily's house that my insurance wouldn't pay for any more chemo treatments. That I did my best, but I was done. I was going to let the cancer do its thing and just be done with it once and for all. My only excuse for blabbing was that I was missing Rayne. I haven't seen her in ages (if she saw me losing my hair again, she'd know what was going on, and I can't risk it). I've only talked to her here and there on the phone. So I was lonely. And I word vomited my plan to go to the beach and die peacefully. Alone. (OK, I know it wouldn't be peaceful, but I'm trying to fool myself so I don't scare myself half to death.)

So there I was, about ready to accept Truck's proposal. Happy beyond anything I've ever felt because this perfect, amazing man wanted to marry me. What were the odds?

Well, then he explained that if I married him, I would qualify for all his Army benefits...including his health insurance. Talk about a buzzkill. I was ready to tell him that I wanted to be Mrs. Ford Laughlin, and he had to go and tell me he was only asking to save me.

Fuck my life.

Truck closed his eyes and concentrated on breathing.

Mary loved him.

He'd been pretty sure, but there it was in black and white.

Then he wanted to kick his own ass. She would've said yes if he hadn't opened his mouth and told her it was so she could be on his insurance, which he was pretty sure had only been a desperate ploy on his part to *get* her to say yes.

His head was pounding now. With every sentence he read, flashes of Mary sparked in his brain. She'd lived here. With him. They'd slept in the same bed every night. They'd watched TV together. He'd fixed her meals. Forced her to eat when she was so sick she didn't want to do anything but sleep.

Mary loved him and had wanted to say yes to his proposal as a result. Yeah, things between them had definitely been "complicated," as she'd called it.

Wanting to know what else he'd fucked up, Truck read on.

Truck won't give it up. He calls me every day and orders me to marry him. Tells me he's not ready to let me go. That he loves me and wants to see my smiling face every day for the rest of his life. I know he's full of shit because I haven't exactly been smiling lately.

Why did he have to bring health insurance into it?

I told him to fuck off.

Truck shook his head. Yeah, he'd really screwed up by bringing insurance into things. Mary was proud. She'd never agree to marry him for his insurance.

He should've been freaking out that he'd asked a woman to marry him and couldn't remember it, but the only thing he was worried about was if she'd finally given in or not. He kept reading.

I thought I was dying today. I hoped I was dying. I've never felt so terrible. Not even the first time I went through chemo. I couldn't get out of bed. I haven't eaten anything in two days. Nothing feels as bad as your body eating itself from the inside out. I have no idea if that's what's going on or not, but it feels like it.

I was lying there, praying for death, and all of a sudden Truck was here. My "perfect man" broke into my damn apartment (although I have to admit, it's kinda hot that he can pick locks!). He used his medic training and told me I was dehydrated and had to eat. Duh.

He stayed with me all day. Forcing me to drink. Making me eat, even though twice what I ate came back up. (Good Lord, can I not throw up in front of the perfect man for once in my life?!?)

Then I broke.

He told me that he'd researched it and we could be married in three days. All he had to do was get the application and we could go down to the courthouse and get it done. Easy-peasy. He told me that his insurance would kick in immediately and I could start the chemo again.

That's the last thing I wanted, but for some reason, I let him convince me. I'm just tired. Tired of fighting him. Tired of being sick. Tired of worrying about every-fucking-thing. Truck said he'd take care of me, and I believe him. He might be marrying me so I don't croak, but I have no doubt that he'll do anything necessary to take care of me.

I think I gave in because no one (other than Raynie, and that's different because she doesn't actually live with me) has ever given the littlest shit about me. Mama sure didn't. Neither did all those uncles.

If I wasn't so tired and sick, I know I probably would've stuck to my guns. Had some pride. But when you're at rock bottom, what's a little pride?

Mary agreed to marry him?

Holy fucking shit!

Truck put his head back on the couch and closed his eyes.

Had they gone through with it? He had to think they did, since she was still alive today. If she was that bad off, there's no way she wouldn't been able to beat the cancer without the chemo.

He was married? Mary was his *wife*?

Eager to find out what happened next, Truck opened his eyes and read the next entry as fast as he could.

Well, it's done. I married Truck today. It wasn't exactly romantic, we were in and out of the courthouse in thirty minutes, but I'm now Mrs.

Ford Laughlin. How did I celebrate? I barfed all over the bathroom floor. Again. FML.

Truck brought me to his apartment and got me in bed, then left to go to post and file the paperwork so I could get on his insurance. He's been distracted because all the guys left to go out to Idaho. Something to do with Fish and his new woman. But of course I don't know what's going on because I haven't talked to Rayne or the others as much as I've wanted to.

Then, while he was gone, I christened our married life by puking on the bathroom floor.

I'm pathetic.

And hideously ugly (it's a good thing sex is off the table because Truck would take one look at my flat-as-fuck chest and run screaming from the room, saying he was no child molester).

And married.

Fuck. What did I do?

I married a man for love and he married me for pity.

Fuck!

Looking down at his ring finger, Truck had a distinct memory of Mary sliding a ring on it. Where was it now?

Suddenly, finding his wedding ring was more important than reading. Putting the journal aside, Truck stood and headed back into his wrecked bedroom. He went straight to the bathroom.

Instinctively knowing exactly where his ring was, he opened the bottom drawer to the left of the sink, crouched down, and rifled through the junk there, pulling out a small velvet bag in the back. How he'd known right where to look, Truck had no idea, but when he dumped the bag into his hand, two rings clinked together as they landed in his palm.

Their wedding rings.

Closing his eyes, he suddenly remembered everything about the day he'd put them away.

"I'm not going to wear my ring," Truck told Mary.

Her eyes were sad, but she nodded. "Okay."

"Not because I'm not happy to be married to you, but because it's not smart while we're on a mission."

"Okay," she repeated, then pulled her own off. "If you're not going to wear yours, then I won't wear mine either. If you have a naked finger, so do I."

"That's not necessary," he said.

"It is. And this goes for more than just this mission. If you take off your ring, mine comes off too. Got it?"

Truck remembered nodding at her, but not worrying about it much because he had no intentions of taking his ring off otherwise, except for missions. He'd never cheat on Mary and he'd never willingly leave her. He'd thought the idea romantic, her not wanting to wear her ring if he couldn't. He'd taken both rings, put them into the small bag, and placed it on the counter. Later, he'd moved the rings to the bottom drawer for safekeeping.

He meant to tell her where he'd stashed them, but they'd both gotten busy and he'd forgotten.

Truck slipped his wedding ring on his finger and couldn't believe how right it felt. He fingered the smaller band wistfully. Reluctantly, he took his own ring off and put it back into the velvet bag with Mary's. He wanted to haul her back to his apartment and demand to know when she'd planned on telling him about their marriage, then make her wear the ring proclaiming her as his. Just as he would wear *his* ring, making sure bitches like the chick from the bar knew he was taken. But instead, he put the bag in his pocket.

He needed to figure out how to get Mary to confess that they were husband and wife, but in the meantime, he couldn't bear to be separated from their rings. Somehow he felt, if he had them with him, it would somehow make their marriage more real.

Truck went back into his living area and detoured to the kitchen to get a glass of water. He drank it down, then went back to the couch.

His memory was definitely returning. With every word he read, and with every hour that passed, Truck was more and more certain he'd eventually remember everything. His head was throbbing, but nothing could keep him from reading his wife's words.

I have to admit that I'm feeling better. I finished the chemo treatments (which sucked) and have started on the radiation again. Every weekday for fifteen minutes, I get zapped. I can't feel it, which is good, although I have a permanent tan mark on my back from the rays. That can't be healthy, can it?

And my skin is slowly starting to burn. I remember this from before.

Truck has been super attentive the entire time, and I have to admit I love it (although I'd never tell him that. It would go to his head or something. Ha!).

There are times I just don't understand how he can love me. I'm a pain in the ass. It can't be fun to be around me right now with my health issues and the way I'm always so bitchy. He could do so much better than me.

But if he decided that he couldn't deal with the cancer, or me, it would break me. More so than Brian did when I was a teenager.

More so than all the other men who let me down. Truck means everything to me, even though I've never told him. I have no idea what I'd do without him.

Truck closed his eyes and took a deep breath. Mary might only be able to admit to herself in her journal how much she cared about him, but seeing the words meant more to Truck than he'd ever be able to put into words himself. He didn't like knowing that he had the power to break Mary, but he wasn't surprised...simply because she could easily break him as well. When he opened his eyes, he had to blink a few times to clear the tears from his vision so he could keep reading.

Oh, God. I forgot how bad radiation was. I can't stand for anything to touch my chest, which makes it awkward because I'm basically living full-time with Truck in his apartment. He's helped me goop up my chest with the lotion they've given me, but it burns so bad. And it's so humiliating having him see me.

Intellectually, I know boobs don't make me who I am, but how will Truck ever see me as anything but the poor pathetic shell of a woman I am now? Not that I have the slightest desire to have sex, but what about the future? If Truck stays married to me, I'm gonna want to jump his bones, but even I wouldn't want to bone someone if they had the kind of scars I do. They simply aren't attractive in any way, shape, or form.

Nights are the worst. I swear I can feel my skin peeling and cracking. I lie in his bed on my back, without a shirt on because that shit hurts, and Truck sleeps next to me. He scoots down until his feet are hanging over the edge of the bed and he throws his arm around my waist. He nuzzles against my hip and tells me how proud he is of me. How strong I am.

What he doesn't know is that it's all a lie. I'm a fraud. I'm not strong at all. If I was, I'd tell him that I love him. That I want him to be with me for me, not because I needed his fucking insurance. But I don't say a word. I lie awake most of the night memorizing the feel of him next to me because I know when this is all said and done, and I'm better (God, please let me get better!), I'm gonna lose him.

Truck remembered sleeping with her like that. Remembered the helplessness he felt of not being able to do anything for her. Hating how much pain she was in. Hating that sometimes even the breeze from the ceiling fan on her chest was too much for her to take. Mary was so fucking strong. He couldn't even fathom how she'd made it through.

But seeing the words "I love him" in black and white, again, made him more determined than ever to make her believe that she was beautiful inside and out.

She loved him.

Mary fucking loved him.

Truck smiled.

It's been a while since I've written in here. Things are...weird.

The doctor told me my cancer is gone (yeah, like I'll believe that. I've heard it before).

I'm still with Truck, have basically moved in.

But Truck's friends found out we're married. And they weren't happy. They were pissed he kept it from them, because they don't keep secrets from each other. I'm afraid Truck is gonna tell me to go home, that we should get a divorce, but so far he hasn't.

But worse than that, Rayne hates me. I can't blame her, really. We promised to get married together, and I went behind her back and did the deed without her. Of course, the promise was bullshit. We were both drunk when we made it, but still. I know Rayne, and I know she had dreams of me marrying Truck and her marrying Ghost in a double wedding ceremony, and learning that I'm already married killed those dreams. I killed her fucking dreams.

Many times, I've thought about how everyone would be much happier if I wasn't around.

If I hadn't married Truck and gotten the treatment, they might've mourned me, but Rayne would be married, Truck might've found someone who was less annoying than me, and the others wouldn't all be fighting.

God. This sucks.

Mary and Rayne had a pact to get married together? The guys were fighting because he'd married Mary and hadn't told them? He couldn't imagine why he didn't tell his best friends about it...unless he was protecting Mary. Yeah, he could see himself not wanting to make her feel awkward around the others.

But he didn't believe for one second that any of the women, or his friends, would be happier without her around. That was bullshit. She'd better not still believe that.

Things still suck. At least Annie is still talking to me. We're practicing our sign language together. She's so fucking cute. Says she's gonna marry Frankie, the deaf kid she met who lives out in California. They "talk" over the Internet all the time.

I miss my best friend.

Truck seems to have patched things up with his friends, thank God, but Rayne still hates me. I don't know how Harley feels, but since she's super close to Rayne, she probably does too. Kassie is about to give birth.

Emily is not far behind her (and she's having a boy! One of the nurses I got to know in the hospital spilled the beans to me. I promised not to tell, but it's been hilarious telling Emily that I just "know" she's having a boy because Annie wants a brother. She's going to be so happy).

I don't really even know Casey or Wendy that well, which sucks because they seem to be really nice. Rayne's brother is now with a woman named Sadie. Truck's talked about how hilarious Bryn is, Fish's wife, but again, I wouldn't know because I'm not in the inner circle anymore.

Truck is...Truck. He's so nice to me and now that I'm not sick anymore, sleeping next to him is akin to torture. Right before he comes to bed, I steal his pillow so I can smell him on it all night. He doesn't know though. He always smells so good.

Oh, and...I miss sex. It's silly. I mean, I was sick for so long, I couldn't imagine ever wanting it again. But one night when Truck was at work, I masturbated. I climaxed so hard, because I was thinking of Truck's big hands on my body. How his tongue would feel eating me out.

I'm so pathetic. But, man...now that I've started thinking about it, I can't stop.

Truck swallowed and felt his dick twitch in his pants. Reading about Mary wanting sex, and masturbating, was so damn sexy, he almost couldn't stand it.

He had no idea how old the journal entries were though. They might be years old, or they might have been written shortly before that last mission when he got hurt. Truck had no idea since they weren't dated. He was glad he and his friends had patched things up, but it sucked that Mary had still felt ostracized. Obviously they'd made up, because Rayne was in constant contact with Mary now, but he hated that they'd had a falling out in the first place, especially since it centered around their marriage.

Rayne and me are BACK!

I decided that enough was enough and I was going to apologize for everything. But then the bank got held up, and I had to hide in the vault with her.

I spilled my guts and she FORGAVE ME!

God. Nothing feels as good as having Rayne back.

I also kinda told Truck that I wanted him. That I wanted to be a real wife to him.

Things have been weird with us lately, but I'm hoping that I haven't ruined our chances altogether. I'm working on being nicer, not only to him but to everyone. It's been hard (especially when that skank paramedic hit on him), but I don't want to always be the bitch.

He has to go on a mission this weekend, but when he gets back, I'm going to tell him that I like him. A lot. I want to tell him that I love him, but I have to work up to that.

Thank God, I don't have to worry about telling him about my lack of boobs, since he already knows (duh!). I can just go straight to telling him I want to suck his cock. Hahahaha!

All guys want that, right? If I had to seduce him from scratch (that sounds weird, but you know what I mean), I'd utterly fail. No boobs, no long hair to swish around, and my prickly attitude...what a recipe for failure. But since I know he already likes me (loves me?), this should work out.

He's working late tonight, so I'm going to masturbate again. I love putting his pillow under my ass and pretending he's pounding into me. God. I'm so pathetic. This girl needs to get her some! But maybe it'll be like a subliminal thing...he'll smell me on his pillow and jump my bones. That's the plan at least. We'll see if it works.

Holy shit. He *had* smelled her on his pillow. Truck remembered the first night back in his apartment, how he'd held his pillow close all night because it smelled so fucking good and he couldn't figure out why.

That little sneak.

He grinned.

It seemed as if there was a lot he and Mary still needed to talk about. He didn't like hearing about the bank being held up, she hadn't told him anything about that, but he wondered if it was related to the sketchy men she'd been talking about lately.

But more than that, she told him she wanted to be a real wife for him.

That she wanted a real marriage.

That took guts. He'd never doubted her strength, but that just proved it all over again.

And her coming over tonight and telling him about her cancer was also extremely brave of her, especially in light of what he'd just read. He didn't know when she'd been all set to seduce him, but he had a feeling it had been fairly recent. And if that was the case, him losing his memories had changed everything.

But what really struck Truck was that she hadn't given up. She'd pushed through her insecurities and worries and stuck by him. Standing up for him when she thought he needed it and not giving up on them as a couple.

She loved him.

He'd realized it before reading her journal, but reading her inner thoughts, knowing what she'd been through, made it all the more clear.

He and Mary were married.

Suddenly, Truck knew what was missing in his bedroom. In that spot on the wall by the door, the one he looked at all the time, thinking it was too empty. Their wedding certificate. He remembered hanging it, and Mary rolling her eyes at him when he'd proudly placed it where they'd see it every day.

He wondered where it was. Wanted it back where it belonged.

He wanted *Mary* back where she belonged.

With him. Here. In their bed. Under him.

Then something else hit home. He and Mary had *really* never had sex. She'd told him that, but it hadn't sunk in because they were still getting to know each other. After reading her last two journal entries, he realized that she'd been serious. At some point, she'd wanted to change the nature of their relationship, but it didn't sound like that had happened before he'd gotten hurt.

They hadn't consummated their relationship yet.

It sucked, because it gave her a hell of a good reason to get their marriage annulled, but on the other hand, he was glad they hadn't. That he hadn't had her and forgotten. One part of him wanted to believe that he'd never forget sinking into her for the first time, but another part wasn't so sure. He couldn't imagine how she'd feel if he'd forgotten them having sex.

Truck understood Mary's reaction tonight a little better after reading her journal. She was insecure about the way her body looked. She was afraid he was going to reject her as a result. But she had nothing to be worried about. Nothing.

Mary was his. Eventually, he had no doubt he'd regain all his memories, but in the meantime, he needed to make sure she knew that he wasn't giving up on them. That he truly loved her. She never needed to say it out loud. He knew she loved him back, and not just because of the words she'd written on the paper.

Truck stood and straightened the living area. Then he

went into his bedroom and picked up as much as he could and vacuumed up the broken glass. He placed her journal on the table next to the bed. He wasn't going to lie about reading it. She had nothing to be ashamed of. Ever.

As he was in the bathroom getting ready for bed, he fingered the velvet bag holding their wedding rings. He didn't see a diamond in there, but he'd be remedying that as soon as he could. He wanted to get her something huge, so there was no mistaking that she was taken, but he knew she'd hate that. He'd have to be creative in designing her ring, make it something low-key yet beautiful at the same time.

Hating that he had to put the bag with their rings back into the drawer, away from view, Truck consoled himself with the thought that Mary would soon be back here. Living with him. That their rings would be back on their fingers for the world to see.

But this time there would be no misunderstandings between them. No sickness. Just the two of them and their love.

He grinned.

CHAPTER FOURTEEN

Mary didn't want to go to work. She wanted to call in sick...or just quit. But she knew she'd need the unemployment payments to survive once she was laid off, and she wouldn't get them if she quit. So she reluctantly got dressed and ready to leave.

She thought about what she wanted to do with her life. She'd thought about it a lot already, and finally decided that she wanted to help women like her. Women who had, or had survived, breast cancer. She didn't know how, but that was what she wanted.

When she'd been sick, there had been a lot of offers from complete strangers to bring her food, sit with her while she was getting chemo, and even offers to pick her up to do errands. She hadn't really needed any help once Truck had insinuated himself into her life, but without him, she would've been in big trouble, and those offers of help would've been extremely important.

She wanted to do that. Wanted to help others. Tell them that she knew what they were going through because she'd been there, done that. Wanted to be a shoulder for people to cry on, to be the one they could let down the façade of strength with.

Mary still had no idea what her decision was going to be about the reconstruction of her breasts, but she didn't need to decide right that minute. Even though she'd been mean, again, to Truck the night before, she'd taken his words to heart.

He loved her exactly how she was. She wasn't looking forward to letting him see her naked, but she knew without a second's doubt that he wouldn't like her any less because she had no boobs.

If she decided to get the reconstruction, she'd do it for *her*. Not because she wanted to be prettier for Truck. Not because she wanted others to look at her and like what they saw.

Feeling better about that part of her breast cancer journey, Mary headed out of her apartment to her car. Still feeling guilty about the way she'd treated Truck the night before, she pulled out her phone. Before she chickened out, she sent him a text.

Mary: I'm sorry about last night. I was a bitch. Again. Want to have lunch today? Talk?

She got in the car and turned it on. She was about to pull out of her parking spot when her phone vibrated. Surprised that Truck had returned her text so quickly, she smiled as she read what he wrote.

Truck: Good morning, beautiful. Yes, I'd love to talk. There's a lot we have to discuss.

Mary didn't know what Truck meant, but at least he wasn't ignoring her.

Mary: I've only got thirty minutes for lunch today.
    Truck: I'll bring you something, if that's all right.
    Mary: Perfect.
    Truck: What time?
    Mary: 11:30?
    Truck: I'll be there. Love you.

Mary stared down at the phone in her hand. She couldn't believe he'd just typed that. Well, maybe she could.

Mary: Later.

Smiling, she put her phone away and headed for the bank in a much better mood than she'd been in five minutes ago. For the first time in a really long time, she thought that things with Truck just might work out. Of course, she had to tell him at some point that they were married, but that could wait.

Halfway through the morning, a woman came into the bank. Mary only noticed her because she stood by the front doors for quite a while. She looked like she was either going to get sick or pass out. When there was a break in customers,

Mary left her station behind the counter and walked up to the woman.

She was around Mary's height, and had long brown hair and brown eyes. She was wearing a pair of blue jeans and a T-shirt that said, "People. Not a fan." It made Mary want to laugh, but the closer she got to the woman, the more she could tell something was wrong.

"Are you all right?" Mary asked quietly when she got close.

The woman jerked, as if she hadn't seen Mary coming toward her at all. She blinked twice, her face pale. "I'm okay," she said quietly.

"Do you need to sit down?" Mary asked, looking around. "I can grab a chair, it's no problem."

"I'm nervous," the woman blurted. Then she closed her eyes and took a deep breath. She wrapped her arms around herself and Mary could see that she was pinching the skin on both of her biceps. "I came to see *you*," the woman said after a moment.

"Me?"

"My name is Macie Laughlin. Ford Laughlin is my brother. You're married to him, right?"

Mary could only stare at her. *This* was Truck's sister? But the longer she looked, the more she recognized the family resemblance. She had no idea where she'd come from or how she knew where Mary worked, or even who she was. But none of that mattered at the moment. "Oh my God, you're really Macie?"

The other woman nodded.

Mary beamed. "He's going to be so happy!"

It was Macie's turn to stare. "He is?"

"Yes! He asked his commander to see if he could find out where you were, so he could talk to you. Catch up. He's hated that he hasn't talked to you in so long. He feels guilty about it."

"It's not his fault. It's mine. I'm pretty sure it's *all* my fault," Macie whispered.

Mary shook her head, thrilled that she was face-to-face with Truck's sister. "How did you find me? I need to call him!"

Macie shook her head frantically. "No! Don't do that. I mean...I want to talk to him, but not today. It took everything I had to come talk to *you*. I couldn't possibly meet him today."

Mary took a long look at the woman in front of her. Now that she was paying attention, she could tell that Macie was on the verge of having a panic attack. Was very possibly *having* a panic attack. She was breathing hard and squinting, a sure sign she had a headache or a migraine. "Okay," she said, trying to calm Macie down. "I won't call him."

"I live near here. In Lampasas. I know someone who's good with computers, and he's kept me up to date on Ford. He's a hacker, really. I know that's illegal, but I've missed my brother so much and felt guilty for losing touch with him. My friend found your marriage certificate online, and I decided that now was the time to try to make contact. I know I shouldn't have pried, but I love him. He's my big brother and I was such an idiot for so long."

Macie's words were quick and rushed, as if she was trying to hurry up and get them out before her body refused to let her say anything at all.

"I...I moved to Texas about two years ago, and I've wanted to come see him ever since, but I didn't think he'd want anything to do with me. But after he got hurt...again...I decided I needed to suck it up and do it. But I didn't know if he remembered me or not, with his amnesia and all. So I thought I'd come and talk to you and see if you thought he might be willing to hear me out. To let me apologize. So... here I am."

"Macie," Mary said gently, wanting to reach out and hug the other woman, but holding back, "your brother will be over the moon to be able to talk to you. I told you, he's had his boss looking for you too. He'll be so happy to know you live close. And to answer your question, yes, he remembers you. He'll *definitely* want to talk to you."

Macie relaxed a fraction, but she was still way too tense. "That's good," she finally said.

"It is," Mary said with a smile. "Can I tell him you were here? Let me give you my number, so you can call and we'll set something up, okay?" She had a hundred more questions, but it was more than obvious Truck's sister was ready to bolt.

Macie nodded. "I'd like that."

Mary turned and grabbed a business card off a nearby desk and scribbled her cell phone number on the back. She handed it to Macie. "Seriously, Truck has told me so many stories about you two. He loves you, Macie."

"Truck?" she asked with a small frown.

"Sorry, Ford. Truck is his nickname...for obvious reasons."

Macie smiled then. It was a small quirk of her lips, but Mary blinked at the transformation that came over her face. The other woman was beautiful. She had too many worry lines and it was obvious that life had been hard on her, but Mary wanted to do everything she could to keep that smile on her face.

"If he's Truck, I guess I'm Car," Macie said with smile.

Mary chuckled. "I'm thinking Truck fits your brother better than Car fits you."

"No doubt. Thank you for talking to me," Macie whispered.

"Truck's coming here for lunch," Mary told her. "If you wanted to stay, I'm sure—"

"I can't," Macie interrupted. "I'll get in touch and we can work something out. Somewhere to meet. Just tell my brother I'm sorry."

"For what?"

"Just tell him, okay?"

"I will," Mary said quickly, seeing that Macie was getting agitated again.

And with that, the other woman nodded, ducked her head, and turned around and left the bank without a backward glance.

Mary wanted to immediately text Truck and tell him that she'd just met his sister, but she decided to wait and tell him in person. She couldn't wait to give him the good news.

Truck pulled into the parking lot of the bank and closed his eyes. His head was killing him. He really needed to call the doctor and let him know that he'd begun to remember more and more. Mostly things that had to do with Mary, but even driving around town was starting to make him remember things suddenly.

Seeing the grocery store made him remember shopping there for something Mary might be able to keep down.

He'd driven by Fletch's old house, and he'd had a flash of a memory of a wedding in the backyard—and taking down assholes who'd thought it would be cool to rob it.

Even seeing the JCPenney store at the mall made him abruptly remember that was where Kassie worked.

It was as if his mind was one of those old films that spun round and round on the reel. It had been stopped, but now it was slowly starting up again in fits and spurts. It was confusing and jarring, but oh so welcome.

Seeing he was early, Truck put his car in park and picked up his phone. He called Ghost.

"Hey, Truck. How're you?"

"Good. I have a question."

"Shoot."

"Was the French diplomat's daughter okay? And the other girls?"

There was silence on the other end of the line for a second before Ghost said, "You remember."

"Not all of it. Just bits and pieces. I do remember we were specifically looking for that little girl, but that there were lots of others who needed rescuing too."

"There were. She's okay."

"How many did we lose?" Truck asked.

"Three."

"Damn."

"What else do you remember?" Ghost asked.

"Most of it is a big jumble in my brain at the moment," Truck admitted. "Flashes here and there that don't make much sense, but I'm confident it's just a matter of time before it all comes back."

"Thank fuck," Ghost said.

"Yeah. So...you guys were all pissed at me for marrying Mary, huh?"

"You remember that?"

"Not the being pissed part, but the marriage, yes." It was a little lie. Truck didn't actually remember the ceremony yet, and he'd had to find out about it from Mary's journal, but that didn't matter.

"That's awesome. You call the doc yet?"

"No, but I will after lunch. I'm here at the bank with

Mary. Ghost, I hope like hell you're all really okay with my marriage to Mary, because I love her. I'm not giving her up. She's going to be in my life for a really fucking long time, and you all need to be okay with that."

"We're more than okay with it," Ghost reassured him immediately.

"Good."

"She know you remember?" Ghost asked tentatively.

"No. But I'm gonna remedy that as soon as I can. I want to talk to the doctor first and hear what he says. Then I'll have a chat with my wife tonight when she gets off work."

"You do that," Ghost said, and Truck could almost hear the grin in his tone. "Good to have you back, Truck."

"Not all the way back yet," Truck warned.

"But you will be."

"Yeah. I understand Fletch wants to have a thing at his house this weekend?"

"Yup. He's bringing Emily and their baby home on Thursday. Emily insisted on having a small get-together—her words —on Saturday so they could share what they named their son."

"What's wrong with a text?" Truck grumbled.

Ghost chuckled. "What Emily wants, Emily gets," he quipped.

Truck could totally understand that. He'd give Mary the world if she asked. "Okay, I need to get inside. Mary only has thirty minutes for lunch. Oh, and she's gonna need to find another job."

"Why?"

"The bank is reorganizing. Getting rid of tellers and going to machines."

"That's stupid."

"Agreed. Anyway, I'd appreciate it if you kept your ears open for something that she might be interested in."

"Will do. Can I tell Rayne?"

Truck hesitated, then said, "Maybe not yet. I'm sure Mary will tell her, but I'd rather she not have something else to be pissed at me about."

Ghost laughed. "She's always pissed at you, *Trucker*, adding one more thing won't matter."

Truck snorted. "Ain't that the truth. But she's so fun to piss off. She doesn't act like most women, she gets right in my face and tells me off. Weirdly enough, I like it."

"Obviously."

"Seriously, I always know exactly what she's thinking. It's refreshing. She's not scared of me at all. Which, because of my size and looks, is a fucking miracle as far as I'm concerned."

"I can see how that could be a good thing."

"It is. Of course, I'd never do anything to hurt her...and she knows it. Makes it hard to get her to do what I want and need her to do, to keep her safe. And now I *really* need to go. I don't want to miss a minute of our lunchtime."

"You'll call after you talk to the doctor?"

"Yup. Later, Ghost."

"Later, Truck."

Truck clicked off his phone and stuck it in his back pocket. Then he grabbed the two lunch bags he'd packed back at his apartment and climbed out of his car and headed for the entrance.

He opened the door and stepped inside the bank—right into the middle of complete chaos.

The second the five men came into the lobby of the bank, Mary knew they were in trouble. All her warnings had gone unheeded by Jennifer and now it was time to pay the price.

The men were dressed in jeans and T-shirts and none had coverings over their faces, which didn't bode well in Mary's mind. They should've been worried about concealing their identities. The fact that they weren't was a bad sign. She recognized three of the men from giving them tours of the vault, but the other two were strangers. All five men were white, and she could see they had tattoos up and down their arms.

She should've been freaking out, but Mary was strangely calm. She and the other employees had trained for situations like this, and while she was scared, Mary wasn't about to do anything that would put her life, or anyone else's life, in danger.

Three of the men branched off and immediately began to corral the customers and employees. The other two came up to the counter where she and Rebecca were sitting and pointed pistols right in their faces.

"Up, bitches," one said.

Mary immediately held her hands in the air, making sure both men could clearly see them. She scooted off the chair she'd been sitting on and stood. While one man held them at gunpoint, the other leaped over the counter, knocking off the odds and ends that had been on the surface. Mary could hear Rebecca sniffing as if she was crying, but she didn't take her eyes from the man in front of her.

"We meet again," he sneered as he stared at her.

Mary's chin went up. She wasn't going to cower to anyone. She'd already faced down death twice and won. No punk-ass kid was going to make her break now.

Mary knew she'd have to work really hard to hold her

tongue and not antagonize the men though. She might be able to harangue and be a bitch to Truck and his friends, but that was only because she knew they wouldn't hurt her... because they were honorable, good men.

These guys? She instinctively knew they wouldn't hesitate to put a bullet into her. She'd seen a lot of men and boys just like them growing up. They'd been taught to think women were beneath them, and any attempts to show them they were wrong were met with swift and immediate retribution.

"Get the keys to the vault, bitch," the one boy sneered.

Mary didn't think he was much older than eighteen, if that. She nodded to a drawer at the end of the counter. "They're in there," she told him.

"Then get them," he spat impatiently.

"I didn't want you to think I was reaching for a weapon or a secret panic button," Mary said calmly, even though inside she was anything but calm.

"I don't care if you do or not, I'll blow your ass away before you can try anything. Now hurry the fuck up," he growled.

Mary shivered, but hurried to do what he wanted. She vaguely heard others around her crying and the thugs yelling, but she was focused on her task. Once she had the keys in her hand, the man grabbed her arm and forced her toward the back. The other herded Rebecca into an office with the other hostages. Mary didn't like that she was separated from everyone, but she tried to keep herself calm.

Just as they were about to go into the vault, the last place she wanted to be alone with a gun-wielding gang member, the door to the bank opened.

She turned to see who had entered—and stared in shock as Truck walked into the bank.

She glanced at the clock. Eleven twenty-six. He was right on time for their lunch together. Dammit.

"Truck." His name came out involuntarily, and the second it did, she winced.

"Get your hands up!" one of the gang members yelled, and Truck immediately did as ordered. Two brown paper bags dropped at his feet as he complied.

"Who the fuck didn't lock the door?" one of the men yelled.

"Snake was supposed to."

"Shut the fuck up, Grass," snarled the man Mary guessed was Snake.

"*Both* of you shut the fuck up!" the man holding Mary's arm yelled. Then he turned and shouted, "Jennifer, lock the door!"

Mary stiffened. *Jennifer?* He knew her?

Before she could fully process the implications, the man holding her arm asked, "You know him?"

Mary was afraid to say yes, so she said nothing at all. That was apparently the wrong thing to do, because the man wrenched her arm up behind her back, and Mary couldn't help the yelp that escaped. The pain was intense, and she went up on her tiptoes to try to take the pressure off her arm.

"I asked you a question, bitch."

"He's a customer," she gasped.

"I don't believe you," the man holding her sneered, and tightened his hold on her arm. The pain was so intense, Mary couldn't help but blurt out the truth. "Yes, I know him! He's my boyfriend."

"Nice," the man drawled. "You, get your ass over here!" he yelled at Truck.

"Not sure that's a good idea, Deuce."

"Did I ask you, Fez? *No.*"

Mary tried to memorize the names the men were using, but it was hard to concentrate with her arm wrenched behind her like it was and with Truck's pissed-off vibe hitting her.

"I'm here," Truck said. "Let her go."

"You shagging this bitch?" Deuce asked, yanking up on her arm as he asked.

Truck nodded once.

"You want to *keep* shagging this bitch?" he asked.

Truck nodded again.

"Good. You look strong. I'm gonna need you. But if you do *anything* I don't like, I'm gonna put a bullet in her knee. Then her other knee. Then her fucking head. Got me?"

"Got you," Truck said evenly.

Mary glanced up at his face and didn't see one ounce of emotion. His lips were pressed together tightly and he didn't so much as glance in her direction. All his attention was focused on the man holding her.

"Good. Come on." Deuce walked sideways, never loosening his grasp on Mary's arm, keeping Truck in his line of sight. He hauled her to the vault that held all the safety-deposit boxes. Once inside, he grabbed the key ring out of her hand then flung her to the side of the space. "Sit over there and don't fucking move or say a word," he ordered.

Without hesitation, Mary lowered herself to the floor in front of a set of the boxes in the vault and hugged her knees to her chest. Her arm was throbbing, but she silently massaged it, trying not to bring any more attention to herself than she'd already received.

"You, go over there," Deuce ordered Truck, pointing to the other side of the room. "Snake, let the others in when they get here. Should be two more minutes."

Mary bit her lip even as the pit in her stomach got bigger.

The others? Shit, how many more? This was getting worse and worse by the minute.

"Bet you're wondering what we've got planned," Deuce said to Mary.

"Yeah, I am."

"The Ladbrook Boys don't take kindly to not gettin' what they want. And last time two of my boys were here, they most *certainly* didn't get what they wanted. So we're here to make sure everyone knows not to fuck with us and that we always get what's comin' to us."

Mary blinked. Did this guy know how stupid he sounded? They were going to get what was coming to them for sure. Didn't they realize that lunchtime was one of the busiest times for a bank? That there were going to be plenty of people who knew the bank wasn't supposed to be closed at lunch and would call the cops? They'd never get out of the bank alive.

"And in case you're wonderin', we put a sign on the door saying there was a training meetin' going on right now and the bank is closed. And we've got some of our boys keepin' the cops busy with calls about holdups all over town. There's even gonna be a fire or two and some traffic accidents. No one's gonna come here until we're done and gone. The Ladbrook Boys are gonna make sure this town knows we mean business."

Mary could only stare at him. Shit, they'd actually thought things out pretty well after all. But why would they spend so much time worrying about the safety-deposit boxes when they could hit the other vault and be in and out in a matter of minutes with stacks of cash?

"I can't open the boxes," Mary told him softly. "I told you that when you toured this place. We really do only have those three master keys, and the owners of the boxes have the other keys to open them. I wasn't lying about that."

"I know. Doesn't matter," Deuce said as he threw the keys to the side.

Mary was confused. Why did he have her get them in the first place if he knew they wouldn't work? "It doesn't?"

"Nope. My girlfriend says the money in the vault is rigged with ink bombs. The second we get too bar from the bank, they'll go off and the cash will be useless. But Jen told me about the jewels and cash people store in here."

Mary shook her head in confusion. "When customers open a box, we don't stay in the room while they put their belongings inside. Jennifer can't know what's in here and what's not."

Deuce had the pistol pointed at her face before she could blink. "You sayin' my bitch is lying?"

Mary immediately shook her head. "No."

"Right, didn't think so. She said there's a camera in here—and she's been watching it. Says there's been a bunch of customers lately who have stored away diamonds and cash. *Clean* cash. Not like that shit in the other vault."

Deuce glanced at Truck, making sure he hadn't moved closer, then back at Mary. "The other reason this is happening is because of *you*, bitch. Jen told me all about how it was *you* who called the cops on my friends the last time they were here. She'd convinced the other bitches to hand over the cash in their drawers, but then the cops fucking showed up. Because of *you*, my friends are locked away. You called the pigs from inside this very vault! Fitting then, that this is where you'll learn the error of your ways. You should've just huddled back here and let my homies do their thing."

With that, Deuce stood up and pointed his pistol at the

phone in the corner. He fired a shot and the phone exploded, plastic pieces flying everywhere.

Mary shrieked and cowered down, covering her head and praying that Deuce wasn't about to turn the weapon on her or Truck.

Just then, five more men came into the safety-deposit vault. All five were carrying boxes with them. "Fucking awesome!" one of them exclaimed when he saw what Deuce had done. "Good shot! Guess no one is calling the cops *this* time." Then he laughed.

"Watch this," Deuce said with a smirk. And he turned the weapon toward the door to the vault. He shot several times, and two of the other men pulled out their own guns and joined him.

When the dust settled, Mary saw that the bullets had disabled the lock mechanism on the thick door. The metal of the door itself was hardly dented, but there was no way it would properly lock anymore. During the last robbery, Mary had been able to shut herself and the other women inside, but Deuce had effectively taken away that option.

"Where do you want us to put these boxes?" one of the men asked once Deuce had reloaded his pistol.

Mary turned to him—and saw what they were carrying for the first time.

Truck obviously noticed as well, because he said, "Fuck," in a low, disbelieving voice.

Deuce smiled. "That's right, Scarface. We're gonna blow this fuckin' place up. We don't need fucking keys to get into these boxes. We'll just blow them open."

Mary stared at all the men in horror. They put the boxes down and began to unpack them. She wasn't sure what she was looking at, but Truck obviously knew. His hands had curled into fists and it was clear he was pissed off. He wasn't trying to hide his emotions now.

"You're gonna get everyone in here killed," Truck told Deuce.

"Nah. Maybe you two, but it's all good as long as we get into the boxes and get the loot."

He smirked as he kept his pistol aimed at Mary. The other men began to pile what looked to Mary like little green boxes against the wall of safety-deposit boxes.

They jammed a wire into each one and started to go back for more of what she could only assume were explosives when Truck said, "Look, I'm in the Army. Demolitions. Let me help. I don't give a shit if you steal the crown jewels, I just don't want anyone to get hurt. And if your plan is to blow open the boxes to steal what's inside, you aren't going to achieve that with what you have going on there." He used his head to indicate the two gangbangers setting up the explosives.

"Yeah?" Deuce asked. "Why should I believe you?"

"Because I want to get out of this alive. And if you set that off," he gestured to the explosives once more, "like that, *none* of us will make it out of here in one piece. You've got enough TNT to take down this entire *block* of buildings. There'll be nothing left of anyone but tiny little pieces."

Deuce studied Truck for a long moment, then turned to the others. "Whaddaya say, Shoebaloo? Think we should let him help?"

Shoebaloo? Mary would've laughed if there was anything remotely funny about this situation.

"Fuck yeah, might as well use 'im. We want to get out of here with the fucking jewels *and* the money."

"Come here," Deuce said to Mary.

She blinked. "Me?"

"What'd I say, bitch? Come. *Here*."

Mary scrambled to her feet and tried to ignore the twinges of pain in her arm where he'd so cruelly gripped her earlier. She walked over to where Deuce was standing and the second she got close enough, he reached out and wrapped a hand around her throat.

Mary immediately reached up to grab his wrist, but he put his pistol to her forehead. She froze as her life flashed before her.

Deuce turned to look at Truck. "You make one move I don't like, and your girlfriend's brains will be splattered all over the inside of this vault. Hear me?"

"Yes," Truck said between clenched teeth.

"You better not be lying to me," he said. "The only chance you have of getting out of this alive is if you help us. Got it?"

"Got it," Truck said. "I'm not lying. I know what I'm doing when it comes to explosives."

Deuce nodded but didn't take the gun away from Mary's forehead. His hand was still wrapped around her neck as well, making it difficult, but not impossible, to suck in air.

Mary's eyes sought out Truck's and they met for a split second, before he looked away and bent to look into the boxes the other gang members had brought in.

What she'd seen in his gaze made her close her eyes and hardened her resolve. She didn't see regret. Or even worry. She saw unadulterated rage. She saw one pissed-off, deadly Delta Force soldier. She had no idea if he'd be able to get them out of this. She didn't doubt his skills when it came to the explosives, but it was still at least ten against one.

But she'd take those odds any day of the week...as long as the one was Truck.

For the first time in her life, Mary put her full trust in a man. She didn't worry about what she should do to get out of the situation. She wasn't concocting a Plan B in her mind. Truck would either get them out of this, or they'd die together. It was that simple...and that complicated.

Truck racked his brain to come up with a way to alert his team that he needed them, but nothing came to mind. Deuce had taken both his and Mary's cell phones, and since he'd disabled the phone inside the vault, that option was out.

He was on his own. He normally wouldn't care, he could handle himself just fine, but Mary was there. If he screwed up, *she* was the one who would pay the price, and that was unacceptable.

The asshole Deuce had finally moved the gun away from her forehead, but that didn't make him feel any better. Now he had one of his gangbanger friends guarding her...and the guy was extremely handsy. Every time the fucknugget touched Mary, Truck wanted to fucking kill him.

But he couldn't. Not yet. He had to bide his time.

Deuce had zeroed in on the one thing that could control him. Mary.

The TNT the gang had brought in could do some serious damage but they obviously had no clue how powerful the stuff was. The assholes packing it against the safety-deposit boxes had been using way too much. He hadn't lied; if the gang members had set it off, everything would've been blown to bits. He wouldn't stand by and risk Mary's life like that. He'd had to speak up. He didn't regret it, he just hoped he could rig the explosives to do the least amount of damage possible while still doing what Deuce wanted it to do... namely, open as many of the miniature safes as possible.

It took twenty minutes or so to remove most of the explosive materials the other men had placed against the side wall of the vault. He put it all back in the boxes and put the boxes by the door of the vault so the gang members could remove it from the general area. It took another ten to rig up the electric blasting caps and attach the wires. It was a crude job, but Truck thought it should work.

Truck stood up holding the detonator, which was connected to the wires coming out of the explosives. "There. It's done."

Deuce clasped his hands together in glee. "Awesome. Shoebaloo? Want to have some fun before we get our loot?"

Truck stiffened. He better not mean what it sounded like he meant.

The other gang member smiled and nodded. "Abso-fuck-ing-lutely."

"Snake, out. Get Cheese, Grass, and Nightshop in here."

"Want me to take this guy out too?" Snake asked, gesturing to Truck.

"No. He stays. I want him to watch. Keep your eye on him, Shoebaloo."

Every muscle in Truck's body tensed as the extremely overweight gangbanger raised his pistol and aimed it at him. They weren't going to hurt Mary in front of him. No fucking way.

He thought about setting off the explosives right then and there, but he couldn't risk Mary getting hurt. Then he thought about bum-rushing Deuce, but there was the pesky matter of the gun the other man was holding. Shit...he'd probably be okay if he got shot once, but there were more gang members on their way in. They'd fill him with holes, and then he'd never be able to help Mary.

Truck felt helpless—and it pissed him off even more.

Deuce went over to Mary and grabbed her shirt,

stretching the neck far enough that he could see the lace of her bra.

Truck growled and took a step toward the gangbanger and Mary—but stopped when Mary calmly reached into her shirt and pulled something out.

She held it out to Deuce and said with only a small tremor in her voice, "If you're hoping to get a look at my tits, let me make it easier for you. Here."

Deuce stared at her hand and dropped his own from her shirt. "What the fuck is *that*?"

"It's my boob," Mary said, as if she were offering him a piece of candy or something equally innocuous. She then reached inside her shirt again and pulled out the other one, and tried to give *that* to him too. "I had breast cancer. My tits tried to kill me so I had them chopped off. Now I wear fake ones. See? It's squishy, just like the real thing."

Truck would've laughed at the look on Deuce's face if there was anything remotely humorous about the situation. The gangbanger looked horrified and disgusted.

"You don't have any tits?"

In response, Mary pulled her shirt taut so it flattened to her chest, proving that no, she had no boobs at all.

"Are you one of those trans people or somethin'?" Shoebaloo asked in horror. "Are you a *dude*?"

Mary took a deep breath and shrugged. "Does not having tits make you trans?"

"She's got short hair, dude," Shoebaloo said. "I bet she's a guy."

"Fuck," Deuce said, stepping away from her.

Mary dropped her hands and let her inserts fall to the floor of the vault. She didn't cower from the gang members, but she didn't outwardly antagonize them either. She'd done exactly what she should've. It couldn't have been easy for her, and Truck wanted to take her in his arms more than he wanted to breathe. His hands shook with the effort it took to stay where he was.

"We gonna blow this shit up or what?" Truck asked, trying to turn the men's attention back to the matter at hand. Namely, their greed.

"I should kill it," Deuce said—and raised his pistol so it was once again pointed at Mary's head.

Truck's heart stopped beating.

Mary didn't say a word, kept her eyes bravely on Deuce's.

The inside of the vault was silent for a moment as everyone held their breath.

"Deuce, there are people outside on their cells—" a gang-banger started as he entered the vault. "What the fuck's going on?" he asked when he saw Deuce pointing his gun at Mary.

"Bang!" Deuce yelled, then laughed when Mary jerked in fright. "Fucking weirdo," he muttered, then kicked one of Mary's fake boobs into a corner. He turned to Truck. "If you've in any way fucked this up, your freak girlfriend is gonna die. Then *you're* gonna die. Got it?"

"Got it," Truck said as calmly as he could. "The explosives I've set should blow up the boxes, but not the wall behind it. I don't know what this vault is made of, but I'm assuming it'll absorb the shockwave well enough."

"For your sake, I hope so," Deuce said, then walked over to Truck and grabbed the detonator out of his hand. He motioned Shoebaloo and the other man out of the room with a tilt of his head.

Truck narrowed his eyes. "Why?"

"Because you and your freak are gonna be in here when it goes off. You better *hope* you didn't fuck it up," Deuce said. "If you disable it in any way when we leave and it doesn't go off, you'll be sorry." Then he saluted Truck with an evil grin and backed away with the crude, hastily built detonator in his hand.

"You can't leave us in here!" Truck blurted. He'd reduced the amount of explosives, yes, but it definitely wasn't safe to be in the vault when they went off.

"Watch me," Deuce sneered, then backed out of the vault. After making sure the wires were situated so the door could still shut most of the way, he closed them inside with the explosives.

Truck stood there staring at the closed door for one precious second, not believing the asshole had actually left them inside *with* the explosives. If they hadn't shot out the lock, he could've slammed the door shut, locking him and Mary safely inside the vault, and disconnected the detonator. But now there was no way to keep the thugs out.

Truck didn't have time to completely disable all the explosives, either. Even if he did, Deuce would come back in and shoot them both on sight.

Making a split-second decision, knowing at any time Deuce could hit the detonator, Truck moved *toward* the explosives rather than away from them.

He heard Mary shout his name in protest, but he ignored her, all his attention on the bricks of explosives. He quickly yanked two wires out of the bottom row of explosives, hopefully making the inevitable explosion survivable. If it was just him, he'd take his chance with Deuce and the others. But it wasn't. He had to think about Mary.

Truck turned away and rushed toward her. Other than a small "oof," she didn't make a sound, just clung to Truck as hard as she could. He picked her up off her feet and brought her to the far corner of the vault. Placing her down as gently as he could, he said, "Curl up into a ball, Mare. Cover your ears."

He waited until she did as ordered, then he rushed back for the table in the middle of the room. His only choice was to do what he could to protect them from the explosion that Truck knew was coming any second.

He knocked the now empty boxes and various other things he'd used to set up the explosives to the floor, then tried to lift the table—before realizing it was bolted down. He'd hoped to use it to hide behind. Swearing, he made his way back to Mary.

He gathered her into his arms and wrapped himself around her as best he could. He wanted every inch of her body covered. For the first time, Truck was glad he was as big as he was. He was made this way to protect his woman. He was a big-ass scary dude for this moment right here.

Her hands came up and covered his ears instead of her own, and without picking his head up from where it was tucked against her body, he did the same for her.

He was huddled over the woman he loved, praying harder than he ever had in his life, his entire body tense and waiting for the explosion, when Mary blew his mind.

"I love you," she whispered.

He didn't hear her, but he felt the words against his neck.

That was all she said. She didn't elaborate. Didn't go on and on about if they didn't make it out of that vault alive...she just wanted him to know.

It made her words all the more poignant and meaningful.

Truck opened his mouth to reciprocate, when the world around them exploded.

CHAPTER FIFTEEN

"Heads-up!" the Delta Force team commander, Colonel Colton Robinson, yelled when he stomped into the meeting room the team was in. "That downtown bank has been held up again. Robbery still in progress."

Within seconds, Ghost, Fletch, Coach, Hollywood, Beatle, and Blade were on their feet and running for the door. As they ran for their vehicles, their commander told them what he knew.

"Shit's hit the fan in the city. Fires, robberies, shots fired, and general chaos. The police are in way over their heads and can't keep up. Dispatch called me when they got reports of something going on at the same bank that was hit last month. Doors are locked and there's a crude note on the door saying something about training. But one customer saw someone with a gun inside and called it in."

"Fuck, is this the bank Mary works at?" Fletch asked.

"Truck's wife? Yeah," their commander said grimly.

"Truck was there having lunch with her today," Ghost said. "He called to tell me he's been getting some of his memory back. He remembers being married to her. Was going to see his doctor after lunch then let me know what he said."

"Could be good if he's inside," Hollywood said.

"Or bad," Beatle countered. "If whoever is in there knows he's Army, they might kill him outright."

"Truck doesn't exactly look nonthreatening," Blade added.

"Take the truck," the commander ordered, throwing a pair of keys to Ghost. "I'll round up the other team and we'll meet you there."

Ghost nodded but didn't bother to respond. He and the rest of his team peeled off and headed for the deuce-and-a-half truck assigned to their unit.

No one spoke much on the way to the bank. Partly because Ghost was driving like a bat out of hell and they were all holding on for dear life, but also because they were all worried about their friends.

Truck and Mary were like...peas and carrots. Peanut butter and jelly. Cookies and cream. They were meant to be together. They might've had their ups and downs, but no one ever doubted they were soul mates.

Mary didn't seem to see Truck's scarred face or his big scary countenance, and Truck didn't give one little shit about Mary's prickliness. From the first time Mary had stood up to Truck on behalf of Rayne, he'd known she was it for him.

No one could fathom one being without the other. It was unthinkable that *neither* would be around. It was bad enough Truck had gotten hurt and lost his memory, but at least he was there.

Little Annie needed him. She needed Mary to teach her how to take no shit from anyone.

Fletch's new baby needed his uncle Truck to look up to.

Casey needed Truck to help with her PTSD because he knew exactly what she'd been through in the jungle.

And Rayne. Fuck. Rayne needed Mary as much as Mary needed her. She wouldn't be the same if Mary didn't make it out of that bank in one piece.

No one spoke, lost in their own heads, until the truck pulled into the bank parking lot. Within minutes, a second deuce-and-a-half pulled in and Trigger, Lefty, Oz, Grover, Lucky, Brain, and Doc hopped out. They were all armed and quickly passed out the extra rifles they'd brought for Ghost's team.

Doc had just headed off to herd the bystanders away from the building when there was a loud explosion from inside the bank.

Without hesitation, the thirteen men headed for the doors. They hadn't had time to make a plan, but they didn't need to. They were Delta Force. They each knew what the others were going to do without having to ask. Without having to plan.

───────

Mary struggled to breathe. Truck was lying on top of her, covering her from head to toe. Her head was under his chest and he had his arms wrapped around it, protecting her from debris. Her ears were ringing, but that was the least of her worries.

She'd been so scared when Truck had walked toward the explosives rather than away from them after Deuce left them alone in the vault. But he hadn't lingered, had just fiddled with some of the wires before coming back for her.

Currently, she couldn't breathe. The smoke in the vault was thick enough she couldn't see anything, and Truck's weight was bearing down on her, heavier than when he'd first thrown himself around her.

"Truck," she croaked, then immediately started coughing.

He didn't respond. In fact, she couldn't feel him moving at all.

Frantic now, Mary wiggled until she was able to get an arm out from under her body. Not thinking about how close she'd come to being raped, or how she'd practically thrown her fake boobs at Deuce, or that he might return any second to gather what valuables he could, Mary kept doing whatever was necessary to get out from beneath Truck.

When she was finally able to get her torso out from under him, she realized why he was so heavy. Through the smoke, she saw the table he hadn't been able to manhandle over to their corner had been blown off the floor and had landed on top of him.

Using all her strength, Mary was able to shove it off his back. It thudded to the floor next to him—and Mary stared in dismay at the blood on the back of Truck's head.

"Shit, Truck," she wailed. "Not again!"

She wanted to turn him over, but didn't want to hurt his head any more than it already was. Her hand moved without thought and she pressed it against the cut on his scalp, feeling the wetness of the blood there. She carefully turned his head to the side so he could breathe, hoping like hell she was doing the right thing. That she wasn't paralyzing him for life.

She waved her hand in front of his face, trying to clear the air of the smoke. Mary continued to cough herself, not able to pull in a deep breath. "Come on, Truck. Breathe," she ordered.

The door to the vault was pushed open, but she didn't even turn around.

A flashlight flickered over her and Truck, but Mary's attention stayed on the man lying so still next to her.

"It worked!" Deuce shouted. "Motherfucker, it *worked*!"

Mary spared a quick glance up and saw that the explosives Truck had set had indeed done exactly what he'd designed them to do. The boxes that were directly next to the explosives were mangled beyond recognition, but the ones around those merely had their fronts blown off. She could see jewelry and cash strewn about on the floor. There were lots of papers too, but Deuce obviously didn't care about those.

He opened a backpack and began to stuff as much as he could into it. "Hey, Shoebaloo!" he yelled, looking up toward the door.

Mary looked toward the door instinctively—and gasped.

Ghost and Trigger were standing there.

She remembered the other Delta from the last time the bank had been held up. Neither man had made a sound. Both Deltas had their rifles up and pointed at Deuce.

Before she could do anything, Deuce had obviously looked to see what she'd gasped at and had dropped his backpack and raised his weapon to point it at her.

"Drop it," Ghost ordered.

"Now, motherfucker," Trigger added.

"Back away—slowly," Deuce countered. "Or I'll blow her away."

Mary held her breath, not liking that she was in the middle of the standoff.

She was fairly sure Ghost and Trigger would take care of Deuce, but just in case he got off a lucky shot, she threw herself over Truck's back, trying to protect him as much as she could.

Just as she'd covered him, Trigger fired and Deuce fell to the floor.

Unmoving. A hole in the middle of his forehead.

Ghost strode over and kicked away his pistol, even though the man was obviously dead.

"Dammit, Trigger," Ghost complained when he'd stood up. "You know how much paperwork we're gonna have to fill out now?"

Mary could hear the humor in his voice. She could tell that Ghost didn't really care that Deuce was dead. She'd make sure the cops knew that Trigger didn't have a choice. The gang member could've easily shot her, or Truck, or either of the Deltas.

Trigger shrugged. "Don't care. They call me Trigger for a reason." He smirked. "Trigger-happy, you know. Besides, he pointed a gun at Mary. No one points a fucking weapon at a teammate's woman and gets away with it."

Mary wanted to smile at the other man, but didn't have it in her at the moment. She looked at Ghost and said, "Truck won't wake up. The table hit him in the head and he's bleeding."

Ghost didn't say anything, but immediately came over to where she was kneeling over Truck. Trigger slipped out of the room, but Mary's attention was on the man lying still as death beside her.

"Lift your hand," Ghost said.

"He's bleeding badly," Mary told him.

"I can see that." Ghost looked her in the eye. "I got this, Mary. Trust me."

She nodded and slowly slipped her hand away from Truck's head. She watched as Ghost parted Truck's hair and checked out the wound before reaching into a pocket and pulling out a pair of gloves. He put one on his hand and covered the wound on Truck's head once more. "He's going to be okay, Mary. It's not that deep. A couple stitches at the most. Maybe even only one staple."

"Are you sure?"

"I'm sure," Ghost told her. "I'm more worried about his

brain. It hasn't been that long since he rattled it the first time."

Mary chewed on her lower lip and couldn't think of anything to say. Truck had to be all right. He *had* to.

Just as she had the thought, Truck moaned.

She leaned down and asked, "Truck?"

His eyes fluttered, and Mary said his name again.

This time his eyes opened all the way. He saw her, but then closed them again immediately. "Fuck," he swore. "Fuck, fuck, *fuck*."

"You're okay," Ghost told his friend. "Just a little bump on the back of the head."

As soon as he finished speaking, the rest of the team crowded into the vault. Fletch and Hollywood picked up Deuce and hauled him out, handing him off to someone Mary couldn't see. Beatle and Blade stood above her, Truck, and Ghost. Coach moved the table out of the way to give everyone more room.

"He okay?" Fletch asked.

"How're *you*, Mary?" Hollywood chimed in.

"Fine. It's Truck I'm worried about," Mary said, looking back down at the man she loved with all her heart. It was hard to believe she'd actually said the words. She didn't know if Truck had heard them or not, but lightning hadn't struck her down as a result of voicing them. She was taking that as a win.

"Can you all shut the fuck up?" Truck said in a whisper.

"Truck?" Ghost asked.

"My ears are ringing and my head hurts like a motherfucker," Truck said.

Mary bit her lip again in worry. He'd looked at her, but hadn't seemed to recognize her. Had he lost the rest of his memory? Had he relapsed? Fuck, she couldn't go through everything again.

Okay, that was a lie, she *could*, she'd do anything for Truck, but she sure as hell didn't want to.

"It's a good thing you've got such a hard head," Beatle quipped. "Otherwise your brain would be mashed potatoes by now."

Mary winced at the imagery. "You aren't helping," she muttered.

"If you're not careful, I'll get Casey to find some of those bullet ants and put them in your fucking bed, Beatle," Truck said.

No one said a word for a moment, letting Truck's words sink in.

"As if," Beatle said, extreme emotion making his voice thick. "She loves me."

"Yeah, she does," Truck said. Then his eyes opened again, and he stared at Mary. "Come here," he said, trying to lift his hand and pull her down to him, but he couldn't move that well with Ghost's hand on the back of his head, holding him still.

Mary leaned down until she was almost nose to nose with Truck. She held her breath as she stared into his beautiful brown eyes. "Yeah?"

"Reach into the front pocket of my jeans, babe."

He rotated his hip enough so Mary could get to his pocket. Confused, she did as he asked, not wanting to do anything that might stress him out. It was obvious how much pain he was in, and she had no idea how badly he was hurt.

She reached into his pocket, ignoring Hollywood's smartass comment about watching what she was grabbing down there, and pulled out a small velvet bag.

"Open it," Truck ordered.

Mary sat back on her heels and loosened the tie at the top. She turned it over, and two rings fell into her palm.

Frozen, Mary stared at Truck.

"Our wedding rings," Truck said. "I'm back from my mission, so we can both wear them again. I won't wear mine if you're not wearing yours."

"Truck," Mary whispered, overwhelmed.

"Help me sit up," Truck asked, and Ghost immediately helped Truck into a sitting position. His hand never left the back of his head and he had a firm grip on Truck's arm to keep him upright.

"I love you, Mary," Truck said. "I asked you to marry me because I love you. Not because of my insurance. Well, that too, but it was a convenient way to get you to say yes *and* to save your life."

"You remember," Mary said.

"All of it," Truck confirmed. "Every second. You're mine, Mary Laughlin. There's a wedding certificate somewhere that proves it. And I'm not letting you go. Ever."

Mary licked her lips and tried not to break down. She ducked her head and slipped her wedding band on the ring finger of her left hand. Then she reached for Truck's hand and put his ring back on his finger as well. He clasped her hand with his before she could pull away.

"Are you okay?" he asked.

Mary nodded. "You took the worst of it."

"Good." His eyes moved from hers to someone above her head. "I assume all the gangbangers are taken care of?"

"Of course," Blade reassured him.

"And Jennifer?" Mary asked. "She was in on it. She was dating Deuce."

"The cops have her in custody," Blade said.

"Good," Mary breathed.

"The paramedics should be here soon," Blade told her, and the second the words were out of his mouth, they heard sirens from the open door of the vault.

"We have to stop meeting in here like this," Truck told Mary, gazing into her eyes once more.

"I'm quitting. Effective right now," Mary returned.

"Good."

"Make way!" a feminine voice said. "Paramedics!"

"Oh, *fuck* no," Mary exclaimed. "No fucking way is she putting one hand on my man!"

The Deltas all chuckled but Mary was serious. When Ruth stepped into the vault, Mary stood and put her hands on her hips. "No. Turn the fuck around."

"Move aside," the other woman said snottily. "I need to see the patient."

Mary's hands curled into claws and she would've leapt on the woman, but Truck's teammates moved too quickly. Beatle grabbed her around the waist and Hollywood took hold of Ruth's arm and moved her backward and out of the vault altogether. Mary heard him informing her in no uncertain terms that she was going to see to the wounded gang members, not Truck.

"My Mary," Truck murmured and pulled on the leg of her pants.

She immediately forgot about Ruth and went back to her knees next to Truck. His eyes were only open in slits and it was obvious he was still in a great deal of pain. "Shit, sorry, Truck. I forgot about your head. I didn't mean to yell."

He smiled at her. "I love seeing you get all protective and jealous over me."

Mary rolled her eyes. "Whatever," she denied.

A man dressed in a navy-blue shirt and a pair of khakis

entered the room with his medical kit. "Everyone step away from the patient," he said in a tone that meant business.

Everyone but Mary and Ghost moved away from Truck, giving the paramedic room.

"Who're you?" he asked, looking at Mary.

"My wife," Truck answered for her. "She goes where I go."

"Fine, but I need to examine you first."

And with that, Ghost proceeded to tell him what he knew about Truck's injury.

Within five minutes, Truck was loaded on a gurney and was ready to be transported to the hospital. Mary refused to let go of his hand, and couldn't take her eyes away from their rings on their fingers.

Just as they were about to walk out of the vault, Truck called out, "Beatle?"

"Yeah, man?" Beatle answered.

"Be a pal and pick up my wife's boobs and make sure they get sterilized and returned to her at the hospital, would ya?"

Mary couldn't stop the laugh that escaped at the looks on the others' faces.

For the first time since her surgery, Mary didn't give one shit about what she looked like without her boob inserts or what others might think of her. She and Truck were alive, and he remembered. Everything else was unimportant.

CHAPTER SIXTEEN

Truck had been in the hospital for two days, which was two days longer than he wanted to be there. He was the worst patient, and Mary was about ready to strangle him. She'd spent almost every minute of those two days with him, refusing to leave his side. The doctors had taken MRIs and bloodwork and put him through a battery of tests to make sure his brain wasn't irreparably damaged.

But it seemed like Beatle was right. Truck had a hard head, thank God.

The night he'd been admitted, Mary had told him about Macie. How she'd shown up out of the blue at the bank before everything had gone down, and how she lived in nearby Lampasas and wanted to meet with Truck. He'd wanted to call her right then, but Mary realized she didn't have Macie's number. She'd given her number to Truck's sister, but hadn't gotten Macie's in return.

But it turned out that not having Macie's number wasn't an issue. She'd shown up at eight in the morning, before official visiting hours, having heard about the incident about the bank, probably from her hacker friend, and had burst into tears when she'd seen Truck lying in bed. She'd been extremely nervous at first, but eventually, with Truck's obvious enjoyment at seeing her, she'd relaxed. Mary had left them alone to talk and when she'd returned forty-five minutes later, they'd still been catching up.

Macie left when Truck's commander, Colt, had shown up. The other man had been glad to meet Macie as well, especially since he'd put out the initial feelers to try to locate her. Mary noticed the instant attraction the two seemed to have toward each other, but because Macie looked so nervous and unsure of herself, she didn't say anything about it. Truck's sister had left after they'd exchanged numbers, with Truck promising to call and catch up when he got home from the hospital. The long, heartfelt hug the siblings had given each other made tears form in Mary's eyes.

Then there had been a nonstop parade of people in to see Truck ever since his sister had left.

Truck tried to bribe Beatle to sneak him out of the hospital, but luckily Mary had returned from getting something to eat in the cafeteria just in time to put the kibosh on the "great escape."

Then Emily and Fletch had come by to see him. Rayne was at their house watching over the new baby so they could visit.

Annie had marched over to the side of Truck's bed and asked, "Do you know me now?"

Truck smiled. "Yeah, squirt. I know you."

"You 'member?"

"Yes."

And with that, Annie crawled onto Truck's bed and lay down next to him. She once again put her little hand over his cheek and snuggled in.

Mary would never forget the look on Truck's face. She'd

seen the exact same look when she was sick and hurting, and he'd snuggled next to her at night. Love.

The adults didn't try to make Annie move, they simply had a conversation as if she wasn't breaking hospital policy by lying in Truck's bed. Mary couldn't exactly protest, as she'd done the same thing the night before, crawled right up beside Truck and held him as tightly as he'd held her.

"We're postponing the baby-naming party one week," Emily informed them.

"You don't have to do that," Truck protested.

"Yeah, we do. We're not having it without you, so deal," Fletch said. "But no longer. I don't care if you go out and get yourself run over, we're not putting it off again. I can't keep calling my son 'Baby Fletch' forever."

Everyone chuckled and Annie lifted her head and looked at Truck. "His name is awesome."

"You know what it is, squirt?"

She nodded.

"I'll give ya a hundred bucks if you tell me right now," Truck teased.

But Annie shook her head. "Nope. My lips are sealed," she said, and pretended to zip them closed. Then she lowered herself back down next to Truck once more.

After another forty-five minutes of chitchat, the Fletchers left.

Mary was thankful for the steady stream of visitors who had come to see Truck. It kept him occupied and less grouchy. Kassie and Hollywood had also been there, and had brought Kate. Mary thought she was going to melt into a puddle of goo when Truck had taken the tiny infant into his arms. He looked down at her reverently and whispered, "No dating until you're twenty-five, little one."

Kassie and Mary had laughed, but Hollywood and Truck didn't. "I told her thirty," Hollywood informed his teammate.

"Sounds about right," Truck responded. Then told his friend, "She's perfect. Congratulations."

Hollywood beamed and had put his arm around his wife and responded, "Thanks."

When Harley and Coach visited, Harley let Truck try out the latest video game she was developing. That killed two full hours, allowing Mary to get a much-needed shower and break from her grumpy alpha man who was ready to go home.

Casey, Beatle, Blade, and Wendy all stopped by together. Wendy's brother, Jackson, had tagged along. They talked a little bit about the large group wedding they were planning, but Mary changed the subject quickly, not ready to talk about wedding ceremonies yet.

Of course Ghost and Rayne stopped in, and Chase and Sadie followed quickly behind them. Mary could tell Truck was enjoying seeing his friends, especially now that his memory had fully returned. But she could also tell when he started to get tired.

It wasn't until all seven of the Deltas from the other team showed up—and spent an hour harassing Truck for not being able to overpower all of the gang members singlehandedly and for having to be rescued—that Mary decided it was enough.

She shooed everyone out of the room, telling them it was time for Truck to take a nap.

Of course, that made all of the other Deltas laugh even harder and start up with the mommy jokes, but throughout it all, Truck didn't seem to give one little shit.

He'd simply said, "I'd much rather spend my time with Mary than with you assholes."

But it was the conversation with her doctor that had been the most emotional for Mary.

He'd heard she was in the hospital and had taken the time to track her down. He'd wanted to talk about her reconstruction, since she'd skipped her appointment.

The three of them, Mary, Truck, and her doctor, had a long conversation about her options. Truck asked a million questions about safety and long-term repercussions of having the implants inserted. He wanted to know the odds of the cancer returning, and whether having silicone implants would make those odds worse, or if they would somehow impede detection if the cancer did return.

By the time the doctor left, Mary still hadn't made a decision but she'd realized exactly how much she'd kept from Truck—and how amazing it was to have someone to talk to about it all. She'd kept a lot of things about her sickness from him, having felt awkward and uncomfortable sharing intimate details. Heck, she wasn't comfortable peeing without shutting the door; she wasn't going to discuss how she sometimes forgot what state Las Vegas was in when she got hot flashes, or ask him for help when the drain she had in suddenly started leaking all over her shirt.

When Truck had asked the doctor about sex and children, it hit home to Mary that she'd been treating Truck unfairly for months. She'd been holding back. Scared that he didn't really want to be with her. That he might *think* he cared about her, but if he knew all the gritty details about her disease, he'd bail.

He'd made it more than clear that he loved her and she was it for him. Mary just hadn't been paying attention. She'd been too convinced that he'd leave her, too busy keeping her shields up just in case he decided she wasn't worth the effort, like every other man in her life had.

She owed him an apology, but she had to get him home and settled first.

"Ready to go?" his doctor asked in a cheery voice as he came into Truck's hospital room late in the afternoon of his second day.

"A day and a half ago," Truck grumbled.

Mary hid her smile. Truck had been bitching about the fact that the doctor hadn't signed him out yet for the last hour and a half.

"You were incredibly lucky," the doctor said, not fazed in the least by his grumpy patient. "Pulling those wires right before the explosion saved your life. Only the upper explosives went off, blowing the table from where it was bolted to the floor. When it crashed into you, it protected you from the worst of the blast, but landing on your head wasn't exactly the ideal outcome. Since your noggin took two pretty intense hits only a few weeks apart, you need to be extremely careful for the next three months."

"Shit," Truck said.

"That's right. You're grounded. No missions for at *least* that long. We'll do another MRI in two months and make sure the bruising on your brain is gone and that everything looks okay in there. Then we'll give it another month just to be on the safe side. If you start having any of the side effects we talked about yesterday, you need to get in here to see me ASAP. I'm serious about this, Ford. Traumatic brain injury isn't something to mess around with. Blackouts, anxiety, aggression, repetition of words or actions, dilated pupils, nausea, sensitivity to light or sound, blurred vision—"

"I remember, Doc," Truck said, interrupting the litany of symptoms of a TBI.

"Right." He turned to Mary. "Just keep your eye on him. Soldiers frequently try to hide their symptoms because they feel like they should just tough it out or because they're embarrassed."

"Don't worry, I will," Mary told him.

"Good. Now, Ford, do you still have a headache?"

Truck nodded reluctantly.

"I don't think it's anything to be worried about right now. They should dissipate after a week or so. I'd like for you to stay in bed for another week, just to let your brain heal."

"Not happening," Truck said. At the same time Mary said, "I'll see to it."

The doctor grinned. "I don't envy you, young lady. Here's his prescription for painkillers. He'll need to come back in about a week to get those staples looked at and hopefully removed. They can get wet, but not immersed. No washing your hair, just brief rinses."

Mary nodded, knowing the next week was going to be tough on both her and Truck. Ways to keep him entertained ran through her head even as the doctor kept talking about what to expect in the upcoming week. She could have Annie come over after school, and make sure the guys took turns visiting him as well.

"If anything happens that concerns you, don't hesitate to contact me," the doctor said, and he handed Mary a business card. "That's my answering service, but just tell them that it's an emergency and they'll get to me right away and I'll call you back. Okay?"

Mary nodded, relieved that she'd have access to someone if Truck needed it.

"I'm fine," Truck said again.

"Right. And in case I didn't say it before...thank you for your service, and good job on stopping those assholes at the bank." Then the doctor turned and walked out of the room. Before Mary could say anything, his head popped back in.

"And wait for the nurse with the wheelchair, Laughlin. I know you manly types don't like to be pushed out of here, but it's policy. Give her a break, okay?" Then he disappeared once more.

Mary chuckled at the look on Truck's face. "It won't be so bad," she soothed.

It took the nurse another half hour to appear and once they were finally on their way, Mary breathed a sigh of relief. She'd brought up the subject of Truck going back to her apartment once he was out of the hospital, so she could look after him, but he'd said he was going home to his place in no uncertain terms, and she was coming with him.

Mary didn't protest too hard, since that's exactly where she wanted to be. She'd have to go back to her place and get her things. But first she'd get Truck settled, make him some dinner and, once he was asleep, she'd run back to her apartment. He'd never even know she was gone, especially when she forced him to take one of the pain pills the doctor prescribed.

She parked, and by the time she went around to help Truck out, he was already standing by the door.

Mary frowned. "You're supposed to let me help you," she told him, wrapping her arm around his waist.

"Why? My legs are just fine. It's my head that was hurt."

"Because," Mary groused. She ignored Truck's chuckle and walked with him to his apartment. She let him unlock the door, and when he held it open for her to go in ahead of him, she didn't even complain.

The second Mary walked into his apartment, she gasped.

She vaguely heard him close the door, but she didn't wait for him. With her mouth open in shock, she walked into his living area.

"How...when?" she stammered.

Truck pulled her back against his chest and rested his chin on top of her head. "When you were showering at the hospital, I talked to Ghost. He said the girls got your stuff packed up and helped you move out of my place after I lost my memory, so I told him he could move you back in, thank you very much. The guys did all the laboring, and the girls put everything away."

Mary's eyes filled with tears as she looked around. All of her things were back. The picture of her and Rayne was on the bookshelf. Her favorite blanket was on the back of the couch. Her knickknacks were everywhere, and she even saw that her coffeepot was on the counter in the kitchen.

"Truck—"

"You're my wife," Truck interrupted. "You belong here with me. The second I walked in here after losing my memory, I knew something was wrong. It *felt* all wrong. It was too empty, too...something. *You* were missing, Mare. You and all your things. You've made this place a home for me. They might have removed your things, but your presence could never be removed from my life. That first night, when I lay in my bed alone, I felt off, but I couldn't figure out why."

Mary took a deep breath then turned in Truck's arms and looked up at him. "Are you sure?"

Instead of answering her, Truck said, "I found your journal."

"What?"

"I was really frustrated when you left that last time, and I kinda went a little crazy. I kicked things and knocked them over like a little kid. I flipped my mattress, and it dislodged your journal that was hidden under it."

"Oh, shit," Mary whispered, and lowered her eyes to the buttons on his shirt.

Truck wouldn't let her hide. He put a finger under her

chin and forced her gaze back up to his. "I said it back in the vault and I'll say it again. I asked you to marry me because I love you, Mary. Yes, I wanted you to be able to use my insurance, but that was just an excuse. I would've said anything to make you mine for real."

When she didn't respond, he smirked. "No comment?"

Mary shook her head.

He got serious again. "I love you, Mary. I love your snark. I love the way you stand up to people. I love that you have Rayne in your life. I'm sorry that you doubted my love for one second. Do not be embarrassed about puking in front of me, or anything else about your cancer. I love you exactly how you are. Boobs, no boobs, hair, no hair. It doesn't matter to me."

"I...you're important to me too, Truck. But...the words. They're really hard for me."

"I know," Truck said.

Mary shook her head and gripped his shirt tighter. "I want to say them, but I can't. They freak me out."

"You said them in the bank," Truck reminded her.

Mary grimaced. "I thought we were about to die," she said. "That it might be my only chance to tell you."

"Mare, you tell me every day that you love me," he said. "Your actions speak loud and clear. I don't need the words."

"But it's not fair," Mary protested.

"Do you love me?" Truck asked. "All you have to do is nod or shake your head."

Mary pressed her lips together and nodded.

"That's all I need," Truck reassured her. "Come on," he said, turning her and taking her hand in his. He led them to the bedroom and went inside. Then he turned and looked at the wall.

Mary stared up at their wedding certificate.

"I knew something was missing from there," Truck said quietly. "I'd lay in bed at night and stare at that spot and try to force my brain to give it up. The happiest day of my fucking life was the day you said I do, Mare. I'd face a hundred gangbangers and blow up a thousand more banks for the right to have you by my side. I'll never cheat on you. I'll never decide I don't want you anymore. I'll fight tooth and nail to keep you safe and happy. If that means I have to go toe-to-toe with fucking cancer again, so be it."

Mary lifted a hand and placed it on his cheek. "I believe you."

"Good."

They stared at each other for a long minute before Truck sighed. "I hate to admit this, because I have a feeling you'll be throwing it in my face for quite a while, but I need to lie down."

Mary blinked, then shook herself out of the haze she'd been in. "Shit! Of course. Are you dizzy? Come on, the bed's right here."

Truck chuckled. "I'm not about to keel over, woman. Chill."

"I just...I'm worried about you. Maybe I should sleep on the couch tonight," she fretted.

"Absolutely not," Truck said sternly. "I know you worry about me, and you have no idea how much that means to me." Truck sat on the bed and pulled her to him. Holding her hands and looking at her, he said, "But there's no way I want to spend even one night away from you if I can help it."

"I think I can manage that," Mary said with a smile. "Are you hungry? I can make you something to eat."

"I could eat," he told her as he settled back on the bed.

Mary hurried out to see what was in the kitchen that would be easy to make. She wasn't the best cook, but she'd be able to come up with something to keep him satisfied. Later, when he was more up to it, they could cook together. For most of the time she'd lived with him, he'd done all the cooking, simply because she either wasn't hungry or was too sick to do it herself.

Mary still wasn't convinced she would make a good wife, but she'd do her best. She trusted Truck, and that was what mattered. Smiling, she opened the fridge and bent over to see what there was to eat.

CHAPTER SEVENTEEN

It was the night before Fletch and Emily's naming party, and Truck had decided that Mary's time was up. The first two days after he'd gotten out of the hospital, he'd done a lot of sleeping. Then his days had been filled with shooting the shit with his friends. He knew Mary had arranged the visits and he loved her even more for it.

She and Rayne had gone grocery shopping one day and had bought enough food to feed an army. And that's pretty much who had been at his apartment in the last week. An army of their friends. Little Annie spent the night and they'd watched *Cinderella*, twice. Another night, Mary had invited Trigger over and the three of them talked until midnight before the other Delta had finally excused himself to go home.

Even Macie had come over for dinner. Truck hadn't really gotten a good explanation of what had happened all those years ago, and why she'd never contacted him, but she had definitely changed over the years. Of course, it *had* been two decades since he'd last seen her, when they were both basically still kids, but she used to be outgoing and smiled nonstop. Now she seemed nervous and uneasy, even around him, which he hated. He found himself doing everything he could to keep conversation light and easy, not to bring up anything that might distress her.

He wanted to know everything about his sister. About her job designing websites—primarily for authors, but really for anyone who contacted her. He wanted to know why she wasn't married. He wanted to know everything about her high school years, and her college ones too. He *really* wanted to know about their parents. If she still was in touch with them, if they'd had anything to do with her not talking to him after he'd left home, as he suspected.

Basically, Truck wanted to know every little detail about her life, but he could tell that asking anything too personal would make her clam up. So he kept things simple, talked mostly about himself and his teammates. He even talked about his commander and the other Delta Force team he was in charge of, as Macie seemed especially interested when he brought up Colonel Robinson.

There would come a time when he'd need to have a heart-to-heart with Macie, and they'd need to clear the air once and for all. They'd have to discuss what happened all those years ago. But for now, he was content having her back in his life.

There hadn't ever been so many people in and out of their apartment, and Truck suspected Mary was doing her best to avoid being alone with him, especially at bedtime. She'd told him one evening that she was trying out a new recipe, and she'd be in bed soon. Of course he'd been fast asleep by the time she'd finished.

Another night, she'd called Rayne just as he got off the couch to head to bed, and then she'd had the nerve to spend the night on the couch.

He was done.

Truck knew Mary was freaking out about sleeping with him, but she was done avoiding him. She needed to face this hurdle head on, like she did just about everything else in her life, including her job.

She hadn't needed to resign from the bank, as the regional manager put everyone on paid leave until they could rebuild the vault and reassess their security measures. They'd reassured all the employees that if they wanted to "pursue other options," the bank would do whatever they could to help them.

Mary had been brainstorming what she wanted to do with Rayne and the others, but she hadn't made a decision. She was moving on with her work life, now it was time to move on with her personal life too.

Mary was currently sitting on the other side of the couch from him, her attention stubbornly fixed on the television. She was flicking channels, but Truck could tell she wasn't really paying attention.

He stood, and hated that Mary flinched slightly, but he ignored her discomfort, walked right up to her, and leaned over and picked her up.

"Truck!" she exclaimed, wrapping her arms around his neck. "Your head! Put me down!"

"No," he said calmly. "It's time for bed."

"I have things I need to do first," she said somewhat desperately.

"No, you don't."

"Yes, I do."

"Nope."

"Trucker," she warned, tensing.

Truck continued to ignore her and walked into their bedroom and put her down in front of the bathroom. "You've got five minutes to do what you need to do in there."

"And if I need more time?" she asked belligerently, hands on her hips.

Truck leaned over and ran a finger down her nose. "Then I'm comin' in to get you."

She huffed out a breath and entered the bathroom, slamming the door behind her.

Truck merely smiled. He loved when Mary got riled up. It was a much more honest reaction than the careful concern she'd been showing him for the last week.

He felt much better. His headache was almost all the way gone. The staples itched, rather than hurt, and he felt much stronger. There was no way he wanted to take three months off, but if he could break through the barrier Mary had put up between them, it would be fun having her all to himself without having to worry about being sent out of the country on a mission.

Truck hurried to the guest bathroom and did his thing before climbing into the bed. He'd taken off his shirt and sweats, but kept on his boxers. They'd be going too, but he needed to tame his skittish wife first.

Mary opened the bathroom door with twenty seconds to spare and stood there uncertainly.

Truck sucked in a breath at what she was wearing. He'd put the nightie on the bathroom counter earlier that night, but it looked a hundred times sexier on her than on the hanger.

Her short brown hair was in disarray on her head, the pink streak calling to him like a siren's song. Her hair had grown in much thicker after the second round of chemo. He loved how it felt tickling his palm when he held her to him.

She had on a black chemise with spaghetti straps. She was still too slender, at least in his opinion. He could see her collarbones clearly. Truck made a mental note to make sure she ate three good meals a day...and had plenty of snacks. The black garment hit her at mid-thigh and he could see the red polish on her toes. She never wore it on her fingernails, but she loved painting her toenails.

"Take a picture, it lasts longer," she quipped.

Truck knew she was nervous, and he smiled. "Come here," he said, holding out a hand.

She hesitated, but Truck didn't rush her. She'd come to him in her own time. That was one of the things he loved most about her.

Finally, she took a deep breath and padded across the room until she could touch him. She placed her hand in his and Truck felt his heart lurch in his chest. Everything this woman did slayed him. She was nervous and uneasy, but she still showed him how much she cared by trusting him.

Truck brought her hand up to his mouth and kissed it. Then he scooted over in the bed, pulling her up onto the mattress after him.

Mary lay back and yawned huge. "Boy, I'm tired. I can't wait for tomorrow. I wonder what Em and Fletch named their son. Don't you? I mean—"

Her words stopped abruptly when Truck placed his hand on her belly.

She immediately grabbed his wrist with both hands and bit her lip as she looked up at him.

"I love you," Truck said gently. "I've seen you naked, Mare. I smoothed that lotion all over your chest when you were going through radiation. I slept with my head on your belly when you were in so much pain you didn't want me anywhere near your chest, yet still wouldn't let me move away from you. We've cried and laughed together. We faced cancer head on, and beat it, *together*. When I lost my memory, you didn't give up on us. In fact, you went toe-to-toe with that paramedic bitch. Nothing means more to me than knowing you were willing to stick by me when I didn't remember who you were. Don't be afraid of me after everything we've been through. I love you and would never hurt you. Physically or emotionally."

"It's different now," she whispered, not removing her hands from his wrist and staring at him with her big brown eyes.

"Because you're not sick? Because you want me as much as I want you?" Truck asked.

Mary blinked in surprise but then nodded.

"Would you feel better with the lights out?"

She immediately shook her head. "No. It makes no sense, and it's totally fucked, but I want to see you. I've dreamed about you making love to me for so long, there's no way I want to miss one second of the experience. But, I'm scared that you're going to take one look at me and not be able to get it up. Between the weight I lost and my flat-as-a-pancake chest...I'm not pretty."

"The hell you aren't," Truck said in a huff. "Let go."

Surprisingly, Mary loosened her grip on his wrist. He immediately got up on his knees and straddled her. He slowly pulled her nightie up over her hips. Mary didn't move to help but he didn't need her to. When the material was bunched at her belly, he kept pushing it up and over her chest.

Truck didn't take his gaze from hers. She lifted her arms and allowed him to remove the garment altogether. The second it cleared her head, Truck leaned over her. He saw her struggle to keep from covering herself. She grabbed onto his biceps instead. Her fingers didn't come close to touching around his large muscles, but she clung to him as if he was the only thing between her and certain death.

"Breathe, babe," he said softly, then leaned down and

kissed her forehead. He moved to the tip of her nose. Then her cheeks. He skipped her lips and moved his mouth to her left ear. "Feel how hard I am for you, Mary. *You.*"

And he was. His cock was as hard as steel inside his boxers. He had a feeling the tip was sticking out through the slit in the material, but he didn't bother to adjust himself. He lowered his hips down far enough that she could feel him against her belly, then he continued his caresses.

Truck nuzzled the sensitive skin under her ear, then moved his nose to her neck and inhaled deeply.

He felt more than heard her chuckle under him and he relaxed a fraction. "That's it, just relax. It's me. I'd sooner shoot myself in the head than hurt you in any way, shape, or form."

Taking a risk, Truck scooted farther down her body and laid his head on her chest. He could hear her heart beating way faster than normal and her breaths came out in rapid puffs, but he felt one of her hands rest on the back of his head, staying clear of his injury as she held him to her.

"I can't feel anything," she said after a while. "The nerves are completely dead. So if you're thinking about kissing me there, or otherwise trying to arouse me that way, don't."

Truck lifted his head and took her face between his palms. "It's okay. I know other places where you're sensitive." And with that, he took her earlobe between his teeth and bit down. He felt her shudder under him, and he smiled.

Deciding he'd teased her long enough, Truck grabbed a pillow and shoved it under her hips. Then he eased himself down her body, still staring into her eyes as he settled between her legs. He could smell her excitement but he still didn't look at the core of her.

"That first night I spent here after coming home from Africa, I smelled the most amazing thing when I got into bed. I ripped off the pillowcase and held this pillow to my face, trying to get more of it. I didn't know what it was or why I was so desperate for it until I read your journal. You masturbated on my pillow," he accused.

For the first time that night, Mary smiled. It was coy and a little bit naughty. She shrugged. "I couldn't help it. I wanted you so bad, but didn't know how to go about changing the nature of our relationship. I had to do something to get relief."

"Consider our relationship changed," Truck said before lowering his eyes. He took in the pulse hammering in her throat. He took in the still slightly red skin of her chest where she'd been burnt by the radiation. He was actually a little surprised to see how good her skin looked compared to the last time he'd seen it after the treatments. It was still a bit odd to see her chest completely flat, but it evoked feelings of love and pride instead of disgust. His Mary was one tough chick. When shit happened in her life, she met it head on and didn't let anyone, or any disease, dictate how she was going to live.

He took in the sight of her clearly definable ribs, her concave belly, her cute belly button. Then he ran his fingers through the tufts of pubic hair above her slit.

"Truck," she whined, and arched her back while spreading her legs wider.

He took the hint, and didn't hesitate to use his fingers to separate her folds and lick her from her slit to clit.

The first taste of Mary on his tongue made him moan. Truck knew he'd remember this moment forever. He might have made Mary his in the eyes of the law, but *this* was the date he'd celebrate as their anniversary from now until he was no longer on this earth. She tasted so fucking good.

Using his hands to hold Mary's thighs open as far as was

comfortable for her, Truck buried his face between her thighs and concentrated on making her come.

It didn't take long. The second Truck latched onto her clit and started a combination of sucking and licking, Mary began to thrash. Her hips pressed up toward him, then shied away as her orgasm got closer and closer.

"Truck, oh my God...more...there...oh, shit...too sensitive...don't stop...yes, right there. Fuuuuuck!"

And with that, she lost it. Her thighs shook, her belly tightened, her head went back, and she exploded.

Truck shifted and eased one of his thick fingers inside her body even as he kept licking the small bundle of nerves. She was slick and hot, but so fucking tight. She squeezed his finger and began to hump against it even as she came a second time.

Her wetness was all over his face when Truck finally lifted his head, and he reveled in it. There was a wet spot on the pillow under her ass and his finger and palm were also soaked.

Truck moved up and over her, leaving her ass propped up as he leaned to grab the condom he'd placed on the table next to the bed in preparation. He ripped open the foil and shoved his boxers down under his balls. He rolled on the condom then waited for Mary to open her eyes and look at him.

The second she did, he notched his cock to her opening and pushed just the head inside.

She groaned and stretched her arms over her head and arched her back.

"I want to take you bare at some point," he told her.

"Okay."

"We'll talk to your doctor about the best form of birth control for you."

"I'm not sure I can have kids," Mary warned him. "Or that I even want them."

"All the more reason why it's important to talk to your doctor," Truck said, holding himself still by sheer force of will.

"Do you want kids?" she asked.

"I want what you want. If that's kids, then I'll do whatever it takes to give them to you. If you want a house full of dogs, cats, and hermit crabs, then that's what we'll have."

Her eyes sparkled with unshed tears, and Truck knew they'd have to have this conversation again at some point, but when his cock was desperately throbbing and he wanted to be balls deep inside her *wasn't* the time. "I'm big," he warned.

"I can take you," Mary said immediately.

"I'll go slow."

"I can take you," Mary repeated. "Fuck me, Truck. I've been waiting for fucking ever."

"That's my line," Truck snarled. "From the second I heard you berating Ghost for not looking for Rayne faster after their one-night stand, I wanted you. When I put my hand over your mouth and you turned around and saw me, you didn't flinch. You didn't even look at my fucking scar. I knew then you were mine. I can't explain how I knew, but through everything that's happened between then and now, I never doubted that. I did whatever it took to have you right here."

Truck pushed inside her body a bit more and moaned. She was incredibly tight, and he knew he wasn't going to last long this first time.

"Your scar is just what's on your skin, it's not who you are," Mary whispered, even as she hiked her knees up higher.

Truck slipped inside her another inch.

"Just as yours aren't who *you* are," Truck said between clenched teeth.

"If you don't stop talking and fuck me, I can't be responsible for my actions," Mary told him.

Moving a hand between their bodies, Truck used his thumb to manipulate Mary's clit. She arched even more, and as she clenched around his dick, he pushed to the hilt inside her.

Truck immediately froze. His thumb stopped moving on her clit and he threw his head back and held his breath, trying to gain some control. He could feel her muscles like a vise around his cock. She was so hot, and nothing in his entire life felt as good as being inside her. *Nothing.*

When he felt as if he could move without immediately blowing his wad, Truck looked down at Mary and saw her smirking up at him. He loved the mischievous look on her face, loved how satisfied she looked.

Her arms were still above her head, opening herself up to him. She might've been unsure about them making love earlier, but if her posture and relaxed position under him were an indication, she was anything but unsure right now.

"That was close, wasn't it?" she asked smugly.

Truck grinned. "Yup. The second I felt you clamp down on my cock, I wanted to blow. Wanted to fill you up with my come until it overflowed and you were dripping with it."

That wiped the smug look off her face. It was replaced by a look so passionate and needy, Truck groaned.

"I never thought we'd end up here," Mary said seriously, bringing her arms down to clasp around his neck. "I mean, even when we got married, I never imagined that you would want me like this."

"I've always wanted you like this," Truck said. "Always."

"Can you deal with *this*?" Mary asked, her chin dipping to indicate her chest.

Instead of answering, he asked, "Can you deal with me being Delta, and the possibility that one of these days I might come home with something more serious than a banged-up head and a few more scars like the one on my face?"

"Of course," she said with a huff.

"Right. So why would you think *I'd* not be able to deal with the aftermath of your cancer?"

Her mouth opened and closed. Then opened again. Truck could see the conflict in her eyes. He leaned down and kissed her hard on the lips. "Don't," he whispered when he was light-headed from lack of air. "I know you love me, you don't need to say it."

"I don't deserve you," Mary said.

"Bullshit," Truck retorted. "We deserve each other. Who else would put up with us?"

"True," she agreed. "Now...will you please fuck me already?"

Truck smiled. "With pleasure."

His hips drew back and then, without warning, he plunged inside her.

Mary groaned and threw her head back again.

"Hands back over your head," Truck ordered.

She complied immediately, fisting the sheet under her hands as she arched her back.

Truck pushed up to his knees and lifted Mary's ass. His first few strokes were smooth, but he soon lost control and began to pound into her. Not so out of it that he didn't want her to get off too, his hand went back to her clit and he roughly thumbed it while he fucked her.

Within seconds, he felt his balls tighten and knew he was on the verge of coming.

"I love you, Mary," he grunted.

Love you, Mary mouthed as she stared up into his eyes. She might not have said the words aloud, but the sentiment behind her actions went straight to his heart.

And that was all it took. Truck shoved into her as far as he could get and frantically thumbed her clit. He began to come a heartbeat before her. And the way her body clenched around his cock made his orgasm all the more intense.

They were both breathing hard by the time Truck recovered enough to straighten his legs behind him. The pillow under Mary's ass stayed in place as he pulled out of her with a groan and put his head back on her chest. Truck felt her playing with his short hair. His head was back to throbbing, but he didn't dare mention that to the woman under him. She'd have a pill stuffed down his throat so fast he wouldn't know what hit him.

"Thank you," Mary said softly.

That made Truck lift his head. He rested his chin on his hand on her chest and asked, "For what?"

"For seeing *me*, and not a breast cancer survivor."

"You've always been just Mary to me," Truck told her. "A pain-in-my-ass Mary."

She rolled her eyes and shook her head. "Whatever."

Truck laid his head back down. He should probably get up and take care of the condom before it made a mess all over the sheets, but he couldn't summon the energy.

They fell asleep that way. Truck woke sometime later and got up and cleaned himself. He brought a warm washcloth into the bedroom and got a sleepy Mary cleaned up as well. Then he took the pillow out from under her ass and smiled as he turned it over and stuffed it under his head. He'd do laundry tomorrow, but he hoped her scent would permeate the pillow itself so he'd always have her with him.

Not bothering to get dressed, and feeling thrilled beyond belief that Mary didn't make any move toward her chemise, he pulled her into his arms.

The redness on her chest still looked painful, even though

Mary insisted she couldn't feel anything from her collarbones to the bottom of her rib cage.

He had absolutely no opinion about the reconstruction of her breasts, except that he wanted what was safest for her. She could get Dolly Parton boobs or a modest B cup, he didn't care. He also didn't care if she decided she didn't want to go through reconstruction at all. He could totally see her sporting a beautiful tattoo across her chest to celebrate her femininity and to say fuck you to the cancer. Whatever she wanted, it didn't matter. He'd love her no matter what her decision.

Truck kissed the side of Mary's head and smiled when she grumbled and turned her back to him. He snuggled up behind her, loving how she pushed her ass against his groin. Mary was prickly, but she was his. That was all that mattered.

CHAPTER EIGHTEEN

Truck held Mary's hand tightly as she knocked on Emily's door with her free hand. They were late, but he didn't think anyone would say anything about it. Mary looked like she'd recently been fucked to within an inch of her life...and she had.

He'd woken up horny as hell and ready to show his wife how they were going to spend the next three months of his recuperation. He'd eaten her to an orgasm, then put her on her hands and knees and taken her from behind. Then he'd dragged her into the shower, and she'd gone to her knees and shown him that she wasn't going to let him call all the sexual shots in their marriage, which was more than all right with him.

Truck would've gotten them out of the apartment on time if she hadn't teased him when they were making breakfast. In retaliation, he'd spread her out on the table and feasted.

"We're late," Mary mumbled.

"Yup," Truck said without an ounce of remorse.

Mary glared at him. "You could at least attempt to look sorry," she scolded.

Truck buried his nose into the skin at the side of her neck and wrapped an arm around her waist. "But I'm not. And our friends are gonna take one look at us and forgive us for being late."

"They will not, Trucker, you better not—"

"Where have you been?" Emily asked huffily when she opened the door. "Everyone's waiting to...oh..." Her voice trailed off when she got a good look at them.

"Hi, Emily," Truck said, straightening but not moving his arm from around Mary's waist. "Sorry we're late."

"That's okay...we were just sitting around talking anyway...come in."

Truck winked at Mary when Emily's back was turned and she rolled her eyes at him.

They walked into the house, and Truck marveled once more at the view from the living room. There were floor-to-ceiling windows that overlooked miles of Texas's rolling hills. He had to admit that he'd been bummed when he remembered Fletch's old house. The team had a ton of great memories there, not to mention Fletch's great neighbors, but he didn't blame his teammate for wanting to start anew.

There may have been a lot of good memories in his old house, but there were also a lot of bad ones too. Scary ones. And Fletch had told him that he didn't want his baby anywhere near whatever bad vibes might still be lingering around the old place.

He was surprised to see Fish and Bryn there. Smiling, Truck went over to the couple.

"Fish! I didn't know you were going to be here!"

"Wouldn't miss it for the world."

"Well, we almost *did* miss it," Bryn corrected. "We had tickets for last weekend, but when you got hurt we had to cancel them, and it was almost impossible to get another flight. There aren't any direct flights from Spokane to here, so we had to fly to Denver, then Dallas, then we had to rent a car to drive down here."

Truck smiled. He liked Bryn. He knew her Asperger's made it hard for her to understand the right things to say and do socially, but to him she was refreshing. He never had to worry about where he stood with her. She'd tell him straight out. "Well, I'm glad you made it anyway. How long are you staying?"

"Probably only another couple of days. Bryn needs to get back. She's giving a presentation at the local library on preppers."

"Really?" Truck asked, raising an eyebrow in surprise. She'd gotten in trouble a while back because she'd gone out to meet who she'd thought was a prepper, but in reality was a mentally unbalanced domestic terrorist. Truck hadn't been able to assist in saving her because he was marrying Mary, but he'd heard all the details after the fact.

"Really," Bryn confirmed. "Most preppers are misunderstood. They aren't bad people. A little paranoid, but what they do is fascinating, and the general population can learn a lot about sustainable living and being prepared from them."

"We'll let you say hi to the others," Fish said with a smile.

Truck nodded and steered him and Mary farther into the room. He saw that they were definitely the last ones to make it to the party. Rayne and Ghost were standing near one of the windows holding plates and talking to Chase and Sadie. Harley and Coach were sitting on one of the couches. Hollywood was standing behind Kassie, who was in a large, comfortable-looking leather chair, holding little Kate. Beatle and Casey were in the attached kitchen, and Blade and Wendy were being entertained by Annie.

But when Annie saw Truck and Mary enter, she popped up and ran over to them. "You're finally here!" she yelled enthusiastically.

"So we are," Truck said with a smile.

Mary greeted Annie with sign language. The little girl responded in kind, and they smiled at each other before Mary gave her a big hug.

"Are you hungry? We have a ton of food. Mommy didn't make it though. She's been too tired. My brother's keeping her up late and Daddy says it's a good thing there's takeout, otherwise we'd starve."

Truck tried to hide his smile behind his hand, but knew he'd failed when Emily said, "Thanks for spilling all the Fletcher secrets, baby."

Everyone chuckled at that. Truck settled into the corner of the couch and pulled Mary down next to him. Conversation started up again, and he got an update on what was going on at work. He laughed when Ghost told him Trigger and the other Delta Force team were more than happy to take up the slack with missions while he was out of commission. None of the men on the other team were married or seriously dating. Truck remembered when he and the others were the same. They lived for missions and hadn't given settling down a second thought.

Looking around, Truck couldn't imagine ever going back to that life. He might have forgotten the last three years for a while, but nothing felt better than seeing the families he and his friends were making. And having Macie back in his own life was like icing on a big chocolate cake.

He listened to the general chitchat going on around him and closed his eyes in contentment and let the relaxed and happy vibe settle into his gut.

"You okay?" Mary whispered.

"More than," Truck told her, opening his eyes and looking into hers. "I'm happy. Being with *you* makes me happy. But also, being here with our friends, seeing how content and settled everyone is, makes me happy."

She smiled up at him and Truck felt his dick twitch. Yeah, he had a feeling he'd never get tired of making love to his wife.

"Everyone settled and comfortable?" Fletch asked in a loud voice, addressing the room in general.

When everyone agreed, and after Beatle and Casey left the kitchen to join them, Fletch took his son from Emily's arms and held him close to his chest as he spoke. "Thank you all for coming today, and a belated thank you for being there for us when Em went into the hospital. Knowing you all were there meant the world to us both."

Everyone nodded, and Truck tightened his arm around Mary and kissed the side of her head.

"I know everyone's been wondering what we've named this little bean." He looked down at his son with a gentle smile. Emily went to his side and Fletch put his arm around her shoulders. Annie snuggled up against her mother, and the family of four stood in front of their best friends for a long moment.

Then Fletch cleared his throat and continued, "We had quite a few family conversations about names. Annie, of course, refused to participate in any kind of discussion that included female names." He stared down at his little girl with mock disapproval, and she giggled. "But we had quite a few male names to weed through and narrow down."

"I thought Franklin was perfect," Annie said with a little grin.

Everyone chuckled, as they knew Frankie was her "boyfriend" who lived out in California.

"We thought about honoring our parents, but that didn't feel right," Fletch went on. "I refused to name my child after me, because he would've gotten beaten up on the playground every day if his name was Cormac."

Everyone laughed again.

"I wouldn't have let that happen!" Annie protested. "I'll beat up anyone who dares hurt my brother!"

"Shhh," Emily soothed. "No one is gonna be hitting anyone."

Fletch reached over and smoothed a hand down Annie's head. "Anyway, so we threw out a few more names and none really seemed to fit. After much back and forth, we decided on Ethan."

Everyone oohed and aahed and said the name was perfect.

"Now, Daddy?" Annie asked once everyone had quieted down.

"Yeah, squirt, now."

Annie walked over to where Truck and Mary were sitting on the couch. "I liked Ethan, but he needed a middle name. Mommy and Daddy suggested lots and lots of names, but none really felt right. I thought and thought and thought about what little Ethan should have as his middle name. It needed to be something strong. Something that would remind him to always be brave. He needed a hero's name."

Then the little girl climbed up into Truck's lap. Mary shifted, giving her room. Truck put both his arms around Annie and didn't take his eyes from hers.

"We named him Ethan Ford," Annie said. "All of Daddy's friends are heroes, but you're the first person I thought of. We couldn't name him Ethan Truck, but your real name is just as good, even if it's not as cool."

Truck blinked. His eyes went from Annie to Fletch and Emily. His chest got tight, and he swallowed several times, trying to keep the emotion at bay. He thought he'd conquered it—but then Annie put her hand on his scarred cheek.

"You're brave. You tooked care of me when the bad guys came and stole me and Mommy. You take care of everyone, and even if you're hurt, you just keep doing it. That's what I want for my brother. I want him to know he was named after the strongest person ever. He probably won't grow up as big as you, but that's okay, because me and you will be there to beat up anyone who's mean to him."

"Squirt," Truck whispered, but couldn't say anything else.

Tears filled his eyes, and he couldn't have prevented them from falling if his life depended on it. He was a big bad Delta Force soldier, and this little slip of a girl had brought him to his knees.

"I'm glad you and Mary are together now. I'm not as dumb as people think I am. I know when she was babysitting me and you came over that you guys liked each other, but since she was sick, you were both pretending you didn't. But she's better now. So you can get married like Daddy and Mommy did and live happily ever after."

Truck heard Mary sniff from next to him, but couldn't take his eyes off of the precious little girl in his lap. He cleared his throat several times and finally got himself under control. Annie wiped the tears that had fallen from his cheeks and smiled at him.

"Ethan Ford, huh?" he asked.

Annie nodded. "Yup."

"Cool."

"Yeah, cool," Annie agreed. Then she climbed off his lap and asked, "Can we have cake now, Mommy?"

Everyone chuckled. Truck turned when he felt Mary's

hand on his thigh. Everyone began to stand, to congratulate Fletch and Emily and to coo over the still sleeping Ethan. But Truck couldn't move.

"I can't think of a better tribute for the greatest man I've ever known," Mary said softly.

"I don't know what to say."

Mary smiled and leaned up and kissed him gently on the lips. "That's the thing about best friends. You don't have to say anything. Fletch knows how much you love him. Knows that you'll do anything to keep him and his family safe."

"I will. Just as I will you," Truck vowed.

Mary leaned up again, but Truck met her halfway this time.

"I need to go see my namesake," he said after a minute.

Mary nodded. "Go. I'll find Rayne and see if there's anything I can help with."

Truck stood and helped Mary up then wandered over to Fletch. He was surrounded by the other Deltas. He went right up to Fletch and pulled him, and his son, into a brief hug. "I don't know what to say," he told his friend.

"Nothing *to* say," Fletch reassured him. "You've always been there for me, and every one of us," he said, gesturing to the men around them. "Without question, without fail, you're there. I can't imagine a better namesake for my son."

The other Deltas nodded and added their agreement.

"We're all so fucking thrilled that things with you and Mary worked out," Fletch continued.

"So am I," Truck said with a grin.

"And in case you've forgotten with all the head banging you've done over the last month, Rayne still wants to get married at the same time as Mary," Ghost informed him. "Even if you're already officially man and wife."

"And the biggest wedding ceremony this town has ever seen is currently being planned," Beatle said.

"And it's not going to be in my backyard," Fletch quipped.

Everyone chuckled.

"How'd we get so lucky?" Truck asked, looking around at his friends. "Seriously, not too long ago we were like Trigger's team. Ready and willing to sleep with any women who wanted us. We didn't have any connections, we were free and easy, living for our next mission. And now look at us."

"Yeah. Look at us. We've got the best fucking friends, children, homes, family. I don't care how it happened, but I'll fight anyone to the death who tries to take it from me," Coach said vehemently.

"Me too," Beatle agreed.

"Me three," Blade chimed in.

Fletch held out the hand that wasn't holding his son. "To friends and family," he said softly.

Truck put his hand on top of Fletch's. "To friends and family."

One by one, the other men did the same until they were all standing in a circle with their arms outstretched, hand to hand.

"Look at them," Rayne said with a contented sigh. She and the other women were in the kitchen, laughing and talking.

Everyone turned and stared at the men in the living room. They were standing together, obviously having a moment.

Rayne put her arm around Mary and pulled Kassie, who was still holding Kate, into their little embrace too. The other women quickly followed suit, linking arms and staring at the men in the other room.

Mary smiled when Casey reached out and pulled Bryn into their huddle. The other woman hadn't realized what was going on, and probably didn't understand why Casey was suddenly holding her hand, either.

"Thank you all for being so amazing," Rayne said softly. "I didn't have many friends, other than Mary, before I got together with Ghost, and now I can't imagine not having you all in my life. We need to promise not to let anything come between us. I know the thing with me and Mary got out of hand and involved all of you, and I promise not to do that again. I need you all in my life. Any kids I might have need all you aunts in their lives. We need to swear right now we'll always be friends, no matter what happens in our futures or where we might end up, even if it's in the middle of nowhere."

"Like Rathdrum, Idaho?" Bryn asked. "That's in the middle of nowhere."

Everyone chuckled.

"Exactly like Rathdrum, Idaho," Rayne told her.

"I've never had friends," Bryn commented. She didn't seem upset about it. She was just stating a fact. "I didn't really think I was missing much, as I don't like painting my nails or don't really see the need to sleep in someone's else house when my bed is super comfortable. But when Fletch called last week to say the party was postponed, I talked to Annie after he and Fish were done. She cried." Bryn was whispering now. "She said that she'd been so looking forward to me coming to visit, so we could talk about how deafness occurs and what kind of life the deaf lead. No one has ever been so upset that they wouldn't get to see me that they cried. And all of you gave me that. I know I'm different and weird, but it's like you guys don't even care."

"We *don't* care," Harley said softly. "We're all weird in our own way."

"True enough," Sadie said with a laugh.

"So we're agreed?" Rayne asked.

"Agreed!" everyone chimed in.

EPILOGUE

"I now pronounce you husband and wife," the officiant announced. Then turned to the second couple and repeated his words. Then he said, "You may kiss your brides."

Beatle leaned down and kissed Casey, while Blade took Wendy in his arms and tilted her backward and kissed her.

The congregation cheered and clapped as the two couples straightened and faced them.

Rayne dropped the curtain she and Mary had been hiding behind and smiled at her friend. "Are you ready?"

"The question is, are *you* ready?" Mary countered. "Truck and I are already married. Renewing our vows isn't the same as getting married the first time."

"Are you sorry?" Rayne asked.

"About what?"

"About having a quickie courthouse wedding the first time?"

Mary immediately shook her head. "No. First off, I didn't think I was going to live long enough to really enjoy being a wife in the first place. Secondly, I was sick as hell. I couldn't have done this even if I'd really wanted it. And third, even though I knew what I was doing would hurt you...I wanted to marry Truck. I wanted something beautiful for once in my life, and that was it."

Rayne's eyes filled with tears.

"Oh, shit, don't cry!" Mary ordered. "You'll ruin your makeup before the pictures!"

Rayne chuckled and looked up and blinked quickly, beating back the tears. Then she looked back at her best friend. "Nothing could be more perfect than this day," she declared. "When we met at that bar all those years ago, I never ever thought I'd be standing here with you like this. I mean, we promised we'd get married together, but I never *really* thought it'd happen. I love you, Mare."

Mary rolled her eyes. "You're awfully sappy today, Raynie."

Rayne smiled at her. "Yup. It's my wedding day. I'm allowed to be."

"I guess."

"And it's more than that too."

"Yeah?" Mary asked.

"I'm pregnant," Rayne whispered.

"Holy shit! Really?"

"Really."

"You better tell Ghost. He's gonna expect you to get shit-faced at the reception, and if you refuse to toast him, he'll get worried."

"Oh, don't worry. I'm planning on telling him in the limo on the way to the reception hall. It's my wedding present for him."

"Oh, jeez," Mary huffed. "You're *so* going to be late."

"As if *you* should talk, Miss I'll Be at the Church in Plenty of Time to Get My Makeup Done."

Mary couldn't help the blush that blossomed across her cheeks. She'd had every intention of being at the church early, but Truck had different thoughts. He'd refused to sleep away from her, claiming that since they were already married, he didn't have to cater to the tradition of the groom not seeing his wife before she arrived at the church. He'd kept her up late the night before, and then that morning, showing her several times how much he loved her.

"Yeah, okay, you're right," Mary told Rayne. Then she hugged her tightly, and refused to let her go when the hug went on a little too long. "I love you, Rayne," Mary said quietly. "I'm so happy for you."

Rayne sniffed, but said, "I love you too, Mare."

"Come on, you guys," Kassie said as she entered the little room right off the nave. "It's time."

"How's everyone doing?" Rayne asked. "Do they need a break?"

"Hell no," Sadie said, entering behind Kassie. "There's no way I'm letting anyone free until this thing is done. With all those hot, single and not-so-single men in attendance, I'd never get them all back in before the single women jumped their bones."

The four women chuckled.

"Was it too much to invite the SEALs and their wives from California?" Rayne asked, obviously not catching the teasing note in Sadie's voice.

"No," Mary told her.

"Maybe we shouldn't have included the other Delta team," Rayne mused, still obviously worried about Sadie's comment.

"Rayne," Mary said, taking her friend's shoulders in her hands. "Trigger and the others are fine. They're making sure Truck's sister is okay. She looks like she'd rather be eating snakes in Borneo than sitting out there. And I've noticed the commander is taking particular interest in her. The SEALs and their wives are also fine. So are the Taggarts from Dallas.

And the cops and firefighters who came too. No one is gonna have a sexual orgy in the pews."

"Yeah, they'll wait until the reception," Sadie muttered.

Mary mock glared at their friend and continued talking Rayne off the ledge. "The only thing you have to concentrate on is becoming Mrs. Keane Bryson."

"Why is that a thing?" Rayne asked.

"Why is *what* a thing?" Kassie asked.

"Why would I be Mrs. Keane Bryson? I mean, that's not my name. That's Ghost's name. I'm going to be Mrs. Rayne Bryson. That's never made sense to me."

Mary chuckled. "Right. Okay, enough talk. It's time."

"We're walking down the aisle together, right?" Rayne asked nervously.

For some reason, Rayne was completely freaked out. Mary had thought it humorous at first, but she knew she needed to comfort her friend. "Of course. Arm in arm. Just like we planned."

"Good."

"Good," Kassie echoed. "I'll make sure everyone is ready."

"I'll help," Sadie said, and followed Kassie out.

Rayne took Mary's hand in hers and the two best friends stared at each other. "Remember how this all started?" Rayne asked.

Mary nodded. "Yup. You sent me a text from London and told me you were hooking up with a hot guy and if you were never heard from again, you gave me the deets you had on him."

"Of course, they were all lies, so you never would've found him *or* my dead body."

Mary chuckled. "You're beautiful, Raynie. Ghost is the luckiest man alive."

Her best friend smiled back. "I think Truck might have something to say about that."

"What do you think?" Mary asked. "Want to go get married?"

"Absolutely."

And with that, the two women linked elbows and walked arm in arm out of the small room, and to the beginning of the aisle of the church.

The music started, and all the guests stood and turned to face them.

Mary saw Truck smiling huge at the end of the aisle, waiting for her. His smile was lopsided, but she'd never seen anything more beautiful in her life.

All their friends were there. Annie was already standing at the altar. She didn't want to wear a dress and no one had the heart to make her. She had on her favorite combat boots and a pair of jeans with a white frilly shirt...the only concession she'd made to the occasion. She didn't have her basket of flowers mixed with small plastic Army men this time, like she had for her parents' wedding, but Emily had warned them that the wedding cake at the reception may or may not have an Army theme.

"Ready?" Rayne asked.

"Ready," Mary said firmly.

Then the two friends walked toward their men just like they'd always planned...together.

Trigger and the rest of his Delta team, the morning after the weddings.

"Holy shit," Lefty groaned. "My head hurts."

"Maybe if you didn't drink a keg of beer all by yourself, it wouldn't," Doc quipped.

Grover laughed and Lefty smacked him. "Shut up, Grover. Too loud."

"Come on," Trigger said. "We've got five miles to run before we hit the gym."

The others all groaned, but fell in beside Trigger as they set off.

"What time did you guys get home?" Brain asked his friends.

"About three," Oz answered. "Me and Doc made sure everyone had rides before they left."

"Luckily, most people were staying at the hotel next door, so it wasn't a big deal," Doc added.

"Did you guys see the commander leave with Truck's sister?" Lefty asked. "It's a good thing Truck didn't see that."

"Right?" Doc asked. "He would've lost his shit. But then again, I think he would've lost his shit no matter *who* it was that left with her."

"Shut it," Brain ordered. "The commander is a good guy. Truck trusts and respects him. Besides, Macie didn't look so good."

"Was she sick?" Trigger asked, concerned now.

Brain shrugged. "Not in the way you think. She just looked...anxious. Like, *really* anxious. Almost freaked out. If the commander hadn't gone up to her, I would've."

"Think she's all right?" Doc asked. "Do we need to tell Truck?"

Brain shook his head. "I'm sure the commander has it under control. If he thinks Truck needs to be informed, he'll tell him. Even if it *is* his honeymoon. Or second honeymoon, as the case may be."

Everyone nodded in agreement.

"It was one hell of a party, wasn't it?" Lucky asked no one in particular. "I mean, if I was going to get married, that's how I'd want to do it."

"What do you mean, *if* you're going to get married?" Trigger asked. "You don't want that?"

Lucky shrugged. "It's not that I don't want it, I just don't see it happening. We're not at home much, we're always sent off to do the dirty shit that the regular units in the Army won't touch. I just don't see it happening."

"It happened for Ghost and the others," Trigger noted.

"Yeah, they all got lucky," Brain chimed in.

The seven men continued their run in silence. Partly because they were all a bit hungover from the reception the night before. But also because seeing four of their fellow Delta Force soldiers get married at once had struck a chord within all of them.

They'd talked about it in the past. How the chances of them living long enough to have families were slim. How the missions they went on were slowly sucking the life right out of them. How no women would likely take a chance on them. They were the baddest of the bad the US Army had, and lived life moment by moment.

But seeing Ghost, Truck, Beatle, and Blade pledge their lives and love to their women had made them start to rethink things. Seeing Fletch and Hollywood with their children had made them yearn, deep down, to have the same.

They might be badass soldiers who weren't scared of anything, but they were also human.

"Maybe all hope for us isn't lost," Trigger said out loud. "If they found love, maybe we can too."

His teammates didn't respond, but no one laughed and said he was crazy either.

Commander Colt Robinson and Macie Laughlin, the morning after the weddings.

Macie opened her eyes and stiffened, trying to figure out where she was.

Recalling the night before, she immediately squeezed them closed again. She felt as if she'd been run over by a truck...exactly how she always felt after she'd had a major anxiety attack. She should be used to the feeling by now, as she'd had more than her fair share of them over the years.

She wanted nothing more than to keep her eyes shut and stay under the covers all day...but that was impossible, because she wasn't at home. The bed she was in wasn't hers. The chest her cheek was resting on belonged to Colonel Colt Robinson. *Shit.*

Feeling her fingers start to tingle once again and her heart start to race, Macie recognized the signs of anxiety rearing its ugly head.

Colt had been amazing the night before. He'd somehow realized that she was on the edge of a massive attack at her brother's reception, and he'd taken her outside so she could get some space and air. She'd continued to shake and feel dizzy. She'd started hyperventilating and couldn't catch her breath.

When being outside and away from all the guests hadn't helped, he'd put her in his car and driven her to his house.

She hadn't been worried. She knew who Colt was, Truck talked about him all the time. Ford trusted his commander, and he'd told her that she could too.

But she couldn't stop thinking about what he must think

of her. How weak she was. How pathetic. How he probably wanted to be anywhere and be doing anything other than babysitting her.

Part of the hell of her brand of anxiety was second-guessing everyone's motives and whether or not they really wanted her around. She constantly had a war going on in her head that things weren't really the way she thought they were.

But Colt had done everything right last night. He'd let her hang on to him to help her feel grounded. He'd put her in his bed and simply held her close. He'd talked about anything and everything for hours, rubbing her arms and letting her physically recover at her own pace.

She still internally questioned what he was doing and why he was helping her, but she'd put on the brave face she wore every day of her life and did her best to try to act normal. But eventually she'd fallen asleep, which was a miracle in itself.

Macie never slept well. Especially after taking a Vistaril. Those pills were reserved for when she really, *really* needed them. Normally her Lexapro tablets did the trick. But last night, in Colt's arms, she'd slept like a baby for the first time in a very long time. It was a rare night that she slept more than four hours in a row.

Easing herself out of Colt's arms as slowly and carefully as she could, Macie stood by the side of his bed, staring down at him for a long moment. His hair was graying at the temples, making him look distinguished rather than old. While he didn't have a defined six pack, he wasn't overweight by any stretch of the imagination. Macie remembered the way his chest and stomach had felt under her hand as they lay talking the night before. He was taller than her by a few inches, but at around six feet, he didn't tower over her like her brother did.

His eyes were a unique shade of gray, and when she spoke,

he looked her right in the eye. He never seemed to be bored or impatient with her when she had a hard time explaining how she felt. He was older than her by at least a decade, but at no time had Macie felt as if the difference in their ages was an issue.

Macie was drawn to Colt. She hadn't felt the kind of chemistry she felt with him in a very long time. It excited her while scaring her to death at the same time.

They were both still dressed in the clothes they'd worn to the wedding and reception the day before. Colt hadn't touched her inappropriately and hadn't done anything out of line.

And that made Macie's anxiety rear its ugly head once more. Was she not pretty enough? Did he not see her as a woman? Did he only see her as someone he had to rescue? Maybe he'd only helped her because he was Ford's commander.

She closed her eyes and wrapped her arms around herself, pinching her biceps to try to stop the ugly thoughts in her head.

When she felt more under control, Macie opened her eyes and looked around the room. She remembered something Colt asked her the night before. Making a split-second decision, and for once not analyzing it to death, she moved toward the table next to the bed. She remembered Colt saying last night that he always kept a pad of paper and pen next to his bed, so he could jot down any thoughts that came to him in the middle of the night.

She ripped off the top piece of paper and wrote a quick note.

Colt. Thank you for last night. If you were honest about wanting to have lunch sometime, I'd like that. -Macie

She scrawled her phone number under her name and left it on the small table. Then, taking a deep breath, she did what her body and mind had been telling her to do from the second she woke up. She fled.

An hour later, Colt stirred in his bed and, when he realized he was alone, quickly sat up and looked around. He couldn't see any indication that Macie was still there, and he didn't hear her anywhere in his house.

Feeling disappointed, he threw back the covers and strode into his bathroom. He liked Mercedes Laughlin. More than liked her. Felt a need deep down in his bones to keep her close and to do whatever he could to make her life easier.

Because it was more than obvious Macie suffered from anxiety, and he hated that.

Colt had a cousin who suffered from the same condition, and he knew he had an uphill mountain to climb. He knew it was unlikely that she'd have gotten up the nerve to leave him a note or her number. Oh, Colt knew he could ask Truck for his sister's phone number, but for now, he wanted to keep things just between them. He had a feeling Macie needed some time to process the night before and come to terms with what had happened. He'd give her some space...for now.

But he would see Macie again. He'd felt something between them, and had a feeling she'd felt it too. Simply holding her in his arms did more for him last night than actually making love to a woman had in the past. He'd loved how she fit against him. How soft her skin and hair was. He'd loved listening to the sound of her voice. And he'd especially loved knowing it was *his* touch that soothed her and the cadence of *his* voice that had finally lulled her to sleep.

Macie Laughlin had touched something deep inside him. And he wanted to explore whatever it was.

He walked into his closet and changed into a pair of jeans and a T-shirt. Then he moved to his door to head downstairs and fix himself some breakfast. Feeling strangely charged, even though Macie had snuck out on him, he opened his bedroom door and pulled it closed with a little too much force. It slammed shut behind him, and Colt winced. Shrugging, and glad he wasn't living in an apartment anymore and his carelessness wouldn't wake anyone else up, he headed down the stairs toward his kitchen.

Colt never realized that when the door had slammed shut, a slight breeze moved through the room, picking up the note Macie had so nervously written and blowing it to the back side of the table and off the edge. It slid down to the floor and ended up under the bed with the multitude of dust bunnies that lived there, destined to remain unfound and unread for weeks.

Harley and Coach, two years after the weddings.

"You still want to do this?" Coach asked Harley.

"Absolutely," she said confidently.

"Then on the count of three," he said. "One. Two. Three!"

On the last number, he pushed them both out of the

plane, and Coach smiled as he heard Harley scream in glee as they plummeted toward the ground.

She'd come a long way since that first jump they'd taken together. Him being hit in the face by a bird was truly a freak accident, and once he'd convinced her to try again, she'd decided she loved it.

Coach monitored their altitude throughout the jump and when it was time, he tapped Harley on the shoulder. She reached back and he helped guide her hand to the parachute cord. They pulled it together, and he laughed when she grunted after being jerked upward by the parachute opening.

They glided toward the ground with Coach steering. They landed without any issues right in the middle of the landing zone.

The second they were on the ground, Coach unclipped her harness from his and turned them until Harley was under him. Her brown eyes sparkled with life as she smiled up at him. He loved her even more than he had the day they got married. She hadn't changed in the least since that day. She was still slender, still had the same shoulder-length light brown hair, but her confidence had grown tenfold.

"Like that?" Coach asked.

"Of course," Harley said. "It was just the thing I needed to get my day started."

"That and the orgasm, you mean," Coach corrected with a grin.

"Oh, yeah. Maybe that too."

Coach tickled her as best he could through the jumpsuit she was wearing. When he took pity on her and let her go, he loved how she clung to him.

"I love you," Harley said.

"Love you back. Are you ready for today?"

"Yes. There's no way they'll turn me down," Harley said

with confidence. "I've been carrying the *This is War* line for years. If they want me to keep working there, they'll have to pay for the privilege."

Coach loved how passionate Harley was for her job. She loved creating the video games. But when one of her games had been altered significantly to make it unnecessarily violent, *after* she'd submitted the final code, she'd lost it.

They didn't have children, a mutual decision, but Harley was more than aware of how kids were being desensitized to violence through social media and games like the ones she designed.

She'd found the nerve to tell the president of the company that if he didn't rewrite her contract to say that she was the only person who could approve changes to the final product, and give her a hefty raise in the meantime, she'd quit and go work for his biggest competitor.

Coach knew she'd have no problem doing just that too. It wasn't a bluff. Harley was good. More than good. She'd continued to learn a lot throughout her career and she was the best programmer the company had. Bar none. She'd also gotten a lot more confident over the years. Coach attributed that to being happy, and to having kick-ass female friends who always had each other's backs and celebrated each other's successes rather than tearing each other down.

Today was her meeting with her boss, and the president of the company. They'd either give her what she wanted or she was out of there.

"Are you up for some breakfast before you have to call in?" Coach asked.

Harley worked remotely, which allowed her to stay home with their cat and two dogs all day. Many times he'd come home to her sitting on the couch with a dog on either side of her, the cat draped over her shoulders, and her fingers moving with the speed of light over her keyboard.

"Of course," she said. "Omelet with all the good shit I like?" she asked.

"As if I'd make you anything else," Coach told her. "What did Davidson and Montesa say last night? Are they good?" He truly liked her siblings, and was always interested in what they were doing.

"Oh, yeah. Montesa is heading off to St. Thomas on vacation today. She told me to call her after my meeting to let her know how it went."

"Her husband finally convinced his workaholic wife to go?"

Harley smiled. "Yup. Crazy, huh?"

"Absolutely. And Davidson?"

"He offered to beat up the president if he didn't give me what I wanted," Harley said with a laugh.

"Sounds like something he'd do."

"Thank you for giving me everything I didn't know I was missing in life," Harley said as she brought up a hand and curled it around the back of Coach's neck.

"You're welcome, Harl. Anything you want is yours."

"Anything?" she said with an arched brow.

Coach pressed his hips into her belly, letting her feel his erection. "Anything," he said.

"You know what adrenaline does to me," Harley said coyly, peering at him from beneath lowered lashes.

Coach had her up and walking toward her Highlander before she knew what was happening. She giggled and gathered up the parachute trailing behind them as they walked. "In a hurry?" she asked.

"If you want to have time to eat before your call, yeah."

Coach was aware they had plenty of time. Even though

he'd had her that morning, he knew he wouldn't last more than a couple minutes the second he got inside her. She always did that to him. Every time they made love, it felt like coming home.

On their way to the parking lot, he held out his hand and sighed in contentment when she took it. "Love you, Harl."

"Love you too."

They both smiled all the way home.

Chase and Sadie, three years after the weddings.

Chase sat at his desk and looked over at his wife. Sadie was in the conference room with a potential customer. She was always the one to conduct the initial meetings with the women who came inquiring about their services.

A year ago, he'd chaptered out of the Army, and even though his friends had told him he'd be sorry, he hadn't regretted one second of his decision.

He and Sadie had opened a branch of her famous uncle's bodyguard services here in the Fort Hood area. With his background in investigations, Chase was easily able to discover information on the exes of their clients. They had a staff of four men who rotated through jobs, and Sadie did most of the paperwork in the office, especially now that she was pregnant with their first child. Chase supervised the bodyguards and occasionally offered backup when needed.

Chase still had a hard time wrapping his head around the fact that he was going to be a father. He'd watched his sister get married and have babies, and had enjoyed being an uncle, but it was completely different knowing he'd have a son of his own soon.

Sadie patted the distraught woman on the shoulder and awkwardly stood up, her eight-months-pregnant belly preventing her from moving anywhere quickly anymore. He met her at the door to the conference room and put his arm under her elbow to help balance her as she waddled to the leather chair in the corner of his office. She'd long since stopped sitting at her desk, as it was uncomfortable for her.

"Is she okay?" Chase asked.

Sadie nodded. "She will be."

"I guess we've got a new client then?"

Sadie smiled. "Yup. She has two kids and is scared her ex is gonna try to snatch them and take them back to Kuwait, where he's from."

"Roger is between jobs right now. I'll get him on it. You have the ex's information for me so I can start researching?"

"Yup."

Chase leaned down and kissed the tip of his wife's nose. "Relax for a bit while I get her home and check out the security at her place. You'll be all right for a while?"

She shook her head at him in exasperation. "Yeah, Chase. I think I'll be fine here by myself for ten minutes until Rayne stops by and collects me for lunch."

Chase didn't even care Sadie had realized three months ago that anytime he couldn't be with her, he'd arranged for one of their friends or his sister to be by her side. The last thing he wanted was her going into premature labor or getting hurt when he wasn't there to help her.

He wasn't going to tell her that her uncle was also keeping tabs on her with an invisible app he'd installed on her phone.

"Nothing's going to happen," she said softly, running her hand over her belly. "We've made it this far, we're fine."

The worst day in Chase's life was the day a year and a half ago when Sadie had miscarried their child. He had only been ten weeks old, and it hammered home how fragile life was... and how precious.

"Of course you are. Call me if you need anything," Chase ordered as he stood and began to gather the things he needed to assess their new client's safety at her home.

"Hand me my laptop?" Sadie asked.

He did.

"And my cell?"

Chase happily retrieved that from the edge of his desk.

"Can you get me a bottle of water before you go too?"

With a smile, Chase walked over to the small fridge in the corner of the office and pulled out a water for her. He also grabbed a serving of string cheese, and a piece of chocolate cake left over from the night before that he'd brought into the office, just in case.

Sadie smiled up at him as he handed her everything.

"Anything else?" he asked, having no problem fetching things for her.

"No, I'm good now. Thanks."

Without a word, Chase pulled the small ottoman over and picked up her feet and placed them on it. He made sure the blanket on the back of the chair was within reach and he scooted the small table next to her chair until so she could reach it better.

"You're too good to me," Sadie said.

"Never," Chase vowed, then kissed her one more time before standing and heading out. He stopped in the doorway and looked back at her. "I'll spend the rest of my days doing any and everything to make your life, and that of our son, perfect." Then he blew her a kiss and left.

Truck and Mary, five years after the weddings.

"Are you ready?" Truck asked his wife.

Mary didn't take her eyes away from the doorway as she nodded her head eagerly.

They were in Banbasa, India, a little over two hundred miles east of Delhi. Before meeting with the adoption agency, they'd never heard of the small town, much less the orphanage named The Good Shepherd.

At first, Mary had been opposed to having any children, or even pets. She was deathly afraid the cancer would return. But after a year had passed and she'd gotten the all-clear from her doctors, then two years, then three, she began to make comments in passing about children and how cute they were.

Truck had finally sat her down and point blank asked her if she wanted kids.

She'd cried but admitted that she hadn't thought she did. After her awful upbringing and experiences, she was afraid that she wouldn't know how to be a good mother. But after spending a lot of time with her friends' children, she realized how much she wanted to have a family. They'd had several conversations with her doctor, and while he said her having kids wasn't impossible, there were risks. They'd decided to adopt.

"Do you think they'll like us?" Mary asked fretfully.

"Eventually, yes," Truck said, and took her hand in his as they waited for the employees to bring their children into the room. "But I also think it'll take a while. You know they've had a hard life so far. As good as this orphanage is, it's still not like a home. There are people who look after the children here, but we were warned that they might be standoffish. They won't understand what's going on."

"We sent that photo album with our pictures," Mary said, looking up at Truck with big eyes. "Maybe they'll recognize us."

"Don't get your hopes up," Truck warned. "I don't want you to be disappointed if they don't."

"Disappointed?" Mary asked incredulously. "Truck, I was disappointed when you made spaghetti for dinner the other night and I was in the mood for steak. I was disappointed when Rayne had to cancel our girls' day out because she had morning sickness. I don't give a crap if Aarav and Deeba recognize us today or not. They'll get to know us because we'll be there for them every day of their lives. We'll comfort them when they cry and feed them when they're hungry. They'll learn to trust us, just like I learned to trust you. If I did it after thirty years of being disappointed and let down by the people I thought were supposed to love me, they can do it after only two and three years."

"Fuck, I love you," Truck whispered. "I don't know what I did to deserve you."

"Well, for starters, you love to rub my feet," Mary quipped.

Truck still didn't mind in the least that she didn't say the words as frequently as he did. She showed him every day they spent together how much she loved him. She had no problem telling Rayne or her other girlfriends how she felt about them. She was constantly whispering words of love to the babies and children in their circle, but Truck still didn't care for one second that the words didn't come out of her mouth all that often.

Because when she did say that she loved him...it was as if the angels came down from heaven and bestowed upon him an otherworldly gift. She'd said the words twenty-two times in the five years since they'd renewed their vows. But she'd told him in a million and one nonverbal ways as well.

"I do love to rub your feet," Truck agreed. "And other things."

Mary blushed and smacked him on the arm. "Shut up. Don't get me all worked up right before we meet our children for the first time."

Before Truck could retort, the door opened and two Indian women walked in, each holding a small toddler in her arms.

Truck let go of Mary's hand as they both instinctively went to their knees when the women bent over and placed the children on their feet. His heart in his throat, Truck took in the sight of his kids for the first time. He'd seen pictures, but they hadn't done these precious babies justice.

Aarav was the older of the two. He had dark brown hair that was too long and fell onto his forehead, almost covering his eyes. He was wearing a pair of loose brown pants held up with a drawstring. His feet were bare, and he had on a white short-sleeve shirt.

Deeba was only two, and she wobbled on her feet when the woman holding her took a step back. She wore a gray dress that came down to just below her knees. Her hair was black and was shorn close to her head. Truck knew it was because she'd had a bad case of lice not too long ago, but her hair barely even registered.

He gazed into the eyes of his children and for the first time, he understood the big undertaking they had in front of them. The kids looked scared to death; he couldn't blame them. Not only were he and Mary white—he had no idea if the kids in the orphanage had ever seen a white person before—but he was big. And he had the awful scar on his face.

Truck wanted to cover it up with his hand, but he didn't dare move. He didn't want to do anything that would scare these precious children in front of him. *His* children.

"*Namaste*," Mary said softly and held out one hand.

Neither child moved. Aarav stuck his hand in his mouth and sucked on it, and Deeba just stood there, wavering on her feet.

"*Maa*," Mary said, pointing to herself. "I'm your mom. And this is your *pita*. Your dad."

Truck held his breath, then whispered, "Maybe I should go. Leave you alone with them for a while."

The second he said the words, Deeba looked at him and tilted her head.

"We played the tapes you sent every night," one of the women said in the quiet of the room. "We thought maybe if they heard your voices, they'd be more comfortable when they actually met you."

"Every night?" Truck asked.

Before the woman could answer, Deeba moved. She teetered toward him with her arms outstretched.

Without thought, Truck leaned forward and held out his hands, wanting to catch her if she fell. But she didn't. Deeba walked right up to him and didn't flinch when Truck's large hand wrapped around her tiny back. She was small for her age. Underweight and undernourished, but the only thing Truck could see was the yearning in her eyes.

"*Pita*," she said softly.

Truck nodded. "That's right. I'm your father."

Aarav, not to be outdone by his sister, followed behind her and came toward Mary. Without a word, he burrowed into her, dropping his forehead on her chest as if he'd done it every day of his life.

Truck's eyes came back to his daughter when he felt her little hand pat him on the cheek. "*Chot?*"

Having no idea what she'd said, he looked to the women.

One translated. "She wants to know if you're hurt."

Truck closed his eyes and counted his blessings for what seemed like the millionth time since he'd met Mary. When he felt little Deeba patting the cheek with his scar impatiently, he opened his eyes and covered her hand with his own. He shook his head. "It doesn't hurt."

Then she melted his heart even more when she held up her arms in the universal sign to be picked up.

Truck stood up with his daughter in his arms then reached down and helped Mary stand with their son. They stood there looking into each other's eyes, ignoring the warnings from the caretaker of the orphanage. She was telling them that the kids would probably be scared later, and that they shouldn't take it personally. She was instructing them on what the kids liked to eat and cautioning them to take it easy for a while on new foods so they didn't get sick. She also told them last-minute things they needed to do in order to get clearance from the Indian government to take Aarav and Deeba out of the country and back to Texas.

But Truck barely heard any of it. His eyes were glued to his beautiful wife and their son.

"I love you," Mary whispered as she gazed into Truck's eyes.

Twenty-three.

"I love you too, baby."

Then Mary turned to her son and kissed his forehead gently. "I love you, Ford Aarav Laughlin." She then leaned forward and kissed her daughter's temple. "And I love you, Elizabeth Deeba Laughlin. Welcome to the family."

Truck's throat closed up with emotion once more. He reached forward and pulled Mary toward him with a hand on her nape. He kissed her on the lips and whispered, "Love you."

Ghost and Rayne, five and a half years after the weddings.

"Give him to me," Ghost ordered, wiggling his fingers at his wife. She was holding their four-year-old and struggling to walk with him.

She gladly handed him over and winced, arching her back.

"I told you to take it easy today," Ghost said, shaking his head at his wife.

She smiled at him but shook her *own* head. "Yeah? What was I supposed to do, lie around while your son single-handedly clogged up every toilet in the house? Or when your daughter decided to take the permanent marker she found and draw pretty pictures all over the wall in her bedroom?"

Ghost winced. "That's it. I'm calling that girl Chase recommended tomorrow."

"We don't need a nanny," Rayne whined. "I can look after my own kids just fine. I don't need someone else to do it for me."

"It's not that I don't think you can do it," Ghost said patiently. "It's that I hate seeing you so exhausted. And when this one is born," he put his hand on Rayne's enormous belly, "it's just going to get more hectic."

When tears sprang to her eyes, Ghost didn't panic. He put his son down and swatted him on the bottom. "Go wash your hands and get ready for dinner, sport."

"Okay, Daddy!" the little boy said happily and ran off toward the bathroom.

Ghost pulled Rayne into his embrace and held her as she sniffled. "I feel like the world's worst mom. I'm awful. They're going to grow up to be delinquents, I just know it."

"You aren't," Ghost reassured her. "You think every mother is all hearts and rainbows all the time? I don't give a shit what people post on social media, I'd bet everything I have that there are times when they want to duct tape their kids. This is normal."

"I'm just so tired," Rayne said softly.

Ghost kissed her forehead. "I know. And I haven't been helping, being gone so much lately, have I?"

When Rayne didn't respond, Ghost felt even guiltier. The team had been on three missions almost back to back recently, and he knew he hadn't been helping with his family nearly as much as he should be.

"Go lie down," he told Rayne. "I've got the kids tonight."

"No, it's okay. I'll get some nuggets in the oven for Billy, and Greta still only eats hotdogs, so I can boil some of those and—"

"I got this," Ghost interrupted. "Seriously."

The tears returned to Rayne's eyes and Ghost felt awful. "I'm sorry, Princess. I'm gonna get you some help so you aren't so exhausted by the end of the day."

"I...okay," she said softly. "I hate to admit it, because it makes me feel like a failure, but Billy has so much energy he sometimes makes me tired just looking at him. And Greta is so picky, I swear to God I spend most of my day pleading with her to eat something, anything, so she doesn't blow away in a stiff wind. I sure as hell hope this one is a little more easygoing." Rayne put a hand on her belly and rubbed.

Ghost leaned down and kissed her pregnant belly, then

spun her around and gave her a gentle push toward the stairs. "Go on. Relax. I've got this. And tonight, if you're up for it, I'll give you a back rub."

"Oooh." Rayne turned back and her eyes lit up. "*Just* a backrub?"

"I'll give you whatever you want, Princess. You know that."

She stood up on tiptoes and untucked his shirt. Putting her hand on the small of his naked back, she whispered, "I'm so fucking horny, Ghost. I swear I don't know how it's possible when I'm this big, but I am."

"I'll take care of you."

"I know you will. I'm gonna take a nap, but call me if you need me."

"I'm not going to need you. I can survive one night with them."

She nodded. "Make sure you wake me up when you get the kids put down for the night."

"I will. Now go."

Ghost watched as his wife waddled up the stairs toward their bedroom. The pregnancy had rounded her out once again, much to her chagrin. Ghost knew she'd worked really hard to get rid of the weight she'd gained when Greta was born, but he liked her this way. Lush and curvy. He wasn't sure what the night would bring; sometimes Rayne only wanted to get off, with either his help or with her vibrator, and other times she wanted actual intercourse. But whatever she wanted and needed, Ghost was happy to provide. He was more than able to get himself off, and in fact, Rayne loved watching him masturbate in front of her.

Life certainly wasn't easy or calm, but it was exactly what Ghost had dreamed about. He loved having a hectic life. Loved watching his kids grow up and explore the world. This was why he'd become a soldier. Why he'd joined Delta Force in the first place. To keep families safe and ignorant of the evils of the world.

When Greta screeched and came running into the living room, Ghost quickly scooped her up and flung her over his shoulder. Billy, who'd been tormenting his sister with his soapy hands, wanted in on the fun, and sat on his dad's foot and wrapped his arms around his calf.

With two squirming kids hanging off him, Ghost smiled and made his way into the kitchen. He needed to get them fed, play with them for an hour or so, read them a story, put them to bed, and *then* he could take care of his wife.

His smile grew as he thought about what that entailed. He couldn't wait.

Hollywood and Kassie, Seven years after the weddings.

"That kid's a menace," Hollywood groaned as he watched Fletch's little boy chase Kate around the backyard. They were hanging out with their friends and watching the kids play.

"No, he's not," Kassie told her husband. "I bet he's just like *you* were at that age. Besides, he likes her. That's what kids do when they like someone else but don't know how to tell them."

"Kate is only seven!" Hollywood said in horror. "She's too young to have a boyfriend."

"Annie knew Frankie was the boy for her when *she* was seven," Kassie said calmly.

"No. Just no," Hollywood said, folding his arms across his chest.

Kassie giggled and turned into her husband and wrapped her arms around him.

Hollywood kept his eyes on his daughter and the little boy who seemed enamored with her, even as he hugged his wife to his chest. The kids had grown up together, spending a lot of time playing, but the thought of them *liking* each other hadn't even dawned on him until right this moment.

Just then, Kate fell. She'd been running from Ethan and laughing and had tripped over something in the yard. Hollywood jerked and moved to go help her, but Kassie held him tightly.

"She's fine," she whispered.

Hollywood clenched his teeth and forced himself to not run to his daughter to make sure she was all right.

He watched as Annie went over to the children and made sure Kate was okay. She had the little girl laughing within seconds. Hollywood didn't miss the way Ethan patted Kate on the shoulder lightly, as if comforting her.

"Fuck, I'm in deep shit, aren't I?" he asked.

Kassie merely chuckled. "Yup. Are you seriously just noticing for the first time how pretty our daughter is?"

"No," Hollywood admitted. "I already knew she was the most beautiful girl in all the world...second only to her mom. But I *am* just realizing that it's a problem. The boys are gonna be all over her."

"Look at me," Kassie ordered.

Hollywood continued to stare at his baby girl—who wasn't so much a baby anymore—as she played with Ethan. When he felt Kassie's fingers on his cheek, he tore his eyes away from the child who meant so much to him.

She'd been sickly as an infant, and when she was two, they'd found out she had sickle cell anemia. The doctors had been surprised, as it mainly affected African-American children in the United States, but somehow Kate had inherited the sickle cell gene from each of her parents, resulting in the anemia.

It had been a tough road for a while, with tons of doctors' appointments and trying to get her medicine right. But today she was a happy and beautiful child. As a result of everything they'd been through with Kate, Hollywood and Kassie had decided to not have any more children. They didn't want to risk passing on the disease to another child.

Hollywood wasn't sorry. He loved Kate with all his heart, but it wasn't easy being a parent. He was more than okay with only having one kid.

"She's smart," Kassie told him. "I have a feeling you're right, and in a few years she's going to be fighting off boys with a stick..."

Hollywood growled, but Kassie ignored him and continued. "But by then, she'll have learned from observing her dad how a man is supposed to treat a woman, because she watches you with me. She sees how your teammates treat *their* women. She's gonna want that for herself. She's not going to put up with anyone treating her badly."

"She's not allowed to date until she's eighteen," Hollywood said with a frown. "I know how boys are...I *was* one, you know. They're gonna want to get in her pants and they don't like hearing no."

"So we'll teach her how to protect herself if there's a boy who doesn't take no for an answer."

Hollywood growled. "If anyone touches my little girl, they're gonna wish they hadn't."

"I love you," Kassie said with a smile.

"I love you too," Hollywood said immediately. "But I don't know why you're smiling like that."

"Fifteen," his wife told him. "And only if she's at either our house or his when adults are home. When she's sixteen, she can start going on dates."

Hollywood closed his eyes. "Why can't she stay this age forever?" he whined.

Kassie turned in his arms until her back was against his front and Hollywood interlaced his fingers together over her stomach.

"Because as much as we want to stop time, we can't. She's going to grow up and be a beautiful woman. I wouldn't be surprised if she got into modeling, she's literally that pretty. But she could also decide to go into construction and I'd be just as happy if she wore a hard hat every day and was covered in dirt."

Hollywood lowered his head until his lips were next to Kassie's ear. "Thank you, sweetheart."

"For what?" she asked.

"For loving me. For being amazing. For just being you."

Kassie chuckled, and Hollywood knew he'd never get tired of hearing that laugh. "It's not a hardship loving you... except when you come back from a mission and smell like you've been crawling through shit for a month."

Hollywood huffed out a laugh...she wasn't exactly wrong. Some of the places he'd been and some of the things he'd had to do weren't far from what she'd described.

"I talked to Karina this afternoon," Kassie told him.

"Yeah?"

"Uh-huh. She's dating a new guy."

Hollywood rolled his eyes, knowing Kassie couldn't see him. His sister-in-law was a serial dater. He knew Kassie worried about her, but she was still young. She had plenty of time to settle down. Better she figure out what she really wanted in a partner now than regret a hasty decision later.

"When is she coming to visit? Kate was saying the other day that she missed her aunt Karina."

"I'm not sure. She loves it out there in California. I told her that maybe she'd meet some hunky Navy SEAL and could bring him home for you to check out."

Hollywood grunted. "You better believe she's bringing home any man she wants to marry for me to check out. I'll call Tex and make him do the complete workup on him."

Kassie turned in his hold again and laughed. She ran her fingers up his chest suggestively, and licked her lips as she looked at him. "Think we can talk Emily and Fletch into keeping Kate for a sleepover tonight?"

"You have something you need to do tonight?" Hollywood asked, knowing exactly what his wife was thinking.

"Oh, yeah," she agreed. "There's someone I need to do tonight."

Hollywood leaned down and kissed his wife. Not caring who was around. Having a child meant they didn't get as much private time together as he liked. Anytime he could have his wife to himself, he'd take it.

After he'd kissed her senseless, Hollywood lifted his head. "Fletch'll take Kate for the night. I'm sure she'll be thrilled."

Kassie sighed in contentment. "Good."

"Love you, Kass."

"Love you too. Now go," she said, pushing him away gently. "Tell your friend he's on babysitting duty. I want to go home."

"Yes, ma'am," Hollywood said, and immediately turned around to find Fletch. He couldn't keep the small smile from his face though. He was as much in love with his wife today as the day he'd married her. More. Life was amazing.

Fish and Bryn, ten years after the weddings.

Fish yawned and stretched, reaching out his good arm for his wife. When he encountered nothing but cold sheets, he frowned. It wasn't unusual that Bryn got up before him, she didn't need a lot of sleep, but he couldn't deny that he hated waking up without her.

He quickly got up and pulled on a pair of jeans, not bothering with a shirt. He did what he needed to do in the bathroom and went looking for Bryn.

He found her in the living room. She was sitting on the floor cross-legged, hunched over what he thought was their toaster, with their six-year-old son.

Fish had known Bryan was different from most kids when he was talking at nine months. By the time he was two, he was using complete sentences and he'd even picked up Spanish from their nanny.

Fish had hired the woman when Bryan was six months old, when Bryn had gotten so involved in researching something she'd literally forgotten about her son. She hadn't meant to, and she was devastated when she'd realized Bryan had been screaming his head off for quite a while and she hadn't even noticed.

Maria was a godsend. She came in every day and spent time with Bryn and their son. She made sure both were eating properly and she also kept the house clean.

Fish loved his wife, but was aware of her quirks. Wanting to keep her safe, as well as his son, had made the decision to hire Maria easy. Now neither of them could imagine life without her. She was like Bryan's second mother, and everyone was happy with the arrangement.

At the moment, Bryn was explaining to their son how the

heating coils in the toaster worked. Bryan was sitting exactly like his mother and their heads were almost touching as they bent over the electronic. There were parts strewn on the carpet around them and it looked like they'd been at it for quite a while.

Fish grinned.

He must've made some sort of noise, because Bryan looked up and saw him standing in the doorway.

"Hi, Papa!" he said happily. "Mama is teaching me how the toaster works!"

"I can see that," Fish said, pushing off the doorway and walking toward his family. He settled himself on the floor next to them then leaned over and kissed Bryn on the temple. "Good morning, love."

"Morning," she said distractedly. "So you see, Bryan, when electricity flows through a wire, energy is transmitted from one end to the other. Think of it like water flowing through a pipe. The electrons in the wire get jostled around and run into one another over and over, giving off heat. The thinner the wire is, the greater the electrical current and the more the electrons run into each other...thus..."

"Making more heat!" Bryan said energetically.

"Exactly!" Bryn said approvingly.

"But how does it know when the toast is done?" their son asked.

Fish smiled as Bryn went into an explanation of thermostats inside the toaster and how the dial for the different level of toasted-ness worked. Every day, his wife amazed and impressed him. He had no idea how he'd managed to create a human as smart as Bryan, but he figured it was mostly Bryn.

His wife had been opposed to kids for a while, but Fish had known she was just scared. She hadn't had the best upbringing and didn't trust herself. But after spending time with Annie and the other children of his Delta Force buddies, she'd loosened up.

Hiring Maria had eased all her worries, and she'd since taken to being a mother better than anyone he'd ever seen. She never got upset with Bryan. Instead, she tried to analyze and figure out why he was crying, unhappy, frustrated, etc. It was fascinating to see her take an academic approach to motherhood.

But it wasn't all facts with her. Every day, she told Bryan how much she loved him and how proud she was of him. She made his lunches for school, including little notes letting him know he was loved. She frequently took him to the library, and to Coeur d'Alene to visit the zoo, museums, and even to antique stores, so they could find things to take apart to learn how they worked.

"Hungry, Bryan?" Bryn asked.

"Yes, Mama."

"Want Daddy to make you pancakes this morning?"

"Yes!" Bryan leaped up, forgetting about the toaster, and threw himself into his father's arms. Fish caught him with his good arm then leaned over and snagged Bryn around the waist with his stub. He hadn't put on his prosthetic this morning, which he only did when he left the house.

He rolled around on the floor with his wife and child and did his best to tickle them, and to keep them from tickling him in return. When they were all winded, they lay on the floor, trying to catch their breath.

Fish turned to Bryn and said, "I love you."

"I know," she returned.

Fish merely smiled. He turned to his other side. "I love you, son."

"I know," Bryan replied, unconsciously echoing his

mother. "I'll go get the stuff ready for pancakes!" And with that, he leaped up and headed for the kitchen.

"How'd you sleep?" Bryn asked once they were alone.

"Good. Although I hate when you get up without waking me."

"I heard Bryan up around five. I figured I'd get up to see what he was into."

"Probably smart. Maria would have a fit if she came to work on Monday and the house had burned down."

"Yeah, she wouldn't be happy."

Bryn still had a hard time understanding when someone was being sarcastic or kidding with her. But it didn't matter to Fish. He loved her exactly the way she was.

Bryn sat up and pushed her hair out of her face. Then she began fiddling with the pieces of the toaster that were still strewn about. "Oh, I took that pregnancy test this morning. It was positive."

Fish gaped at his wife.

He knew she had missed her last two periods, but had thought it was because she'd been sick recently. She'd had a nasty bout with the flu and had lost a lot of weight as a result.

She didn't seem to realize the magnitude of the news she'd just shared with him. Fish reached out and took her hands in his good one, making her physically stop fiddling with the electronics. He knew he'd never get her attention otherwise.

"You're pregnant?"

"Yes. I believe I just said that."

"You're having my baby?" Fish was having a hard time wrapping his head around the bomb she'd just dropped on him.

"Well, technically it's half mine, but yes, it looks like I am."

"Oh, Smalls," Fish said, and put his hand on her cheek,

making her look at him. He couldn't even come up with the words to tell her how he felt.

"Are you...okay with this?" she asked.

For the first time, Fish saw the trepidation in her eyes. She was worried he wouldn't be happy?

Turning them so she was under him, Fish looked her right in the eyes and told her what she needed to hear. He'd learned that beating around the bush with her wasn't good. "I'm ecstatic. I'm more than happy. I'm over the moon."

"Did you know that the expression 'over the moon' originated from the sixteenth-century nursery rhyme called 'Hey Diddle Diddle'?"

"Hadn't thought about it," Fish told her.

"Hmmm," Bryn hummed. Then she leaned up and kissed him. "Love you, Dane."

"Love you too, Smalls."

"Hey! Are you guys comin'? I'm hungry!" Bryan said as he came back into the room and saw them still on the floor.

"We're comin', keep your pants on," Fish said.

"Of course I will! Why would I take them off to have breakfast?" Bryan asked before heading back into the kitchen to wait for them.

Fish chuckled, and made a mental note to call Ghost and the others and let them know the good news later that day. He sat up and helped Bryn to her feet as well. Then hand in hand, they walked into the kitchen together, ready to start a new day.

"I'm the luckiest man alive," Fish said later as he watched his son eat his chocolate chip pancakes.

"Maybe so. But if you are, then I'm the luckiest woman alive," Bryn said with a small smile.

Fish had no retort to that. She was absolutely right.

Beatle and Casey, eleven years after the weddings.

"I can't do it again," Casey said, looking up at Beatle with huge tears in her eyes.

Beatle thought his heart was going to break. They'd done everything they were supposed to this time. Just as they had the last three times, and it hadn't worked.

They'd started trying to have kids a few years after they'd gotten married. They'd wanted to wait until Casey's university job was a bit more secure. After she'd gotten tenure, they'd started trying to get pregnant right away.

After a year with no results, even though the attempts were more than enjoyable, they'd seen a specialist. Thus had begun six years of doing everything they could to have a child.

They'd just found out that the last round of in-vitro fertilization had failed. Again.

Beatle held Casey as close as possible and didn't say anything as she cried on his shoulder. His own eyes welled with tears. He hated seeing his wife so upset. Nothing tore at his heart more than not being able to give her what she most wanted, their child.

It wasn't that they were opposed to adoption. They'd talked about it, and had followed Truck and Mary's journey to adopt overseas closely. But Casey had really wanted her own child.

Knowing now wasn't the time to bring up adoption again, Beatle closed his eyes and simply held his wife and thought about the calls he needed to make. He needed to call Blade and let him know that the procedure had once again failed.

Needed to tell their parents. Needed to let the other women know, so they could do their thing and surround Casey with love and friendship.

But for now, he'd simply hold her.

How long they sat on the couch and soaked up the much-needed love and affection from each other, Beatle had no idea, but he jerked in surprise when his phone started ringing in his pocket. He was going to ignore it, but Casey pulled away and wiped her eyes.

"You should get that," she said softly.

Nodding, Beatle pulled the phone out and clicked to answer. He didn't recognize the number, but he always answered, just in case. "Hello?"

"Is this Mr. Lennon?"

"Speaking."

"This is Doctor Harris from the fertility clinic."

"Yes?" Beatle wasn't sure why their doctor was calling them. They'd just seen him a couple hours ago, when he'd told them the bad news.

"This is highly unusual...but I just received a call from a colleague who's an OBGYN. He just delivered a baby to a teenaged single mother who wants to give her up for adoption."

Beatle froze. His eyes whipped to Casey, who was staring at him curiously. "And?" he asked, needing more information before he said anything to clue his wife into what was happening.

"She's been adamant from the beginning that she didn't want the child. Her parents refused to allow her to get an abortion. The father isn't in the picture at all. Child services is looking for a foster home ASAP. I just thought... Can I be frank here?"

"Please," Beatle said, still in shock.

"We've been through a lot together. The last thing I wanted to do today was break the news that the procedure once again didn't work. You and Casey are the kind of people who deserve to be parents. You'd be amazing, I have no doubt. I know you both want children more than anything. So, I pulled some strings... You could pick up the baby tomorrow. But you'd have to go in and fill out the application to be a foster parent first. They'll do background checks, and you'll have to put up with home visits for a while too. Then there will be court dates to make sure the mother and her family have relinquished all rights to the child.

"It won't be easy, but then again, what the two of you have gone through in the last six years hasn't been easy either. This little girl needs you, Troy. Needs you and Casey."

"When do I have to give you an answer?" Beatle asked, not taking his eyes from Casey.

"Sooner rather than later would be better, but I know you need to talk it over with your wife. Tomorrow morning would be best, as I can make arrangements for you to meet with child services and sign the paperwork, then you can take the baby home as soon as tomorrow afternoon, if everything checks out."

"Tomorrow?" Beatle choked out, wanting to make sure he'd heard the doctor right.

"Tomorrow," Doctor Harris confirmed.

"I...shit..." Beatle stammered.

"Talk to Casey. I'll wait for your call in the morning."

"Right."

"Troy?"

"Yeah, Doc?"

"You deserve this. I know it's scary, but it's nothing you can't handle."

"Ten-four. I'll call tomorrow."

"You do that. Bye."

Beatle clicked off the phone and stared at his wife. She still had tracks on her face from her tears, and she furrowed her brows in concern.

"What did the doctor want?"

Beatle ran a hand down his face and took a deep breath—then told her everything he'd just heard from the doctor.

For several moments, they stared at each other in shock.

"Tomorrow?" Casey whispered. "We can take her home *tomorrow?*"

"That's what the doc said. What do you think?"

"What do *you* think?"

"I'm sorry that I couldn't give you a biological child. But I think we both knew before we even started on this last round that the possibility of it failing was high. I want to give you everything your heart desires, and I hate that I couldn't. But...I think this is a sign from God. What're the odds that this girl gave birth today of all days? And that her doctor was friends with ours? I think we should do it."

"Me too," Casey whispered.

Beatle kissed her, then pulled back and asked, "Did we just become parents?"

Casey chuckled. "Well...foster parents for now, but...yes, I think we did." Then the smile fell from her face and her eyes got huge. "Oh my God. We don't have *anything*. The house is a mess and we don't even have a room to put her in. We need clothes. And diapers. And formula. Oh, shit...we need to go shopping!"

Beatle grabbed her right before she leaped up from the couch. "Calm down, Case."

"I can't!" she screeched. "We're gonna be parents!"

He simply held her and arched his brows.

"Oh my God, Troy. We're gonna be parents," Casey whispered, then she burst into tears once again.

As he pulled his wife back into his arms, Beatle beamed. It was so strange how the world worked, but he knew they were meant to be this little girl's parents. He already loved her. It was crazy. Insane. But true.

After Casey had gotten herself under control, he said, "Come on, let's go call your brother. Then our parents. They need to know they're going to be grandparents."

Blade and Wendy, thirteen years after the weddings.

"I'd like to make a toast," Jackson Tucker said as he raised his champagne glass.

Blade stared at his brother-in-law proudly. After his rough start to life, he'd not let anything stand in his way. Wendy had done a hell of a job raising him to be an amazing, smart young man. He was now thirty, and had just gotten married.

They were at his wedding reception, and before anyone could eat, they had to get through the toasts. His best man had done his thing, telling stories about a wild and crazy Jackson at college.

But now it was Jackson's turn for a toast.

Wendy leaned into Blade's side and he wrapped his arm around her. The thirteen years they'd been married had been amazing. They didn't have children; Wendy said raising her kid brother had been more than enough child-rearing for her, and Blade didn't protest.

He liked kids, but didn't really want any of his own. He

was content spoiling his friends' children...then giving them back.

"Today, I not only married the most beautiful woman on the planet, I married my best friend," Jackson began. "I met her in high school, and knew there'd never be another for me."

Blade half-listened as he leaned down and whispered to Wendy, "How long do we have to stay?"

She elbowed his side and glared up at him. "Hush," she admonished.

"Seriously, how long?" Blade asked.

Wendy pressed her lips together and refused to engage him in conversation.

"Because seeing you in that dress has had me hard all night. All I can think about is whether your panties and bra match."

"Aspen, hush," she said, but he could tell she wasn't exactly mad at him. Her hand moved to rest on his thigh, then slid so her fingers were caressing his inner thigh. If she moved even an inch higher, she'd see for herself how badly he needed her.

"...all I ever needed to know from my brother-in-law, Aspen."

Blade tore his eyes away from Wendy's cleavage—prominently yet tactfully displayed in her custom-made light gray dress—to look at Jackson.

He stared at him as he continued his speech.

"I learned how to treat the woman I loved, and that nothing was more important than making her feel safe and protected. That's probably not a popular sentiment in today's age, with women still fighting for equal rights, but I don't care." He turned to his bride. "Jenny, I promise to always be there when you need me. I'll do everything in my power to make sure you can achieve your dreams and support you however you need me to. I'll fight dragons for you, and stand between you and anyone who dares try to hurt you. I love you. Thank you for loving *me*, and for saying yes."

"Oh, Jackson," Jenny said, and stood up to kiss her new husband.

"Why'd it take them so long to get married again?" Blade asked as he tightened his arm around Wendy. He was trying to distract her because she was about to lose it—again. She'd been crying on and off all day, and he would do anything to keep those tears from her eyes...even happy tears.

"You know why. He didn't want to hold her back."

"But she went to the same college he did and they dated throughout."

"I know."

"And they've been living together for years," Blade went on.

"I know."

"So explain it to me?"

"I can't," Wendy finally said. "They've loved each other since they first met, but I think they were both afraid something was going to happen and ruin it. It just took them a while to take the plunge. But it's always been the two of them."

"Hmmm," Blade said, and nuzzled the skin by her ear.

"Besides, I think they would've gone on forever simply being common-law married...except she's pregnant."

Blade's head whipped up and he stared at Wendy. "Really?"

"Yup."

"Holy shit! I can't believe that kid is gonna be a parent."

"He's thirty, Aspen. He's not exactly a kid. In fact, he's older than I was when *we* met."

"Damn," Blade said again. "I can't wrap my head around it. I'm gonna be an uncle."

Wendy chuckled. "Yup. And I'll be an aunt."

The waitstaff began to circulate in the room and serve the first course for dinner. Blade looked around and mentally said, *fuck it*.

He grabbed Wendy's hand and stood.

Ignoring the knowing looks from his teammates—and the confused ones from their wives—he towed Wendy out of the ballroom. He went straight to the elevators and impatiently stabbed at the up arrow.

"Aspen, what on earth?" Wendy asked.

The elevator opened and Blade pulled her inside, pressing the door-close button so the businessman coming their way with a suitcase had to take the next one. He backed Wendy against a wall of the elevator after pushing the button for their floor and said, "I can't go another minute without being inside you."

"For God's sake, Aspen, my brother's reception is going on!"

"Right, and he doesn't give a shit who's there and who isn't. All he's thinking about is getting Jenny up to the honeymoon suite and making love to his wife."

"Ew, gross," Wendy said, covering her ears with her hands.

"I love you, Wen," Blade said. "I can't think about your brother being thirty. I can't think about the fact that thirteen years has gone by since we met. I love you just as much as I did when we said our own vows, and I want you just as badly. I'll always want you. Even when I'll have to take those little blue pills to get it up."

Wendy giggled and Blade relaxed. He was afraid he'd really pissed her off this time.

"You're lucky I love you," she told him, unbuttoning the

first button on his shirt. "But this has to be quick. I'm hungry and we're missing dinner."

"I'll make sure you get dinner," Blade told her. "I'll track down the wedding coordinator and tell her you had an allergic reaction and missed it."

"She knows I'm not allergic to anything," Wendy said. "She made sure before planning the dinner menu."

"Then I'll tell her you were so horny and needed my cock that you couldn't wait, so you missed dinner."

"Allergic reaction sounds good," Wendy muttered.

Blade smiled and kissed her palm. The doors opened and they quickly walked hand in hand to their room. Then he felt her hands push under the waistband of his slacks as he stuck the card in the door, and smiled.

Twenty minutes later, they lay on the bed, trying to catch their breath.

"I knew they'd match," Blade said with a small smile.

"Horndog," Wendy complained, but she grinned at him while she said it.

"Love you, Wendy Carlisle."

"Love you back, Aspen. Now can we please go and have dinner and pretend to be a respectable couple at my brother's wedding?"

"Anything you say, babe, anything you say."

Emily and Fletch, fifteen years after the weddings.

"John, so help me God, if you don't put your butt down on that seat, it's gonna get smacked," Emily hissed at her youngest son.

"I'm boooored!" their seven-year-old whined. "When is this gonna be over?"

"I told you to bring a book," his older brother, Doug, told him.

Fletch smiled at his sons. Douglas was only eleven, but sometimes he acted years older. He was their studious child. He'd loved to read by the age of five and it seemed like he'd had his head in a book ever since.

"She's almost up," Ethan said, sitting as straight as he could to try to see the stage better.

Fletch reached for Emily's hand, and she latched on and squeezed his fingers hard.

It seemed like only yesterday Annie had been zooming around their yard in her homemade tank. But now they were at her college graduation, and she was going to be sworn in as the newest member of the US Army. She'd never lost her enthusiasm for the armed forces and had joined the ROTC at the university as a freshman. Over the years, she'd excelled, and was on her way to being in the medical field in the Army.

Fletch worried about her—he'd be a shit parent if he didn't—but he couldn't help but be proud.

He looked over his shoulder at the group of people sitting in the few rows behind his family. Seeing all his Army friends and their families made him smile in contentment. He knew they loved Annie almost as much as he did.

"There she is," Ethan said excitedly as he pointed to the student preparing to go across the stage. Fletch turned to look at the stage, and the entire family stood up and yelled when her name was announced.

Annie Elizabeth Grant Fletcher.

Fletch heard the shouts and excitement from Ghost and the others as they celebrated her achievement along with his family.

Annie walked proudly across the stage and, once she had her diploma in hand, looked up into the stands at her family. She raised her hand in a fist above her head, which only set her brothers off more.

Fletch knew the swearing-in ceremony would take place after everyone received their diplomas, so they had more time to wait.

"This is awesome," Ethan said after they'd sat down again.

Fletch couldn't argue. It *was* awesome. Even better was how close brother and sister were. Annie loved all of her brothers, but there was a special bond between her and Ethan. It probably stemmed from the hours Annie read to him and played with him when he was only a toddler. Even when she'd been in high school, she'd never been irritated or short with him. She loved everything about being a big sister, and had reveled in teaching him how to play soldier and running around with him in the woods behind their house.

Later, Fletch held Emily as she cried when Annie recited the oath of service, beaming with pride himself.

He knew the best part of the day was still to come. The present he'd arranged for his daughter was waiting.

The arena was chaotic after the ceremony, but Fletch waited for Annie in the spot they'd staked out ahead of time. After ten minutes, he finally saw her coming toward them. She was wearing her dress green Army uniform, and even though she'd complained about having to wear a skirt when the boys could wear slacks, Fletch thought she looked amazing.

She hugged everyone and teased Doug about whether he'd seen any of the ceremony or if he'd read his book the entire time. She let John pin her name badge, Fletcher, on his own shirt, even though she knew she'd get in trouble if any instructors saw her in an incomplete uniform. Ethan gave her a big hug, and Fletch wasn't surprised to see tears in his daughter's eyes. She was about to head off to complete the Officer Basic Course and her medical training with the Army, and it would be quite a while before she was able to spend any amount of time with her family again.

Annie was just as amazing today as she'd been when he'd first met her, and Fletch was more proud of her than he could say. She'd grown into a beautiful, thoughtful, smart young lady who knew what she wanted in life and wasn't afraid to go after it.

Smiling when he saw someone coming up behind Annie, he handed her name badge back and told her they'd see her at the house. They were having a huge graduation party there in a couple hours. Fletch knew all his teammates would be there, as well as a few other Delta Force men, Fish and Bryn, and even a couple of the SEALs from California.

And a huge party wouldn't be complete without the man Annie loved.

As Fletch walked away, he looked back and saw Annie turn and see Frankie for the first time. He knew the young man had told her he couldn't make it because of his work schedule.

Annie's screech of delight could be heard above the crowd still milling around, and Fletch couldn't help but smile as he watched the reunion.

"She really loves him," Emily said softly. "She's loved him since they were seven years old."

"Yup," Fletch said, because there really wasn't anything else to say.

They watched their daughter's hands move lightning fast as she signed her happiness to Frankie. He laughed and signed back. The two stood in the middle of the crowd of happy graduates, reconnecting.

Things hadn't been easy for the couple, and unfortunately, it would continue to be difficult. They were still young and had different roads ahead of them, but Fletch hoped they made it.

Frankie was a good man. He was smart and respectful, and it was easy to see how much he loved Annie. But he also refused to hold her back from her dreams. The pain in his eyes when he thought Annie wasn't watching was clear to see, but he stayed the course, refusing to let Annie settle on anything less than her dream of being a medic in the Army.

Fletch made sure his sons were settled in the car and walked Emily to the passenger side. Before she could open the door, he leaned in and kissed her. Hard and deep. Right there in the parking lot for all to see. He heard John groaning from inside the car at their public display of affection, but he didn't pull away until he was good and ready.

When Em groaned and pressed against him, he finally pulled back. He didn't want to do anything that might embarrass Emily in public, but damn, he loved knowing he could still turn her on as much as he had when they'd first met.

"I love you, Em. I couldn't imagine a better life than this right here."

"Me either. Thank you for renting out that room over your garage."

He grinned. "Thank you for applying."

"Thank *you* for coming to find me when I was sick."

"I could do this all afternoon. Thank *you* for raising our daughter to be compassionate, funny, and so fucking amazing, I'm in awe just being around her."

Emily chuckled. "Okay, okay, you win. We need to get the boys home before John starves to death and Doug finishes his book. He didn't bring an extra and you know how he gets when he doesn't have anything to read."

"He could read electronic books like a normal person," Fletch said. "Then he'd never run out."

"You know he likes the feel of a real book in his hands," Emily scolded.

"But they take up so much room," Fletch returned.

Emily laughed. "It would suck if the caterers beat us to the house."

"Right. I'm gettin' the hint. If I forget to say it later, thank you for suggesting we fly Frankie out here. I have a feeling that's the best present we could've gotten our daughter."

"I have a feeling you're right."

Fletch leaned down and kissed his wife briefly on the lips, then helped her into the car and waited until she'd fastened her seat belt before closing the door. He looked over at where he'd left his daughter and her boyfriend, and saw them kissing passionately.

Frowning, Fletch took a deep breath. Annie was more than old enough to be kissing, but it still weirded him out. He remembered when she was a little girl, his little sprite. Intellectually, he knew she wasn't that seven-year-old anymore, but emotionally, she'd always be his little girl.

Deliberately turning his back on the couple, Fletch climbed into the car and turned around to face his family. "Ready to go home?"

"Yeah!"

"Yes."

"Whatever."

The last came from Doug, who was obviously lost in the world of warlocks and witches from the latest series he was reading.

"Let's go home," Emily said softly.

Fletch raised a hand and ran his fingers over his wife's

cheek gently, before turning his attention back to the road and heading out.

Mary and Rayne, twenty-five years after the weddings.

"To friends," Rayne said as she held up her glass.

"To friends," Mary echoed.

Then both women brought their shot glasses to their mouths and downed the shots.

Rayne coughed and sputtered, but Mary merely smiled at her and threw her arm around her friend's shoulders.

"Can you believe it's been twenty-five years since we had our wedding?" Mary asked.

Rayne shook her head. "Nope. Sure doesn't seem like it."

"I think it's so romantic that Ghost is taking you back to London and the same hotel you had your one-night stand in all those years ago."

"Yeah, he's pretty amazing," Rayne agreed.

"What time are you and Ghost leaving tomorrow?"

"Our flight doesn't leave until ten in the evening, but Ghost hates to be late, so I'm sure we'll leave here around three in the afternoon."

Mary rolled her eyes. "At least you're going first class."

"Right? Although Ghost is all upset that they have those pod things. I think he wanted to rejoin the mile-high club."

Mary rolled her eyes. "I remember when you told me about you guys going at it and almost getting caught the last time you flew overseas together. You'd think he'd have learned his lesson."

Rayne giggled. "Apparently not. But I have to say, he can't

wait until I get home tonight. He loves when you and I go out together."

"Why, because you come home drunk and he gets to have his wicked way with you?"

Rayne laughed again. "As if you don't get the same thing when you get home!"

"That's true. And it's much easier since the kids are out of the house and on their own. We don't have to be quite so creative."

"Preach it, sister," Rayne said, nodding. "Last month, I barely made it through the door before Ghost was on me."

Both women giggled.

"I love you, Mare," Rayne said, sobering up.

"Don't start," Mary said, holding up a hand.

"Seriously, I do. I have no idea what I'd do without you. When I thought I was the worst mom ever, you talked me off the ledge. When Ghost got hurt on that one mission, you were there for me, making sure my kids didn't starve to death. When Greta called from college crying because she'd almost been raped at that party, you and Truck not only kept Ghost from going down there and killing the asshole, you drove the four hours with me to get to her. Then you scared that pissant frat boy so badly by threatening to not only kick his ass in front of all his buddies, but swearing if he so much as looked at another girl cross-eyed after that, you'd know and ruin him."

"I was bluffing," Mary mumbled.

"But *he* didn't know that. And you showed Greta that there's nothing you wouldn't do for her. My life wouldn't be the same without you, Mare."

"Oh, shit," Mary said, pressing her lips together, trying not to cry.

"I know why you did what you did all those years ago, but

I swear to God, if you ever do something so stupid again, I'm gonna kill you myself, hear me?"

Mary nodded.

Rayne turned her head and yelled for the bartender. "We need another, Jimmy!"

With a smirk, the good-looking, young, buff bartender poured two more shots and pushed them across the bar.

Mary knew when the college kid looked at them, he saw two middle-aged women way past their prime, probably desperate and looking for a hookup. But he'd be wrong. Oh, they might be middle-aged, but they were nowhere near their prime. They still had years and years to cause trouble together. And looking for a hookup? No way. Their men were at home waiting for them.

Mary knew as much about Rayne's love life as she did her own—that's how best friends operated, they didn't keep secrets from each other, even when it came to things like menopause, or how well and often their men still made love to them. She also knew for a fact that her best friend was still having as much amazing sex as she had twenty-five years ago.

"I love you, Raynie," Mary told her best friend. "The day we met at that bar was the best day of my life. I would go through cancer all over again, twice, if it meant having you in my life."

"Don't say that!" Rayne protested immediately. "No more fucking cancer for you, bitch!"

Mary laughed. When Rayne got drunk, she always got sappy...and swore like a sailor.

Just then a song came on. It was an oldie, way older than most of the people in the bar at the moment, but Rayne immediately turned to Mary and screamed, "Black Eyed Peas! We have to dance!"

The song was "The Time (Dirty Bit)," and she and Rayne

had danced to it time and time again over the years. It had such an awesome beat, it was almost impossible not to get up and dance. Not to mention, it reminded them of the movie *Dirty Dancing*, which, even though another old classic, was still one of their favorites.

"I've had the time of my life!" Rayne sang at the top of her lungs, pointing at Mary. Then she threw the shot back and pulled at her friend's hand. "Come on! Let's dance!"

"Go on, I'll be right there," Mary assured her. She downed her own shot and watched with humor as Rayne went to the dance floor and began gyrating and shaking her ass. Mary saw several young women and men rolling their eyes at the "old woman" dancing, but didn't give a shit.

She hoped in another twenty-five years, she and Rayne were still doing shots and dancing their ass off on the dance floor. The hell with what anyone else thought. She and Rayne had been through a lot of shit in their lives. This was them. They weren't going to change now, and didn't feel one ounce of regret for being who they were.

Mary plunked the empty shot glass on the bar and hurried out to join her best friend in the world. As they danced, laughing and embracing life, and ignoring the stares from the much younger clientele, Mary couldn't help but think about her life.

She'd had a horrible mother, and had learned at a young age not to trust anyone, especially men. But then she'd met Rayne, and learned that there were good people out there. Then through her best friend, she'd met Truck. The man who'd changed her entire life. Thinking about her husband made Mary smile once again.

Her man.

He made her crazy and pissed her off all the time.

But he also went out of his way to make sure she knew

how much he loved her, and to make her happy. He'd raised their two children to be amazing human beings, and Mary felt content in the knowledge they wouldn't have the same issues she'd had when trying to find a life partner.

At the end of the song, Rayne pulled Mary into an intense embrace. The two women hugged each other long after a new song started. Finally, Rayne pulled away and looked Mary in the eyes. "We did good, didn't we?"

Mary smiled. "We sure did."

"You ready to go?"

"Fuck yeah."

"Let's go get us some," Rayne said.

Mary laughed. "You're gonna be hungover tomorrow for your flight."

Rayne merely shrugged. "Don't care. I'm having fun with my best friend. I've got one of the hottest men on the planet in my bed. And we're happy and healthy. What else could I ask for?"

Mary simply shrugged. "Nothing."

"Exactly."

"Now call your man and tell him to get here to pick your ass up," Rayne ordered.

Mary did as ordered, even as Rayne made her own call to Ghost.

They stood outside the bar, under the watchful eye of the bartender, while they waited for their husbands to pick them up.

"Mary?"

"Yeah, Rayne?"

"Thanks for not dying."

Mary didn't laugh. She knew Rayne was completely serious. "You're welcome."

The two friends linked their arms together and settled

back against the side of the bar to wait for their men to arrive...and their beautiful lives to continue.

Thank you ALL for going on this Delta Force ride with me!

Keep reading for my Author Note to find out what's coming next!

AUTHOR NOTE

Readers,

I can't say how happy I am that you have embraced the Deltas and their women. I've loved writing about them, and while this chapter is ending, you'll soon get to see more about the new team of Deltas that you were introduced to in this book...starting with Commander Colt Robinson and Macie, Truck's sister, in April with *Rescuing Macie*. And yes, you'll get glimpses of Ghost and Truck and their team in those new books too.

I've loved writing Annie's character in this story as well. If you've read my free short story, *The Gift*, you know she's always had her eye on little Frankie (from *Protecting Kiera*). And you saw a glimpse into their life after college graduation. I'm not sure when they'll get their story, but you'll get it. Promise.

This was a tricky book to write because Truck is such a well-loved character. I needed to make sure I did his and Mary's story justice. I hope I did. In the end, while there were lots of obstacles in their way, neither gave up on the other, and I think that's what love is all about.

You might think that I forgot to close the plot point of Mary's choice on whether or not to get breast reconstruction. I didn't forget. I didn't disclose what her decision was on purpose, because I didn't want to seem like I was endorsing one decision over another. It's a *very* personal choice breast cancer survivors have to make, and one that has repercussions no matter what's decided. I showed Mary agonizing over the decision, but ultimately, whatever she decided to do doesn't matter. She's the same Mary who Truck loves, and the same Mary who Rayne loves. Whether she has boobs or not has no bearing on that love. *That* is why I didn't specifically say what she chose to do.

Ruth, you know I love ya, but sorry...Truck was Mary's from the very beginning. No matter how snarky or bitchy she was, Truck only had eyes for her (and it turns out, she had a good reason to be that way).

And lastly, Amy. What can I say except that my life wouldn't be the same without you in it. Even though your boobs tried to kill you, you never let a little thing like chemo and radiation keep you down. You kept on being a mom, a wife, and an amazing friend, even when you undoubtedly felt like curling up in a ball on the floor. You are literally the strongest person I know. (And there's nothing like being on vacation with you and looking over and seeing a BOOB lying on the bed next to me to make me laugh like a loon.) From the tips of your tingly fingers to the bottom of your beautiful toes...I love ya.

PLAYLIST

https://spoti.fi/2vK4unM

I never do this, but for this book, I felt as if I *needed* to share some songs that I love that really resonated with me in regards to Truck and Mary, as well as Rayne and Mary's friendship. If this was the '80s, I totally would've made you all a mix tape and you could play it over and over...but because we're in the digital age, I encourage you to look up all of these, play them, and think about Mary as you do.

Play List for *Rescuing Mary*:
    Perfect, Ed Sheeran
    I'll Fight, Daughtry
    Rise Up, Andra Day
    Little Me, Little Mix
    Can't Hold us Down, Christina Aguilera, Lil Kim
    Scars to Your Beautiful, Alessia Cara
    What Makes You Beautiful, One Direction
    Warrior, Demi Lovato
    The Fighter, Keith Urban & Carrie Underwood

F**kin' Perfect, Pink

This One's for the Girls, Martina McBride

This is Me, Keala Settle

Holding out for a Hero, Tara Leigh Cobble

Isabelle, Unlabeled

Beautiful, Christina Aguilera

Bless the Broken Road, Rascal Flatts

Just the Way You Are, Bruno Mars

I Won't Give Up, Jason Mraz

Stand By You, Rachel Platten

Fighter, Christina Aguilera

I Will Remember You, Sarah McLachlan

Fight Song, Rachel Platten

Brave, Sara Bareilles

Who Says, Selena Gomez & The Scene

The Time (Dirty Bit), The Black Eyed Peas

Lean on Me, Club Nouveau

Count On Me, Bruno Mars

https://spoti.fi/2vK4unM

Also by Susan Stoker

Delta Force Heroes Series

Rescuing Rayne
Rescuing Aimee (novella)
Rescuing Emily
Rescuing Harley
Marrying Emily
Rescuing Kassie
Rescuing Bryn
Rescuing Casey
Rescuing Sadie
Rescuing Wendy
Rescuing Mary
Rescuing Macie (April 2019)

Badge of Honor: Texas Heroes Series

Justice for Mackenzie
Justice for Mickie
Justice for Corrie
Justice for Laine (novella)
Shelter for Elizabeth
Justice for Boone
Shelter for Adeline
Shelter for Sophie
Justice for Erin
Justice for Milena
Shelter for Blythe
Justice for Hope
Shelter for Quinn (Feb 2019)
Shelter for Koren (June 2019)
Shelter for Penelope (Oct 2019)

SEAL of Protection: Legacy Series

Securing Caite (Jan 2019)
Securing Sidney (May 2019)
Securing Piper (Sept 2019)
Securing Zoey (TBA)
Securing Avery (TBA)
Securing Kalee (TBA)

Ace Security Series

Claiming Grace
Claiming Alexis
Claiming Bailey
Claiming Felicity

Mountain Mercenaries Series

Defending Allye
Defending Chloe (Dec 2018)
Defending Morgan (Mar 2019)
Defending Harlow (July 2019)
Defending Everly (TBA)
Defending Zara (TBA)
Defending Raven (TBA)

SEAL of Protection Series

Protecting Caroline
Protecting Alabama
Protecting Fiona
Marrying Caroline (novella)
Protecting Summer
Protecting Cheyenne
Protecting Jessyka
Protecting Julie (novella)

Protecting Melody
Protecting the Future
Protecting Kiera (novella)
Protecting Dakota

Stand Alone

The Guardian Mist
Nature's Rift
A Princess for Cale
A Moment in Time- A Collection of Short Stories
Lambert's Lady

Special Operations Fan Fiction

http://www.AcesPress.com

Beyond Reality Series

Outback Hearts
Flaming Hearts
Frozen Hearts

Writing as Annie George:

Stepbrother Virgin (erotic novella)

ABOUT THE AUTHOR

New York Times, *USA Today* and *Wall Street Journal* Bestselling Author Susan Stoker has a heart as big as the state of Tennessee where she lives, but this all American girl has also spent the last fourteen years living in Missouri, California, Colorado, Indiana, and Texas. She's married to a retired Army man who now gets to follow *her* around the country.

She debuted her first series in 2014 and quickly followed that up with the SEAL of Protection Series, which solidified her love of writing and creating stories readers can get lost in.

If you enjoyed this book, or any book, please consider leaving a review. It's appreciated by authors more than you'll know.

www.stokeraces.com
www.AcesPress.com
susan@stokeraces.com

 facebook.com/authorsusanstoker

 twitter.com/Susan_Stoker

 instagram.com/authorsusanstoker

 goodreads.com/SusanStoker

 bookbub.com/authors/susan-stoker

 amazon.com/author/susanstoker